Henry Morford

Shoulder Straps

A Novel of New York and the Army in 1862

Henry Morford

Shoulder Straps
A Novel of New York and the Army in 1862

ISBN/EAN: 9783337048334

Printed in Europe, USA, Canada, Australia, Japan

Cover: Foto ©Andreas Hilbeck / pixelio.de

More available books at **www.hansebooks.com**

SHOULDER-STRAPS

Henry Morford

T. B. PETERSON & BROS.
PHILADELPHIA.

SHOULDER-STRAPS.

A

NOVEL

OF

NEW YORK AND THE ARMY,

IN

1 8 6 2.

By HENRY MORFORD.

PHILADELPHIA:

T. B. PETERSON & BROTHERS
306 CHESTNUT STREET.

TO

DR. R. SHELTON MACKENZIE,

WHO

HAS ALREADY RECEIVED SO MANY DEDICATIONS,

THAT THEY HAVE BECOME

AN OLD, OLD STORY,—

THIS VOLUME IS

RESPECTFULLY DEDICATED

BY

HIS GRATEFUL FRIEND AND CO-LABORER,

THE AUTHOR.

New York City, July, 1863.

(1)

PREFACE.

—◆—

SEVERAL months have necessarily elapsed since the commencement of this narration. Within that time many and rapid changes have occurred, both in national situation and in private character. As a consequence, there may be several words, in earlier portions of the story, that would not have been written a few months later. The writer has preferred not to make any changes in original expression, but to set down, instead, in references, the dates at which certain portions of the work were written. In one instance important assistance has been derived from a writer of ability and much military experience; and that assistance is thankfully acknowledged in a foot-note to one of the appropriate chapters. Some readers may be disappointed not to find a work more extensively military, under such a title and at this time; but the aim of the writer, while giving glances at one or two of our most important battles, has been chiefly to present a faithful picture of certain relations in life and society which have grown out, as side-issues, from the great struggle. At another time and under different circumstances, the writer might feel disposed to apologize

15

for the great liberty of episode and digression, taken
with the story; but in the days of Victor Hugo and
Charles Reade, and at a time when the text of the
preacher in his pulpit, and the title of a bill in a legislative body, are alike made the threads upon which to
string the whole knowledge of the speaker upon every
subject,—such an apology can scarcely be necessary. It
should be said, in deference to a few retentive memories,
that two chapters of this story, now embraced in the
body of the work, were originally written for and published in the *Continental Monthly*, last fall, the publication
of the whole work through that medium, at first designed,
being prevented by a change of management and a contract mutually broken.

NEW YORK CITY, July, 1863.

CONTENTS.

apparent concession to the season, for his glossy round hat
would have been quite as much in place in January as in June,
and his well-fitting and glossy patent-leather boots would
have been thought oppressively warm by a hotter-blooded and
more plethoric man.   Those who should have seen the bap-
tismal register recording his birth some five-and-thirty years
before, would have known his name to be Walter Lane Harding ; and those who met him in business or society would have
become quite as well aware that he was a prosperous merchant,
doing business in one of the leading mercantile streets running
out of Broadway, not far from the City Hospital.   So far as
the somewhat precise mercantile appearance of Harding was
concerned, a true disciple of Lavater would have judged
correctly of him, for there were few men in the city of New
York who displayed more steadiness, or greater money-making
capacity in all the details of business ; and yet even the close
observer would have been likely to derive a false impression
from this very preciseness, as to the social qualities of the
man.   There were quite as few better or heartier laughers
than Harding, when duly aroused to mirth ; and those persons
were very rare, making the characters of mankind their professional study, who saw slight indications of disposition more
quickly, or better enjoyed whatever gave food for quiet merriment.   Once away from his counting-house, too, Walter
Harding seemed to assume a second of his two natures that
had before been lying dormant, and to enter into the permitted gaieties of city life with a zest that many a professed
good fellow might have envied.   He visited the theatre, as we
have seen ; went to the opera when it pleased him, not for
fashion's sake, but because he liked music and was a connois-
seur of singing and acting ; liked a stroll in the streets with a
congenial companion (male or female) ; could smoke a good
cigar with evident enjoyment ; and sometimes, though rarely,
sipped a glass of fine old wine, and indulged in the freer
pleasures of the table ; though he was scrupulously careful
of his company, and no man had ever seen his foot cross the
threshold of a house of improper character.   It is sufficient,
in addition, at the present moment, to say that he was still a
bachelor, occupying rooms in an up-town street, and enjoying

life in that pleasant and rational mode which seemed to promise long continuance.

Harding's companion, who has already been indicated as
his opposite, was markedly so in personal appearance, at least.
He was two or three inches shorter than Harding, and much
stouter, displaying a well-rounded leg through the folds of his
loose pants of light-gray Melton cloth, and being quite well
aware of that advantage of person. He had a smoothly rounded
face, with a complexion that had been fair until hard work,
late hours, and some exposure to the elements, had browned
and roughened it; brown hair, with an evident tendency to
curl, if he had not worn it so short on account of the heat of
the season, that a curl was rendered impossible; a heavy
dark-brown moustache, worn without other beard; a sunny hazel
eye that seemed made for laughter, and a full, red, voluptuous
lip that might have belonged to a sensualist; while the eye could
really do other things than laughing, and the lip was quite as
often compressed or curled in the bitterness of disdain or the
earnestness of close thought, as employed to express any
warmer or more sympathetic feeling.

Tom Leslie, who might have been called by the more
respectful and dignified name of "Thomas," but that no
one had ever expended the additional amount of breath necessary to extend the name into two syllables, was a cadet of
a leading family in a neighboring state, who at home had
been reckoned the black sheep of the flock, because he would
not settle quietly down like the rest to money-getting and
the enjoyment of legislative offices; a man who at thirty had
passed through much experience, seen a little dissipation,
traveled over most States of the Union in the search for new
scenery, or the fulfilment of his avocation as a newspaper correspondent and man of letters; been twice in Europe, alternately flying about like a madman, and sitting down to study
life and manners in Paris, Vienna, and Rome, and gathering
up all kinds of useful and useless information; taken a short
turn at war in the Crimea, in 1853, as a private in the ranks
of the French army; seen service for a few months in the
Brazilian navy, from which he had brought a severe wound as
a flattering testimonial. He was at that time located in New

York as an editorial contributor and occasional "special correspondent" of a leading newspaper. He had seen much of
life—tasted much of its pains and pleasures—perhaps thought
more than either; and though with a little too much of a
propensity for late hours and those long stories which *would*
grow out of current events seen in the light of past experience, he was held to be a very pleasant companion by other
men than Walter Harding.

Perhaps even the long stories were more a misfortune than
a fault. The Ancient Mariner found it one of the saddest
penalties of his crime, that he was obliged to button-hole all
his friends and be written down an incorrigible bore; and who
doubts that the Wandering Jew, with the weight of twenty
centuries of experience and observation upon his head, finds
a deeper pang than the tropic heat or the Arctic snow could
give, in the want of an occasional quiet and patient listener
to the story of his wanderings?

On the present occasion it may be noted, at once to complete the picture and give additional insight of a character
which did very independent and *outre* things, that Tom Leslie
had gone to Niblo's with his carefully-dressed and precise
friend Harding, and sat conspicuously in an orchestra chair,
in a gray business sack, no vest and no pretence at a collar.
In other men, Harding would have noticed the dress with
disapprobation: in Leslie it seemed to be legitimately a part
of the man to dress as he liked; and neither Harding, or any
one else who knew him, paid any more attention to his outward appearance than they would have bestowed upon a
harmless lunatic under the same circumstances. Wherever
Leslie boarded, (and his places of boarding were very numerous, taking the whole year together,) it was always noted
that he filled up the hat-rack with a collection of hats of all
odd and rapid styles, with a *few* of the more sedate and
respectable; and on this evening's visit to Niblo's, when
there was not a shadow of occasion for a hat with any brim
whatever, he had completed his personal appearance by a fine
gray beaver California soft hat, of not less than eighteen or
twenty inches in the whole circumference, which gave him
somewhat the appearance of being under a collapsed um-

brella, and yet became him as well as any thing else could have done, and left him unmistakably a handsome fellow.

An oddly mixed compound, certainly—even odder than Harding ; and yet what a dull, dead world this would prove to be, if there were no odd and *outre* characters to startle the grave people from their propriety, and throw an occasional pebble splashing into the pool of quiet and irreproachable mediocrity !

The two companions, whose description has occupied a much longer time than it needed to walk from the door of Niblo's to the Houston Street corner, were just passing the corner of that street on their way up to Bleecker, when they were momentarily stopped by a very ordinary incident. A girl, evidently of the *demi-monde* from her bold eyes, lavish display of charms and general demeanor, was turning the corner from Broadway into Houston Street immediately in front of Harding and Leslie ; and as she swept around, her long dress trailing on the pavement, a careless fellow, loung-ing along, cigar in mouth, and eyes everywhere else than at his feet, stepped full upon her skirt, and before she could check the impetus of her sudden turn, literally tore the gar-ment from her, the dark folds of the dress falling on the pave-ment and leaving the under-clothing painfully exposed. The girl turned suddenly, one of those harsh oaths upon her lips which even more than any action betray the fallen woman, and hissed out a malediction on his brutal carelessness. The man, probably one who literally knew no better, instead of remembering the provocation, apologizing for the injury he had done and offering to make any reparation in his power, replied by an oath still more shocking than that of the lost girl, hurled at her the most opprobrious epithet which man bestows upon woman in the English language, and one by far too obscene to be repeated in these pages,—and was passing on, leaving the poor girl to gather her torn drapery as she best could, when his course was suddenly arrested.

A tall figure had come up from below during the alterca-tion, unnoticed by either ; and the instant after the man had disgraced his humanity by that abuse of a fallen woman, he found himself seized by the collar with a hand that managed
2

him as if he had been a child, and himself full off the side-walk
into the street, and among the wheels of the passing omnibuses, with the quick sharp words ringing in his ear :

"The devil take you ! If you can't learn to walk along
the pavement without tearing off women's dresses and afterwards abusing them, go out into the street with the brutes,
where you belong !"

The two friends noticed, casually, that a policeman stood
on the upper corner, and at this act of violence on the part
of the new-comer, they naturally expected to see him interfere
to preserve the peace, if not make an arrest; but he was
either too lazy to cross the street, (such things have been,) or
too well satisfied that the coarse ruffian had met the treatment he deserved, to make any step forward. The fellow,
thus suddenly sent to the company of worn-out omnibus-
horses and swearing stage-drivers on a slippery pavement,
turned with an oath, when he recovered himself, made a
movement as if to return to the sidewalk and seek satisfaction for the violence, but evidently did not like the looks of
his antagonist, when he caught a fair glance of his proportions, and solaced himself with a few more muttered oaths as
he dodged across to the other side of Broadway and disappeared in the crowd.

The second and prudential resolve of this person seemed
fully justified by even a hasty survey of his assailant, who
happened to be thrown under the light of the lamp at the
corner, and in full view of our companions. He was perhaps
six feet and an inch in height, cast in a most powerful model,
and evidently possessing herculean strength—with a dark
complexion, high cheek bones, showing almost as if he had a
cross of the old Indian blood in his descent, fiery dark eyes
set under brows of the pent-house or Webster mould, heavy
massed black curly hair worn a little long, and a very heavy
black moustache entirely concealing the mouth, while the
beard shorn away from the lower portions of the face left the
square, strong chin in full prominence. He was dressed in
dark frock coat with white vest and pants, and wore a dark
wide-brimmed slouched hat almost the counterpart of Leslie's,
except in color, which harmonized well with his personal

appearance in other regards, and while it left him looking the gentleman, made him the gentleman of some other locality than the city of New York.

The new-comer, the moment he had sent the other whirling into the street, approached the girl, who still remained standing on the corner, her ungathered dress sweeping the pavement, and said :

"Madame, your dress is badly torn. Allow me to offer you a few pins." He drew a large pin-cushion from his large vest pocket, (every thing seemed to be of a large pattern about this man,) and was handing it to the girl, who stretched out her left hand to receive it, when he suddenly seemed to recognize her.

"Why, Kate!" He spoke in tones of the most unfeigned surprise—"Kate, what the deuce! I thought you were in—"

"Yes, Deck!" answered the girl, with a coarse familiarity, "but you see I am here! And you? I thought *you* were in—"

"Hush-h-h!" said the man, in a quick, sharp, decided tone, prolonged almost to be a hiss. "That will do! Now use some of these pins—quick, fasten up your skirt, and then go with *me!*"

He spoke as if he was in the habit of being obeyed, or as if he had some peculiar claim that he should be obeyed in this instance. And the girl seemed fully to understand him, for only a moment served to supply so many pins to the torn gathers of the dress as enabled her to walk and hid her exposed under-clothing; and the instant that object was accomplished she thrust her arm into his, he making no attempt to repel the familiarity, but walking with hasty strides and almost dragging her after him, down into the partial gloom of Houston Street.

When they had disappeared, and not till then, the two friends removed from the spot where they had been standing entirely silent, and passed on up Broadway.

"A strange person—a very strange person, that!" said Harding, the moment after, to Leslie, who appeared to be thinking intently, and who had not uttered a word since the affair commenced.

Y—a—es !" said Leslie, in that slow, abstracted tone which indicates that the man who uses it is doing so mechanically and without knowing what he says.

"Poor devil! how the new man whirled him out into the street!" Harding went on, *his* attention on the incident, as Leslie's apparently was not. "Just the treatment he deserved for being brutal to a woman, no matter how lost or degraded she may be! Tearing off her dress was all right enough, however, for all the woman deserve nothing better than to have their dresses torn into ribbons for thrusting them under our feet and sweeping the streets with them, as they do!"

Harding was thinking, at the moment, of a little adventure of his own a few weeks before, in which, hurrying along to an appointment, early in the evening, not far from the St. Nicholas, he had come up with a party of theatre-goers, trodden upon the dress of one of the ladies in attempting to pass—in extricating himself from that awkwardness, trodden upon the dresses of two more—and left the whole three nearly naked in the street ; while three female voices were screaming in shame and mortification, and three male voices sending words after him the very reverse of complimentary.

"You think that a singular person ?" at length said Leslie, as if waking from a reverie, but proving at the same time that he had heard the words of his friend. "You are right, he is so !"

"What! do you know him ?" asked Harding, surprised.

"I do, indeed," was the reply of Leslie ; "but I should as soon have thought of meeting Schamyl or Garibaldi in the streets of New York, at this moment, as the man we have just encountered. Fortunately, he did not recognize me—perhaps, thanks to this hat—(it *is* an immense hat, isn't it, Harding ?) What can be his position, and what is his business here at the present moment, I wonder ?" he went on, speaking more to himself than to his companion, as they turned down Bleecker from Broadway towards Leslie's lodgings, on Bleecker near Elm.

"Well, but you have not yet told me his name, or any thing about him, while you go on tantalizing me with speculations as to how he came to be here, and what he is doing!" said Harding.

"True enough," answered Leslie. "Well, he is not the sort of man to talk about loosely in the streets; so wait a moment, until I use my night-key and we get up into my room. There we can smoke a cigar, and I will tell you all I know of him, which is just enough to excite my wonder to a much greater height than your own."

Less than five minutes sufficed to fulfil the conditions prescribed; and in Leslie's little room, himself occupying the three chairs it contained, by sitting in one, and stretching out his two legs on the others, while Harding threw off his coat and lounged on the bed, Leslie poured out his story, and the smoke from his cigar, with about equal rapidity.

"The name of that singular man," he said, "is Dexter Ralston, and he is by birth a Virginian. You heard the girl call him 'Deck,' which you no doubt took to be 'Dick,' but which she really meant as a familiar abbreviation of his name. It is a little singular that I should have met him first at a theatre, and not far from the one at which we just now encountered him. It was in the fall of 1857, I think, going in with a party of friends, one night, to Laura Keene's, that one of the ladies of the party was rudely jostled by a large man, who caught his foot in the matting of the vestibule and fell against her with such violence as nearly to throw her to the floor. He turned and apologized at once, and with so much high-toned and gentlemanly dignity, that all the party felt almost glad that the little accident had occurred. This made the first step of an acquaintance between him and myself; and when, in the intermission the same evening, I met him for a few moments in a saloon near the theatre, we drank together, held some slight conversation, exchanged cards, and each invited the other to call at his lodgings. His card lies somewhere in the bureau there at this moment, and it read, I remember, 'Dexter Ralston, Charles City, Virginia,' with 'St. Nicholas' written in pencil in the corner. He was a wealthy planter, living near Charles City, as I afterwards gathered from conversation with him, and had an interest in tobacco transactions at the North which kept him a large proportion of his time in this city.

"Of his own choice Ralston attended the theatres very frequently, as I did from professional duty ; and the consequence was that we met often, and sometimes supped together. I liked him, and he seemed to be pleased with me, though I should be perverting the truth to say that I ever became very cordial or intimate with him. There was something about the man which forbade familiarity ; though I remember thinking, several times, that if one only *could* penetrate beneath the crust made by that evident pride and haughty reserve, he was a man to be liked to the death by a man, and loved by a woman with eternal devotion. After a time, and without my receiving any ' P. P. C.' to say that he was going to leave the city, he disappeared, and I saw him no more in the street or at any of his favorite places of amusement.

"Well, I went down to Mount Vernon with a party of friends from Washington, on board the steamboat George Page. Did you ever know Page himself, the fat old Washingtonian who invented something about the circular-saw, and has some kind of a patent-right on all that are made above a certain number of inches in diameter? No? Well, he is an odd genius, and I will some day tell you something about him. But I was just now speaking of the steamboat named after him. The Rebels had her last year, you remember, using her as a gunboat somewhere up Aquia Creek, until they got scared and burned her one night,—though she was about as fit for that purpose as an Indian bark-canoe. The Page was running as an excursion boat to Mount Vernon, and sometimes going down to Aquia Creek in connection with the railroad, in the winter and spring of 1858–9. I was doing some reporting, and a little lobbying, in the Senate, at the beginning of March, and, as I have said, ran down with a party of friends to see the Tomb of Washington, curse the neglect that hung over it like a nightmare, and execrate the meanness which sold off bouquets from the garden, and canes from the woods, at a quarter each, by the hands of a pack of dirty slaves, to the hands of a pack of dirtier curiosity-hunters.

"Going down the river I found no acquaintances on board, outside of my own party; but when we had made the due inspection, and were returning in the afternoon, just when we were off Fort Washington, an acquaintance belonging to the capital came up, in conversation with a thin, scrawny, hard-featured man, dressed in black, and looking like a cross between a decayed Yankee schoolmaster and a foreign Count gone into the hand-organ business. As we exchanged salutations he stopped, made a step backward, and astounded me by this introduction:

"'Col. Washington, my friend, Mr. Leslie—Mr. Leslie, Col. John A. Washington, proprietor of Mount Vernon.'

"I do not suppose that there was any merit in it, any more than there would have been in refusing to drink a nauseous dose; but, really, I felt that I was fulfilling a stern duty (no pun intended) in turning my back short upon the Colonel, and saying:

"'Much obliged to you, Mr. ——, but I have no desire whatever to know Col. John A. Washington!'

"I will do the Colonel (though he did afterwards die a rebel as he deserved) the justice to say that I do not think he cared much for the cut. I noticed that his sallow face looked a shade nearer to green than before, but he merely drew himself up and took no other notice of my decidedly cavalier conduct. Not so, however, with some of the passengers, who had been near enough to hear the words, and who seemed to think that the memory of the great dead was insulted, instead of honored, by this rebuff to the miserable offshoot who kept Mount Vernon as a cross between a pig-stye and a Jew old-clo' shop. Some of them, I suppose, were Virginians, and neighbors of 'the Colonel.' At all events, I heard mutterings, and the ladies in my company (they were all ladies) looked a little alarmed.

"Directly one of the F. F. V.'s, as I suppose them to have been, stepped forward immediately in front of me, and said:

"'D—n it, sir, the man who insults a Washington must answer 'o me!'"

"'Must he?' I said, not much scared, I think, but a little flustered, and quite undecided whether to get into a row on the spot by striking the last man.

"'He must!' replied the F. F. V., with another curse or two thrown in by way of emphasis. 'You may be some cursed Yankee, peddling buttons, and afraid to fight; but if not—'

"'He will have no occasion to fight,' said a voice coming through the crowd from the side of the vessel. 'I will take that little job off his hands. Eh, Leslie, is that you? They tell me you have been giving the cut-direct to that mean humbug who calls himself John A. Washington. Give me your hand, old boy; you have done nothing more than your duty. I am a Virginian, and no d—d Yankee—does any-body want to fight me?'

"It was Dexter Ralston. How many of the people on board knew him I have no idea, or what they knew of him. He seemed to exercise some strange influence, however, for Col. Washington turned away, with the friend who had offered to introduce him; and the man who had offered to fight me also disappeared. The crowd at that spot on the deck seemed to be gone in a moment. Ralston and myself exchanged a few words. I thanked him for having extri-. cated me from a possible scrape, as well as for his good opinion of my conduct, all which he waived with a 'pshaw!' He received an introduction to the ladies with all due cour-tesy, chatted with them a few moments, and then strolled off, smoking a cigar. I was engaged with my party for the re-mainder of the trip, and did not see him again until we had reached Washington and the passengers dispersed from the steamboat, when of course I lost him, without any inquiry being made as to his address or present residence. I went to Europe, the last time, as you know, the summer following, and so perhaps lost him more effectually. Tired?"

The latter word was especially addressed to Harding, who gave symptoms of going to sleep. Refreshed, however, by a cigar which Leslie thrust between his lips and insisted upon his smoking, Harding managed, even in his recumbent po-sition, to keep awake for what followed.

"Confound you!" said Leslie, "you might manage to get along without yawning at my story, when you asked me to tell it! However, who cares! You are not the only man who does not know a good thing when he sees or hears it! Some of my best things in print have probably been received in like manner, by people just as stupid!"

"Very likely," said Harding, drily; and Leslie continued.

"I came home from Europe in the winter of 1860–61, as you may likewise remember if you are not too sleepy; and I was one of the ten thousand who went down from this city to Washington, to attend the inauguration of Abraham Lincoln. Nine thousand nine hundred and ninety odd went armed to the teeth, carrying each from one revolver to three, and a few bowie-knives, in anticipation of there being a general row on inauguration morning, if not an open attempt to assassinate the President. One man whom I could name actually carried four revolvers and a dirk, without knowing any more about the use of either than a child of ten years might have done. There *was* danger of a collision, of course, growing out of the very fact that everybody went down armed. I was one of the very few who could not borrow a revolver or did not want one—no matter which.

"Suffice it to say that I reached Washington on Sunday morning.—the day previous to the inauguration—found the hotels full and took lodgings at a private house a few hundred yards from the Capitol, and spent the early part of the day in inspecting the preparations made for the holiday show, in and about the Capitol building. The courtesy of Colonel Forney, then Clerk of the House, arranged for my admission to the building during the ceremonies of the next day; and that of Douglas Wallach, of the *Star*, furnished me a seat in the reporters' gallery of the Senate for that evening when the last session of the expiring Congress was to be held and a last effort made for putting through those 'compromise resolutions' which it was then believed might 'save the Union,' but which we now know to have been as useless, even if they could have been passed, as so much whistling against the wind.

"Although it was Sunday, time was pressing, and the fate

of the nation seemed to be hanging upon a breath; so the
Senate had arranged a session for five o'clock, which seemed
very likely to last well into the night, and was almost certain
to be crowded to suffocation. As you will remember, it *did*
last until seven the next morning—after daylight, and witnessed one of the most exciting debates in the history of that
body,—in which Baker of Oregon flashed out even more than
usual of his patriotic eloquence; and white-haired, sad old
Crittenden of Kentucky moaned out words of fear for the
nation, that have since been but too truly realized; and Mason
of Virginia showed more boldly than ever the cloven foot of
the traitor who would not have reconciliation at any price;
and Douglas rose above his short stature in alternately lashing one and the other of those whom he believed to be
equally enemies to his type of conservatism. No one who
sat out that session will ever forget it—but enough of this,
which should be written and not spoken.

"Of course after dinner that day I went down to the
Hotels on the Avenue, to take a peep at the political baro-
meter and see what was the prospect for violence on the
morrow. It was a dark and stormy one. Most of the
avowedly Southern element had disappeared from the street,
and there were not many of the secession cockades to be met;
but a few were flaunted by beardless young men who should
that day have been arrested and thrown into the Old Capitol;
and every foot of space in Willard's and the other leading
houses was full all day long of a moving, surging, anxious
and excited crowd, all talking, nobody listening, everybody
inquiring, many significant hints, a few threats, an occasional
quarrel and the interference of the police, but not much violence and no bloodshed. The evening shut down stormy, as
to the national atmosphere, and I went home to supper impressed with the belief that the morrow could not pass off
quietly—a belief strengthened by the fears of Scott, which
were shown in the calling out of the volunteer militia in
large force,—by the tap of the drum and the challenge of the
sentry, which could be heard all around Capitol Hill,—
and by the knowledge that files of regulars were barracked
at different places on the Hill, ready for service in the morn-

ing and so posted as to command every avenue of ingress to the inauguration.

"One of the high winds which belong to the normal condition of Washington began blowing at dark, and it increased to a gale during the evening, rattling shutters, creaking signs and filling the air with clouds of blinding dust which went whirling around the Capitol as if they would bury it. This added materially to the appearance and feeling of desolation, especially when the white stone being worked for the Extension would gleam and disappear through the cloud, and suggest graveyards and monuments for the national greatness that seemed to be falling. Then at dusk we had the report that several hundreds of armed horsemen had been discovered by one of Scott's scouts, lying in wait over Anacosti, and ready to make a descent upon the doomed city the moment that it should be buried in slumber. Many doubted this report, but some believed it; and I have an impression that hundreds went to bed in Washington that night with a lingering doubt whether they would not be involved, before morning, or at all events before the noon of the next day, in such scenes of violence and bloodshed as the continent had never yet witnessed.

"I went over to the Capitol after tea, and took the place that had been kindly kept for me in the reporters' gallery of the Senate. No matter what occurred there—history has made it a part of our painful record, and that is quite sufficient. It was between one and two o'clock in the morning, Crittenden had just concluded his heart-breaking appeal to the North to be generous and not let the Union go by default, and Baker had just closed his noble appeal to the new dominant party (of which he was one) not to peril a nation by the adoption of the old Roman cry of '*Vae Victis*,'—when I left the Senate gallery for an hour, intending to return when I had breathed for awhile outside of that suffocating atmosphere. I passed to the front through the entrance under the collonade, and was just about to step out into the open air, when a voice arrested me. Surely I had heard it before.

"'Straws against a whirlwind!' I heard it say. 'The work is already done, and no human power can undo it!'

"'I yet believe that the Union can be saved by the adoption of the plan proposed by Crittenden;' said the other voice. 'Mason is right when he says that Virginia will join the seceding States if no concession is made; but—'

"A laugh, deep, sonorous, and yet hollow and mocking, broke out from the lips of the first speaker, and rung through the arches—such a laugh as we may suppose to have rung from the bearded lips of the Norse Jarl when the poor Viking asked his daughter's hand and the father intended to stun if not to kill him with the bitter scoff. I had heard that laugh before, more moderately given, and minus the accompaniment of the rushing wind without and the ringing of the hollow arches within. It was that of Dexter Ralston, and I now detected that he and his companion were standing just within one of the embrasures, so as to be partially sheltered from the wind, and I could trace their outlines. Ralston was enveloped in a large cloak, and wearing his inevitable broad hat; and his companion seemed much smaller, dressed in dark clothes, and wearing the usual 'stovepipe.' I had no intention to play listener, but there really did not seem to be any wish for privacy on the part of the man who could laugh in that manner; and, at all events, I stood still in the doorway and listened to the discussion of that topic, as I might not have done to another.

"'Well, what does the laugh mean?' asked the other, in a tone that did not indicate remarkable good humor, when the sound had ceased.

"'Excuse me, I was not laughing at you!' said Ralston, 'but at the blind, besotted fools who believe that they hold in their hands the destinies of this Republic, and who really have no more power over them than so many children playing at marbles! Hear Crittenden and Baker begging and pleading within there, to save what is lost; and Mason, the sly old fox, threatening them with what is already done!'

"'What do you mean?' asked the other? 'Virginia—'

"'Virginia has seceded!' spoke Ralston, with an accent that sounded like a hiss. I do not to this moment know whether it expressed triumph or anger.

"'Seceded!' spoke the other, startled, as was evident from

his voice. As for myself, I was trembling like a leaf, for I felt that the words were true, that the treason was already unfathomable, and that the Capitol was tumbling down about my ears long before it was finished.

"'Seceded? Yes, I spoke the word!' said Ralston, 'and you are not very likely to believe that I am mistaken.'

"'No, no, certainly not!' replied the other, in a tone of energetic disclaimer which showed that he knew *why* Ralston was not deceived. 'But then, if this is so, why does Mason remain, and why is the fact kept in the dark?'

"'To gain time!' answered Ralston, 'and to procure more arms. Virginia is a 'loyal State,' and arms may be shipped to her, while they cannot to the States that are known to have seceded. You can guess that the arms go further south almost as fast as they reach Richmond, and that Colt's pistols, especially, will pretty soon be beyond the reach of many men who live north of Mason and Dixon's line. Do you understand *now?*' he concluded.

"'Humph! Yes, I begin to know something more than I did a while ago!' answered the other. 'Then, as you say, all that is going on in yonder is a farce, and—'

"'And to-morrow's proceedings will be a more notable one!' Ralston broke in. 'Some of _them, I believe, have been afraid of violence to-morrow. No fear of that—the game is to be played differently, and it is not yet ripe for blood. Well, I have had enough of it. Good-night!'

"At the word Ralston stepped out from the arch, and his companion followed him. By the lamp-light in front I caught a view of the face as the former went out, and saw that I had not been mistaken as to the voice. I had intended, when I first knew it was Ralston, to accost him before he left, but I had now lost the desire, while my head was in that whirl and his own position seemed to be so ambiguous. He stepped toward the gateway, and, I believe, entered a carriage and drove off. The other, whose face I recognized by the lamp-light to be that of a certain New York Congressman of more than doubtful antecedents, went back again the moment after, and I suppose returned to the Senate Chamber.

"As for myself, I may say that within half an hour after,

late as it was, I had placed myself in communication with a
leading member of the new party in power, with whom I
happened to be well acquainted and who was well known to
have the ear of the new President, even if he did not receive,
within the next week, the portfolio of a Cabinet officer. I
need not say, at present, whether he received the Cabinet
appointment or not, as it is a matter of no consequence to my
story. Without mentioning any names, I told him what had
fallen under my notice, and gave him my opinion that Government ought to act as if Virginia had already seceded. He
thanked me for the trouble I had taken, and for my earnestness; said that if the assertion was true, it would be highly
important, as guiding the immediate policy of the administration; but, pshaw!—and the whole story is that he did not
believe it. Of course the new administration did not act as
if Virginia had seceded; the Rebels were allowed to gather
arms at will and at leisure, Fortress Monroe came very near
to falling into their hands, and Norfolk Navy Yard did so,
with the destruction of half our best vessels, and ten millions
of dollars worth of Government property—all which might
have been avoided if they had taken a hint from a fool.
Everybody understands now,* that Virginia *had* formally
seceded before the inauguration, and that she played loyal
for the very purposes indicated by Ralston.

"Now," Leslie concluded, "you know as much of Dexter
Ralston as I do. And I think you will quite agree with me
that he is one of the last men I could have expected to meet
in the streets of New York at the present moment, when
martial law is so prevalent and Fort Lafayette so convenient."

"Humph!" said Harding, getting up from the bed where
he had lounged so long, examining his watch to see that it
was nearly midnight, and lighting a fresh cigar to go home.
"Humph! well, what do you make of him? A leading
traitor, deep in the counsels of Jeff. Davis, Yancey and Company?"

"Humph!" said Leslie in return, "what else can he be?"

* September, 1862.

"Or a Virginia Unionist, faithful among the faithless, and too brave to be afraid anywhere?" suggested Harding.

"Ah!" answered Leslie, in that tone which suggests a new idea, or the corroboration of an old one.

"Or a trusted agent of the Federal Government, giving up old prejudices for the sake of patriotism, and better acquainted with Seward than Slidell—eh?"

"By George!" exclaimed Leslie, "there is something in that idea! He must be one of the three—but which?"

"That we may know better one of these days," said Harding, as Leslie accompanied him out to the street. "Meanwhile he is certainly a most singular person, and I shall not be sorry to know more of him, whether as friend or foe to the nation!"

How soon and how remarkably his wish was fulfilled, to some extent, we shall see hereafter.

<hr />

CHAPTER II.

The Invalid and the Wild Madonna—A Brave Heart Beating the Bars of its Prison—Odd Comfort and Doubtful Consolation—The Dawn of a Terrible Suspicion.

In the neat and tastefully-furnished back parlor of a house on West 3—th Street, one afternoon, at very nearly the same period mentioned in a previous chapter—the latter part of June, 1862—lay on the sofa a young man, of perhaps twenty-five, with a countenance that would have been strikingly handsome if it had not been drawn and attenuated by suffering. He had a well-chiselled face, clear blue eyes, and light-brown, curling hair, closely shaven of beard or moustache; still showing, spite of sickness, the manly nature that lay within, and which always makes, when it radiates outward, a pleasanter picture for the eye of a true woman than can be

supplied by even high health and the most perfect physical
beauty without it. The limbs, extended upon the sofa as he
lay, though a little attenuated like the face, showed that they
were well-formed and athletic. And the hand, drooping over
the side of the couch, though too thinly white to suggest a
love-pressure, indicated, in the taper of the fingers, and the
fine round of the back, without any coarse protruding
knuckles, what a handsome little Napoleonic hand it must
have been when the owner was in full health and the life-
blood coursing freely through his veins.

By the appearance of the little back parlor, it seemed to
be half sick-room and half study, for, in addition to the sofa
and an easy-chair, there was a well-filled book-case, in wal-
nut, and a writing-desk open on a small table, with blank
paper, some manuscripts, pens, ink, and a book or two lying
open, as if the occupant had been writing not long before,
and lain down from pain and weariness, without waiting to
replace his writing materials in their proper position.
Through the open door of a small room adjoining, some
pieces of bed-room furniture could be seen, showing that
when the invalid wished to find more complete repose, he
could do so without painful removal to any distance. Close
by his side lay a daily newspaper fallen upon the floor, with
the sensation-headings of war-time displayed at the top of
one of the columns; and in his hand he held a palm-leaf fan,
with which he had apparently been trying to wave off some
portion of the sultry heat of the afternoon. At length the
fan grew still, the weak hand fell down on his breast, and he
seemed to be dropping away into quiet slumber.

Suddenly a strain of martial music floated through the open
windows—at first low and gentle, then bursting loud and
clear, with the rattle of drums, the screaming of reeds and
the clash of cymbals, as a band came nearer along the
avenue and approached the corner of the street. The invalid's face lit up—he made a motion to rise hastily from the
sofa—a sudden spasm of pain crossed his countenance, and
he fell back exhausted, with a slight cry which instantly
brought the sound of sliding doors between the little back

parlor and the large room that adjoined it in front, and sent a pair of light feet flying into the room.

"Trying to get up again, eh, old fellow? I know you! Couldn't lie still when that music was going by! Now you great big boy, you ought to know better!" Such were the words with which the young girl greeted the sufferer, as she dropped down on her knees by the side of the sofa and took one of his hands in both hers.

"Yes, Joe, I *was* trying to get up and listen to the music," was the reply. "You know how I have always loved the brass band, and how it seems to rack my frame even worse than disease, just now! See what a wreck I am, when I cannot even attempt to rise from the sofa without screaming in that manner and alarming the house!"

"Oh, never mind alarming the house!" replied the girl, whom he had called "Joe," the very convenient and popular abbreviation of the Christian name of Miss Josephine Harris. She was, it may be said here, an almost every-day visitor from the house of her widowed mother, a lady in very comfortable circumstances, living not many blocks away up-town from the residence of the Crawfords. In ordinary seasons Joe and her mother (the young lady is made to precede the other, advisedly)—had a habit of getting away from the city, early in the season, to one of the watering-places or some cool retreat in the country; but this year perhaps the illness of Richard Crawford had something to do with retaining at least the daughter late in town. "The house can get along well enough—it is *you* that is to be taken care of, and I should like to know, Dick Crawford, how any body is going to do it if you do not manage to moderate your transports and lie still when you have not strength to do any thing else!"

How her tongue ran on, and what a tongue she had! Not a bit of sting in it, except when she was fully aroused to anger, and then it would suddenly develope the faculty of morally flaying her victim alive, with words of indignation that tumbled over each other without calculation or order, in the effort to escape the tears of vexation that were sure to follow close behind. At such moments Joe's tongue was actually cruel, though without premeditation; at other times
3

it was simply a very rapid and noisy tongue, that spoke very
sweet words most of the time and exercised an influence all
around it that no one could attempt to describe. But perhaps the tongue was not alone concerned in the matter.
There may have been something in the rather tall and lithe
form—the brown cheek with a dash of color shining through
it the moment she was in the least degree warmed or excited
—the eyes dark but sunny, wavering between hazel brown
and Irish gray, and the most difficult eyes in the world to look
into and yet keep your head—the profile uneven and partially
spoiled by the nose being decidedly pert, retroussé and too
small for the other features—the pouting red lips that never
seemed to fade and grow pale as the lips of so many American
women do before one half their sweetness has been extracted
by the human bee—the wealth of glossy black hair, coming
down on the low forehead and plainly swept back in the
Madonna fashion over a face that otherwise had the purity
and goodness of the Madonna in it, but very little of her devotion,—perhaps there was something in all this, besides the
influence of her flood-tide of language, to make Josephine
Harris the delight, the botheration and the absolute tyrant
of more than half the persons with whom she was thrown in
contact. Perhaps there was even more than all, to those
with whom she came into closer intercourse, in the breath
that always seemed as if it came over a bank of over-ripe
strawberries dying in the sun, late in summer—and that
intoxicated with its aroma as rare old wine does with its flavor.

It is not difficult to believe (par parenthese) that the
pearls and diamonds that dropped from the mouth of the
good little princess in the old fairy story, every time she
opened the ruby portals of her lips, dissolved themselves into
air and came out in breath suggestive of spice-fields and
orange-groves, and that the toads and scorpions falling from
the mouth of her wicked sister manifested themselves in a
corresponding rank and fetid odor. So bear with us, lady
of the fevered breath, if we take the privilege of age and long
sight to drink in your flood of pleasant wisdom from a distance; and think not your lover overbold, Edie of the Red

Lips, if he bends so near you when you speak, that the waves of brown and the curls of black even nestle together!

"Another sermon, eh, Joseph?" said the invalid, trying to smile and apparently soothed away from his pain by the very presence of the young girl. "Another sermon just be cause I cannot *always* remember that I am a poor miserable wreck!"

"Miserable fiddlestick!" said Joe, smoothing down his hair with both hands and accidentally stooping down so low that her lips came near enough to his forehead to breathe on it and send a pleasant creeping chill to the very tips of his toes. "I read you sermons, as you call them, because you are very impatient and very imprudent, and because I really have no one but yourself who is tied down so as not to be able to run away when I begin preaching. Don't you see that?"

"Yes, I do!" said the invalid, whom she had unconsciously introduced to us in calling him Dick Crawford—"I see!" and his face grew into a transient smile in spite of himself. "But where is my sister, and what was the music?"

"Two questions at once, like all the men!" the saucy girl answered. "But go ahead, for asking questions won't hurt your rheumatism. Bell has gone out shopping, I believe. She discovered an hour ago that there was a shade of cerise ribbon somewhere or other that she had not managed to get hold of, and of course she ordered the carriage at once and posted after it. As for the music—oh, the music was a brass band accompanying the One Hundred and Ninetieth Regiment. They are going to leave to-morrow, and they came up the avenue to receive a set of colors from Mrs. Pearl Dowlas, the ugly old woman with all that brown-stone incumbrance and three flags in the windows, round the corner."

"Going to-morrow!" said the invalid, and the old pained expression came back to his face. "Going to-morrow!— everybody is going!—and I lie here like a crushed worm, unable to move from my couch, useless to myself or to any one else, when the country is calling upon all her children to aid her! Pest on it! I would trade life, hopes, brains if I have any, every thing, for a sound body to-day!"

"And make a great fool of yourself in doing so!" was the flattering response of Josephine. "Now I suppose that music and my gabble have started the mill, and we shall have nothing else during the rest of the day than the same old weepings and wailings and gnashings of teeth. Just as if, because a war exists, there was nothing else in the world to do but to go to the war! Just as if we did not require some attention paid to the needs of the country at home, as well as on the battle-field! Just as if we did not need that the trade, and the literature—yes, the *literature* of the country—should be sustained."

"Pshaw!" said Crawford, impatiently, and making an effort to turn over, with his face to the wall.

"No you don't, old fellow!" cried the young girl, exercising the little restraint that was necessary. "You don't get away from me in that manner. I will stop your grumbling before I have done with you, by a remedy a little worse than the disease—plenty of my own gabble! I said literature—do you see that desk littered with papers, you ungrateful wretch?" (It will be seen that Josephine Harris had a habit of using strong Saxon words, as well as some that were "fast," not to say bordering upon popular slang; and the reader may as well be horrified with her, and get over it, first as last.) "You have sent out from that desk words that have done more good to the patriotic cause than the raising of ten regiments, and yet you have not the grace to thank God for giving you the strength to do *that!* You *dare* to lie there and call yourself useless! Out-upon you—I am ashamed of you!"

"Words are not deeds!" said the young man, again moving uneasily.

"Words, when they come from the furnace of a true heart, shape themselves into deeds in others," was the reply.

"In the days of the Revolution, my ancestors did their deeds, instead of shaping them," said the invalid. "Two of them dead in the Old Sugar House and the prison ships at the Wallabout, and another crippled for life at Saratoga, bore witness that patriotism with them was no hollow pretence. And look at the present. My brother John going through battle after battle with Duryea's Zouaves, in Virginia, like a brave man and a soldier; and I lying helpless here, while my cousin Egbert has his regiment almost raised."

"*Almost,*" said the young girl, in a tone which showed that she did not think he had quite accomplished that laudable endeavor.

"And will be going down directly," Crawford continued.

"Yes, going down, clear down, that is if he ever starts!" commented saucy Josephine.

"Yes, I remember, you do not like my cousin Egbert," said the invalid.

"I do not like humbugs anywhere!" sharply said the young girl. "Why don't you call him 'Eg.,' as you do sometimes? Then I should be tempted to make a few bad puns, and to say that in my opinion he is not a 'good egg,' but a 'hard egg,' if not a 'bad egg,' and that I hope if he ever gets among the Virginia sands he will come out a 'roast egg' or a 'cracked' one!"

"Shame, Joe, what do you mean!" said the invalid, really pained by her flippancy.

"Mean? why, mean what I say!" was the answer, "and that is a good deal more than most of the people do now-a-days. Your cousin Egbert is a big humbug! I never see him strutting about, with his shoulder-straps and his red sword-belts, but I have a mind to take the first off his shoulders, with claws like a cat, and use the second to strap him with, like a truant schoolboy!"

"Why, Josephine, Josephine!" cried the invalid, still more surprised.

"Don't stop me!" said the wild girl. "I have intended for some time to say this to you, but you have been very sick, and somehow I could not begin the conversation. Now that it is begun, I am going to out with it, if it costs a lawsuit. I do not like that man, nor would you if you could know him half as well as I do. In the first place, I believe he is a coward, and worth no more to the cause than just what his gimcracks would sell for."

"Shame;" again said the invalid. "Josephine, you are really going too far. If he was a coward, why would he have placed himself in a position which must by-and-by be one of danger?"

"Bah!" said the young girl, "I do not see that he has done any thing of the kind. Officers have the right of resigning, and some of them have the habit of skulking, I have heard. I will bet my best bonnet against your old worn-out slippers there, that if ever brought to the test your shoulder-strapped cousin would do one or the other! Besides—" and here she paused.

"Well, what is the 'besides'?" asked the young man, a little impatiently.

"Besides, he hates you like a rattlesnake, and would do any thing in his power to get you out of his way," the young girl said, giving out the words as if she was performing a painful operation and only doing it under a strong sense of duty. "Tell me: is there any point in which your interests would run counter to each other? I have seen daggers and poison in that man's eyes when looking at you, and when you have not observed him!"

"Interests?—in conflict? Good heavens, what are you saying, Josephine? Hate me—he?" and a terrible shadow passed over the face of the invalid. A moment before he had been unable to raise himself from the sofa, or bear the least motion, without agony. Now, in the excitement produced by her words and by some horrible doubt which they seemed to have awakened, he forgot the pain, or did not heed it, and struggled up to a sitting posture, his hands to his head and the whole expression of his face changed to one of intense mental suffering.

"Mr. Crawford—Dick!" the young girl cried in alarm; "what has happened—what have I said?—tell me: are you in sudden pain?" and she threw her arm around-him to sustain him in his sitting position.

"Do not ask me!" he said, hoarsely. "I cannot speak just now, but you have agitated me very much. My cousin —in his way—heavens!"

At this moment, and when the young girl, frightened at

what she had done, scarcely dared to speak another word, and was altogether at a loss what to do, there was a rattle of carriage wheels at the door, the sound of a latch-key applied to the lock, then steps and voices in the hall.

"Talk of the Prince of Darkness, and he is not very far from your elbow!" said Josephine, whose ears were sharper than those of the invalid. "I hear Bell's voice and that of the puissant and patriotic Colonel Egbert Crawford, who has evidently come home with her."

"*His* voice with hers, after what you have said!" the invalid gasped. "Lay me down quick, and hurt me as little as possible. I have not strength to sit up, and this pain— this pain—it drives me to distraction!" One hand was still at his head, and the other had fallen, whether accidentally or otherwise, over his heart. Whether the one hand or the other covered the pain of which he had that moment spoken, was difficult to tell. One thing was certain—that something in the last few moments had broken him down in health and spirits, even more than his long previous sickness. What was it?

Josephine, ever an excellent nurse in sickness (spite of her rapid tongue), and the one of all a crowd who was certain to have the head of the fainted woman on her breast, and her hands chafing the pallid temples,—assisted the invalid back to his recumbent position as quickly and as easily as possible; and at the moment when she had once more arranged the pillow under his head on the sofa, the glass doors between the front and back parlors slid gently apart, and Isabel Crawford and her cousin the Colonel, who had lately been the subject of so much speculation and agitation, approached the sofa of the rheumatic. His eyes were closed, and Josephine was standing at the open window with its closed blinds. Still she saw what the new-comers did not—a quick, convulsive shudder pass over the recumbent form, and the hand that lay on his heart close with a nervous spasm, as if it was crushing something hateful and dangerous that lay within it.

But the personal appearance of the two who had just entered, and the after events of that interview, must be recorded in a subsequent chapter.

CHAPTER III.

MOTHER AND DAUGHTER—LOVE, HATE, AND DISOBEDIENCE—·
JUDGE OWEN IN A STORM—AUNT MARTHA AND HER RECORD
OF UNLOVING MARRIAGE AND WEDDED OUTRAGE.

IT was a very pleasant picture upon which Mrs. Maria
Owen, wife of Judge Owen of the ——th District Court,
was looking just at twilight of a June evening; but something in that picture, or its surroundings, did not seem to
please her; for her comely though matronly face was drawn
into an expression of displeasure, and the little mice about
the wainscot, if any there were, might occasionally have
heard her foot patting the floor with impatience and vexation.

The time has been already indicated. The place was the
back parlor of Judge Owen's house, on a street not far from
the Harlem River—the window open and the parlor opening
into a neat little yard, half garden and half conservatory,
with glimpses over the unoccupied lots beyond, of the junction of Harlem River with the Sound, up which the Boston
boats had only a little while before disappeared on their way
eastward, and where a few white sails of trading-schooners
and pleasure-boats could yet be seen through the gathering
twilight.

But this did not comprise all the picture upon which
Mrs. Maria Owen looked; for in the window, with the last
rays of the dying daylight falling upon face and figure, sat
her daughter Emily, listlessly toying with the leaves of a
book that she had been reading until the light grew too
indistinct, and with a slight pout on her lip and an expression
of dissatisfaction generally distributed over her pretty face,
which showed that her own vexation and that of her mother
had some kind of connection more or less mysterious. The
face was not only pretty, as every one could see,—but softly
rounded, womanly and most loveable while yet girlish, as
only those could fully realize who had known something of
the comparative characters of women. The eyes (in a better
light) were hazel, with a depth and transparency which made

the very thought of a mean action in her presence apparently
impossible ; the cheek that showed against the fading light
had been rounded to perfection in the soft atmosphere floating
about eighteen, as a peach is rounded and colored by the
genial air and sunshine of late summer : the heavy masses
of hair that had partially fallen out of their confinement and
swept down to her shoulders, were scarcely darker than nut-
brown ; and the hand toying with the book would have
shown, even without a better glimpse of the half recumbent
figure, that that figure was of medium height, fully rounded
and delicately voluptuous. It is not to be supposed that
Emily Owen knew quite all this of herself. Some others
realized all her perfections, however, as will more fully and
at large appear (to use the conveyancers' phraseology) ;
and for the purposes of this narrative it is necessary to have
the lady distinctly before us.

And now what had caused the shadow on the matronly
face of Mrs. Owen, and the pout on the red lip of Emily ?
The old—old story : told over at some period or other in
almost every household on earth. Old eyes and young eyes,
seeing very differently ; old hearts and young hearts, beating
to very different tunes, and informing the whole being with
very different aspirations. There was a love—there was a
dislike—and there was a certain amount of parental soli-
citude and determination—excellent materials from which to
construct a serious disagreement and an eventual family row.
Not Hecate, when she threw " eye of newt and tail of frog"
into the infernal brew on the blasted heath, could have been
more certain of the final nature of her compound, than may
the presiding genius of any " well regulated family" be of
the eventual result when the two acids of love and hate are
brought chemically together in the heart of budding womanhood.

There was a certain John Boadley Bancker, a man of a
family exceedingly respectable, though decayed, who had
himself been a speculator in lands and stocks and amassed
more or less money, and who was popularly understood to
have been intrusted by Major General Governor Morgan
with the authority of Colonel and the permission to raise a

regiment for the war. There was a certain Frank Wallace, a young man of no particular family that any one had ever heard mentioned, a fellow of infinite jest and agreeableness, but very little money and no commission at all except to make love when necessary and extract as much comfort as possible from the passing hour,—who carried on a small printing business which just made him a comfortable livelihood, in a narrow street within a stone's throw of the Museum. It was the bounden duty of Miss Emily Owen, seeing that the portly Judge, her father, and the pleasant matron, her mother, had formed the very highest opinion of one of these gentlemen, to fall in love with him as quickly as possible. Of course she had contracted for him a most unconquerable aversion! It was her bounden duty to ignore the other, even if she did not hate and despise him—seeing that he found no other friend in her family: could there have been a stronger guaranty for her going madly in love with the scapegrace?

A moment after the period when we saw them sitting in silence and mutual discomfort, mother and daughter resumed the conversation which had brought about that state of feeling.

" You will be sorry for what you have said, Emily!" said the mother.

" So will you, for what *you* have said!" was the reply of the daughter, with that species of iteration which displays no wit but a great deal of earnestness.

" You know, as well as I do, that your father has set his heart upon this match," continued the mother, " and you know how much he is in the habit of allowing others to oppose him."

" Yes, I know," replied the young girl, " and I know one thing more."

" Indeed! and what is that?" asked the mother, with the slightest perceptible shade of a sneer in her voice.

"—That both you and my father made a serious blunder in bringing *me* into the world, if you meant to get along entirely without opposition!"

" Hoity toity!" exclaimed the mother, quite as much sur-

prised as nettled at this original and forcible way of stating
a domestic fact. "What has become of your modesty? Do
you mean to insult both your father and myself?"

"No!" said the young girl, in a sharper tone and with
her words cut off much shorter and more decidedly than was
her habit. While those plump little white fingers had been
toying with the leaves of the book, sitting there in the
twilight, heart and hand had evidently both been busy, and
they had produced any other effect rather than making their
owner more tractable. "No! mother, no! But I tell you,
once for all, that the match you are talking of is hateful!
I have tried to keep still while the affair seemed at some
distance, but now that you bring it closer it fills my whole
being with disgust! Do drop it if you do not wish to drive
me mad or make me disobedient. Oh, mother!" and the
whole manner of the young girl seemed to change and melt
in a moment, as she rose hastily from her chair, ran to that
on which her mother was seated, threw herself on her knees
with her arms around her parent, and buried her face in the
sheltering lap,—"oh mother! do be my friend instead of
my enemy, in this! I cannot—indeed I cannot marry that
man!"

There are a good many things they think they cannot do—
these young girls—and they never know themselves until
they are tried. Perhaps it may not always be well to try
them to their full capacity, however!

What Mrs. Maria Owen might have answered to this
appeal, under other circumstances, is uncertain. She was,
or intended to be, a good and tender mother, and would have
cut off her right hand rather than do any thing which could
make against the ultimate happiness of her daughter; and
she really, at that moment, must have caught a glimpse of
the fact that the heart of the young girl was very much
interested in her refusal. But if there was any sentiment
which the worthy woman entertained more deeply than
another, it was the belief that Judge Owen, her husband,
was the most wonderful man in the world. She thought of
him with pride when his portly figure disappeared down the
steps of a morning, when he was starting to go to "Court."

She thought of him with a respect amounting to reverence
when she contemplated him sitting

> "At once mild and severe,
>   On his seat of dooming,"

(to quote good old Esaias Tegner) a local Rhadamanthus
from whose judgment there could not be any possible appeal
(although, sooth to say, there *were* a good many appeals, and
quite effectual ones, from the very unimportant decisions to
which only his authority extended). And when he came
home at night, after dispensing justice for the whole day
(to wit—three hours on the average) she looked with almost
holy reverence on his broad brow, under which there must
lie such a store of legal knowledge, and thought what a
blessed and honored woman she was to have been allowed
to mate with so much wisdom and so much dignity.

Does this sound like sneering at the wife's pride and devotion? If so, let there be a word to qualify it. God knows
that there are not too many women who respect and look up
to their husbands, and that the sanctity and the happiness of
the domestic circle would be much seldomer invaded if there
was more of this feeling. Only those poor women, on an
average, make such terrible mistakes as to the instances that
should demand or allow the full indulgence of this pride; and
miserable humbugs are looked up to and worshipped so
much of the time, while those who could deserve and should
command that feeling are treated with indifference or even
despised by inferior minds to which they have been mated!
They do not "manage these things" any "better in France,"
probably; but they manage them ill enough in republican
America at about this period, and the result is not a pleasant
or even a moral one!

The check to any possible motherly concession to the
weakness of Emily, which Mrs. Owen experienced on this
occasion, arose from the coming of the ponderous man of law,
whose heavy footstep and loud cough were at that moment
heard in the hall. Had the daughter been less absorbed
than she was in her own feelings, she too might have heard

those tokens of the Judge's presence; and had she been as wise as her mother, any further discussion of the subject would have been stopped and the coming catastrophe averted.

Either she did not observe or she was too much absorbed to heed who heard her, for at the very moment when Judge Owen, a large-framed, portly, broad-browed, iron-gray man of fifty, entered the back parlor and stood full in the presence of his wife and daughter, the latter was looking up to her mother with clasped hands and half sobbing out a repetition of her former declaration: "I cannot—indeed I cannot marry that man!"

"Hush! Emily, hush!—no more of this!" said the mother, half in hope that her husband might not have caught the words; but she was widely mistaken. The ears so much in the habit of listening to the least quaver in the tone of a witness's voice, were not to be trifled with in the present instance.

"Hey? What is this?" asked the Judge, in a tone that admitted of no trifling in the answer.

"Nothing—that is—Emily was talking of—" began the abashed wife, with a stammer.

"Of—I know," said the father, who had heard quite enough of his daughter's words to know without asking, and who was more behind the curtain than his wife, in some other respects. "I heard what this school-girl muttered. She cannot marry the man whom I intend she shall marry, and she has taken this opportunity, when she supposed I was absent, to acquaint you with her determination."

"Not determination," said the mother, willing to smooth affairs as much as possible—"say wish."

"No, mother, determination!" said the young girl, springing to her feet with an energy which was really not an ordinary part of her nature,—under the impression that now, if ever, was the time to give utterance to her true sentiments. "Father used the right word—determination! I cannot marry Boad Bancker, and I won't! There you have it!"

There was nothing classic or even romantic in the young lady's mode of expression, or the nickname which she bestowed upon her would-be lover; but they were at least

natural, which is something gained in this world of pre-
tences and deceptions.

"You won't? and why, I should like to know?" broke in
the Judge, for the moment surprised out of the violence that
might have resulted, by the very audacity of the declaration.

"Because he is hateful, and ugly, and I do not like him,
and—" answered Miss Emily, with a charming return to the
system of the school-girl which she had just been called by
her father.

"Silence!" thundered Judge Owen, who had recovered
from the blow and thought that he had a refractory juryman
or an insolent attorney to put down. "Silence! I have had
enough of this. John Boadley Bancker is the man I have
selected for your husband. He belongs to an excellent
family, has wealth enough to keep a wife in comfort and
even luxury, and has lately proved himself a true patriot by
springing up at the call of the President—" (Judge Owen
had by this time forgotten his indignation, and fancied himself
for the moment addressing an immense assemblage at Union
Square or in the Park)—"by springing up at the call of the
President, girding on his—"

"—Shoulder-straps!" put in Miss Emily, who had recovered from her agitation and began to be mischievous the
moment her father began to be didactic and ponderous.
Whether he heard the interpolation or not, is somewhat
doubtful.

"—Girding on his sword," the Judge went on, "and
marching—"

"—Up and down Broadway!" put in the young girl, in a
second parenthesis, not more audible than the other.

"That is, he has not marched, but is going to march to the
seat of war, to fight for—"

"—The niggers!" again and finally interpolated the incorrigible, who had somehow managed to get a peep behind
the curtain of national affairs and to see towards what the
great struggle seemed tending.

"—For the defence of the country," the Judge concluded
his peroration. Then he went on with the pith of his remark,
to the effect that the girl who could be mad enough and dis-

obedient enough to refuse the hand of such a man as that,
might go to—mumble—mumble—mumble—for she could
never more be daughter of his!

By this time Emily had recovered her equanimity, and
almost her spirits, and her mother shared in the feeling of
relief, for the explosion had not been half so violent as expected. But there are pauses in storms, the moment before
the coming of the most destructive blasts of all, and the temper of Judge Owen was gusty. Miss Emily fancied that the
whole ought to be said while the subject was under discussion, and, to use a vulgarism, she "put her foot in it."

"Boad Bancker," she said (she had the common weakness
of supposing that the use of a nick-name belittled the person
spoken of)—"Boad Bancker may be a soldier, but nobody
knows it. I know he is a fool; and he is a miserable humbug, pretending to be a young man, when he is as old as
you, Pa!"

If Judge Owen had a weakness unworthy one of the
shining lights of the bench, it lay in thinking that his fifty
years were only thirty, and that he was yet a young man.
Other men than the Judge have labored under the same
delusion, and found sick rooms and decrepitude necessary to
disabuse them. Probably nothing in his daughter's power
to utter would have made him so angry. He had only muttered before—this time he thundered.

"Old! You are talking about age, are you, you shameless,
impertinent hussy—insulting me as well as my friends, are
you! I know you, and by G—" (he was a dignitary of the
legal profession, and he was speaking in the presence of his
wife and daughter; but the truth must be recorded)—"I
know what you are driving at, and I'll break you of your
fancy or I'll break your stubborn neck! You don't like
Bancker, the husband I pick out for you, because he is not
a beardless boy, and you choose to consider him old. And
you think I will permit you to encourage that miserable
beggar, Frank Wallace, because he is young! Let me see
one more sign of familiarity between him and yourself, and I
will kick him out of the house, as I would a dog—and you
may go after him! Do you hear me? Now look out!" And

the Judge rang the bell for the servant, scolded her for not lighting the gas that no one had before wished lighted, and stormed out of the room, leaving his wife to follow him, and his daughter to drop again into her chair and muse over the pleasant prospect for after-life lying so broadly before her.

But if the young girl had passed through an agitating and unpleasant scene, and if the prospects for her future life had been sensibly narrowed within the preceding half hour, the depths of her being had not been stirred as they were to be before she slept. Perhaps she had occupied the position of depression into which she had fallen, in the chair by the window, with her head upon her hand, for five minutes—a bitter sea of thought surging through her mind, and her flash of resolution so giving way before her father's terrible anger, that she felt almost ready to sacrifice her happiness, life, every thing, to obey him and secure peace—when a hand was laid gently upon her shoulder, and the quiet face of Aunt Martha, framed in its widow's cap, peered into her own.

"Oh, Aunt, I am so glad you have come down! I was so lonely and so wretched!" broke out Emily, the moment she felt the touch and saw the face.

"I have been down some time, sitting in the front parlor by the window, and trying to make music out of that very-badly-cracked hand-organ that was playing on the other side of the way," said the widow, taking her seat by the young girl's side. Perhaps five-and-forty years had passed over the widowed younger sister of Judge Owen, who made her home in a quiet upper chamber of his house. But they had not much thinned her tall and magnificent form, or entirely destroyed, though they had completely *subdued*, the quiet beauty of her face, which must once have been strikingly like that of her niece. She had been in youth the underling of her family, as her elder brother had been the tyrant; and it was perhaps a fitting sequel, that at this period of her life she should have become, to some small extent, a pensioner on his bounty, as well as a peace-maker in his household.

"You have been in the front parlor some time?" echoed her niece, surprised. "Then you must have heard—"

"I heard quite enough," was the answer, as Aunt Martha

possessed herself of both the young girl's hands, and finally
drew down the nut-brown head so that it rested upon her
bosom. "I heard a few of your words—enough to tell me
what are your feelings toward the man whom they wish to
make your husband. I heard your father's fierce resolution,
and I made my own." ·

"And what was that?" asked the young girl, rising from
her recumbent position, and showing something of the surprise she felt at hearing her gentle and pliant aunt speak of
forming resolutions. She had cause to be more surprised in
a moment.

"What was my resolution?" echoed Aunt Martha. "A
strange one, perhaps, but one quite as immovable as my big
brother's!"

"Yes, yes—tell me, Aunt, *dear* Aunt!" pleaded Emily, feeling that there was some shadow of hope in such words from
such a source.

"My resolution?" said the placid woman, placid now no
longer, but starting to her feet, speaking with rapid energy,
and seeming, for the moment, half a foot taller than usual—
"My resolution is that you shall never marry the man whom
I have heard you say that you loathe and detest—not if
sacrificing myself can save you—not if I can prevent the
wrong, by even taking his life!"

"Aunt! Aunt! what are you saying!" broke out the young
girl, surprised, and even horrified. "Do not say so, Aunt,
for heaven's sake! I *do* dislike Col. Bancker; I cannot
marry him without misery; but his life! You do not know
what words you use."

"Do I not?" said the aunt, and there was a bitterness in
her tone which her niece had never before heard there, and
which perhaps no one else had heard there for many a long
year. "Do I not? His life—pshaw! what is his life, or the
life of any man, compared to some other lives that are sacrificed without punishment or even the knowledge of any
crime being committed!"

"Aunt, dear Aunt, it is for me that you are saying this,
and you know that I thank you; but you are excited, you
are not yourself—"
4

"I *am* myself—perhaps for the first time in years!" said
the widow, the tones of her voice still betraying the same
bitterness. "In the last half hour I have lived over again
half a life-time of misery. Close that door!" And she
pointed to the door leading into the front parlor, with a gesture of command that shamed her brother's most forcible
attempt at dignity. Her niece closed the door, and stepped
back to her chair. The aunt retained her standing position,
and a part of the time walked the floor of the little back
parlor with strides that the shorter limbs of Emily could not
have compassed, as she went on :

"I had you close that door because I did not wish to speak
to the whole house : though the whole house might hear me
without disadvantage to themselves. You do not know why
I am so much excited : I will tell you. That man—your
father and my brother—did an unwise thing in recalling the
past by that brutal speech and that rough oath ; but he did
recall it, and he must take the consequences. I have said
that you should not marry that man whom you detest, and
you shall not—no matter how I prevent it! But do not
mistake me, Emily! I am not arranging that you shall
marry another man, and one whom your parents dislike.
That is your business, not mine."

"I will not marry against my parents' will or against
yours," said Emily, as her aunt paused for a moment—"only
prevent my marrying this man whom I dislike, without doing
any crime !"

"Hush, and listen to *me!*" said the aunt, almost sternly.
"Do you think that it is of yourself alone that I am speaking?
No—I am thinking and speaking more of myself than of you.
Do you guess the riddle? No, you cannot. Emily, *I have
myself once married a man whom I loathed, and I know
what it means!*"

"You, Aunt? good heavens!" was the pitying reply of
the young girl, while the usually placid widow, occasionally
with both hands to her head as if in severe suffering, still
walked the room as she spoke.

"You begin to understand me, and you begin to perceive
how that man threatening to marry *you* to a man you hate,

has opened again the wounds of my own sacrifice—a sacrifice *he* made nearly twenty years ago—heaven. forgive him ! Richard West was a gambler and a libertine. There was an indefinable something which told me as much, very soon after I met him. He was tall and fine-looking, and he had political influence. My brother had a motive for courting him. He carried out that object by introducing him to *me*. I can scarcely say that I loved elsewhere, though I certainly had a preference. From the first I had a dislike to West, which soon grew into absolute aversion. Meanwhile I was allowing myself to be more and more in his company, and my whole family, with my big brother at their head, were importuning me to marry him. I was a little reckless and did not know myself; and I think it was more to get clear of his importunities and theirs, than for any other purpose, that I at last permitted myself to be engaged to him. I hated to be teased —I had no other settled hope in the world—and so I promised to marry a man whom I despised. Are you listening ?"

" Yes, dear Aunt, listening with my whole heart as well as my ears !" said the young girl, creeping up to her as she made a momentary pause, and taking one of her aunt's hands in both of her own. Strange to say, the aunt did not permit her hand to be retained. She drew it away as if for the moment she had no care for human sympathy,—and went on with her agitated walk and her narration.

"I had a shuddering horror of the marriage, very soon after my engagement was formed, though I knew nothing, except from my own perception, against the character of West. That feeling grew as the marriage day approached, and I found that instead of schooling myself to meet with calmness what was now inevitable, every day increased an aversion which was both mental and physical. I commenced to make my wedding clothes. I began to think that I would rather be making my shroud. And yet I worked on, stolidly, and bore the caresses of the man who was so soon to be my husband. He grew warmer and warmer in his manifestations as the marriage day approached. I suppose he thought he was flattering and pleasing me ! God help him, if he did ! I was handsome, I know it—and the sensualist began to gloat over the charms he would so soon have in possession. I began to think how soon the slimy worms would crawl over me! At length all this culminated. West was fool enough to take me one night to the Old Park Theatre, where Ellen Tree was then playing. She played *Julia*, in "The Hunchback," and I heard her make that agonized appeal to *Master Walter* and allude to the expected horrors of an unloving marriage-bed. My eyes were opened. I saw it all, now, as I had never done before. It was not alone my existence and my mentality that I must sacrifice, but my *body*. That too was to be given up! To what horrible profanation and outrage was I to be subjected! My head grew dizzy and my eyes blind. I shared in the torments of *Julia*—I was *Julia* herself. I was on the brink of a precipice, with hell beneath me and devils goading me on to the leap. I went home stunned and half crazed. West spoke to me, but I believe that I never answered him a word. If I could have killed him suddenly and without reflection, I should have done it.

"The next day I implored my brother to assist me in breaking the hateful engagement. He refused, insultingly, and threatened me with á ruined reputation and the scorn of every one who knew me, if, after being so notoriously engaged to West, and in his private society so much, the marriage should now be broken off. I had no one else to whom to appeal, and appeal to my *bridegroom* would have been worse than useless. I could not combat every thing and everybody. My God! my God!—that I should have given up!—but I did. I went on finishing my wedding-clothes; with only a week between me and their use. Oh how I shuddered as my needle ran over the soft white laces and ruffles! They were to deck my dainty limbs for *outrage*—such outrage as I did not then know—and such as you can only dream. I only saw before me a vague horror, but that horror was enough to set me on the dizzy verge of madness, of suicide or of *murder*.

"A week went by, and in the presence of a minister of God I swore to a lie. Richard West swore to another, for he was no more capable of love than of honor. Then followed what, woman though you already are, I cannot tell you of—prostitution, outrage, that left me a poor dishonored *thing*—my womanhood a curse, and the creeping horror of physical repugnance to a loathsome touch my bridal portion ! God forgive those who forced me to this ! God forgive them !' —I do not know that *I* ever can ! Ten years afterwards I saw one happy day—the first since my engagement. It was when Richard West was shot down in a gambling-house by one of his victims, and brought home dead !

"Now, Emily, you know, better than any other living, the heart of the woman who is supposed to be so calm and placid ! Now you can have some idea what I have suffered to-night, when I saw the same pit opening for *you?* Do you understand me ? Have I said enough ?"

"Enough, dear, dear Aunt, but not one word too much ! I understand you, I know you, now ! Oh, save me, save me at any sacrifice from this marriage !" And the young girl was sobbing in the arms of Aunt Martha, who now that her story was told grew her gentle self again, and smoothed down the brown hair with a promise of aid and sympathy which was not likely to be forfeited

---

CHAPTER IV.

ANOTHER ADVENTURE OF THE TWO FRIENDS—THE LIGHT IN THE WINDOW—A SINGULAR SPOT ON THE WALL—A CLIMB, A TUMBLE AND A PURSUIT—HOW IT ALL ENDED FOR THE TIME.

WE left Walter Harding and Tom Leslie, at the conclusion of a former chapter, coming out from the lodgings of the latter, on Bleecker Street near Elm, Leslie accompanying Harding out to a car on the Bowery before betaking himself to bed. "Man proposes but God disposes," says the French proverb: There is "a divinity that shapes our ends," even in the matters of going to bed and getting into railroad cars.

It was somewhat longer than either had expected, before he reached the "desired haven" of home and a bed-chamber.

It was past midnight when the two friends reached the Bowery, and the Third Avenue cars, on one of which Harding was going up, were running less frequently than early in the evening. There was not one of the green lights in sight down the Bowery from the corner of Bleecker Street, and the friends chatted a moment while waiting for one to make its appearance. Then they grew tired and restless, as people very soon do who are waiting for cars (or boiling tea-kettles, or marriage-days, or any thing of that kind); and they walked down to the corner of Prince to meet the tardy conveyance. There was a green light coming up, some blocks down the Bowery, but it seemed to the two sleepy fellows as if it would never reach the corner. They walked listlessly a block or two down Prince Street toward Broadway, still arm in arm as they had left the house on Bleecker. They wheeled to walk back. Suddenly the eyes of Harding were attracted by the very bright light in one of the upper windows of an old brick house on Prince Street, large and stately and giving evidence of having once been the residence of some person of fortune, though now a little dilapidated.

"People in that house must have an interest in one of the Gas Companies," said Harding, "by the quantity of light they show at this time of night! Why, the window is all ablaze!"

Tom Leslie looked up, as his friend spoke. They were on the opposite side of the street from the house in question, and consequently had a fair view of the lighted window. It *was* very light indeed, a perfect flood of gaslight pouring on a white curtain that partially covered the whole sash. Partially, not altogether. Whether accidentally or by intention, it was swept away at the lower right-hand corner, leaving a little of the top of the white wall of the room visible, with the edge of the ceiling. Was there ever a man (or woman) who did not look in through a half-closed curtain, precisely because there is no propriety whatever in doing so? Willis has made some of his most taking verbal photographs, during his "lookings on at the war" at Washington, from the

glimpses caught of the lower half lengths of notables, more
or less undressed, through windows supposed to be closed
against outside observation.

Both Walter Harding and Tom Leslie took an eager look
up at the white wall and the edge of the ceiling, in the upper
chamber of the house on Prince Street. Harding either had
sharper eyes than Leslie, or stood in a more favorable position, for he saw what Leslie did not, and his discovery was
communicated in the brief exclamation:

"By Jupiter!"

"What?" asked Leslie.

"Look!" said Harding, drawing his friend's head into
position for a better view. "If that is not a secesh flag
draped up near the ceiling, may I never brag of my eye-
sight again!"

Tom Leslie took a nearer look. "If it is *not* a secesh
flag," he said, "draped over some kind of a gilded ornament
like a star, may I never find another opportunity to look at a
pretty girl through this double-barrelled telescope."

And with the word he had whipped out an opera-glass
from his pocket, large enough to have been formed out of
two moderate-sized specimens of the optical instrument he
had named, and levelled it at the object on the wall. His
observations and those of Harding through the same powerful instrument resulted in the same conclusion. The two
red bars and one white one of the Confederate flag, with the
blue field in the corner and meagre number of stars, were all
plainly visible, and beneath the flag was a gilded circle, some
four or five inches in diameter, with a radiating centre.

"A nice house that, I don't think!" was Tom Leslie's not
very classical comment, as he took the double-barrelled telescope finally down from his eye, after a second inspection.
(It may be mentioned, in a parenthesis, that the Third
Avenue car had some time since rumbled by, and that the
very existence of that entire line of communication had been
forgotten by the two friends.) "Where is Provost Marshal
Kennedy, I wonder?"

"Oh, it may not be quite so bad as you think," said
Harding, reading the whole of his friend's thought. "Who

knows ?—that secesh flag may be a trophy won by one of
our soldiers, and brought or sent home."

"Humph !" said Tom, significantly. "That won't do,
Harding ! If the flag was a trophy, and in the house of a loyal
man, it would not be quite so neatly draped on the wall,
with the lodge emblem of the Knights of the Golden Circle
under it !"

"Phew !" said Harding, "is that really the emblem ?".

"*The* emblem, and nothing else," answered Leslie. "There
is mischief in that house, and the nest must be looked after."

Suddenly, and while the two friends yet looked, there were
dark shadows flung on the white curtain, as if of moving figures,
and then one shadow, as if of a human arm, began to move
up and down on the curtain and kept moving steadily.
Directly there was one quick sharp scream, followed by no
other sound, though both listened intently. Then a figure
came to the window, and apparently looked out, disappearing
again in a moment and leaving every thing as before.

"By George, I cannot stand this !" said Leslie.

"Nor I," said Harding, moved by quite a different feeling.
"I am getting sleepy and must go home."

"Must you ?" said Tom Leslie. "Well, you are not going
a step. You cannot be spared just yet. Do you see that
tree ?"

Harding had seen the tree for some minutes—a tall one
with wide branches, standing a little to the left of the window.
But he did not see anything special in the tree, while Leslie
did, and that made the great difference.

"I am going on a perilous expedition," continued Leslie,
in a bantering tone, but his voice sinking lower, almost without his being aware of the fact, and jerking off his boots
meanwhile on the sidewalk. "If I never come back, comfort my bereaved wife and children. If I break my neck,
see me comfortably buried, *without* a coroner's inquest if
possible."

"What are you going to do ?" asked Harding, with a fain
premonition, however, of his intention.

"I am going to get a peep in at that window," was the
reply, "or I am going to break the most precious neck in

America in making the attempt. I used to be able to climb, though some years ago. Keep still, here goes!"

There seemed to be at the moment no passers in the street, and Harding's anxious gaze around showed no policeman in the vicinity. By the time he had fairly spoken the last words, Leslie had thrown off his broad hat, crossed the street, and commenced climbing the tree. Harding followed and stood under the tree, as if Leslie was going to throw down apples and he must catch them. Leslie was a little awkward, but hugged the bark handsomely, and was soon on a level with the window. Harding saw him distinctly, by the reflected light from the window, clutch his arm around one of the main limbs, and throw his head and body forward so that his face was not more than a foot from the window. He had not looked in more than a moment, when Harding heard him utter a quick, short cry, and the next instant he seemed to be trying to regain his hold of the tree. Then there was a rush, a tumble, and he seemed to be falling. Harding threw himself beneath him, and Leslie half slid and half fell to the pavement, with such violence as to send both sprawling into the middle of the street. Harding was not much hurt; Leslie seemed to be injured, and limped a little as he sprang up.

"Are you hurt, Tom? What made you fall?" was the double question that Harding attempted to ask.

"My God! can that be possible?" was the inconsequent answer, and his hand went up to his head as if the organs of thought were for the moment disordered.

"What do you mean? What did you see, Tom?" was Harding's next double question. Leslie was pulling on his boots.

"See? Nothing—every thing! I will tell you all about it when my brains get settled!" was the reply. "I have simply been frightened out of my boots—no, I left my boots down here. But I was frightened out of the tree, and came devilish near to killing myself and *you*. Eh, didn't I?"

"Never mind about that! Tell us what you saw?" said Harding, whose bump of curiosity now began to be seriously agitated.

"The red woman! witch! devil! What does it all

mean?" was the torrent of incoherence which next burst
from Leslie, not affording Harding a very close solution of
the mystery, but promising at least something.

"Well?" said the latter, expecting more. They had again
crossed the street, and stood opposite the house of mystery.
Leslie was endeavoring to brush his soiled clothes with that
most difficult of all brushes, the hand. Harding was looking
full at the window, and waiting for the further explanation.
Suddenly, a carriage whirled through Prince from the direction of Broadway, and pulled up immediately before the
house. Leslie stopped brushing his clothes. At the same
moment, a head was again thrust against the window, and
immediately withdrawn. Then the light against the curtain
dimmed suddenly. Leslie "put that and that together" with
the celerity of a lawyer and the confidence of a man of the
world. The people in that house were going away. Where?
That was something to be looked into.

"You know where the livery stable round the corner is, on
Houston?" he asked hurriedly of Harding.

"Yes," was the reply.

"I am too lame to run fast," said Leslie, speaking very
rapidly. "We must follow those people, if they go to perdition.
Go to the stable, quick—do. There is always at least one
carriage standing ready, and have it here as soon as money
can bring it. I will watch meanwhile. Hurry! hurry!"

Probably Harding, who was rather precise in his ordinary
movements, had not gone so fast in ten years. He was
around the corner before the last words had fairly left Leslie's mouth—going as if an enraged woman and three lively
policemen had been close after him. Leslie stepped across
the street again, took a glance at the number on the lamps of
the hack as he passed, and then ensconced himself in a deserted doorway very near, to watch what followed. Every
moment that Harding was gone seemed an hour. Would
they come out and get away, after all, before the coming of
the other vehicle? What kept him so long? (He had been
gone about half a minute!) Had there been, for once, no
carriage in waiting at the livery? or had Harding concluded
to go to sleep on the road? And what the deuce did it all

mean—the half-dozen persons, and one a woman almost completely stripped, whom he had seen in that moment's glance into that upper chamber? And the red woman!—aye, the *red woman!*—that bothered Tom Leslie the worst, and as he had himself confessed, frightened him.

At this juncture the door of the house opened, and a man and two women came out. The man, from his stature and general appearance, and especially from his hat, struck Tom as strangely like the tall Virginian whom they had seen two hours before on Broadway. One of the women might be the girl, Kate; and the third—Leslie indulged in another bit of a shudder as he thought that possibly the third might be the red woman. They were all muffled up, however, and Leslie dared not quit his shelter to observe them more nearly. The driver kept his seat on the box. The man opened the door of the carriage, all stepped in, and the carriage whirled away out into the Bowery and up town. There they were, going, gone, and Harding not yet returned with the means of pursuit! Confusion, vexation and every cross-grained word in the language! So thought Leslie, as he dodged out to the Bowery and watched the disappearing carriage. It had not turned off into any one of the cross-streets, and seemed making for one or the other of the forks of the avenues at the Cooper Institute. Half a minute more, however, and it might as well be the proverbial "needle in the hay-stack" for any chance they would have of finding it again.

Hark! yes, there came tearing hoofs round into Prince Street from Crosby, and the lamps of a carriage shivered with the speed at which they were going. The horses were on the run. It was *their* carriage after all, for nobody else could be in such a hurry. Twenty seconds brought the flying carriage to the corner—a second's pause—a hail from each of the friends—and Leslie was inside with Harding, and the carriage was dashing up the Bowery about as fast as two good horses could run, with Leslie and Harding each peering out of the opened windows at the side, to see if they could catch any glimpse of a carriage ahead.

There is no doubt that the horses attached to the hinder

carriage, whatever may have been the opinions of those attached to the one before,—thought that the rate of speed was a little rapid for a hot midnight in June ; and certainly one or two pedestrians who came near being run over at the crossings just below the Cooper Institute, had an impression that some rebel prisoner must be running away from Fort Lafayette or some government official trying to stop one. As Harding and Leslie neared that highly respectable but very ugly monument to the profits of iron and glue and the public pride of Mr. Peter Cooper,—of course there arose a question, the carriage being out of sight, which of the two branches it had taken. The Third Avenue being the plainer road, Leslie decided for the Fourth, and with a shout to the driver just before they reached Tompkins Market, the horses' heads were turned in that direction, and away they went up the comparatively quiet avenue.

At the rate they were going they soon overtook a carriage, as they would have overtaken any thing less rapid than a locomotive or a whirlwind. It was lucky that Leslie had taken the precaution to note the number on the hack, as otherwise they would have been at fault after all. As they dashed by the carriage, which was going at good speed, that cosmopolitan saw that the number on the lamps was a wrong one ; and so they kept on. Another carriage was passed at the same speed, their horses by this time dripping as if they had been plunged into the river, but the driver of hack No. 2980 going ahead under the influence of a private five dollars and the promise of an extraordinary glass of brandy. At Twenty-eighth Street they jerked the check-string and the driver pulled up. There was nothing in sight, short of the railroad tunnel.

"We have lost them !" said Harding, whose organ of hopefulness was not so large as that of his friend.

"Humph ! maybe so !" was Leslie's reply, his eyes peering out of the windows on all sides, meanwhile. "One thing is certain, that I am not going to bed until I find that hack and know where it has been to-night !"

At that moment, with better fortune than two such wild-goose chasers deserved, they saw the lamps of a carriage flash across Twenty-eighth Street, going up Lexington Avenue.

"By George ! there they are !" said the sanguine Leslie.

"Maybe so !" was the reply of Harding, echoing the words his friend had used the moment before.

A word from Leslie to the driver, and away went the carriage down Twenty-eighth Street toward Lexington Avenue. On the avenue there was a carriage ahead, driving at good speed but not at such a headlong rate as their own had been pursuing. Leslie pulled the check-string. "Pass that carriage !" he said to the driver, and the horses sprung out at full speed again. The speed of the carriage ahead did not increase : whoever occupied it probably had no idea of being pursued. Before it had gone two blocks further the pursuers had passed it, and Tom Leslie brought his hand down upon Harding's leg with a force that made him wince, as he saw the number on the near lamp.

"Got them, by the tail of the holy camel !"

It was indeed the same carriage that had left Prince Street less than a quarter of an hour before. They were now ahead of it, and it would not answer either to slacken speed so perceptibly as to let it pass, or to turn back to meet it. Either course might excite apprehension, if there was really anything worth watching in the adventure. A word more to the driver arranged all. They wheeled down Thirty-fourth Street to Third Avenue, drove rapidly around the two blocks to Thirty-sixth, and came out again on Lexington, with the carriage just ahead of them and a fine opportunity to dog it at leisure.

Two or three minutes afterwards the leading carriage wheeled out of Lexington Avenue into East 5— Street, not very far from the Eastern Dispensary, which has lately so well supplied the place of a soldiers' hospital. It was driving slowly, now, and unless some peculiar dodge was intended, Leslie knew that the occupants must be near their destination. To follow them further with the carriage would be both useless and dangerous. Stopping the carriage and telling the driver to wait for them in the avenue half a dozen blocks above, the two friends alighted and followed their quarry on foot. They were close behind the carriage, now, but keeping the sidewalk, and even if observed they might have been supposed to be a couple of late wayfarers plodding home, and not *spies* as they at that moment felt themselves to be, in however meritorious a cause ! About half way between Fourth Avenue and Madison, the carriage stopped before a handsome brown-stone house. " Nothing venture nothing have !" is an old motto that never wears out. Before the rumble of the carriage had fairly stopped or the driver could have had time to turn around, the two friends were over the area railings and under the steps. Not a dignified position, perhaps, nor a pleasant one in which to be caught in the event of a sudden opening of the area door ; but other men have risked as much for a much idler curiosity !

Perfect silence under the steps, except two loudly-beating hearts and a little quick breathing. Leslie ventured a look around the corner of the stoop—saw the driver get down and open the door, and the one man and two women alight and go up the steps. For the rest, they were obliged to depend upon the ears. One of the women spoke :

" It will come to-morrow at midnight ?"

Harding could feel that Leslie shuddered, and could distinguish his sharp whisper to himself :

" The red woman's voice ! I knew I could not be mistaken !"

Then the voice of the man said : " Wait a moment !" and Leslie fancied that he recognized that voice quite as well as the other. Then there was a quick pull of the bell, the sound tinkling far back in the still house. Then came two sharp pulls after the pause of a moment, and then a fourth after another pause. Not until the fourth tinkle had been heard was there any other sound within the house. Then a door was heard to open and shut, and feet were heard in the hall. The man's voice said "All right !" and the carriage drove away. An inner door opened, but the outer one (as the friends could easily distinguish by the sound of the voices) remained closed until some one within asked :

" How many ?"

" Seven !" answered the man's voice. Then the outer

door opened, all went in, the doors closed and were locked, the footsteps in the hall died away, and the friends heard no more.

Very gingerly, as if some depredation on personal property had lately been committed, the two volunteer midnight guardians of the public weal climbed again over the area railings, after all had been still for a moment. Not a word passed between them. Harding stepped softly up the stone steps to the door and noted the number on it, then down again, as if he was treading on eggs. Leslie counted the number of houses from the corner, with steps not more sonorous, and looked around to see whether they could possibly not have been watched by a policeman, when getting into and out of the area, because they did *not* intend to steal. All these things accomplished, and apparently nothing more to be done, they went quietly down 5— Street to Lexington Avenue and sought their carriage.

CHAPTER V.

THE MYSTERY OF THE RED WOMAN—ANOTHER OF TOM LESLIE'S LONG STORIES—AN INCIDENT OF PARIS IN 1860 —THE VISION OF THE WHITE MIST—TWO MEN WITH ONE WONDER AND ONE PURPOSE.

" AND who was the red woman ?"

It has been indicated in a former chapter that both Tom Leslie and Walter Lane Harding intended, at one period of the night, to go to bed as soon as possible. The event was that neither found that luxury until the milkman was bawling under the windows. Harding had contrived to raise a large amount of curiosity, especially about the "red woman" and her possible connection with the events of the evening, and Leslie tired and satisfied him, collectively and at intervals, with another long story before they separated. Only

in his own words can that story be so conveyed as to be intelligible.

"I had returned from Vienna to Paris," he said, "late in
1860. No matter what I was doing in Paris; and as we
are upon a serious subject, don't let me hear a word about
'grisettes' or the 'back room of a baker's shop.' I lodged in
the little Rue Marie Stuart, not far from the Rue Montor-
geuil, and only two or three minutes' walk from the Louvre,
for the long picture galleries of which I had an unfortunate
weakness. I had a tradesman with a pretty wife for my
landlord, and a cozy little room in which three persons could
sit down comfortably, for my domicil. As I did not often
have more than two visitors, my room was quite sufficient;
and as I spent a large proportion of my evenings at other
places than my lodgings, the space was three quarters of the
time more than I needed.

"One of my intimates, a young Prussian by the name of
Adolph Von Berg, had a habit of visiting mediums, clairvoyants, and, not to put too fine a point upon it, fortune-
tellers. Though I had been in company with clairvoyants in
many instances, I had never, before my return to Paris in
the late summer of 1860, entered any one of those places in
which professional fortune-tellers carried on their business.
It was early in September, I think, that at the earnest solici-
tation of Von Berg, who had been reading and smoking with
me at my lodgings, I went with him, late in the evening, to
a small two-story house in the Rue La Reynie Ogniard, a
little street down the Rue Saint Denis toward the quays of
the Seine, and running from Saint Denis across to the Rue
Saint Martin. The house seemed to me to be one of the
oldest in Paris, although built of wood; and the wrinkled
and crazy appearance of the front was eminently suggestive of
the face of an old woman on which time had long been plowing
furrows to plant disease. The interior of the house, when we
entered it by the dingy and narrow hall-way, that night, well
corresponded with the exterior. A tallow candle in a tin
sconce was burning on the wall, half hiding and half reveal-
ing the grime on the plastering, the cobwebs in the corners,

and the rickety stairs by which it might be supposed that the occupants ascended to the second story.

"My companion tinkled a small bell that lay upon a little uncovered table in the hall (the outer door having been entirely unfastened, to all appearance), and a slattern girl came out from an inner room. On recognizing my companion, who had visited the house before, she led the way, without a word, to the same room she had herself just quitted. There was nothing remarkable in this. A shabby table, and two or three still more shabby chairs, occupied the room, and a dark wax-taper stood on the table, while at the side opposite the single window a curtain of some dark stuff shut in almost one entire side of the apartment. We took seats on the rickety chairs, and waited in silence, Adolph informing me that the etiquette (strange name for such a place) of the house did not allow of conversation, not with the proprietors, carried on in that apartment sacred to the divine mysteries.

"Perhaps fifteen minutes had elapsed, and I had grown fearfully tired of waiting, when the corner of the curtain was suddenly thrown back, and the figure of a woman stood in the space thus created. Every thing behind her seemed to be in darkness; but some description of bright light, which did not show through the curtain at all, and which seemed almost dazzling enough to be Calcium or Drummond, shed its rays directly upon her side-face, throwing every feature, from brow to chin, into bold relief, and making every fold of her dark dress visible. But I scarcely saw the dress, the face being so remarkable beyond any thing I had ever witnessed. I had looked to see an old, wrinkled hag—it being the general understanding that all witches and fortune-tellers must be long past the noon of life; but instead, I saw a woman who could not have been over thirty-five or forty, with a figure of regal magnificence, and a face that would have been, but for one circumstance, beautiful beyond description. Apelles never drew and Phidias never chiselled nose or brow of more classic perfection, and I have never seen the bow of Cupid in the mouth of any woman more

5

ravishingly shown than in that feature of the countenance of
the sorceress.

"I said that but for one circumstance that face would have
been beautiful beyond description. And yet no human eye
ever looked upon a face more hideously fearful than it was in
reality. Even a momentary glance could not be cast upon it
without a shudder, and a longer gaze involved a species of
horrible fascination which affected one like a night-mare.
You do not understand yet what was this remarkable and
most hideous feature. I can scarcely find words to describe
it to you so that you can catch the full force of the idea—I
must try, however. You have often seen Mephistopheles in
his flame-colored dress, and caught some kind of impression
that the face was of the same hue, though the fact was that
it was of the natural color and only affected by the lurid
character of the dress and by the Satanic pencilling of the
eyebrows! Well, this face was really what that seemed for
the moment to be. It was redder than blood—red as fire,
and yet so strangely did the flame-color play through it that
you knew no paint laid upon the skin could have produced
the effect. It almost seemed that the skin and the whole
mass of flesh were transparent, and that the red color came
from some kind of fire or light within, as the red bottle in a
druggist's window might glow when you were standing full
in front of it and the gas was turned on to full height behind.
Every feature—brow, nose, lips, chin, even the eyes themselves, and their very pupils, seemed to be pervaded and per-
meated by this lurid flame; and it was impossible for the
beholder to avoid asking himself whether there were indeed
spirits of flame—salamandrines—who sometimes existed out
of their own element and lived and moved as mortals.

"Have I given you a strange and fearful picture? Be
sure that I have not conveyed to you one thousandth part of
the impression made upon myself, and that until the day I
die that strange apparition will remain stamped upon the
tablets of my mind. Diabolical beauty! infernal ugliness!
—I would give half my life, be it longer or shorter, to be able
to explain whence such things can come, to confound and
stupefy all human calculation!

" Well, as I was saying, there stood my horribly beautiful
fiend, and there I sat spell-bound before her. As for Adolph,
though he had told me nothing in advance of the peculiarities
of her appearance, he had been fully aware of them, of course,
and I had the horrible surprise all to myself. I think the
sorceress saw the mingled feeling in my face, and that a
smile blended of pride and contempt contorted the proud
features and made the ghastly face yet more ghastly for one
moment. If so, the expression soon passed away, and she
stood, as before, the incarnation of all that was terrible and
mysterious. At length, still retaining her place and fixing
her eyes upon Von Berg, she spoke, sharply, brusquely, and
decidedly :

" ' You are here again ! what do you want ?'

" ' I come to introduce my friend, the Baron Charles
Denmore, of England,' answered Von Berg, ' who wishes—'

" ' Nothing !' said the sorceress, the word coming from her
lips with an unmistakably hissing sound. ' He wants nothing,
and he is *not* the Baron Charles Denmore ! He comes from
far away, across the sea, and he would not have come here
to-night but that you insisted upon it ! Take him away—go
away yourself—and never let me see you again unless you
have something to ask or you wish me to do you an injury !'

" ' But—' began Von Berg.

" ' Not another word !' said the sorceress, ' I have said.
Go, before you repent having come at all !'

" ' Madame,' I began to say, awed out of the feeling at
least of equality which I should have felt to be proper under
such circumstances, and only aware that Adolph, and possibly myself, had incurred the enmity of a being so near to the
supernatural as to be at least dangerous—' Madame, I hope
that you will not think—'

" But here she cut *me* short, as she had done Von Berg
the instant before.

" ' Hope nothing, young man !' she said, her voice perceptibly less harsh and brusque than it had been when
speaking to my companion. ' Hope nothing and ask nothing
until you may have occasion ; then come to me.'

" ' And then ?'

" 'Then I will answer every question you may think proper to put to me. Stay! you may have occasion to visit me sooner than you suppose, or I may have occasion to force knowledge upon you that you will not have the boldness to seek. If so, I shall send for you. Now go, both of you!'

"The dark curtain suddenly fell, and the singular vision faded with the reflected light which had filled the room. The moment after, I heard the shuffling feet of the slattern girl coming to show us out of the room, but, singularly enough, as you will think, not out of the *house!* Without a word we followed her—Adolph, who knew the customs of the place, merely slipping a twenty-franc piece into her hand; and in a moment more we were out in the street and walking up the Rue Saint Denis. It is not worth while to detail the conversation which followed between us as we passed up to the Rue Marie Stuart, I to my lodgings and Adolph to his own, further on, close to the Rue Vivienne and not far from the Boulevard Montmartre. Of course I asked him fifty questions, the replies to which left me quite as much in the dark as before. He knew, he said, and hundreds of other persons in Paris knew, the singularity of the personal appearance of the sorceress, and her apparent power of divination, but neither he nor they had any knowledge of her origin. He had been introduced at her house several months before, and had asked questions affecting his family in Prussia and the chances of descent of certain property, the replies to which had astounded him. He had heard of her using marvellous and fearful incantations, but had never himself witnessed any thing of them. In two or three instances, before the present, he had taken friends to the house and introduced them under any name which he chose to apply to them for the time, and the sorceress had never before chosen to call him to account for the deception, though, according to the assurances of his friends after leaving the house, she had never failed to arrive at the truth of their nationalities and positions in life. There must have been something in myself or my circumstances, he averred, which had produced so singular an effect upon the witch, (as he evidently believed her to be,) and he had the impression that at no distant day I should again hear from her. That was all, and so we parted, I in any other condition of mind than that promising sleep, and really without closing my eyes, except for a moment or two at a time, during the night which followed. When I did attempt to force myself into slumber, a red spectre stood continually before me, an unearthly light seemed to sear my covered eyeballs, and I awoke with a start. Days passed before I sufficiently wore away the impression to be comfortable, and at least two or three weeks before my rest became again entirely unbroken.

"You must be partially aware with what anxiety we Americans temporarily sojourning on the other side of the Atlantic, who loved the country we had left behind on this, watched the succession of events which preceded and accompanied the Presidential election of that year. Some suppose that a man loses his love for his native land, or finds it comparatively chilled within his bosom, after long residence abroad. The very opposite is the case, I think! I never knew what the old flag was, until I saw it waving from the top of an American consulate abroad, or floating from the gaff of one of our war-vessels, when I came down the mountains to some port on the Mediterranean. It had been merely red, white and blue bunting, at home, where the symbols of our national greatness were to be seen on every hand: it was the *only* symbol of our national greatness when we were looking at it from beyond the sea; and the man whose eyes will not fill with tears and whose throat will not choke a little with overpowering feeling, when catching sight of the Stars and Stripes where they only can be seen to remind him of the glory of the country of which he is a part, is unworthy the name of patriot or of man!

"But to return: Where was I? Oh! I was remarking with what interest we on the other side of the water watched the course of affairs at home, during that year when the rumble of distant thunder was just heralding the storm. You are well aware that without extensive and long-continued connivance on the part of sympathizers among the leading people of Europe—England and France especially—secession could never have been accomplished so far as it has been;

and there never could have been any hope of its eventual
success if there had been no hope of one or both these two
countries bearing it up on their strong and unscrupulous
arms. The leaven of foreign aid to rebellion was working
even then, both in London and Paris; and perhaps we
had opportunities over the water for a nearer guess at the
peril of the nation, than you could have had in the midst of
your party-political squabbles at home.

"During the months of September and October, when
your Wide-Awakes on the one hand, and your conservative
Democracy on the other, were parading the streets with
banners and music, as they or their predecessors had done in
so many previous contests, and believing that nothing worse
could be involved than a possible party defeat and some bad
feelings, we, who lived where revolutions were common,
thought that we discovered the smouldering spark which
would be blown to revolution here. The disruption of the
Charleston Convention and through it of the Democracy; the
bold language and firm attitude of the Republicans; the
well-understood energy of the uncompromising Abolitionists,
and the less defined but rabid energy of the Southern fire-
eaters: all these were known abroad and watched with
gathering apprehension. American newspapers, and the
extracts made from them by the leading journals of France
and England, commanded more attention among the Americo-
French and English than all other excitements of the time
put together.

"Then followed what you all know—the election, with its
radical result and the threats which immediately succeeded,
that 'Old Abe Lincoln' should never live to be inaugurated!
'He shall not!' cried the South. 'He shall!' replied the
North. To us who knew something of the Spanish knife
and the Italian stiletto, the probabilities seemed to be that
he would never live to reach Washington. Then the mutterings of the thunder grew deeper and deeper, and some disruption seemed inevitable, evident to us far away, while you
at home, it seemed, were eating and drinking, marrying and
giving in marriage, holding gala-days and enjoying yourselves generally, on the brink of an arousing volcano from

which the sulphurous smoke already began to ascend to the heavens! So time passed on; autumn became winter, and December was rolling away.

" I was sitting with half-a-dozen friends in the chess-room at Very's, about eleven o'clock on the night of the twentieth of December, talking over some of the marvellous successes which had been won by Paul Morphy when in Paris, and the unenviable position in which Howard Staunton had placed himself by keeping out of the lists through evident fear of the New-Orleanian, when Adolph Von Berg came behind me and laid his hand on my shoulder.

" 'Come with me a moment,' he said, 'you are wanted!'

" 'Where?' I asked, getting up from my seat and following him to the door, before which stood a light *coupé*, with its red lights flashing, the horse smoking, and the driver in his seat.

" 'I have been to-night to the Rue la Reynie Ogniard!' he answered.

" 'And are you going there again?' I asked, my blood chilling a little with an indefinable sensation of terror, but a sense of satisfaction predominating at the opportunity of seeing something more of the mysterious woman.

" 'I am!' he answered, 'and so are *you!* She has sent for you! Come!'

" Without another word I stepped into the *coupé*, and we were rapidly whirled away. I asked Adolph how and why I had been summoned; but he knew nothing more than my- self, except that he had visited the sorceress at between nine and ten that evening, that she had only spoken to him for an instant, but ordered him to go at once and find his friend, *the American,* whom he had falsely introduced some months be- fore as the English baron. He had been irresistibly im- pressed with the necessity of obedience, though it would break in upon his own arrangements for the later evening, (which included an hour at the Chateau Rouge;) had picked up a *coupé,* looked in for me at two or three places where he thought me most likely to be at that hour in the evening, and had found me at Very's, as related. What the sorceress could possibly want of me, he had no more idea than myself,

but he reminded me that she had hinted at the possible necessity of sending for me at no distant period, and I remembered the fact too well to need the reminder.

"It was nearly midnight when we drove down the Rue St.
Denis, turned into La Reynie Ogniard, and drew up at the
antiquated door I had once entered nearly three months earlier.
We entered as before, rang the bell as before, and were admitted into the inner room by the same slattern girl. I remember at this moment one impression which this person
made upon me—that she did not wash so often as four times
a year, and that the *same old dirt* was upon her face that had
been crusted there at the time of my previous visit. There
seemed no change in the room, except that *two* tapers, and each
larger than the one I had previously seen, were burning upon
the table. The curtain was down as before, and when it suddenly rose, after a few minutes spent in waiting, and the blood-
red woman stood in the vacant space, all seemed so exactly as it
had done on the previous visit, that it would have been no
difficult matter to believe the past three months a mere imagination, and this the same first visit renewed.

"The illusion, such as it was, did not last long, however.
The sorceress fixed her eyes full upon me, with the red flame
seeming to play through the eyeballs as it had before done
through her cheeks, and said, in a voice lower, more sad and
broken, than it had been when addressing me on the previous
occasion :

"'Young American, I have sent for you, and you have
done well to come. Do not fear—'

"'I do *not* fear—you, or any one !' I answered, a little
piqued that she should have drawn any such impression from
my appearance. I may have been uttering a fib of magnificent proportions at the moment, but one has a right to deny
cowardice to the last gasp, whatever else he must admit.

"'You do not? It is well, then !' she said in reply, and
in the same low, sad voice. 'You will have courage, then,
perhaps, to see what I will show you from the land of
shadows.'

"'Whom does it concern ?' I asked. 'Myself or some
other ?'

"'Yourself, and many others—all the world!' uttered the lips of flame. 'It is of your country that I would show you.'

"'My country? God of heaven! what has happened to my country?' broke from my lips almost before I knew what I was uttering. I suppose the words came almost like a groan, for I had been deeply anxious over the state of affairs known to exist at home, and perhaps I can be nearer to a weeping child when I think of any ill to my own beloved land, than I could be for any other evil threatened in the world.

"'But a moment more, and you shall see!' said the sorceress. Then she added: 'You have a friend here present. Shall he too look on what I have to reveal, or will you behold it alone?'

"'Let him see!" I answered. 'My native land may fall into ruin, but she can never be ashamed!'

"'So let it be, then!' said the sorceress, solemnly. 'Be silent, look, and learn what is at this moment transpiring in your own land!'

"Beneath that adjuration I was silent, and the same dread stillness fell upon my companion. Suddenly the sorceress, still standing in the same place, waved her right hand in the air, and a strain of low, sad music, such as the harps of angels may be continually making over the descent of lost spirits to the pit of suffering, broke upon my ears. Von Berg too heard it, I know, for I saw him look up in surprise, then apply his fingers to his ears and test whether his sense of hearing had suddenly become defective. Whence that strain of music could have sprung I did not know, nor do I know any better at this moment. I only know that, to my senses and those of my companion, it was definite as if the thunders of the sky had been ringing.

"Then came another change, quite as startling as the music and even more difficult to explain. The room began to fill with a whitish mist, transparent in its obscurity, that wrapped the form of the sybil and finally enveloped her until she appeared to be but a shade. Anon, another and larger room seemed to grow in the midst, with columned galleries and a rostrum, and hundreds of forms in wild commotion,

moving to and fro, though uttering no sound. At one moment, it seemed that I could look through one of the windows of the phantom building, and I saw the branches of a
palmetto tree waving in the winter wind. Then amidst and
apparently at the head of all, a white-haired man stood upon
the rostrum, and as he turned down a long scroll from which
he seemed to be reading to the assemblage, I read the words
that appeared on the top of the scroll : 'An ordinance to dissolve the union heretofore existing between the State of
South Carolina and the several States of the Federal Union,
under the name of the United States of America.' My
breath came thick, my eyes filled with tears of wonder and
dismay, and I could see no more.

"'Horror!' I cried. 'Roll away the vision, for it is false !
It cannot be that the man lives who could draw an ordinance
to dissolve the Union of the United States of America!'

"'It is so ! That has this day been done!' spoke the
voice of the sorceress from within the cloud of white mist.

"'If this is indeed true,' I said, 'show me what is the result, for the heavens must bow if this work of ruin is accomplished!'

"'Look again, then!' said the voice. The strain of music, which had partially ceased for a moment, grew louder
and sadder again, and I saw the white mist rolling and
changing, as if a wind were stirring it. Gradually again it
assumed shape and form ; and in the moonlight, before the
Capitol of the nation, its white proportions gleaming in the
wintry ray, the form of Washington stood, the hands clasped,
the head bare, and the eyes cast upward in the mute agony
of supplication.

"'All is not lost!' I shouted more than spoke, 'for the
Father of his Country still watches his children, and while
he lives in the heavens and prays for the erring and wandering, the nation may yet be reclaimed.'

"'It may be so,' said the voice through the mist, 'for
look !'

"Again the strain of music sounded, but now louder and
clearer, and without the tone of hopeless sadness. Again
the white mists rolled by in changing forms, and when once

more they assumed shape and consistency, I saw great masses
of men, apparently in the streets of a large city, throwing out
the old flag from roof and steeple, lifting it to heaven in attitudes of devotion, and pressing it to their lips with those wild
kisses which a mother gives to her darling child when it has
been just rescued from a deadly peril.

"'The nation lives!' I shouted. 'The old flag is not deserted and the patriotic heart yet beats in American bosoms!
Show me yet more, for the next must be triumph!'

"'Triumph indeed!' said the voice. 'Behold it, and re-
joice at it while there is time!' I shuddered at the closing
words, but another change in the strain of music roused me.
It was not sadness now, nor yet the rising voice of hope, for
martial music rung loudly and clearly, and through it I heard
the roar of cannon and the cries of combatants in battle. As
the vision cleared, I saw the armies of the Union in fight
with a host almost as numerous as themselves, but savage,
ragged and tumultuous, and bearing a mongrel flag that I
had never seen before—one that seemed robbed from the
banner of the nation's glory. For a moment the battle wavered and the forces of the Union seemed driven backward;
then they rallied with a shout, and the flag of stars and
stripes was rebaptized in glory. They pressed the traitors
backward at every turn—they trod rebellion under their
heels—they were everywhere, and everywhere triumphant.

"'Three cheers for the Star-Spangled Banner!' I cried,
forgetting place and time in the excitement of the scene.
'Let the world look on and wonder and admire! I knew
the land that the Fathers founded and Washington guarded
could not die! Three cheers—yes, nine—for the Star-
Spangled Banner and the brave old land over which it
floats!'

"'Pause!' said the voice, coming out once more from the
cloud of white mist, and chilling my very marrow with the
sad solemnity of its tone. 'Look once again!' I looked,
and the mists went rolling by as before, while the music
changed to wild discord; and when the sight became clear
again, I saw the men of the nation struggling over bags of
gold and quarrelling for a black shadow that flitted about in

their midst, while cries of want and wails of despair went up
and sickened the heavens! I closed my eyes and tried to
close my ears, but I could not shut out the voice of the sorceress, saying once more from her shroud of white mist:

"'Look yet again, and for the last time! Behold the
worm that gnaws away the bravery of a nation and makes
it a prey for the spoiler!' Heart-brokenly sad was the music
now, as the vision changed once more, and I saw a great
crowd of men, each in the uniform of an officer of the United
States army, clustered around one who seemed to be their
chief. But while I looked, I saw one by one totter and fall,
and directly I perceived that *the epaulette or shoulder-strap
on the shoulder of each was a great hideous yellow worm,
that gnawed away the shoulder and palsied the arm and ate
into the vitals.* Every second, one fell and died, making frantic efforts to tear away the reptile from its grasp, but in vain.
Then the white mists rolled away, and I saw the strange
woman standing where she had been when the first vision began.
She was silent, the music was hushed, Adolph Von Berg had
fallen back asleep in his chair, and drawing out my watch, I
discovered that only ten minutes had elapsed since the sorceress spoke her first word.

"'You have seen all—go!' was her first and last interruption to the silence. The instant after, the curtain fell. I
kicked Von Berg to awake him, and we left the house. The
coupé was waiting in the street and set me down at my
lodgings, after which it conveyed my companion to his.
Adolph did not seem to have a very clear idea of what had
occurred, and my impression is that he went to sleep the
moment the first strain of music commenced.

"As for myself, I am not much clearer than Adolph as to
how and why I saw and heard what I know that I did see
and hear. I can only say that on that night of the twentieth
of December, 1860, the same on which, as it afterward appeared, the ordinance of secession was adopted at Charleston, I, in the little old two-story house in the Rue la Reynie
Ogniard, witnessed what I have related.

"I left Havre in the old Arago only a fortnight afterwards.
Perhaps the incident helped to drive me home. At all events

I was ashamed to remain abroad when the country was in danger. Now you know quite as much of the affair as myself—which is not saying much!"

"Ugh!" said Harding, drawing an evident sigh of relief at the conclusion of so long a story, which had yet been so absorbingly interesting to him, under the circumstances, that he could not go to sleep in the midst of it—"Ugh! your idea—I beg your pardon!—your *relation* of the great yellow worms and their affinity to shoulder-straps, is almost enough to make a man, however patriotic, shudder at the thought of assuming such a decoration."

"I believe you, my boy!" said Leslie, quoting an expressive vulgarism which Orpheus C. Kerr had just been making so extensively popular.

"And that female combination of ghastly red and magical knowledge—"

"That remarkable combination," said Leslie, anticipating and interrupting the half-sneer that was coming—"is the red woman whom I saw to-night in the house on Prince Street, just before I fell out of the tree; and it was her voice that I heard on the piazza yonder just before the door opened. What do you think of it?"

"Think?" said Harding, earnestly this time. "I am altogether too much wrapped in that remarkable white mist that you have been shaking round me, to *think!* Then the events of to-night—so much crowded in a little space, and that woman coming into the midst of it all! My life has been a rather plain one, so far, and I have had to do with very few mysteries; but here I am tumbling into the midst of one thicker than the fog on the East River in a February thaw!"

"And yet the mystery of the two houses, and of the red woman so far as possible, I am going to go through like the proverbial streak of lightning through a gooseberry-bush, before I have done with it!" said Leslie, his habitual good opinion of his own powers coming once more into play. "You are ready to go with me?"

"All the way!" said Harding, graphically; and it was then that after a few words of arrangement the two friends parted, to catch what might still remain of uneasy morning

slumber, in which red women, flying carriage-lamps and respectable young men skulking in doorways and areas, were
very likely to be prominent.

CHAPTER VI.

COLONEL EGBERT CRAWFORD AND BELL CRAWFORD—SOME
SPECULATIONS ON THE SPY SYSTEM—JOSEPHINE HARRIS ON
A RECONNOISSANCE, AND WHAT SHE SAW AND HEARD.

AT any other time than the present, before proceeding with
the relation of the events that transpired in the house on
West 3— Street after the arrival of Colonel Egbert Crawford
and Miss Bell Crawford,—it might be both proper and politic
to indulge in a disquisition on the meanness of peeping and
the general iniquity of the spy system. At any other time—
not now, when the country is deep in the horrors of a war
that principally seems to have been a failure on our side because we have not "peeped" and "spied" enough.* The
rebels have had the advantage of us from the beginning,—
not only because they were fighting comparatively on their
own ground and among a friendly population, but because
they at once applied the spy system when they began, and
nosed out all our secrets of army and cabinet, while we
have neglected spying and scouting, and made every important military movement a plunge in the dark.

Every military commander has blamed every other military commander for inefficiency in this respect, and when
brought to the test he has showed that he himself had a *terra
incognita* to go over in making his first advance. Quite a
number of well-known people who were present may remember a few words of conversation which took place on the
Union Course at one of the contests there between Pri icess

December 15th, 1862.

and Flora Temple (was It not?) in June, 1861. Schenck had just plunged a few regiments, huddled up in railroad cars, into the mouths of the rebel batteries at Vienna, as if he had been taking a contract to feed some great military monster with victims as quickly and in as compact a form as possible. The country was horrified over the slaughter, Ball's Bluff and Fredericksburgh not having yet offered up their holocausts to dwarf it by comparison. An officer of prominence under McDowell, then in command of the Potomac Army under Scott, had come home on a furlough and was present. Many inquiries were made of him by acquaintances, as to the progress and prospects of the war. Among other things, the Vienna blunder was called to his attention.

"Oh," said the officer—"that was one of the most stupid of blunders—all owing to the fact that the ground had not been properly reconnoitered beforehand! They seem to have had neither scouts nor spies, and what else than failure *could* be the result?"

"True," said one of the by-standers. "And the Potomac army—that is going to advance pretty soon, as I hear—is *that* all right in the respect you have named?"

"What? *McDowell's* army?" said the officer, contemptuously. "When you catch *Irwin McDowell* not knowing exactly what is ahead of him and around him, you will catch a weasel asleep!"

So all the by-standers believed, and were confident accordingly. Four weeks afterwards Irwin McDowell fought the battle of Manassas, the result of which showed the most utter ignorance of the opposing fortifications and forces in front, that had ever been recorded in any history!*

So much for the confidence that *one* entertains, of being able to avoid the blunders of the other! Not one of the predecessors of Scherazaide, it is probable, went to the marriage bed of the Sultan without believing that *she* could fix the wavering love of the tyrant and avoid the fate threatened for the morrow! And yet some hundreds of fair white bosoms furnished a morning bauquet to the fishes, before

* December, 1862.

Scherazaide the Wise succeeded in entangling the Sultan in
the meshes of her golden speech !

It may be a little difficult to guess what this has to do with
the narration.. Simply this—that one of the most amiable
and fascinating of women played what might have been
called "a mean trick" on the occasion, and there has seemed
to exist some occasion for making her excuse before relating
the iniquity.   Having settled that during the War for the
Union there has not been half enough of "spying," on the
side of right,—and having before us not only the examples
of John Champe and Nathan Hale, beloved of Washington,
but of the two estimable young men not long emerged from
under the area steps in 5— Street, let us dismiss the contempt with which we have been wont to regard Paul Pry and
Betty the housemaid, listening at key-holes, in our favorite
dramas, and look mercifully upon the peccadilloes of Miss
Josephine Harris.

Colonel Egbert Crawford, who entered the room of the invalid on that occasion, was a tall and rather fine-looking man,
with the least dash of iron-gray in his hair and a decidedly
soldierly bearing.   He had dark eyes, a little too small and
not always direct in their glance, but only close observers
would have been able to make the latter discovery.   Had he
been wise, he would have worn something more than the full
moustache and military side-whiskers, for the under lip and
chin being close shaven the play of the muscles of the lip,
and its shape, were visible.   The lip was heavy and sullen, if
not cruel ; and any one who watched him closely enough
(close as Josephine Harris had sometimes been watching him,
say !) could see that the under lip had an almost constant
twitching motion, and that the hands, when unoccupied,
were always opening and shutting themselves much too often
for a mind at ease.   He was dressed in the full regulation
blue uniform, with fatigue-cap, in spite of the heat of the
weather, and with the eagle on shoulder and the red belts
and gilt hook at waist suggesting the sword that was to come
some time or other.

Miss Bell or Isabella Crawford, sister of Richard, who
made her appearance with the Colonel after her more or less

successful search for the peculiar shade of cerise ribbon,—
demands a word of description, and only a word. She was of
medium height, well formed and rather plump, with a plea-
santly-moulded face and dark hair and eyes, undeniably handsome and ladylike, but with something weak and languid
about the mouth, and indefinably creating the impression of
a woman incapable of being quite content with affairs as they
came, unless they came very pleasantly and fashionably, or
of making any well-directed effort to improve them. She
was faultlessly dressed and irreproachably gloved, and a close
observer would have judged, after a minute inspection, that
she would be better at home in the pleasant idleness of a ball
or an opera-matinée than where she might be required either
to do or to bear.

"A nice couple and belong together! Neither one of them
good for anything!" had more than once been Joe Harris'
irreverent comment, when looking at them as they entered
or left carriage or ball room, a little earlier in her acquaintance and when she had not yet enjoyed so many opportunities for studying the peculiar character of Col. Egbert
Crawford. Just now she would have had her doubts about
sacrificing even the useless Bell to a man whom she herself
began to dislike so much.

"How do you feel, brother?" asked the sister as she came
in,—evidently more as a matter of duty than because she felt
any peculiar interest in the answer.

"You look pale—your face is drawn—you seem to be in
pain!" was the observation of the Colonel, before the invalid
could answer, and taking the hand of the latter without seeming to notice the shudder with which his touch was met.

"Perhaps so—cousin—Egbert—yes—I do *not* feel quite so
well as I have done," muttered the invalid, who seemed all
the while to be making a violent effort to command face and
feeling. "There was music in the street, you know—I heard
it and I suppose that it agitated me."

"Sorry! tut! tut! tut! You ought to be getting better
by this time, I should think!" said the Colonel, laying his
finger on the pulse of Richard and looking up at vacancy as
a Doctor has the habit of doing when he performs that very

6

imposing (imposing upon *whom?*) operation. What was
there in his glance, that met the eye of Joe Harris, as he did
so—and gave her so plain a confirmation of her worst suspicions? What power is it that lets in the daylight on our
darkest wishes and worst motives, just at the moment when
we flatter ourselves that we have them more carefully hidden
away in darkness than ever before? Joe was still at the
window, where she had been joined by Bell, the latter already
half-forgetful of her sick brother and eager to show some
astounding purchase she had just made at one of the dry-
goods palaces.

"There—go away, girls; you bother poor Richard with
your chatter!" said Colonel Egbert, affecting great cordiality
and a little familiarity. (The fact was, as may have been
noticed, that Bell had spoken only five words aloud and Joe
not a word, since the two had entered.) "Richard is not so
well, I am afraid. I will sit by him awhile and you may go
away and gabble to your heart's content."

"Just as you like," answered Isabella, doubling up a half-
unrolled little package and preparing to go. "I have some
little things to look after up-stairs. Will you go with me,
Joe? Of course you are not going away until after dinner?"

"Humph! I do not know that I am going away at all!"
said the wild girl, her words very different from her thought
at the moment. "You are such nice people, and Dick is
such an interesting invalid, and who knows—well, I will not
speculate any more about that, *in public*, just yet! Yes,
Bell, go up-stairs and attend to your finery; I am going
down into the basement to ask Norah for two slices of bread-
and-butter and the wing of a cold chicken!"

And away through the noiseless glass door buzzed Josephine, on her way to the basement, followed by Isabella on
her way to the inner penetralia of the second floor; while
Col. Egbert Crawford shied his fatigue-cap at the desk and
drew up his chair to the side of the sofa occupied by the
invalid. Isabella really went up-stairs, and for the purpose
designated. Shame for Joe Harris, it must be said that
while she really descended to the basement and made an
inroad on Norah's larder to the extent of the wing of cold

chicken and *one* slice of bread-and-butter, yet she thrust both
the edibles into a piece of paper and into her pocket, at the
imminent risk of greasing the latter convenient receptacle,
and was back again on the parlor floor within the space of
one and a half minutes by the little Geneva watch which she
carried so bewitchingly at her belt. If mischief and sad
earnest can both be blended in the expression of one face
at one and the same time, they were so blended in hers at
that moment. What was in the wind and who was to
suffer?—for suffer somebody always did when Josey fairly
started out on a campaign !

From the door leading to the basement, to that opening
into the parlor from the hall, she probably stepped lighter
than she had ever before done since playing blind-man's buff
in early girlhood; and it is doubtful whether that parlor door
had ever before opened and shut with so little noise, since
the skilful hanger first oiled the plated hinges. From the
door to the back part of the room she went on tip-toe—the
fact cannot be denied,—little noise as her light shoes would
have made on the heavy velvet. We all have something of
the cat about us—man and the other animals; though the
quality developes itself under different circumstances. Pussy
treads even softer than usual, when after the coveted cream ;
that larger pussy, the tiger, steals lightly towards the ambushed hunter who is to furnish him the next delicious meal;
and "Tarquin's ravishing strides" are undoubtedly a mis-
nomer, for the Roman must have been something more or
less than man if he did not tip-toe his sandals or cast them
off altogether, when he stole towards the midnight bed of
Lucrece.

The cream for which Pussy Harris—shame upon her for
that same !—was just then making an adventurous foray,—
was *a hearing of the conversation which might take place
between Richard Crawford and his cousin!* That conversation she had determined to hear, at all hazards ; for what,
she scarcely knew herself, but with an undefinable impression
that she *must* hear it—that (Jesuitically, and of course most
horrible doctrine !) the end might justify the otherwise indefensible means—and that—that—in short, that she was going

to do it, and this settled the matter as well as finished up the
reason !

The piano stood on the left, passing down from the parlor
door towards the rear of the room, and behind it was a small
inlaid table covered with books, and a large easy chair
designed for lazy reading. Any person in the chair would
be within twelve inches of the glass doors and not over ten
feet from the two men at the sofa in the little back room.
Josephine distinctly heard, through the thin glass, the hum
of their voices as she approached the table, but not many of
the words were audible. Confound it !—she thought—her
plan of sitting in the chair, pretending to read as a safeguard
against possible detection, and overhearing by laying her
head back against the door—this would never do. Time
was pressing—finesse must give way to boldness; and in
the sixteenth of a minute thereafter the sliding doors were
softly parted by less than half an inch of space—too little to
be readily noticed from the back room, which was the lighter
of the two, and yet enough to see through if necessary, (but
she did not intend to look,) and to *hear* through, which was
the matter of first consequence. And there she stood—an
'eaves-dropper of the first order—a flush of shame and of
half-conscious guilt on cheek and brow, and a wild, startled
look in her eyes, such as a hare might show when listening
for the second bay of the hound—liable to be caught by some
one entering the parlor from the hall, or by the Colonel
taking a fancy to enter the room for any purpose—and yet
chained there, with her ear within an inch of the opening, as
if present happiness and eternal salvation had both depended
upon her keeping that position !

Could anything be more shameful ?—anything more
despicable ? Was ever a heroine so placed, even by English
romancers or French dramatists ? And was not the long
dissertation at the beginning of this chapter, to prove the
applicability of the spy system to war time, an absolute
necessity ?

What might have passed precedently, while she was looking after the chicken and the bread-and-butter, Josephine
had no means of divining. At the time of her assuming her

post of observation, Richard Crawford was still lying back upon the sofa, and looking up, as he had been half an hour before when she was herself conversing with him. If the spasms had not ceased altogether, they were at least conquered by the will and concealed from the eyes of the Colonel, as they had not been from hers. The young girl thought she could detect, too, upon the face of the invalid, a less hopeless look, and some evidence of more determined insight in the glance, than she had marked for a considerable period. Colonel Egbert Crawford was sitting with his chair drawn up reasonably close in front of his cousin, and conversing eagerly with him, yet with his face partially turned away most of the time, and not meeting his gaze directly as most honest and earnest men do the observation of those with whom they converse on important subjects. Perhaps that disposition of the Colonel's face gave both his seen and his unseen listeners better opportunities for close study of his expression than they might otherwise have enjoyed.

"I am sorry to say that things are *not* as we both wish them to be, at West Falls," the young girl heard the Colonel say. "Of course I am not less anxious than yourself to have everything arranged and the property—"

"Ah, there is some *property* involved, then! and at West Falls, of all the places in the world!" commented the uninvited listener, speaking to herself, and with her words very carefully kept between her teeth, as was becoming under such circumstances—always provided there could be anything "becoming" about the affair.

"Uncle John," the Colonel went on to say, "seems to have imbibed some kind of singular prejudice against your mode of life in the city, if not against you, and Mary—"

"Humph! there is a 'Mary'—a woman in the case, as well as the property," commented the listener. "Little while as I have been here, the thing already begins to grow interesting!"

"Well, Mary? what of her? Why does she answer my letters no more?" asked the invalid, calming his voice by an evidently strong effort and speaking as the Colonel paused for an instant. "Does she too begin to share so bitterly in the—in the—"

"In the prejudice? I am sorry to say—yes," the Colonel went on, "though I do not think that either of them could give a reason. I tried to probe the matter a little when there, but the old gentleman answered me so shortly that I had no excuse to go on; and Mary—"

"You did not say anything to *her?*" broke in the invalid, with the same evident suppression in his voice.

"Of course not!" was the answer. "You know me, Richard, I hope, and know that I would not have lost a chance of saying anything in your favor—"

"Trust *you* for *that!*" was the mental comment of the listener. "Wouldn't *you* glorify *him!* Wouldn't *you* make him blue and gold, with gilt edges! I see you doing it!"

"—If I had any opportunity," concluded the Colonel.

"I should think not," said the invalid, his words so forced from between his teeth that his interlocutor, had he been less absorbed in his own calculations, must have noticed the difference from his usual manner.

"Richard Crawford, you are beginning to wake, for you know that man is lying—I see it by your eyes!" was the comment of the young girl, this time.

"I am going to West Falls again in a few days—that is, if we do not get orders for Washington," continued the Colonel; "and if I have your permission—as you are not likely to be well enough to go out even by that time—I shall speak to both on the subject, as it would be the world's pity if you should be thrown out of so fine a property and the possession of a girl who I believe once loved you, by false reports, or—"

"False reports? eh? who should have circulated false reports?" asked the invalid, his face firing for a moment and his voice temporarily under less command. But the momentary flush passed away, and it was only with the querulous voice and petulant manner of sickness that he concluded: "Eh, well, no matter; we will see about all that by-and-by, when I get well."

"That is right—I am glad to hear you speak so hopefully," said the Colonel. "All will be right, no doubt, when you *get well.*" Did he or did he not lay a peculiar stress on the two words, as the old jokers used to do on a few others when they informed the boys that the statue of St. Paul, in the niche in the front of St. Paul's church, always came down and took a drink of water from the nearest pump, *when it heard the clock strike twelve?* If there was such an emphasis, did Richard Crawford hear and recognize it? That some one else in the immediate vicinity did, and duly commented upon it, is beyond a question.

"You must modulate your voice better than that, Colonel Egbert Crawford, before you go on the stage!" said the wild girl. "You think he is dying—you mean he shall die—I have an impression that I did not come here for nothing, after all!"

"And now," said the Colonel, rising, and taking out his watch, "I must leave you. We have a recruiting meeting at —— Hall at six, and I must be there without fail. Oh," as if suddenly recollecting something comparatively unimportant, that had been overlooked in the pressure of more interesting matter—"I had nearly forgotten. Your bandage—is it all right? I hope the Doctor and Bell have not found out the secret, so as to laugh at what they would call our *superstition.* Shall I renew it? I believe I have some of the preparation in one or another of my pockets," feeling in one and then another, as if doubtful. "Ah, here it is," and he took out from one of his pockets which he had hurriedly gone over with his hands at least half a dozen of times, a small black box, four or five inches in length and perhaps two in width by an inch deep.

Were Josephine Harris' eyes playing fantastic tricks with her on that occasion; or did she see, as that little black box met the view, a momentary repetition of the suffering spasm which had crossed the face of Richard Crawford half an hour before, when she first suggested a conflict of interests between them? At all events the spasm, if such it was, passed away, and he merely answered, languidly:

"Yes, thank you, Egbert—yes, if you please."

At this stage of the proceedings, had Josephine Harris been a "real lady," or had she possessed any well-defined sense of "propriety," she would have left her post of observation on the instant. For though the Colonel was partially between her and the patient, she saw him open the little black box, take out a broad knife from his vest pocket, and then proceed to other operations very improper for a young lady to witness. She saw Richard Crawford unbutton his vest, a little assisted by the Colonel. What followed she could not see, very fortunately. All that she could make out, was that some sort of narrow white bandage seemed to have been removed from the breast or stomach of the invalid—that the Colonel took out a dark paste from the box with his knife, spread a portion of it on the opened bandage, then re-folded it and assisted in replacing it on the breast or stomach and re-arranging the disordered clothing. This done, and the box put back into his pocket, he took his cap and stooped down to shake hands with Richard ; whereupon Josephine, knowing that his way out would be through the parlor, shoved the two doors together by a silent but very nervous movement, and managed to escape from the room as silently, before the Colonel's hand had yet been laid upon the glass door to open it.

There were half a dozen unoccupied rooms on the next floor, as she well knew, and up the stairs and into one of these she bounded, her cheeks still more aglow than they had been when she set out on her "reconnoissance," and her eyes still more wild and startled, while a strange tremor creeping at her heart told her that she had been witness to much more than could yet be shaped into words or embodied even in thought ! Poor girl !—how her brain throbbed and how her heart beat like ten thousand little trip-hammers !—the usual and very proper penalty which we pay for an indiscretion !

CHAPTER VII.

INTRODUCTION OF THE CONTRABAND, WITH SOME REFLECTIONS
THEREON—THREE MONTHS BEFORE—AUNT SYNCHY AND THE
OBI POISONING—A NICE LITTLE ARRANGEMENT OF EGBERT
CRAWFORD'S.

HERE it becomes necessary to pause and introduce a new
and altogether indispensable character. Not new to the
world—sorrow for the world that it is not! Not new to the
country—wo to the country that it has filled so large a place
in its history! But something new in this veracious narration—the *contraband*. The negro must come in, by all means
and at all hazards. Time was when romances and even histories could be written without such an introduction ; but
that time is past and perhaps past forever. "I and Napoleon," said the courier of Arves, relating some incident in
which he had temporarily become associated with the fortunes of the Great Captain ; and "I and the white man" may
Sambo say at no distant day, without presumption and without outraging the dignity of position. It was a very harmless monster that Frankenstein constructed, apparently ; but
it grew to be a very fearful and tyrannical monster before he
was quite done with it. No doubt the first black face that
grinned on the Virginian shore, a couple of centuries ago,
seemed more an object of mirth than of terror—and it certainly
gave promise of profit. But he is a man of mirthful disposition
who sees anything to laugh at in the same black face, grown
older and broader and much less comical, on the shore of the
same Virginia to-day. The white race and the black—the
sharp profile and the broad lip—the springing instep and the
protuberant heel—have been having a long tussle, with the
probabilities for a while all on the side of the white : to-day
the struggle is doubtful if not decided in favor of the black
"Here we go, up—up—uppy! Here we go, down—down
—downy!" the children used to sing when playing see-saw
with a broad plank on the fence ; and *they* understood, what
their elders sometimes forget—that the rebound of extreme

height is descent. One more illustration, before this train of thought necessarily ceases.

Is it not recorded in all the books of relative history, that the Normans, under William the Conqueror, invaded and subjugated Saxon England and made virtual slaves of the unfortunate countrymen of Harold? Yet who were the conquered eventually? England was Saxon within fifty years of Hastings : England is Saxon to-day. The broad bosom of the Saxon mother, even when the sire of her child was a ravisher, gave out drops of strength that moulded it in spite of him, to be at last her avenger and his master ! The Saxon pirate still sweeps the seas in his descendants : the Norman robber is only heard of at long intervals when he meets his opportunity at a Balaklava. The revenges of history are fearful; and if the end of human experience is not reached in our downfall, other races will be careful never to rivet a chain of caste or color, or so to rivet it that no meddling fingers of fanaticism can ever unloose the shackle !

Perhaps it is proper as well as inevitable that the negro should have changed his place and mounted astride of the national neck instead of being trodden under the national foot. Everything else in our surroundings has changed— why not he? We do not yet quite understand the fact—it may be ; but the foundations of the old in society have been broken up as effectually, within the past two years, as were those of the great deep at the time of Noah's flood. The old deities of fashion have been swept away in the flood of revolution. The millionaire of two years ago, intent at that time on the means by which the revenues from his brown-stone houses and pet railroad stocks could be spent to the most showy advantage, has become the struggling man of to-day, intent upon keeping up appearances, and happy if diminished and doubtful rents can even be made to meet increasing taxes. The struggling man of that time has meanwhile sprung into fortune and position, through lucky adventures in government transportations or army-contracts ; and the jewelers of Broadway and Chestnut Street are busy resetting the diamonds of decayed families, to sparkle on brows and bosoms that only a little while ago beat with pride at an added weight

of California paste or Kentucky rock-crystal. The most
showy equipages that flashed last summer at Newport and
Saratoga, were never seen between the bathing-beach and
Fort Adams, or between Congress Spring and the Lake, in
the old days; and on the " Dinorah" nights at the Academy*
there have been new faces in the most prominent boxes,
almost as *outre* and unaccustomed in their appearance as
was that of the hard-featured Western President, framed in
a shock head and a turn-down collar, meeting the gaze of
astonished Murray Hill, when he passed an hour there on
his way to the inauguration.

Quite as notable a change has taken place in personal
reputation. Many of the men on whom the country depended
as most likely to prove able defenders in the day of need,
have not only discovered to the world their worthlessness,
but filled up the fable of the man who leaned upon a reed,
by fatally piercing those whom they had betrayed to their
fall. Bubble-characters have burst, and high-sounding phrases
have been exploded. Men whose education and antecedents
should have made them brave and true, have shown themselves false and cowardly—impotent for good, and active only
for evil. Unconsidered nobodies have meanwhile sprung
forth from the mass of the people, and equally astonished
themselves and others by the power, wisdom and courage
they have displayed. In cabinet and camp, in army and
navy, in the editorial chair and in the halls of eloquence, the
men from whom least was expected have done most, and
those upon whom the greatest expectations had been founded
have only given another proof of the fallacy of all human calculations. All has been change, all has been transition, in
the estimation men have held of themselves and the light in
which they presented themselves to each other.

Opinions of duties and recognitions of necessities have
known a change not less remarkable. What yesterday we
believed to be fallacy, to-day we know to be the truth.
What seemed the fixed and immutable purpose of God only
a few short months ago, we have already discovered to have

* December 1862.

been founded only in human passion or ambition. What
seemed eternal has passed away, and what appeared to
be evanescent has assumed stability. The storm has been
raging around us, and doing its work not the less destruc-
tively because we failed to perceive that we were passing
through anything more threatening than a summer shower.
While we have stood upon the bank of the swelling river,
and pointed to some structure of old rising on the bank,
declaring that not a stone could be moved until the very
heaven's should fall, little by little the foundations have been
undermined, and the full crash of its falling has first awoke
us from our security. That without which we said that the
nation could not live, has fallen and been destroyed; and
yet we know not whether the nation dies, or grows to a better and more enduring life. What we cherished we have
lost; what we did not ask or expect has come to us; the
effete but reliable old is passing away, and out of the ashes
of its decay is springing forth a new so unexpected and so
little prepared for that it may be salvation or destruction as
the hand of God shall rule. The past of the nation lies with
the sunken Cumberland in the waters of Hampton Roads;
its future floats about in a new-fangled Monitor, that may
combat and defeat the navies of the world or go to the bottom
with one inglorious plunge.* And this general transition
brings us back to the negro, whose apotheosis is after all
only a part of the inevitable, and may be only the flash before
his final and welcome disappearance.

Our contraband is a woman, and she comes upon the
scene of action in this wise, retrospectively.

Some three months before the events recorded in the preceding chapters, to wit about the middle of March, Egbert
Crawford, Tombs lawyer, doing a thriving business in the
line especially affected by such gentry, and not yet elevated
to a Colonel's commission in the volunteer army by the
parental forethought of Governor Edwin D. Morgan,—had
occasion to visit that portion of Thomas Street lying between
West Broadway and Hudson. The locality is not by any

* Written three days before the foundering of the Monitor off
Hatteras, Dec. 31st 1862.

means a pleasant one, either for the eye or the other senses, and the character of the street is not materially improved by the recollection of the Ellen Jewett murder, which occurred on the south side, within a few doors of Hudson. Garbage left unremoved by Hackley festers alike on pavement, side-walk and gutter; and a mass of black and white humanity (the former predominating) left unremoved by the civilization of New York in the last half of the nineteenth century, festers within the crazy and tumble-down tenements. Colored cotton handkerchiefs wrapping woolly heads, and shoes slouched at the heel furnishing doubtful covering to feet redolent of filth and crippled by disease—alternate with the scanty habiliments of black and white children, brought up in the kennel and reduced by blows, mud and exposure to a woful similarity of hue. The whiskey bottle generally ac-companies the basket with a quart of decayed potatoes, from the grocery at the corner; and even the begged calf's-liver or the stolen beef-bone comes home accompanied by a flavor of bad gin. It is no wonder that the few shutters hang by the eye-lids, and that even the wagon-boys who vend ante-diluvian vegetables from castaway wagons drawn by twenty-shilling horse-frames, hurry through without any hope in the yells intended to attract custom.

Any observer who should have seen the neatly-dressed lawyer peering into the broken doors and up the black stair-cases of Thomas Street, would naturally have supposed his visit connected with some revelation of crime, and that he was either looking up a witness whose testimony might be necessary to save a perilled burglar from Sing Sing, or taking measures to keep one hidden who might have told too much if brought upon the witness-stand. And yet Egbert Craw-ford was really visiting that den of black squalor with a very different object—to find an old darkey woman who was re-ported as living in that street, and in his capacity as one of the eleven hundred and fifty Commissioners of Deeds of the City and County of New York, to procure her "⋈ mark" and take her acknowledgment in the little matter of a quit-claim deed. A very harmless purpose, in itself, certainly; and yet the observer might have been nearer right in his

suspicion than even the lawyer himself believed, when the
whole result of the visit was taken into account.

One of the ricketty houses on the south side of the street,
not far from the Ellen Jewett house, and not much further
from the equally celebrated panel-house which furnished the
weekly papers with illustrations of that peculiar species of
man-trap a few years ago—seemed to the seeker to bear out
the description that had been given him. The door was wide
open, and all within appeared to be a sort of dark cabin out
of which issued occasional sounds of quarrelling voices and
continual puffs of fetid air foul enough to sicken the strongest
stomach. He went in, as one of the lost might go into
Pandemonium, impelled by an imperious necessity. He
mounted the ricketty and creaking stair, with the bannister
half gone and the steps groaning beneath his tread as if they
contained the spirits of the dead respectability that had left
them half a century before. He had been told that the old
woman lived on the third floor, and though he met no one he
concluded to dare the perils of a second ascent, in spite of
the landing place being in almost pitchy darkness. Rushing
along with a hasty step that even the gloom could not make
a slower one, he felt something bump against his knees and
the lower part of his body, and then something human fell to
the floor with a crash that had the jingling of broken crockery
blended with it.

"Boo! hoo! hoo! e-e-e-gh! Mammy! Mammy!" yelled a
voice. "Boo! hoo! hoo! e-e-e-gh! Mammy! Mammy!" and
Crawford could just discern that he had run over and partially demolished a little negro boy carrying a pitcher, the
pitcher and the boy seeming to have suffered about equally.
Neither of them had any nose left, to speak of; and the little
imp did not make any effort to rise from the floor, but lay
there and yelled merrily. The victor in the collision did not
have much time for inspection, for the moment after a door at
the back end of the passage opened hurriedly, and a hideous
old negro woman came rushing out, with a sputtering fragment of lighted tallow-candle in her hand, and exclaiming:

"What's de matter, Jeffy? Here am Mamma!"

"Big man run'd ober me! broke de pitcher! Boo! hoo!

hoo !" yelled the black atom in reply, without any additional effort at getting up.

"Get out ob dar ! d—n you, I run'd ober *you*, mind dat !" screeched out the old woman, catching sight of the dark form of Crawford. "Hurtin' leetle boys !—I pay you for it, honey !"

"I hit him accidentally," said the lawyer, who had no intention of getting into a row in that "negro quarter." "It was dark, and I did not see him. I'll pay for the pitcher."

"Will you, honey ?" said the old woman, mollifying instantly. "Well den, 'spose you couldn't help it. Get up, Jeffy."

"Can you tell me whether Mrs. —— lives on any of the floors of this house ?" asked Crawford.

"Nebber mind dat, till you gib me-de money !" answered the old woman, not to be diverted by any side-issues. "Dat are pitcher cost a quarter, honey !"

Crawford was feeling in his pocket for one of the quarters that yet remained in that receptacle, preparatory to going out of circulation altogether,—when the old crone, eager for the money, stuck her candle somewhat nearer his face than it had before been held. Instantly her withered face assumed a new expression of intelligence, and her hand shook so that she almost dropped the candle, as she cried :

"Merciful Lord and Marser! If dat are ain't young Egbert Crawford !"

"My name is certainly Egbert Crawford !" said that individual, very much surprised in his turn. "But who are you that know *me* ?"

"Don't know his ole Aunt Synchy !" exclaimed the old woman.

"Aunt Synchy ! Aunt Synchy !" said the lawyer, trying to recollect the past very rapidly, and catching some glimmers. "What ? Aunt Synchy that used to live at—"

"Used to live at old Tom Crawford's. Lor bress you, yes ! Why come in, honey !" and before the lawyer could answer further, he was literally dragged through the dingy door by the still vigorous old woman, and found himself inside her apartment, Master Jeffy and his pitcher being left neglected on the entry floor.

Once within the door, and in the better light afforded even by the dingy windows, Crawford had a better opportunity to observe the old woman, and he now found no difficulty in recalling something more than the name. She might have been sixty-five or seventy years of age, to judge by the wrinkles on her face and the white of her eyebrows, though her hair was hidden under a gaudy and dirty cotton plaid handkerchief and her tall form seemed little bowed by age. Two coal-black eyes, showing no diminution of their natural fire, gleamed from under those white eyebrows ; and on the portions of the cheeks yet left smooth enough to show the texture of the skin, there were deep gashes that had once been the tattooing of her barbarian youth and beauty. Her hands were withered, much more than her face, and seemed skinny and claw-like. Her dress, which had once been plaid cotton gingham, was fearfully dirty and unskilfully patched with other material ; and the frayed silk shawl thrown around her old shoulders might have been rescued from a rag-heap in the streets to serve that turn.

The room, as Crawford readily noticed, was almost as re-markable in appearance as the old woman herself. There was nothing singular in the bare floor, the pine table and two or three broken chairs ; for something very like them, or worse, can be found in almost every miserable tenement where virtue struggles or vice swelters, in the slums of the great city. Neither was there anything notable in the smoke-greased walls and ceiling, the miserable fireplace with one cracked kettle and a red earthen bowl, and the wretched bed of rags stuck away in one of the corners, on which evidently both the old crone and Master Jeffy made their sad pretence at sleep.

But what really was singular in the appearance of the apartment, and what Crawford noted at once, although he did not allude to it until afterwards, was—first, a ghastly attempt at painting, hanging behind the chimney, represent-ing a death's-head and cross-bones, which might have been executed by an artist in whitewash, on a ground of black muslin. Second, a hanging shelf in one corner, with a dozen or two of dingy small bottles and vials, and a rod lying across it, apparently made from a black birchen switch, peeled in sections. Third, and most important of all, a string of twine suspended from one side of the room to the other, in front of the fire-place and near the ceiling, and hung with objects that required a moment to recognize. Among them, when closely examined, could be found two or three bats, dried ; a string of snake's eggs, blackened by being smoked ; a tail and two legs of a black cat ; a bunch of the dried leaves of the black hellebore ; a snake's skin—not the "shedder" or superficial skin, but the cuticle itself, peeled from the writhing reptile ; two objects that might have been spotted toads, run over by wagons until thoroughly flattened—then dried ; and one object which could not well be anything more or less than the hand of a child a few weeks old, cut off just above the wrist and subjected to some kind of embalming or drying process.

The purposes of this narrative do not require the recording of all the conversation which took place between the Tombs lawyer and Aunt Synchy, when the latter had dusted off one of the miserable chairs and forced the former down into it, taking another herself, sitting square in front of him, and thrusting her face so close into his that the withered features seemed almost plastered against his own. It is enough to say that that conversation corroborated the suspicion which the first words of the crone would have engendered—that Aunt Synchy, in her younger days, had been a slave in the Crawford family, in a neighboring State where the institution had not yet been entirely abolished—and that, at last manumitted by a mistaken kindness, she had finally wandered away to the crime and misery of negro life in the great city. She retained, as people of that feudal class always do, a vivid recollection of her early life and of all the residents of the section where she had lived ; and Egbert Crawford, who was in the habit of putting many questions to others, was not in the habit of answering quite so many as the old woman put to him concerning the intermediate histories of the families

7

of which she had now lost sight for more than a quarter of a
century.

In this conversation it became apparent, too, that Thomas
Crawford, the father of Egbert, had been the quasi owner of
Synchy, and that she retained for the son something of that
singular attachment which appears to be inseparable from any
description of feudality. Thomas Crawford, it would appear,
had had two brothers, Richard, the father of the present
Richard Crawford and of John, the soldier, both Thomas and
Richard being then dead and their families in the country
broken up. Another brother, John, had become very
wealthy, and appeared to be living, with Mary, an only
daughter, at West Falls, in the Oneida Valley. Finally, it
became quite apparent that the old crone, whatever her
attachment to the family of Thomas Crawford, did not hold
the same feudal regard for some of the other members of the
family—in short, that she had retained the memory of certain
supposed early slights and injuries, quite as closely as she
had done the softer and more grateful sentiments towards
others.

"So Dick am rich, am he, honey? an you am poor? Tut!
tut! dat is too bad for de son of ole Marser Tom!" said the
old crone, after the lapse of half an hour in which both
tongues had been running pretty rapidly.

"He is," said Crawford, his face expressing no strong
sense of satisfaction at the recollection. "He bought
property in the new parts of the city, twelve or fifteen years
ago, and the rise has been so great that it has made him rich.
He is now living on Murray Hill, in style, though, d—n
him!" and the face now was very sinister indeed, "he has
been attacked with inflammatory rheumatism and confined
for some weeks to his house, so that I don't think he enjoys
it all very much."

"An Uncle John's big property," the old woman went on—
"Dick is to have all dat, too, you tink?"

"Yes, and Mary," answered Crawford. "Mary is a pretty
little girl, and worth as much as all the property. Dick has
managed to get around the old man, somehow, and if I can't
stop it—"

"Eh, yes, if you can't stop 'um!" said the old crone, rubbing her skinny hands together as if this, at least, pleased her. " Has you tried, honey ?"

Egbert Crawford, Tombs lawyer, as has before been said, was much more in the habit of putting others under close cross-examination, than allowing himself to be subjected to the same sifting process. But whether he had his own motives for telling the old woman the truth, or whether he saw that those coal black old eyes were looking through him and divining all that he wished or intended—he certainly submitted to the question and told the truth, in the present instance :

" Yes, d—n him once more !"

" You want Mary and de property bofe ?" asked the old woman again.

" Both !" answered the lawyer, after one more instant of hesitation and one more glance into the coal black eyes. " I don't care if you know all about it—you *daren't* betray me, for your life !"

" Don't *want* to, honey !" was all the old woman's reply; and the lawyer went on :

" I have been twice up at West Falls since Dick was taken ill, and I think I have set some reports in circulation there, that may make Miss Mary hesitate, if they do not change the old man's will. How will that do, Aunt Synchy—you old black anatomy ? Eh ?"

" Spose I am an 'atomy," said the old woman, apparently rather pleased with the epithet than otherwise. " But Lor' bress you, chile, dat won't do at all! You ain't ole enough yet !" and there was an unmistakable sneer on the withered black face, to think that any body could be so verdant.

" Ah !" said Egbert Crawford, who neither liked the sneer nor the intimation. " What more could I do, I should like to know ?"

What was it that Jeremy Taylor said—that old silver-tongued Bishop of Down, Connor and Dromore, in Ireland ? —" No disease cometh so much with our breath, drinking from the infected lips of others, as with the vessels of our

own bodies that are ready to receive it." Shakspeare says
the same thing of mirth, when he records that

> "A jest's prosperity lies in the ear
> Of him that hears it, never in the tongue
> Of him that makes it."

Artemus Ward, when he sets whole audiences into broad
roars of laughter over his odd conceits of "carrying pepper-
mint to General Price" or "going to be measured for an
umbrella," may doubt the truth of this assertion; and Lester
Wallack or Ned Sothern, when inspiring chuckles that almost
threaten the life, may share in the infidelity: but let all these
remember that their audiences *come* to be amused, and that
their best drolleries might fall very flat indeed at a Quaker
meeting or in a hospital devoted to men with the jumping
tooth-ache! The conditions of Crime are like those of
Disease and Mirth—the patient must be ready before the
inoculation can take place. Eve was unquestionably wishing
for a break in the already dull routine of her life in Eden,
before the Serpent dared to make his appearance; and
Arnold had some treason crudely floating through his mind,
even if not that particular treason, before the overtures of
the British commander led him to the attempted betrayal of
the Key of the Highlands. Egbert Crawford, Tombs lawyer,
when he said to Aunt Synchy, "What more could I do, I
should like to know?" meant to be understood as asserting
that nothing more was in his power; but there was really in
his heart the wish for aid in some higher crime to effect his
purposes; and the tempter came!

"All dat goin' away from you, and nobody in de way but
dat miserable chile!" was the only comment of the old woman on Crawford's last question.

"So I suppose," was the puzzled answer.

"Why don't you have a good doctor for him, honey!"
asked the old woman, next.

"A good doctor?" queried Crawford, still more puzzled.
"Why curse it, woman, what are you talking about? Won't
he get well too soon, now, and perhaps be up at West
Falls before I am more than half ready for him?"

"Oh, you poor chile—you don't half understan' dis ole woman!" chuckled the crone, delighted to find that she had puzzled the lawyer. "Spose de good doctor so good that he nebber get well? Eh, honey?"

"What? poison?" broke out the lawyer, catching at the old woman's meaning so suddenly that he could not quite control his voice.

"Hush–h–h! you fool!" hissed the old woman, rising at once, hobbling to the door and opening it suddenly—then closing it and returning to her chair. "You call yourself a lawyer, honey, and do such things as dat 'are? Done you know dem policers are sneakin' aroun' ebberywhere, up de stairways as well as ebberywhere else? An if one of dem happened to hear you speak such words, dis ole woman take a ride up to de Islan' in de Black Maria, and you go to de debbil, sure! Know all about 'em, honey—been dare afore!"

"Humph!" said the lawyer, nevertheless using lower voice even for the disclaimer. "No danger, Aunty, I guess! There are no policemen now-a-days—only Provost-Marshal Kennedy's spies, looking for traitors. But what do you mean?—that I should get a doctor to—to—put him out of the way?"

"Dats jes it, honey!" said the old woman, again rubbing her hands. "He is in de way—put him out and have de ole man's money."

"Impossible!" spoke Egbert Crawford, in a tone which would have told a close observer—and probably told the old woman—that he only meant: "I do not see how to do it."

"Give um somefin," graphically said the crone.

"What!" spoke the lawyer, almost in as loud a tone as he had before used, and rising from his chair in apparent indignation.

"Sit down, honey," said the old woman, with the same sneer in her voice that had before been apparent. "Oh, I know you is a good man and wouldn't do nuffin to hurt Cousin Dickey. Didn't kill his dog, nor nuffin, did you, honey, a good wile ago, jes because you didn't like *him*. Don't do nuffin now, if you don't want to! Let him have de girl, an de ole man's money, an—"

"Woman!" said Egbert Crawford, rising altogether this time, and pacing the floor like a man a good deal unquieted. "I hate Dick Crawford, and you know it. I want Uncle John's money and I want Mary, and he is in my way in both cases. You may as well know the whole truth—I hate him enough to 'put him out of the way,' as we have both called it, but the thing is impossible. Any doctor to whom I should speak would have me arrested at once, for though they poison they do not wish to be suspected of such operations; and there is no other way. He will get well and go up to West Falls, and then all is over!" and the lawyer sunk his head on his breast as if he had been the most ill-used of individuals.

"Not while your ole Aunty libs, Marser Egbert, if you dar do what she tells you!"

The words struck some chord previously active in the brain of Crawford. He glanced up at the string of articles on the line of twine, then stopped short in his walk, before the old woman.

"Well?"

"Oh, you see dem tings, and you is coming to it, is you, honey!" chuckled the crone. "You 'member what Aunt Synchy is, now?"

"Yes, I remember," said Crawford, "though I forget the name. You are an O—Ogee—Odee—no, O—"

"An Obi woman!" said the crone, rising and stretching herself to her full height, with a look that was commanding in spite of her squalor. "You 'member somefin, but not much. We be great people in Jamaica. Up in de hills 'bove Spanish Town, we are de kings and de queens. De great Obi spirit come down to us, when de moon am at its last quarter, an he tell us how to cure and how to kill. We mix de charm at midnight, wid de great Obi 'pearin' to us all de time in de smoke dat rises from de kettle, an de secert words all de time a mutterin'; and de charm works, an kills or cures 'way off hunerds of miles, 'cordin' as we want um for our friens or our euemies. Does you hear, honey?"

"I hear!" said Egbert Crawford, for the moment absorbed if not fascinated by the developments of this real or affected

superstition ; but not carried away, it may be believed, from
the influence which this hideous old woman might be able to
exert on his own fortunes.

"Mammy—you don't 'member ole Mammy?"—the old
woman went on. "Captain Lewis brought Mammy an me
from Jamaica more'n fifty years ago. She mus' have died
when you was a little picanninny. She was de great Obi
woman, de queen of dem all ; and she tole me afore she died,
so's I could do mos' as much. Many's de lub potion Mammy
an me has mixed up, dat has made some ob de wite bosoms
fuller afore dey was done workin ; and many's de charm—"

"Poh! nonsense! don't say 'charm'; call it 'dose'!" broke
in the lawyer, at last impatient. "I believe you can kill,
whether you can cure or not, Aunt Synchy ; but I am a man,
with some experience in the world, and I don't believe in
your Obi. All your dead cats and babies' hands and snakes
yonder, are just so many tricks to influence the superstitious.
I know better, and they don't influence me !"

"Oh, dey doesn't, eh, honey ? You is too smart an don't
believe in de Obi ?" For the moment her face was lowering
and threatening—then it changed again to the same wrinkled
Sphynx as before. "Nebber mind—you is my boy, an I lubs
you, an so you 'sult de ole woman widout de Obi payin' you
for it ! Call it ' dose,' then, honey—many's de dose dat dese
hans have mixed, dat has made de coffin-maker hab somefin
to do and sent de property where it belonged."

"I believe you !" was the laconic comment of Egbert
Crawford, when the crone, spite of his interruptions, had
finished her long rigmarole. What followed may quite as
well be imagined as described. Richard Crawford was
doomed to be operated upon by one of those insidious and
deadly vegetable poisons, outwardly applied, in which none
have such horrible skill as the crones of the African race who
have derived their knowledge from the West India Islands.
Whether it should be brought near the head by concealment
in a pillow, or near the more vital portions of the body itself
through use of a bandage worn near the skin,—the effect
would be the same—insensible debilitation, decline, death !
But the latter plan would be much the more rapid ; and in

neither event, when the deed was done, would there be one
mark, perceptible even to the dissecting surgeon, telling that
other than natural decay had brought about dissolution.

Ten minutes afterwards, Aunt Synchy was busy compound-
ing a *black paste*, from various preparations which she found
among the vials on the shelf and under one corner of the
heap of rags which she called her bed—crooning all the
while a dismal attempt at a tune which made even the not-
over-sensitive lawyer shudder, and putting the mixture at
last into his hands with a "Lor' bress you, honey!" which
might have made *any one* shudder if he had understood the
connection. Fifteen minutes later, the Tombs lawyer left
Thomas Street, without the information of which he had
originally come in search, but his mind now full of other
things, and bearing in his mind the mental label of the pre-
scription : " to be used as directed."

So vice buds into crime whenever opportunity offers, and
the Hazaels of the world, who have believed that they never
could be brought to "do this thing," pursue it with an energy
and determination shaming the efforts of older offenders.
Yesterday only an illicit lover : to-day the destroyer of children unborn ! Yesterday only an *ordinary* scoundrel : tq-
day the worst and most deadly of all murderers—the *poi-
soner!*

Three months later—to wit, toward the close of June—.
that state of affairs was existing at the house of Richard
Crawford, which has before been indicated. What was it,
indeed, that Josephine Harris had dimly discovered ?

CHAPTER VIII.

THE TWO RIVALS AT JUDGE OWEN'S—A COMBAT A LA
OUTRANCE BETWEEN THE BANCKER AND THE WALLACE—
ALMOST A CHALLENGE, AND A TRIAL OF EVERY-DAY
COURAGE.

RETURN we now to the somewhat too-long neglected Miss
Emily Owen and the other inmates and intimates of Judge
Owen's pleasant house near the Harlem River.

' Some days had elapsed after the conversation between
Emily and Aunt Martha, bringing the time to the first of
July and the commencement of that fire-cracker abomination
that was to culminate on the Fourth in a general distraction.
Some days had elapsed—as has already been noted ; and
judging by the person who sat nearest to Miss Emily Owen
in the faintly-lighted parlor, at about half past eight in the
evening, the Judge's praises of Col. Bancker and animad-
versions of Frank Wallace had not been without their effect
on the young girl. Both the rival suitors were present, and
so was Aunt Martha ; but Frank Wallace made a somewhat dim and undefined picture as he sat near one of the
front windows, apparently observing the boys deep in the
mysteries of fire-crackers and torpedoes ; while the Colonel
was in altogether a better light as he sat near Emily and
nearly under the half-lighted chandelier. Emily was indulging in the peculiarly American vice of rolling backward
and forward in a rocking-chair ; the Colonel had one leg over
the other and was drumming with the opened blade of his
penknife on the cover of the book he held in his hand ; and
Aunt Martha was ruining what eyes she had left, by some
kind of crochet-work in cotton that may possibly have been
a "tidy."

Frank and the Colonel had come in very nearly together,
yet *not* together, about half an hour before. Some little
conversation had ensued, but very little, for the rivals in-
stinctively hated each other, and Wallace could not manage
to string ten words in his rival's presence without throwing

bits at him in a manner decidedly improper. Perhaps Emily
had taken the Colonel's part a little, spite of her aversion to
him ; and the result was that Master Frank had fallen partially into the sulks and gone off to the end of the room—
quite as far as he intended to go at that juncture, however.

The young man might be pardoned if he felt for the moment a little vexed. Though not forbidden the house of
Judge Owen, and treated with cold politeness when he entered it (of course with *one* exception)—he knew very well
that he was an object of dislike to the portly Judge, and he
always endeavored so to time his visits that he might avoid
that parental potentate. That afternoon he had accidentally
seen the Judge (who had anticipated his summer vacation)
step on board the Hudson River cars, with Mrs. Owen, for a
day or two somewhere up the Hudson ; and he had very
naturally made his calculations upon a quiet evening with
Emily. And now to find the Colonel dividing the opportunity with him—nay more, to find Emily even siding a little
with the valorous Colonel !—it *was* too bad, was it not ?

Perhaps the young lover would not have fallen into his
partial sulks quite so easily, had he been aware that Col.
Bancker had announced his intention of being at the house
in the evening (as *he* had not), and that Emily had begged
her aunt to come down from her room and sit with her in
the parlor, on purpose to prevent the expected Colonel having an opportunity for one word with her in private. But
these men are so unreasonable as well as so blind ! There is
no satisfying them, especially with the amount of attention
shown them by a woman whom they happen to fancy that
they love. Perhaps men do not grow actually jealous any more
easily than women, but they grow "miffed" and "hurt" a thousand times easier—let the fact be recorded. There is one instance on legendary record, of a woman who divided her husband with another, at the time of the chivalrous adventures of
the Crusaders ; but the instance has not yet come to light of
the man who so divided his *wife*. Mormonism at the present
day shows the pitch even of fanatical tolerance to which the
female mind can be wrought in this direction ; while we have
yet to look for the corresponding instance on the other side,

in which the women of a community appropriate to themselves half a dozen or fifty husbands each, and the men consent to the division.

This difference goes much farther even than the regulation (can such a thing be regulated ?) of jealousy. Where no jealousy exists, exclusiveness and the sense of propriety comes into the account—again on the male side of the calculation. Jones and his wife being both wall-flowers at any evening party, Mrs. Jones did not feel aggrieved, but rather proud, at Mrs. Thompson's reunion, that Jones went off for an hour to pay the usual flirting attention to the wives of half a dozen of his acquaintances; while Jones colored to the eyes and could scarcely be restrained from making a fool of himself, because Robinson sat down in the vacant chair beside his wife, and tried to be agreeable. And when the Emperor and Lady Flora were at Niagara last summer, it is not upon record that the lady made any objection to the gentleman lingering an hour too late upon Goat Island with that blonde-haired English girl who was such an unmistakeable flirt,—while the gentleman went on like a madman on the balcony of the Cataract, because Lady Flora ran away for half an hour in broad daylight, to Prospect Point, with an old friend of her father's, *ætat* fifty and incurably an invalid. Ah, well—so it has been from the days of the first flirtation (always *except* that of Adam and Eve, when there was neither male nor female rival in the neighborhood), and so it will be to the last—with those arrogant, unreasonable, unsatisfied "lords of the creation."

A word of description of the two rivals, as yet unintroduced, who on that occasion sunned themselves in the eyes of Emily Owen, though at such different distances from the luminary.

Lt. Colonel 'John Boadley Bancker (let him have his full name once more, for the honor of the service—be the same more or less !) was a rather tall and slight man, gentlemanly in appearance and action, but with an occasional dash of swagger that somehow did not indicate courage, and the undefinable impression of the "old beau." His face was well-formed, except that the nose was too large and too

prominently aquiline. He had faultlessly black side-whiskers
and hair correspondingly black—*too* black, Frank Wallace
said—not to have been "doctored" by Batchelor or Crista-
doro, at least. The dark eyes were a little faded, and there
were crows-feet at the corners of the same eyes, for age has
its own way of telling its story, and not all of us who wish
to be young can alter the record in the old family Bible.   In
dress Colonel Bancker presented no variation from the other
colonels of the volunteer service—wearing the full blue uniform, shoulder-straps and belts, with the number of his regiment
wrought in gold on the front of a broad brimmed hat lying
on a book-table near him. Not an ill-looking man by any
manner of means, in spite of the violent antipathy for him
which Miss Emily had managed to transmute out of her
regard for Wallace.

"Age before beauty!" is a motto somewhat popular, so
the Colonel has had the preference. Frank Wallace, proprietor of a small but thriving job-printing establishment
before spoken of, and would-be proprietor of the heart and
hand of Miss Emily Owen—was altogether a different style
of man from the puissant Colonel. As he lounged at the
window in his suit of loose-fitting gray Melton, he looked
very young indeed and created rather the impression of a
"little fellow." He probably fell at least three or four inches
short of the romantic six feet, in reality ; but was the owner
of a fine erect and well-rounded gymnastic form, not a little
improved by frequent visits to the Seventh Regiment
Gymnasium. A jolly round face with very fair complexion,
a merry blue eye, short, curly brown hair and a full moustache
somewhat darker,—made up the ensemble of the particular
person destined to be the torment of Judge Owen—and of
others. For Frank Wallace, be it understood, had other
penchants besides his attachment to pretty Emily—fun
being the other and leading propensity. He was a capital
mimic, an incorrigible banterer, and in any other company
than that of the woman he loved, and her family, the merriest
and most jocular soul alive. Sometimes when alone with
her, and with the "spooniness" which will attach to male
courtship before twenty-five, fairly shaken off. he could be a

gay, dashing and even a presuming lover. Just now he was unamiable—not to say wicked, and ready for any use of his glib tongue which could send the blue coat out of the house at "double-quick."

It could not have been malice—it certainly must have been want of thought—that induced Aunt Martha to break the temporary silence with the remark, addressed to the Colonel :

"It is a funny question I am going to ask, I know, Colonel, but I suppose I have an old woman's privilage. Mrs. Owen and myself were talking about ages a day or two ago, and she thought you were more than thirty-five. How old *are* you ?"

If half a paper of pins, with all the points upward, had suddenly made their appearance in the bottom of the Colonel's chair, he probably could not have been more discomfited. What reason he had to be unquiet, will be more apparent at a later period. He fidgetted a little and hemmed more than once, before he replied :

"Humph ! hum ! Well, Madame, to tell you the truth, I *am* a little on the shady side of extreme youth—old enough to be through with my juvenile indiscretions—ha ! ha !" (The laugh decidedly forced and feeble). "I am a little over thirty-two—was thirty-two in March last."

"I thought so ! I was sure you could not be older than that !" said Aunt Martha, in the most natural way in the world, while Emily took a quick look round at the Colonel, which said, much plainer than words : "Oh, what a bouncer !"

"No, Madame," added the Colonel, perhaps aware that fibs require to be told over at least twice before they acquire the weight of truths told *once.* "No, Madame, a fraction over thirty-two, as I said."

At that moment the invisible influences, if they have good ears, may have heard Frank Wallace getting up from his chair, and muttering between his teeth something very like :

"Humph ! well, I cannot stand *this* any longer ! If I do not succeed in making the house too warm to hold that respectable individual, within ten minutes, I shall certainly leave it myself !" Just then the words "thirty-two," from the Colonel's lips, met his ear, and though he did not catch the context, so as to know what it was all about, the spirit of malicious (and it must be said, reckless) mischief, prompted him to lounge leisurely forward and take a share in the conversation, although uninvited.

"Ah, Colonel, did I understand you to say thirty-two?"

"Yes, I said thirty-two!" said the personage addressed, with a stiffness contrasting very forcibly with the suavity of his speech to Aunt Martha. Emily, who, as may be supposed, knew Frank Wallace better than any other person in the house, at that moment caught a glimpse of his face under the chandelier, and saw that trouble was brewing. The *sulk* had gone, and the *badger*, a much more dangerous devil in society, had taken its place. Two antagonistic acids were certainly coming together, and an explosion was very likely to be the result. Yet what could the poor girl do, except to wait the crash and be ready to act as peacemaker when the worst came to the worst? The one thing she would have liked to do, was precisely the thing she dared not do for her life—that was, to spring up, catch her young lover by the arm, drag him out into the garden, pet him a good deal and kiss him a very little, and send him home doubtful whether he was walking on his head or his heels—while her old beau might spend the whole evening, if he liked, with Aunt Martha. Millie would give her bright eyes to be able to do the same thing with Tom, stately Madame *mere*, when all she dares do in your presence is to sit still, answer in monosyllables, steal sly glances when you are not looking, and be generally dull and stupid. Would it not be well to let them out occasionally, Madame *mere*, for half an hour's play, with full consent and confidence, as they let out the colts in the country? Who knows but they might behave the better for it, when out of your sight altogether? Think of it, Madame *mere*, and make public the result of your experiment! But all this is grossly irrelevant, and springs out of the fact that Emily, who wished to drag Frank Wallace out of the danger of an approaching *melée*, had not the power to do so.

"Indeed I always thought there were thirty-*nine!*" said the young scamp, in the most natural tone of surprise imaginable, and in response to the Colonel's last "thirty-two."

"Thirty-nine *what*, sir?" asked the Colonel, with the same

sign of intense disgust upon his face that we have sometimes seen on Harry Placide's, when playing *Sir Harcourt Court-ley* and uttering the words: "Good gracious! who was addressing *you*?"

"Oh, I really beg pardon," replied the young man, in a tone which meant that he did nothing of the kind. "I thought I heard Mrs. West and yourself speaking of the religious aspects of the country, and that you were enumerating the articles of faith."

"Oh no, you were quite mistaken, Mr. Wallace!" said Aunt Martha, very calmly, while Emily directed an appealing look at the scapegrace, which might as well have been a putty pellet fired at the brown-stone Washington in the Park, for any effect it produced.

"No sir, we were talking of nothing of the kind!" said the Colonel, with that kind of severe dignity intended to convey: "This closes the conversation."

"Then of course it is my duty to beg pardon once more," said the incorrigible. "But you *might* have been talking on that subject, you know, without any impropriety. The religious aspects of the country are deplorable!" throwing up his hands and eyes in no bad imitation of *Aminadab Sleek*. "Do you not think so, Colonel?"

"Sir!" said the Colonel, still more severely, "I had not been thinking of the subject at all!"

"Oh yes," the scapegrace went on—"deplorable! War desolating the country—all the restraints of society removed or weakened—no Sabbath at all—gambling and libertinism in the army and infidelity among the officers—Colonel, I really hope you will excuse me! of course I do not mean to make any allusion to the present company—but I repeat that the present religious aspects of the country are deplorable."

"And *I* repeat, sir," spoke the Colonel, with even more severity than before, while Aunt Martha's face began to assume an expression that might easily have deepened into a smile, and Emily had serious trouble to keep from a broad grin—"*I* repeat, sir, that we were not speaking of the religious aspects of the country at all!"

"Pshaw! of course not! How stupid I am!" said the

tormentor, who had by this time dropped into a chair a little behind the Colonel's left shoulder, where he could literally talk into his ear. "It was the number that deceived me, as I heard it from the window. I *should* have known what you were saying, at once. You are right in the remark that had we had only thirty-two States instead of thirty-four, this rebellion might never have occurred. Had South Carolina, with its rampant Calhounism, and Massachusetts with its anti-slavery fanaticism, both been left out of the compact—"

"*I* must beg pardon, now, for interrupting *you*, Mr. Wallace," said Aunt Martha, with the calmest of voices and the smile all smoothed away from her face. "You are mistaken again. We were neither discussing religious nor national affairs, when you were so *kind* as to come down and join us." (Emphasis on the word "kind," which made the young man wince a little and for the moment predisposed the Colonel to a chuckle.) "Colonel Bancker was saying—"

"Really, my dear Madame," put in the Colonel, "it is scarcely necessary to repeat—"

"Oh, we have had quite enough of misconceptions," said that estimable lady, with what appeared to be another shot at Wallace. "Let us have the truth at last. I had the impoliteness to ask Colonel Bancker his age, and he had the courtesy to say that he was just turned of thirty-two."

"Ph-ph-ph-ph-ew!" came in a long whistle from the lips of the tormentor. The Colonel sprung to his feet in an instant, and looked angrily around. Frank Wallace was quite on the other side of the room, examining a pastel over the mantel, and whistling very slightly, but he was certainly whistling the serenade from "Pasquali."

"Sir!" said the Colonel, rage in the word.

"Meaning *me?*" asked Wallace, turning around.

"Was that whistle intended for *me*, sir?" demanded the Colonel, tragically.

"Certainly not," answered Wallace. "I was directing my whistle, which is not a good one, and certainly impolite in company—at the cornice. The cornice is a handsome one, you will notice, Colonel, and I think by Garvey. Those festoons of roses—"

" Mr. Wallace, you shall answer to me for this !" broke out the Colonel, now no longer master of himself.

"Gentlemen ! gentlemen !" said Aunt Martha, rising.

"Don't, Frank ! for heaven's sake don't torment him any more !" plead Emily, passing rapidly before her lover and speaking in a low tone. Whether he understood her is a question to be settled between them at some future time. " Don't !" is a very easy thing to say, when Niagara is pouring or a herd of wild buffaloes sweeping down; but if the imploration is addressed to either of the moving bodies, it may not win quick obedience. As the human temper is a combination of the torrent, the herd, and all the other unmanageable things in nature and beyond, " Don't !" even from a voice that we love, with right and reason behind it, is sometimes painfully powerless. There is no intention, on the part of the narrator, of defending the previous or subsequent action of Mr. Frank Wallace on this occasion; but actual events must be recorded.

"Well sir, and what am I to answer ?" asked the young man, without a quiver in his voice, but with much more earnest in it than it had before manifested.

" You made an offensive comment on my veracity, by whistling, a moment ago."

" And what then, sir ?"

" That offensive comment shows that you doubt my veracity !"

" Gentlemen ! gentlemen !" again spoke Aunt Martha; and poor Emily, now half frightened out of her wits, made one more attempt at imploring her lover to be quiet. This done, and both now aware that the tide, on one side at least, had overflowed the bounds of all prudence, they desisted, stepped back from between the rivals, and allowed the quarrel to take its own course.

" And suppose I *do* doubt your veracity !" answered Wallace to the last remark of the Colonel. " You call yourself thirty-two ! Bah ! you are fifty, if you are ten !" The obvious rage on the countenance of the Colonel did not stop the torrent, now, nor even check it ! " Such fine crows'-feet under the eyes, as those of yours, never come much before fifty,

except in case of a nice round of brandy-smashes, late hours
and general dissipation, or—"

"Well, sir, what is the *or*?" broke out the Colonel, still
more furious.

"A severe course of early piety!" concluded the young
man, throwing a terrible sting into the tail of his sentence, not
less by the manner than the voice.

"You should answer for this, Mr. Wallace, as you call
yourself," foamed the Colonel—"but—"

"But *what*, Lieut. Colonel Bancker—as you *try* to call
yourself?" thundered the young man, in reply.

"Oh, gentlemen! gentlemen! do stop, for the sake of the
house!" imploringly put in Aunt Martha at this period;
while Emily, seriously frightened, indulged in a few tears that
were no doubt set down to the account of her brute of a
lover, by the over-watching intelligences. But the quarrel
ceased not, even yet, at the bidding of either; and, marvellous to relate, though the front windows were open and they
were speaking in a tone altogether too loud for the amenities
of society, a crowd had *not* gathered around the area railing
in front.

"But *what*?" demanded the younger combatant.

"But that my sword, sir—" began the elder.

"Oh, you *have* a sword, then!" sneered Wallace.   "I
thought it was all *bells!*"

"I would chastise you for this, sir, severely," said the
officer, "but that my sword is sacred to the cause of the
Union.   When with my regiment, sir—"

"Yes, I know," again interrupted Wallace, who had his
own reasons for believing that the Colonel's regiment was
altogether a myth, as so many others have been—"Yes, I
know—the Eleven hundred and fifty-fifth Coney Island Thim-
ble-rig Zouaves!"

Human patience could stand this no longer. With one dash
for his hat and a surly "Good night, ladies!" coupled with
an intimation to Wallace: "You shall hear from me, sir!"
Lt. Colonel John Boadley Bancker (let him once more have
the full benefit of the name!) strode out of the parlor into the
hall, and was about to vanish from the field. But as he

passed into the hall the hand of Aunt Martha was laid upon
his arm, and her voice—so much pleasanter than that of the
tormentor—sounded in his ear. The good aunt, whatever
might have been her wish to rid her niece of a match so repugnant, certainly did not wish to produce the riddance in
this manner and to send the Colonel out of the house under
a sensation of outrage which could not fail to come to the
ears of her " big brother." So she passed into the hall with
the Colonel, leaving the young people behind her,—and
managed to detain the enraged man in the hall and on the
piazza for several minutes. It was not the first time, beyond
doubt, that she had made peace for others, however she might
have martyred her own.

." Oh, Frank ! what have you done !" exclaimed the young
girl, the moment they had passed out into the hall, her eyes
yet dim with the tears of anxiety she had been shedding ; but
in spite of her fear and even her mortification, laying her hand
in that of the reckless young scapegrace whom she truly
loved. " Father will hear of this—we shall be separated
altogether !" And again she repeated the expostulation of
all dairy-maids to all cats or children that have upset pans
of milk—" What have you done !"

" What have I done !" echoed the culprit. " Why merely
roasted a cowardly humbug who deserves nothing better, and
who has not spunk enough to resent it—that is all !"

" But besides my father's anger—I am afraid he *may*,
Frank," said the young girl, looking into her lover's face with
real anxiety.

" I only wish he would !" was the reply.

" Why, you do not mean to say that you would fight him ?"

" With the sword, if he has one—no !" he said. " Not
with anything more dangerous than a piece of rattan. I
would not mind polishing off his dainty hide with *that!* Besides, if I quarrelled with him, who made me ? You ! He
sat too near you, and you not only talked with him but *looked*
at him. What business had you to look at him ? Eh ?"

" Oh, you cruel fellow !" said the young girl, not disposed
to scold more sharply, even at *folly*, when it had such a sedi-
ment of true love lying beneath the froth.

"Oh, you handsome torment!" was the reply of the lover, as he took that one auspicious moment to enfold the young girl in his arms and give her half a dozen warm, close, voluptuous kisses full on the lips—such kisses as people should never indulge in who do not know exactly the haven toward which they are sailing.

"What are you doing *now*, impudence!" uttered the thoroughly-kissed girl, making just so much resistance as seemed becoming, and yet meeting her lover nearly enough half-way to make the exercise rather exhilarating.

"What am I doing? 'Locking up' a 'form'—you know I am a printer!" said the young man, taking yet another "proof" of affection. But here the alarmed reader will be spared the succession of bad puns, peculiar to the printing-office, with which this specimen was followed, and which has probably been to some extent indulged in by every disciple of Faust more or less in love, since Adam worked off the first proof of his breakfast bill-of-fare, on the original hand-press, in one corner of the Garden of Eden.

The young man was yet standing with his arm around the waist of Emily, just within the door leading from the parlor into the hall, and yet other farewell kisses and reproaches might have been on the possible programme,—when both were startled by a sharp scream from Aunt Martha, who was yet standing on the piazza with the Colonel near her.

"Ough-ough-oh!"

Wallace and Emily at once rushed to the front door, under the belief that some sudden accident had befallen the lady; but at that moment there was a loud crash, followed by other voices screaming; and in the street, almost in front of the door, a painful and threatening spectacle presented itself.

As afterwards appeared, when the various parties became sufficiently collected to ascertain what had really happened— a carriage had been coming along the street from the left, driven rapidly, but with the pair of fine horses under good command. Just before it reached the house of Judge Owen, one of those troublesome boys who ought all to be sent to Blackwell's Island from the twenty-fifth of June until the tenth of July, had thrown a lighted "snake," or "chaser,"

under the belly of the near horse as he passed. The animals
had already become sufficiently frightened by the fire-crackers
thrown under them and the pistols exploding at their ears;
and at this crowning atrocity they became altogether unmanageable. Spite of the exertions of the practised driver,
they shied violently to the left, breaking into a run at the
same moment, and the next instant one side of the carriage
was whirled upon the curb, so that the hind axle and wheel
caught in the lamp-post, happily not tearing apart or over-
turning the vehicle, but bringing-up with such a shock that
the driver was hurled from his seat and thrown to the pavement between the maddened horses.

This state of affairs had drawn the scream from Aunt
Martha, and at the instant when Wallace reached the door
the people in the carriage were screaming but incapable of
getting out, the horses were plunging to such a degree that
they must have broken loose in a moment, after making a
wreck of the carriage and trampling to death the poor fellow
who lay senseless under their feet. At the same time it
seemed worth a dozen lives to plunge into that storm of
lashing hoofs and do anything to rescue driver and riders
from their peril.

"Help! help! oh, save them!—save the poor man—somebody!" cried both the women on the piazza, at a breath; and
"Help! help!" rung in a woman's voice from the inside of
the carriage. Fifteen or twenty persons had already rushed
up, but no one seemed disposed to risk his own life to save
others. The Colonel yet stood on one of the steps of the
piazza, apparently spell-bound.

"Colonel Baucker, you wanted to try courage with me a
little while ago: take hold of those horses, if you *dare!*" cried
Frank Wallace, rushing to the edge of the stoop. The
Colonel neither spoke nor stirred. "Coward!" they heard
the young man cry, and the next instant—how, none of them
knew—he had rushed in upon the horses' heads, spite of
their lashing hoofs, had one or both by the bridles, and in
an instant more both horses were flung prostrate and helpless. The imminent danger over, some of the bystanders
rushed in to assist, the horses were more firmly secured, and

the poor driver was dragged out, bloody and half insensible, but not seriously injured. One ready and daring hand had prevented the certain loss of one life, and the probable loss of more. Fire-crackers, pistols and other abominations had vanished from the street as if by magic; the noise over, the horses came again under command; they were raised, and horses, harness and carriage all found comparatively uninjured; the disabled driver was taken to a neighboring drugstore; one of the bystanders volunteered to drive the carriage to its destination, and took his seat on the box; the owner droned out his thanks from the inside of the carriage, in a fat, wheezy voice, mingled with the sobs of a woman in partial hysterics; and the equipage rolled away almost as suddenly as it had come—perhaps not five minutes having been consumed in the whole affair.

Short as was the time occupied, the Colonel had disappeared. When the trouble was over he was no longer standing on the piazza. Frank Wallace had apparently been once beaten down, and had some soiled spots on his Melton, and a few bruises, but he had received no injury of any consequence. For what violent and even dangerous exertion he had undergone, he was unquestionably more than repaid when Aunt Martha caught him by one hand and said fervently, "God bless you!" and when Emily Owen took the other hand with a warmer and fonder pressure than she had ever given it before, and said—so low that probably not even Aunt Martha heard her: "Good—brave—generous Frank!— I won't scold you again in a twelvemonth!"

All that Frank Wallace replied to both these generous outbursts, was comprised in a snap of his fingers in the direction supposed to have been taken by the Colonel, and the words:

"Bah! I told you that man was a coward and wouldn't fight! If he had not pluck enough to risk the feet of those two horses, what would he do in the face of a charge of rebel cavalry!"

CHAPTER IX.

THE FIRST WEEK OF JULY—A CHAPTER THAT SHOULD ONLY
BE READ BY THOSE WHO THINK—THE DESPAIR OF THE SEVEN
DAYS BATTLES—SHOULDER-STRAPS AND STAY-AT-HOME SOL-
DIERS—AN INCIDENT OF THE SECOND.

THE first week of July, eighteen hundred and sixty-two.
What a time it was!—and who that took part in it, in any
portion of the loyal States to which the telegraph and the
newspaper had reached, can ever forget it ?   Everything was
hopeless, blank despair—dull, dead desolation.   Not even
the fatal Monday following the defeat of Bull Run, when we
believed that all our New York troops had been cut to pieces
or fled ingloriously, produced the same total discouragement
in the great city.   Bull Run was our first signal reverse—
the first blow from the rod of national chastisement, that was
afterwards to cut so deeply.   Though that stroke pained, it
also fired and awakened ; and repeated blows had not yet
produced that weakness and exhaustion so difficult to arouse
to any further effort.   And we had not, at the same time,
passed through the repeated disasters of the few months
following, which stunned and hardened while they pained.
We were quite unprepared for the disaster, coming as it did
after several months of continued comparative victory (the
Austerlitz, Jena and Friedland period of the Lincoln Empire,
if it has had one) ; and the country felt it most keenly.
The heart of the nation had been bound up in McClellan.
The confidence and love reposed in him may have been man-
worship, without ground or reason, but it was no less real and
positive.   While in the Command-in Chief, everything had gone
well, and the Butler and Burnside expeditions, the two great
successes of the war, had been planned and executed.   On
the Army of the Potomac the people had looked as the
bulwark of the country—the central force that should in good
time take Richmond and give the last blow to the rebellion.
The miserable bickering and paltry fears which had detached
McDowell's division from the grand army, to defend Wash-

ington when never threatened, had been comparatively unknown or little understood. Many and disastrous months
were yet to elapse, before the letters of the Orleans Princes
could tear away the curtain of mystery and show the official
action in its naked deformity of malice and misjudgment.
McClellan had left Manassas with a gallant army of immense
force, whose numbers had no doubt been all the while exag-
gerated to the popular ear. They had proved themselves
soldiers and heroes, and had won whenever and wherever
brought to the test. The young commander had had the
Command-in-Chief taken from him, at the moment when he
first moved forward; but it was believed that the change had
been made with his consent if not at his own request, so that
he might be the more unhampered in the field. We did not
know the chain which had been cruelly locked around his
strong limbs, and which he had been dragging through every
mile of that long march. He had complained, it is true, from
Williamsburgh, of the insufficiency of his force for the great
end in view; but he was known to be a cautious man, and
when he had won Williamsburgh, forced the evacuation of
Yorktown and afterwards won Fair Oaks, all fears for him
and for the army had been gradually dismissed.

He had been set down to win—to take Richmond: that
had formed the great culmination of the programme—the
red fire and flourish of trumpets on which the curtain of the
rebellion was to go down. If any one had spoken dis-
approvingly or doubtfully of his long delay in the swamps
of the Chickahominy, the reply had been: "Wait patiently!
McClellan is slow, but sure. He will take Richmond before
he ends the campaign, and that is enough!" Such had been
public confidence—the confidence of a public who perhaps
did not know the General, but who certainly did not know
the government directing and overruling his every action.
At last even the time of the great capture had been fixed.
Officers leaving on short furlough had been admonished to
return quickly, "if they expected to take part in the capture
of Richmond." What else could this mean, than confidence
on the part of the commanding general, that the approaches
to the rebel capital had been made sufficiently close to ensure

its capture, and that the prize was at length in his grasp? Then the Fourth of July had been seized upon as the auspicious period, and the whole country had grown ready to celebrate the National Anniversary in the loyal cities, simultaneously with the shouts and bonfires of the Union Army that should then be treading the streets of the conquered capital and opening the prison-doors of the loyal men who had been suffering and starving in the tobacco-warehouses.

Such had been the supposed aspect of affairs in the field, up to the last week of June, and young orators preparing their Fourth of July orations had introduced rounded periods referring to the added glory of the day and the new laurels wreathing the brows of the Union commanders. Those who contemplated speaking on the great day, and had not made any allusion to the fall of Richmond in their prepared orations, had already seen cause to repent the omission. One, who had incautiously mentioned in a city passenger-car that "he hoped Richmond would not be taken until after the Fourth," and who had lacked time to give as a reason that "if it should be taken before, he would be obliged to write his oration all over again"—had been assaulted for the offensive expression, and only escaped after a hard fight, with a black eye and a sense of damaged personal dignity. It had been settled that Richmond was to be in possession of the Union troops on the Fourth—wo to him who doubted it!

Hark! was there muttering thunder in the heavens?— thunder from a sky hitherto all bright blue? Business men, going down town on the morning of the twenty-eighth of June, found that "fighting had commenced before Richmond," and that "McClellan was changing his front." That "change of front" looked ominous. A few read the secret at once— that heavy reinforcements had come into Richmond from the half-disbanded rebel army Halleck had checked but not defeated at Corinth; and coupled with strange rumors of this came hints about "Stonewall Jackson," which indicated to the same persons that that rebel officer had advanced from the North-west and made an attempt to take McClellan's right wing in flank, necessitating a retrograde movement of that wing to bring him in front. Still, confidence was not

lost, in McClellan or in the army. While his right wing fell
back before an attack in force, his left might swing in towards
Richmond and even take the city—who could say ?

Then the telegraph closed down, and the morning papers
contained "no later intelligence" from the field before Richmond. This was " the feather that broke the camel's back"
of the national spirit. The government had no confidence in
the people—it dared not trust them with the truth—it dared
conceal ! Our army was being cut to pieces, and we were
permitted to know nothing of the calamity except the dreadful fact. No development could have been so injurious as
this concealment—no stroke at the national confidence so
deadly as the want of reliance shown by the government
censors. The nation's heart went down beneath the blow :
to this day* it has never risen to the same proud and cou-
rageous determination shown through all previous disasters.

It is said to be a terrible spectacle when a strong man
weeps—a thousand times more terrible than the grief of the
softer sex and the gentler nature, because it is evident what
must have been the blow inflicted and what the struggle
before the pent waters burst forth. But even the strong
man's grief is tame compared to the spectacle of the grief of
a *nation*—that aggregation of strong men and of vital interests. When the very sky seems dimmed and the bright sunshine a mockery. When the foot falls without energy and
the voice breaks forth without emphasis. When men, who
meet on the corners of streets, clasp hands in silence or only
speak in low and broken words. When the silver moonlight
seems to be shining upon nothing else than new-made graves.
When the sound of revelry from ball-rooms jars upon the
heart until it creates deadly sickness ; and the glare of lights
from places of public amusement seems to be an indecorum
like a waltz at a funeral. When a uniform in the street is a
reproach and a horror ; and the music of the band to which
soldiers tramp, sounds like nothing but the " Dead March in
Saul." When business is impossible, and idleness an agony.
When the old flag is looked up to without pride, and the

* January, 1863.

very pulses of patriotism seem dead because they have no hope to keep them in motion. When all is darkness—all discouragement—all shame—all despair. These are the tears of a broad land—this is the spectacle we witness when a nation weeps. The loyal men of this generation have wept more bitterly and sorely, within the past two years, than those wept who saw the armies of the Revolution starved and outnumbered—who pined in the Prison-Ships and tracked the bloody snow at Valley Forge. God forgive those who have wrung these tears—whatever the ultraism they may represent! The people they have outraged will not forgive until a terrible vengeance is taken.

The first days of July, when fell the President's fifth proclamation, calling for "three hundred thousand more." If ever a cry of despair burst out from an overcharged heart, it went up to heaven from the whole land at that moment. "Have I yet more to give?" cried the depopulated city and the desolated village. "Have I yet more to give?" cried the father with one son remaining of his six brave boys; "Have I yet more to give?" echoed the widow whose last stay was to be taken from her; and "Have I yet more to give?" re-echoed the wife as she buckled the sword or the bayonet-sheath on the side of her husband and sent him forth as one more sacrifice to the insatiate demons of Ambition and Mismanagement. Have not the days following Manassas, and the Seven Days before Richmond, and Fredericksburgh, been hours in a national Gethsemane? And has not the hand been almost excusable, lifted in the prayer: "Father of Nations!—if it be possible let this cup pass from us!" And yet the cup has not passed—we have been draining it to the very dregs!

The introduction of this chapter, which does not in the least advance the action of the story, would be altogether inexcusable, did not every artist have a habit of painting a background for his historical composition, instead of throwing the figures on the naked canvas and thereby losing half his little chance of illusion. The characters here introduced may live and move, but relieved against what? The background of current events, certainly—without a knowledge of which

their actions might be altogether unaccountable. And general as may be a feeling to-day, it must be caught and put
upon record to-morrow, or the very persons who held it most
deeply will forget it by the third day. Ten years hence—
perhaps a year hence—the bitter humiliation through which
the country has been passing between the opening of 1861
and the opening of 1863, will be almost entirely forgotten in
after glory or after shame. A few will remember, but faintly
and dimly, as the old veterans of the Revolution remembered
in their tottering age the conflicts through which they had
passed in youth, beside Washington or with Mad Anthony.
A few will remember something of the truth, but only as
veteran play-goers remember a performance at the Old Park
in its palmy days—a Cooper or a Power prominent, but all
the other actors lost in the mists of time.

When Thomas Wilson left the field of Brandywine, after
that disastrous defeat, and with a bullet-hole through his
neck, narrowly missing the jugular, which had been received
in aiding to rescue and bear off the wounded Lafayette,—
that battle-scene was so imprinted on his mind that he believed he could ever afterwards, to his dying day, recall the
position of every squadron, and even the place of every rock
and tree beside which he had fought; and yet when he saw
him, more than half a century afterwards, hobbling along on
his stout hickory cane to the place where he was to draw
the scant pittance afforded him by a nation grudging in its
gratitude—he remembered Lafayette and that he was wounded
in helping to bear him off—nothing more. No doubt John
Wilson, grandson of the old man, wounded in the assault at
Fredericksburgh, came away from that murderous field with
the same impression of the eternity of his own memory; but
he will forget all except the very event of the action, like his
grandsire. And yesterday evening, coming out from among
the plaudits of the crowd that had been paying honor to
the wonderful renderings of Couldock and Davidge in the
" Chimney-Corner," Wetmore, the critic and habitue, did not
even bring away a play-bill. That little domestic scene was
so daguerreotyped upon his memory that he should never
forget one detail of cast or incident—never! And yet five

years hence, Wetmore will turn to some companion of the present and say: "Ah, confound it—I cannot remember! Who *was* it that played with Couldock at the Winter Garden, in the—the—there, hang me if I have not even forgotten the name of the piece!—that capital little Robson domestic drama—the—the—the 'Chimney Corner'?"

So much by way of explanation, if not of apology, for catching the colors of the background of general feeling at the particular period of this story, before they have time to fade. And yet a few more words with reference to that general feeling, as it took particular directions.

"Vox populi, vox Dei" is a motto so often falsified, at least in appearance, that the world has come to place but little reliance upon it; and yet it is as true to-day as when the old Latin maximist first penned it, with the plurality of the gods of his dependence fully manifest in the original "Dii" or "Deis." The people do not often err materially or long. They may throne a wooden god or a baboon for a short moment, but that moment soon passes. As a political body no demagogue with words supplying the place of brains, can long override them; and as an army they never make a favorite of a fool or a coward. The American people did not err for a moment as to where the responsibility of the sad check to the army of the Potomac did *not* belong; and they erred but little in their calculation of where it *did*. The army was brave—its leader was both careful and capable— the very man for the place: that they knew intuitively. They doubted the existence of brains at Washington, and of loyalty in many of those who had been urging "forward movements" without sufficient force or proper preparation; and they have already been fully justified in the doubt.

But the people saw something more—execrated it, howled against it, spat upon it; and after the Seven Days before Richmond, their abhorrence culminated. That terrible something was *absenteeism*. Thousands and tens of thousands who should have been in their places in the army, were shamelessly absent when their brothers-in-arms were being sacrificed from their very want of numbers. Wounded soldiers who had come home on furlough, and afterwards re-

covered, had never rejoined their commands; and in spite of
the calls of McClellan no steps had been taken to force them
back into the ranks. The Provost Marshals were too busy
looking for summer-boarders at Fort Lafayette and Fort Warren, to think of their obvious duty of protecting the armies
of the Union against indolence and desertion! A still more
serious defection existed among the officers—those who
had been awhile in the service, and those who had merely
entered it in *pretence*. Half the New York regiments,
especially, had originally been officered by men who had no
intention of fighting, and who merely took commissions and
spent a few weeks in camp or in the field of inactive operations, in order that they might have "Colonel," "Major," or
Captain" attached to their names, and be ready to make
more successful plunges into the flesh-pots of well-paid offices,
on the plea that they had been "patriots" and "served the
country" in its need. Hundreds had come home, leaving
their commands half-officered, on one pretext or another, and
their leaves-of-absence obtained by more or less of political
influence or favoritism. They never intended to go back; for
were not the elections coming within a few months? and was
it not necessary to plough the political field with those very
harmless swords in order to raise a fall crop of offices?
    Then the other class—those who had never intended to go
at all—those who had no heart in the cause, from the first,
and who had merely assumed the regulation uniform to feed
vanity or the *pocket*. The former, to strut Broadway in unimpeachable blue-and-gold, be called by military titles, lounge
at the theatres or create sensations at the watering-places,
confident of being able to escape, on some pretext, before their
commands (if they had any) should leave for the seat of war.
The latter, to find profitable employment in raising companies,
regiments or brigades, for Staten Island, East New York or
the Red House, drawing pay and subsistence for twice or
three times the number ever in camp, and coolly pocketing
the difference! It is idle to talk, as exaggerating sensation-
paragraphists sometimes do, of stealing the pennies off the
eyes of a dead grandmother to play at pitch-and-toss, or
forging the name of a buried father to a note and then allow-

ing it to go to protest,—it is idle to talk of these as the extreme of criminal heartlessness: the men who could thus
trade—the men who *have* thus traded, during the whole war
—on the public patriotism and the public necessity, would
deserve the lowest deep in the pit of perdition, following upon
leprosy in life and deaths on dunghills—if there was not a still
deeper guilt on the souls of those who first plunged the country into war and then murdered it by treason or inefficiency.*

The public disgust at these "shoulder-straps" of both classes
culminated during the first week of July. It might be unpatri-
otic and even cowardly to make no movement towards joining
the Army of the Union : it was base and utterly contemptible
to make such a movement merely as an injurious sham. So
thought the people—seeing in this *desire of military repudia-
tion and profit without service or sacrifice*, the worm gnawing
at the very heart of the republic. "If they are not soldiers,
why do they wear those trappings of the battle-field?" asked
the public. "If they are soldiers, why are they loitering here
when their comrades are being overpowered and slaughtered?" Alas! the question has been continually asked and
never answered. "Leipsic was lost, and I not there!" cried
the soldier of the old French Eleventh, bursting into tears.
But: "All the great battles of this war have been fought,
and I have managed to keep out of them!" might the shoulder-
strapped, belted, fatigue-capped, strutting mock-soldier of our
own time say with a corresponding chuckle. God help us!—
Rome had but one Nero fiddling when it burned, if history
tells us true : we have had ten thousand military fiddlers
playing away to admiring audiences during *our* conflagration!
Is this to be a wholesale attack, then, on our national
courage? Had we no brave men, then, that only these apolo-
gies for men are exhibited? Yes!—thousand upon thousand
of brave men, and hundred upon hundred of brave officers—
the world over no better or truer! But they were, as they
are, the men of action, not of *show*, or at least not of show
alone.

One incident of the morning of the Second of July, when

the Seven Days Battles were yet in progress before Richmond,
will at once supply a few figures for this background, and au
illustration of the public feeling for the soldiers of the little
army of action and the great army of sham !

A few words had been permitted by the telegraph-censors
to come through, and they had arrived too late for the morning papers. They were consequently bulletined. They gave
some hint of the abandonment of the White House and the
severe fighting which followed that movement, on Saturday
and Sunday. They were not hopeful—they were discouraging
—much worse, as it afterwards appeared, than the truth demanded ; and the knit brows and set teet of the readers did
not show any symptoms of improvement under the new revelation.

A considerable group of men were standing about the
" World" bulletin, stopping, reading and passing on—all the
more slowly because the shade of the high building was refreshing in that hot, blinding, cloudless July morning sun.
A group of politicians who had read the bulletins and taken
their second breakfast at Crook and Duff's, were digesting the
one and picking their teeth from the fragments of the other,
before the door of that unaccountably-popular establishment,
on the block above. Over the street from the "World" corner,
at the Park fence, a dozen or two of invalid soldiers, with
jaundiced faces and shabby uniforms, who had arrived by
steamer from the South the day before and taken up their
temporary abode in the dirty Barracks,—were standing lounging and listening to what was read from the bulletin ; while
a sentinel paraded up and down the walk, outside, to prevent escapes that did not seem over-probable. Voices were
a little high, though not in disagreement, among the group at
the corner—for they were discussing the very subject noted—
that of *absenteeism and military sham.*

At that moment a good-looking young officer in spotless
full uniform, with his cap so natty that the rain could never
have been allowed to fall upon it, with his hair curled and his
moustache trim as if he had been intended for any other
description of "ball" than one met on the field of battle, and
with a Captain's double-bars on his shoulder,—came across

the Park from the direction of Broadway, over to the Beekman Street corner, as if to pass down that street. Some of
the talkers noticed him, and connected him and his class a
little injuriously with the events of the day. Just as he passed
the corner, brushing very near some of the talkers and casting
a hurried glance at the bulletin-board—one of the crowd, a
rough fellow who might have belonged to the set who growled
and hooted Coriolanus out of Rome,—broke out with :—

"There goes one of them, now !"

"Yes, muttered another, almost in front of the officer.
"D—n 'em all ! Much good those shiny uniforms are doing
the country !"

The officer, who must have heard the words and known
that they were intended for his ears, paid no attention and
was passing on—the part of prudence and propriety, beyond
a doubt. But one of the crowd was not satisfied. He must
make wrong of the right (a thing very common in all causes)
and the insult a personal one.

"See here !" and he laid his hand on the officer's arm,
detaining him, but not roughly. "Do you see what there is
on that bulletin ?"

"I see !" said the Captain.

"Yes, they are cutting our boys all to pieces down there !"
went on the aggrieved citizen.

"Well ?" again said the officer, apparently neither angry
nor frightened.

"Well !" spoke the other, repeating his word, but a little
abashed by the calmness of the officer, whose arm he had let
go the moment he turned to speak to him. "Well !—perhaps it is none of my business, you know—but why the
d—l don't you fellows who have such handsome uniforms,
and commissions, and all that sort of thing, go down and
help ?"

"Humph !" said the Captain, still with no symptom of
being abashed or angry. Perhaps it *would* be as well, for
all of us who *could*."

"Oh, you can't go, eh ?" said another member of the
assemblage, in a sneering tone.

"Not *yet !*" was the reply of the officer

9

"I thought not!" said the man who had first addressed him.

"See here, boys!" said the Captain, haven't you made a mistake in your man? I hate a stay-at-home soldier, quite as much as you."

"Why don't you go, then?" one of the others again interrupted.

"I have *been*, and I am *going again!*" said the Captain, emphatically. "I see what is the matter. I have just put on a new uniform, and you think that looks suspicious. So it does, I suppose; but my old one has been through six pitched battles and looks rough enough to suit you."

"The d—l it has!" said the man who had addressed him. "Really, Captain, I beg your pardon!"

"Never mind that!" said the Captain. "You will probably hit the right man next time, and the quicker you shame the make-believes into doing something or pulling off their uniforms, the better. McClellan wants us all—"

"McClellan's the boy!" broke out a voice.

"You are right,—' Little Mac's' the boy!" said the Captain. "He wants us all. The doctor told me this morning that I might go back, and I am going to-morrow."

"The doctor?—then you have been sick or wounded! What a fool I have been making of myself!" said the first speaker, generous as rough.

"A little!" answered the Captain, and by a dexterous movement he flung back his coat, threw open his collar and bared his neck almost to the shoulder. The whole top of the shoulder seemed to have been shot away, and the blade broken, by a ball that had struck him there and ploughed through into the neck; and the yet imperfectly healed flesh lay in torn ridges of ghastly disfigurement. Thousands of men have died from wounds of not half the apparent consequence; and yet the wearer of this was the smiling and even-tempered man of the new uniform—going back to-morrow! The world has not lost all its heroes yet; and some of them have the same fancy for a clean shirt and spotless broadcloth, when attainable, as Murat displayed for a velvet cloak, or white plume and plenty of gold embroidery

on his trousers, when making the most reckless of charges at
the head of the most dashing cavalry in the world. "That,"
said the Captain, closing up the wound as rapidly as he had
opened it, but not before a general shudder had run through
the crowd at its ghastly character—"that I got at Fair Oaks,
three weeks ago last Sunday. How do you like it? Am I
going back soon enough? Good morning, boys!"

"And your name?" asked the man who had stopped him,
as he attempted to pass on. "Who are you?—Do tell us."

"Nobody that you would know," said the Captain. "My
name is D——, and I belong to the Sickles Brigade."

He passed on, hurriedly, down Beekman Street, as if
"Little Mac" had sent for him and he had been wasting time
in going; but the cheer that went after him was joined in by
the invalids at the Park fence, who had caught a part of the
dialogue; and the people in the "World" office looked up
from their account books, wondering what was the matter in
the street; while the politicians in front of Crook and Duff's,
among whom were some of the City Fathers and their
backers and bottle-holders, losing the other part of the affair
and only hearing the shouts, wondered whether some new
notability had not just arrived at the Astor House, who could
be turned to profitable use in the way of a reception in the
Governor's Room, a few "Committees," gloves, carriages
from Van Ranst and a dinner or two all around—of course
at the expense of the economically-managed city treasury.

And this closes a chapter which has made no direct progress whatever in following the leading characters of this
story, who must now be again taken up in their order.

CHAPTER X.

FOLLOWING UP THE PRINCE STREET MYSTERY—TOM LESLIE'S
PECULIAR IDEAS—A CALL UPON SUPERINTENDENT KENNEDY
—THE DEPARTURE OF A REGIMENT—JOSEY HARRIS IN A
STREET-SQUALL—A RENCONTRE.

IT was not to be supposed that Tom Leslie and Walter
Lane Harding, after the expenditure of ten dollars, a whole
night's rest and a considerable amount of bodily energy, in
the investigation of what they called the 'Prince Street
mystery,' would permit it to remain uninvestigated afterwards, so far as a little more money and a good deal more of
inquisitiveness could go in unravelling it. Even before they
parted, late on the night of the adventure, they had discussed
half a dozen plans for gaining admission to the house on
Prince Street or that on East 5—th, by fair means or foul.
Harding, who was something of a stickler for propriety in
ordinary cases, in spite of the fact that he had on that one
occasion been inveigled into following a carriage and playing
spy under a front stoop—Harding expressed himself satisfied
that there being now in their minds a sufficient certainty of
the existence of a disloyal organization in the city to make
affidavits to that effect a duty—the proper course would be to
lay the matter at once before the Superintendent of Police
and request that a watch might be set upon the houses or
some proceedings taken to "work up" the case for after proceedings. The young merchant no doubt had more confidence
in this plan than he might otherwise have done, from the fact
that a few months previous a robbery had been committed at
his place of business, and that upon his laying the matter at
once before the police authorities, such steps had been taken
as within two weeks secured the detection of the leading culprit and the recovery of most of the missing property. Here
was a detective "bridge" that had once "carried him safe
over" in a commercial point of view: why would not the
same bridge offer both of them a safe footing when attempting to unravel a mystery of disloyalty?

Tom Leslie, as was natural to one of his temperament, took a different view of the whole matter. Mysteries "bothered" the straight-forward Harding; but to Tom they formed one of the necessities of existence—a little less indispensable than his breakfast, but much more important than his cigar. Had he been precisely the sort of man for employing police agency where personal investigation was possible, he would never have climbed the tree in Prince Street or dragged Harding under the stoop of the brown-stone house. He suggested that Harding would not have much difficulty in making himself up for a postman, and getting inside the up-town house in that capacity, trusting to his own skill to *remain* within until he had made the necessary investigations; while as for himself—well, he had no particular objections to entering temporarily upon the occupation of a tinker or a gatherer of old rags and bottles, with a disguise from his friend Williams, the costumer, and working the basement of the house on Prince Street, and the domestics therein employed, in one of those capacities. He had no doubt whatever that if he could only succeed in concealing himself in the sub-cellar or the coal-vault, until the house should be closed for the night, he could then, with the aid of a few matches and a pair of list slippers carried in the pocket, make a "rummage" of the premises which must prove eminently satisfactory. He did not seem to labor under any fear that the little accident of being discovered while lying perdu or while making his explorations, and arrested and sent to Blackwell's Island as an ordinary sneak-thief, might possibly stand in the way. In fact, if all stories of his earlier life were to be credited, he had taken some pains, in more than one instance, to be arrested by the Police under what appeared to be suspicious circumstances, spend a night in the station-house, and astound the Police Justices, who personally knew him somewhat too well for their comfort, by his appearance as a very woe-begone culprit in the morning. "*De gustibus non est*," etc.—there *is* really no disputing about tastes, since St. Simeon Stylites roosted upon the top of a very inconvenient pillar, and the first ostrich inaugurated the dietary proclivities of the race by gobbling down a small cart-load of cord-wood with a garnish of a peck

of paving-stones! A night in a station-house may not be so
very unpleasant a thing, when taken from choice and with a
certainty of the door being laughingly opened in the morning : Whiskey Tom or Scratching Sall, who visit the institution perforce, for small burglaries or big vagrancies, with a
prospect of "six months" or "two years" at the end, may
form a very different opinion of it!

Tom Leslie, as has been remarked, did not seem to have
any fears of such a result as an arrest, to his proposed spy-
movements; but it cannot be concealed that for a moment
Walter Harding, who had before thought that he knew him
well, looked at him out of the corners of his eyes, with some
impression that he must unwittingly have been keeping
company with a genteel house-breaker. At all events,
Harding did not fall in with the spy-proposition, so far as his
own action was concerned, alleging that there might be such
a thing as a business man having other occupations than
traversing the city in disguise as a volunteer detective ; and
so that project, if any there had really been in the mind of
Leslie, was abandoned.

A resort to the police remained ; for neither of the friends,
after what they had seen and heard, could think of the whole
affair being allowed to go by default. Superintendent
Kennedy must be visited, after all ; and though Harding's
business for the next day would interfere, it was more than
half agreed upon before they separated, that they would call
together upon that official on the next day but one and lay
the whole matter before him.

The agreement, though only half made, was better kept
than many that are made more conclusively; for at eleven
o'clock on the day named Leslie made his appearance at the
place of business of Harding, and dragged him away from a
series of mercantile calculations over the desk, in which he
had more than half forgotten the existence of his friend as
well as the whole adventure of the chase and the mystery.
He came up to the work pretty readily, however—the
presence of the rattling, go-ahead Leslie always having the
effect of carrying him a little off his feet ; and half an hour
afterwards the two friends had entered that melancholy-

looking five-story brick building on the corner of Broome and Elm, then and till lately known as the headquarters of the Metropolitan Police,—and were being shown by a policeman in attendance, with the blue of his suit undimmed by exposure to the weather and the brass of his buttons radiantly untarnished, into the presence of John A. Kennedy, Superintendent of the Metropolitan Police District and for the time Provost Marshal of the City of New York. They entered from the hall of the building by a side door to the left, in the rear of what had been the centre of the house when occupied as a private residence before New York moved up "above Bleecker,"—and advancing towards the front under the guidance of the respectful official, passed the table at which sat the half-bald, stern-faced, and iron-gray Deputy Superintendent Carpenter, through the door that had once separated the two parlors, and stood in the presence of another iron-gray man, seated writing at a table covered with books and papers, his back to the front of the building, and the smooth-shaven and round-faced Inspector Leonard busily examining a roll of papers behind him in the corner.

Few men in this whole country have occupied a more marked position in the public mind, during all this struggle, than Superintendent Kennedy, in his legitimate position at the head of the Police and in what we must believe to have been his il-legitimate one as Provost Marshal. He made himself peculiarly conspicuous, and won the enmity of all the secession wing of the Northern democracy, by stopping the shipment of arms to the rebellious States, and blocking the apparent game of Mayor Wood and his aiders and abettors to curry favor with the extreme South by truckling to every one of its arrogant dictations. The enmity then created has never died, and can never die until those who hold it happen to die themselves. At the same time, those who were and are unconditionally loyal to the Union, have never judged the action of Superintendent Kennedy very harshly—aware that *something* needed to be done to prevent the existing evil, and that only a man of his indomitable "pluck" could be found to apply the remedy at such a period.

A somewhat broader and more general charge has since

been preferred against him—that in the exercise of the duties
of Provost Marshal, which he assumed without propriety, he
showed himself a willing tool of governmental despotism and
displayed indefensible harshness and arrogance. There is
something of truth in this charge, beyond a question,—as
the impossibility of " touching pitch" without being " defiled,"
applies to intercourse with wrong-doers high in power as
well as to those in lower station. The station-houses of the
New York police were certainly made receptacles for accused
parties whose crimes were very different from those contemplated in their erection,—just as the forts in the harbors of
New York and Boston have been made " Bastilles" for state-
prisoners whose arrests were signally reckless and improper.
Many of the prisoners, in both cases, have deserved more
than all the punishment received ; but the blind uncertainty
as to their guilt, and the impossibility of discovering even the
nature of the charges against them, have made those imprisonments equally indefensible and dangerous, and brought
them at last to their end.

There is a woman at the bottom of almost every revolution
—political as well as social. Tradition tells us, though history
is silent on the subject, that the sad fate of the daughter of a
French citizen, flung into the Bastille for alleged complicity
in a conspiracy during the early days of Louis XVI., and
dying there—rankled in the minds of the Parisians much more
than the wrongs done to thousands of brave and noble men
during the centuries previous, and furnished the burden of the
terrible cry with which the men of 1789 thundered at the
walls of that old fortress of feudal oppression, and with which
they butchered not only De Launay, the Governor of the
Bastille, but Flesselles, the *Provost Marshal*. The case of a
woman—Mrs. Brinsmaid—was the last drop in the cup of endurance, here, and the event which we believe was finally and
forever to close the melancholy doors of Lafayette and Warren
against arrest without charge and imprisonment without trial
—spite of indemnity bills passed and unlimited powers con-
ferred upon the President by a mad Congress.

Through all this, meanwhile, John A. Kennedy was unquestionably more sinned against than sinning—made the tool of

worse and more unscrupulous men, who used his hard con-
scientiousness and his narrow bigotry of mind, fostered by too
long and too close connection with the lodges of secret socie-
ties—to carry out their own designs of despotism, without the
nobility to stand between him and his possible sacrifice for
obeying the very orders they had given. He is not the first
man who has been misused and placed in a false position, nor
the last, as a later victim of blind confidence and obedience,
Burnside,* is very likely to bear sad witness.

But all this while, for the purposes of this narrative, Tom
Leslie and his friend Harding have been standing unnoticed
in the presence of the Superintendent. Not very long in
reality—scarcely longer than enabled them to note the hair and
closely-cut full beard of iron gray, the keen but troubled eyes,
that had scarcely yet ceased to moisten at the memory of the
loss of a dearly loved brother,† the face care-worn and anxious,
and the shoulders bent over a little as he sat,—scarcely longer
time than this was given them, when the Superintendent laid
down his pen and said, sharply and decisively: .

"Well, gentlemen?"

There was nothing very cordial in the tone, and no indication that the Superintendent considered it peculiarly his place
to listen to all the persons who came to him upon business;
but perhaps this comparative *brusquerie* is necessary, in the
carrying on of any important department, to discourage bores
and send idle people the sooner about their business. It does
not add to popularity, however, and may add materially to the
opposite.

Under such circumstances, it did not need a very long period
of time for Tom Leslie, with the occasional assistance of
Harding, whose memory was much more accurate if not more
retentive—to convey to the Superintendent the main facts of
their midnight adventure, with the impression that adventure
had made, of some disloyal movements going on in the City,
and probably with extended ramifications elsewhere. Except
to say that one of the women seen on that evening had before

* January 25th, 1863.
† Col. William D. Kennedy, of the Tammany Regiment.

fallen under his notice in Europe, Leslie did not allude to the
episode of the "red woman," nor did he enter into the particulars of his previous meetings with Dexter Ralston, though
he asserted his knowledge of him as a Virginian of peculiar
influence and a very ambiguous position. The Superintendent
showed few signs of interest in the narration, though his sharp
eye occasionally glanced at the face of the principal narrator,
and though he two or three times made motions with the pencil
lying before him, which might have been merely listless occupation of his fingers and might have been something very
different.

"Well, gentlemen," said the Superintendent, when they
had concluded. "It is certainly a strange story you have
been telling, and of course I do not question the entire veracity of your narration of what you saw or *thought* you saw.
But there is nothing proved, so far, that could justify any
arrest, even if we could find the persons to arrest. I do not
see that there is anything *I* could do in the matter."

"I told you so!" said Leslie in a low voice to his friend.
He had opposed coming to the Superintendent at all, be it remembered.

"Nothing?—not even to set a watch upon the two houses
we have named?" asked Harding, a good deal surprised and
not a little out of temper.

"Humph!" answered the Superintendent. "This is not
France under the Empire, and I am not Fouché."

"The latter part of that sentence may probably be true : I
have my doubts about the other!" thought Tom Leslie, though
he waited a more prudent occasion for communicating the
thought to Harding.

"And so, Mr. Superintendent, you consider all this of no
consequence?" said Harding, going back to first principles,
and not by any means improving in the matter of temper.

"I did not say anything of the kind!" answered the Superintendent, his face sterner but his voice even as before. "I
said there was nothing upon which I could act, and the police
force of the district is scarcely sufficient to set a watch around
all the houses that may happen to have traitors in them. I
would advise you to say nothing of this affair to any other

SHOULDER-STRAPS. 149

persons, if you have not yet done so; and if you see or hear
of anything more that *will* seem to justify an arrest, communicate with this office again."

He did not say "good morning!" as a sign of dismissal,
but his manner indicated as much, and the two friends left
him with merely an additional nod. Harding was in decided
dudgeon as the policeman of the bright blue cloth and the
unimpeachable buttons accompanied them to the door, and
muttered something very like "I'm d—d if I *do* communicate
with that office again, in a hurry!" Leslie, who had seen
more of police operations, both abroad and at home, than his
friend, and who had expected little or nothing else from the
first,—kept his good humor admirably; and he bored Harding,
before they had walked from the office to Broadway, with the
information that that was about all the thanks any man ever
received for attempting to do a service to government or individuals, and a relation of how at Naples a couple of years
before, he had attempted to save the life of an Englishman
threatened with assassination, and been arrested and very
nearly imprisoned for an attempt to stab the man himself,
with his pen-knife or tooth-pick—he never knew precisely
which!

The two friends were scarcely in the street, when the
Superintendent called sharply:

"Mr. Carpenter!"

The Deputy was in the room in a moment. The Superintendent was writing a few words on a piece of paper.

"You heard the story those men were telling?"

"A part of it—perhaps all," answered the Deputy.

"There may be something in it—I think there *is*," continued the Superintendent. "At all events, put those two
houses"—handing him the slip of paper—"under close watch,
and discover who enters and who leaves them, and at what
hours. Put B—— and another good man in charge of the
Prince Street house, and L—— and another good man at the
one in East 5— Street. That is all."

The Deputy merely bowed and returned to his own table,
beckoning to one of the policemen near the door and giving
the necessary orders to carry out the directions of his superior

So that almost by the time the two friends reached Broadway,
and certainly some time before Leslie concluded his illustra-
tive narration of police management in Naples, the arrangement for which they had especially come, and which had been
apparently denied, was already in active operation. The
reasons which had induced the Superintendent to underrate
to Harding and Leslie the importance of the intelligence he
had just received, or which had led to so sudden a change of
mind, will probably remain a mystery even after the pro-
founder mysteries of governmental management during the
war are brought into broad daylight. There is no Sphynx
like your "man in authority," whether his reasons for silence
be that he does not wish others to know his intentions, or that
he *does not know them himself*.

It was perhaps one o'clock when the two friends reached
Broadway and turned downward to return to their different
places of business—Harding of course to his store near the
Hospital, and Leslie to his little desk in the office of the
Daily Thundergust, or anywhere else in the more frequented
parts of the town, where he might chance to pick up material
for an item or an article. Broadway at that point and at that
moment presented an appearance that used to be extraordinary, but that of late months has been almost as common as
its ordinary crowded condition. One of the Eastern regiments, that had just landed at the New Haven Railroad De-
pot, was on its way down to the Park Barracks, and the
police had been clearing the street of omnibuses and carriages
to make room for them. The sidewalks on both sides were
pretty well filled with spectators—idlers who never find anything better to do than gazing at street spectacles, and people of both sexes, with more or less of business on hand, who
cannot avoid pausing for a moment when the police sweep
by to clear the street and the tap of the bass-drum is heard,—
just to see what the excitement is all about. In this instance
a file of policemen extending almost from curb to curb were
marching abreast to keep the way clear in front of the regiment; close behind them sounded the crashing of brass, the
screaming of clarionet-reeds and the tap of drums; and a
little farther behind, over the heads of the advancing column, a

couple of flags caught the sun and waved softly in the light
summer air—one the glorious old banner, with its three colors
that blend truth, purity and devotion till death,—and the
other a fringed and tasselled embroidery of dark blue silk,
bearing the peculiar arms of the one State that was sending
forth more of its bravest sons to do battle for all.

"A Massachusetts regiment," said Harding. "One was to
come down by the New Haven Road, this morning."

"Yes," said Leslie. "You can afford half an hour more,
while I can afford all day if I wish. Let us wait until the
show passes." They paused accordingly and took shelter beside a lamp-post against the downward pressure of the side-
walk crowd that was coming.

Nearer came the soldiers, their long line of sloped bayonets
glancing off the sunbeams with a peculiarly threatening aspect, and their equipments showing the perfection which has
been accorded by the Old Bay State to all her troops, in con-
tradistinction to the men of some of the other States, that
have been allowed to go down to the conflict looking more
like a mob of scarecrows than a body of trained soldiers.
The Colonel, who rode first, lolled easily on his saddle, like
one who had not mounted a horse for the first time when he
first put on his sword-belts; the Captains of the various companies stepped out boldly and clearly in front of their men,
turning occasionally to see that the line was properly kept;
and the rank and file tramped on, their step almost steady
enough for the march of veteran troops, and the dull thunder
of the fall of each thousand of feet on the solid pavement,
making the most impressive sound in the world except that
supplied by the multitudinous clink of the iron hoofs of a
cavalry squadron passing over the same stony road.

It was an impressive spectacle, like all of the same kind
that have preceded and followed it—a glorious spectacle,
when the faces of most of the men were observed, and nothing
of the despairing dullness of the conscript's eye seen there,
but the vigorous pride and determination of men who were
going forth at the call of their country to battle for that
country to the death. And yet a sad spectacle, as all the
others have been, when waste of life and mismanagement of

power were taken into the account, and when the thinned
ranks that should return, of the full ranks that went so
proudly away, came to be remembered. Something of this
latter feeling, and the peculiarities of the time, made the
waving of handkerchiefs and the clapping of hands less frequent and cordial than the fine-looking fellows and their excellent appointments really deserved.

"The d—l take the politics and policy of Massachusetts!"
broke out Tom Leslie, when the array had half passed. "I
do not like her, and uever did.   But she *does* send out troops
as the old Trojan horse poured out heroes; she *does* know how
to equip and take care of them, as *we* do not; and they *fight*
—eh, Harding, don't they?"

"Not any better than most of our New York troops, I
fancy!" replied Harding, an incarnate New Yorker, to the
last observation.

"Not better, perhaps, but more steadily—not so dashingly,
but more inevitably," said Leslie, going into one of his fits of
abstract philosophy, where he must perforce be followed, like
a maniac by his keeper. "Our New York boys go into the
fight more as a spree—the New Englanders more as a duty.
Our boys enjoy it—they endure it; and some one else than
myself must decide which is the higher order of courage.
Almost all the New Englanders are comparatively fanatics,
while we have very few indeed, unless it may be fanaticism to
worship the old flag—God bless it! If it could have been
possible for England to be plunged into a general war with
some other country, immediately after the Restoration, something like this same distinction would have been seen. Sir
Gervase Langford would have charged upon the foe, his
feathers flying and his lady's colors woven into a love-knot
above his cuirass, singing a roundelay of decidedly loose tendencies, precisely as he had once charged beside Prince
Rupert on the bloody day of Long Marston; and Master
John Grimston would have snuffled a psalm through his nose
and made a thanksgiving prayer over a cut throat, swinging
his long two-handed sword meanwhile, as he had done when
mowing down the 'malignants' at Naseby, under the very
eye of Oliver himself. That would have been an odd mixture

for the same army; but we have an odder, when the neat-whiskered clerk from behind the dry-goods counter in this city—the rough fisherman from Cape Cod—the lumberman from the forests of Maine—and the long, gangling squirrel-hunters from the wilds of Wisconsin,—all meet together to fight for the same cause."

"True," said Harding—"true. And I suppose that fanaticism *does* fight well. It has no fear of death, and very little of consequences. How much difference was there, I wonder, between Ali at the head of his Moslem horde, fresh from the teachings of Mohammed himself, and fully impressed with the belief that if he died he should go at once to the company of the Houris in Paradise,—and Cromwell—or Old John Brown —in a corresponding madness of supposed Christianity? Not much, eh?"

"Not much—none at all!" replied Leslie. "But see how long this one regiment has been in filing past. Only one regiment—not much more than a thousand men, and yet the street seems full of the glisten of their bayonets for half-a-mile. We have grown used to handling the phrases 'thirty thousand,' 'fifty thousand,' 'one hundred thousand,' or even 'a quarter of a million' of men, just as glibly as we speak of one, two or ten millions of money; and yet we realize very little of the force of those numbers. Fifty thousand men are considered to be no army—nothing more than a skirmishing party, now-a-days; and yet to form it, forty or fifty such bodies of men as that which has just passed us must be included. Is it any wonder—after studying a thousand men in this manner —that while we have many generals capable of managing five or ten thousand, very few can command fifty thousand without making a mess of it, and a hundred thousand succeeds in crazing almost every one of our commanders?"

"Wonder? No, I should think not," said Harding, laughing. "I have puzzle enough, sometimes, with even that number of *figures*, and I should make a bad muddle of handling that quantity of men. But, by the way, did you ever read that singular novel, 'Border War,' by a Southwestern writer, Jones, published several years ago?"

"I have skimmed it—never read it," said Leslie. "Remark-

able book, I should say, to be read over now-a-days, when
the event then handled as romance has become reality !"

"The numbers of his opposing forces, as compared with
the actual armies of the present day, are the great point of
interest," said Harding. "He makes terrible blunders in
guessing at the great battle-ground of the war, as he lays the
principal battles in Upper Maryland, Pennsylvania and New
Jersey, and does not seem to contemplate the possibility of
there being any fighting on *Southern* soil. But his numbers—
I think he made each of the opposing forces number some one
hundred and fifty or two hundred thousand men ; and a sharp
reviewer broke out into a loud guffaw over the impossibility
that any such number of men could ever be arrayed against
each other, on the soil of the United States, by any possible
convulsion. Only a few years have passed, and we have three
or four times his numbers in the fight on either side, with
half a million more men to be called for "

"We are travelling fast—that is all," replied Leslie.

"You couldn't exactly inform me *where*, could you ?"
asked Harding. "But,—phew !—w !—w !" looking at his
watch, "the soldiers are gone and time is up; I must look
after my deposits before three."

"And what are we to do about our mystery ?" asked Leslie, as the other was about to leave him. "Give that up altogether?—or will you agree to take a hand in at personal
investigation ?"

"Yes—no—I really do not know what to say, Tom !" was
the reply of Harding. "At all events, I have spent all the
time I can spare to-day, looking after that and the soldiers.
'Business first and pleasure afterwards,' you know."

"Yes," said Leslie, "as the excellent Duke of Gloster remarked, when he first killed the old King and then murdered
the young Princes."

"Pshaw !" replied Harding, "I think I may have heard
that before."

"Very possibly," said Leslie, too much used to slight re-
buffs to pay them any great attention.

"Well, I shall walk down faster than you—bye-bye, old
fellow. Look in at my place to-morrow and let us see

whether we can arrange to do anything more in opposition to
His High Mightiness Superintendent and Provost Marshal
Kennedy," said Harding, moving away.

"Look! look! over there!" said Leslie, just as his friend
was leaving him. "There is a piece of infernal impudence!"

The two friends were yet on the East side of Broadway, as
they had come out from Broome Street. The procession had
passed from the street, and the crowd on the side-walks had
materially cleared away. Leslie had been looking across at
the passengers on the "shilling side." Two ladies, neatly
dressed in street costume, and wearing light gypsies, were
walking together, downward. Behind them, and so close
that he nearly trod upon their dresses, a tall man was walking apparently upon tiptoe and leaning over so that his head
was almost between theirs. He was evidently not of their
party—was apparently listening to their conversation and
scanning the necks and busts before him somewhat too
closely; they all the while unconscious what a miserable
libel on humanity was dogging them. He looked foreign—
perhaps French, especially in the extraordinary curve and
bell of his black round hat,—was well-dressed, and seemed to
be gray-haired enough to know better.

"Impudence? I should think so," replied Harding, as he
caught sight of the two girls and their unobserved follower.
"That dirty hound would rob a church! Oh, if I could only
see that taller one turn around, now, and fetch him such a
slap in the face that it would ring for a twelvemonth! Why,
by Heavens, Leslie!" he said, looking closer. "I ought to
know that figure, and I *do*. Come over, and let us see the
end of this."

"And your bank account?" asked Leslie.

"Oh, never mind that—come along!" and in half a minute
they were across the street and close behind the ladies and
their persecutor. The latter kept his place, dodging his head
around at every opportunity as if to get a sight of the face
of the taller girl, and both apparently yet unconscious of his
presence.

"Do you see a policeman?" asked Harding, in a low voice.
"I will have that fellow taken up."

10

"Not a policeman!" answered Leslie. "If you know either
of the ladies, take the scoundrel by the collar, or let *me*."

"I *do* know the taller girl," said Harding, "and—"

Suddenly he was interrupted. The taller lady on the outside wheeled around so suddenly as almost to throw the tip-
toe follower off his feet, confronted him boldly, flung up the
short light veil that depended from her gypsy and partially
hid her features, ineffable scorn and delicious impudence dancing at the same moment out of her dark eyes and flushed
cheeks,—and burst out with:

"You have followed me long enough. Perhaps you want
a better look? Here it is! How do you like me?"

"Oh, Joe!" said the other lady, almost sinking with fright.

"Upon my honor, miss—ladies—it was all a mistake—I
was not following you—that is—I thought—"

"You are lying, sir, and you know it!" spoke the strange
girl, the words fairly hissing from her red lips and the coming
tears already combating with anger in her voice. "You have
followed us for more than a block, leaning over our very
shoulders, and if I was only a man I would flog you within
an inch of your life!" Here pride and shame overcame anger,
and the tears burst out in spite of her; so that by the time
she had concluded she was nearly as weak and helpless as her
frightened companion.

The sneaking scoundrel attempted to get away, not less
from the anger of the outraged girl than from the passers-by,
a dozen or two of whom had already collected; but before he
could make any movement in that direction, a hand—that of
Walter Harding, was laid on his collar, swinging him violently around; and a small Malacca cane—that of Tom Leslie,
was laid about his shoulders and back with such good will
that the human hound literally yelled with pain. "Serve
him right!" "Give it to him!" and other exclamations of the
same character, broke from those who had heard the girl's
words and who saw the punishment; and in thirty seconds he
was perhaps as thoroughly-flogged a man as Broadway ever
saw. Then Harding released him with a kick, and he made
three howling leaps to an omnibus passing up, and disappeared inside. The impression on the minds of the specta

tore was that he would not much enjoy his ride ; and they no doubt had another impression in which we may fully share, that though vulgarism is "bred in the bone and will come out in the flesh," yet the flogged man would be very careful of the locality in which he again indulged in the same atrocious habit

All this time the taller girl, though endeavoring to control her emotion, was literally sobbing with shame and anger, while yet half-laughing at the sudden punishment of her persecutor. The other lady had been too much frightened to utter a second exclamation, and neither had paid any attention to the personality of their defenders.

But at this stage of the proceedings, Walter Harding lifted his hat (his hands having been too busy before) and approached the taller lady.

"Miss Harris, if I am not mistaken."

"Harris—that is my name, certainly," said the lady, "and you do not know how much we thank you for your kindness, but—"

"But you don't remember me, eh ?" This was said with a smile that brought some new expression to his face, and the wild girl instantly cried:

"Yes, I do remember you—you are—you are—" but she had not yet recovered the name from the mists of forgetfulness. if she remembered the face.

"Walter Harding, merchant, of this city, Miss Josephine. and very glad to meet you again. even under such circumstances."

"Mr. Harding—oh yes, what a crazy head I have !" said the lady, smiles now altogether taking the place of the struggling tears, and giving him both her hands with the freedom of a school-girl—either in acknowledgment of his late service or as an apology for her momentary forgetfulness. "Mr. Harding, of course ! Newport—Purgatory—Dumpling Rocks —everywhere—what fish we caught and what a jolly month we had—didn't we ? And then to think that I should have forgotten you, even for a moment !"

The explanation of which is, that Walter Lane Harding had met Miss Josephine Harris at Newport, in the summer of 1860, and that they had been much pleased with the

society of each other and companions in many a stroll and
fishing-excursion. Probably neither believed, when they
parted, that two years would elapse without another meeting;
but in the great Babel of city life it is only occasionally that
we can manage to make ourselves heard by each other, above
the clattering of the hammers and the confusion of tongues.
Had they been lovers, they would have found each other
before, no matter what stood in the way; but friendships,
even the warmest, have little of the fierce energy of love, and
a very cobweb mesh of circumstances or business engagements can bind the sentiment, while there is no cord spun in
the long rope-walk of life, strong enough to fetter the free
limbs of the passion. That Walter Harding and Josephine
Harris had only met by accident after two years, and yet
both living in the same city and moving in the same walk of
society—proved that they might have *liked* but had never
loved.

The few passers-by who had collected around the ladies at
the time of the insult, had separated when they proved to be
in the company of male acquaintances; and in a moment
after the recognition between Harding and Joe Harris, the
latter had introduced Miss Bell Crawford, the heroine of the
cerise ribbon, to both the gentlemen ; and she had received
an introduction which caused her to start and color singularly
the moment their eyes met—to Mr. Tom Leslie, traveler,
newspaper-correspondent, Jack-at-all-trades and general good
fellow. Was that interested and conscious look repaid by
another on the part of Tom Leslie, or had he had sufficient
time after seeing the young girl and before speaking to her,
to recover from any agitation, pleasurable or the contrary,
incident to the meeting? Did they know each other or only
something *of* each other? Had they met before, and if so,
when and where? Perhaps some light may be thrown on
all these questions, a little later in the progress of this story.

At the present juncture two of the parties were hungry;
the third what is called "peckish," which means a *little*
hungry and quite capable of bolting a sandwich or the wing
of a cold turkey ; and the fourth very much in a hurry and
anxious to get away to his business.

"We sent our carriage home, knowing that we could not
get through Broadway while the troops were passing," said
Bell Crawford, "with orders to have it call for us late in the
afternoon, at a friend's house near Union Square. We were
just going down to Taylor's for a little lunch, when this
awkward affair occurred : may we ask you to join us, gentlemen ?"

"Oh yes," said Josephine Harris, with her school-girl
pleasure at the proposition ill-concealed. "That will be—
yes, well, I may as well say out what I think—that will be
jolly."

"As for my friend Leslie here," said Harding, "*he* has
nothing to do, and can certainly ask no greater pleasure than
to join you. We were just about separating when we saw
you. For myself, I *must* forego the pleasure, for I have the
misfortune to be a busy man, and I must really wish you a
hurried good-morning, leaving you in my friend's care."

With a promise to call upon the ladies at his earliest con-
venience, the young merchant hurried away, with every
evidence that his thoughts were intent upon the balance at
his banker's and the question whether certain regular
customers who were to have called during the morning had
been duly impressed by his clerks with the merits of certain
choice styles of goods, rapidly on the rise, that he would
himself have commended to their particular attention. And
yet there are odd mixtures, sometimes, even in the minds of
merchants—mixtures in which customers become blended
with curls and profits with profiles ; for Walter Lane Harding,
as he wasted yet one more moment to step into Gilsey's and
light a choice Havana, indulged in a train of thought which
might have been shaped into words something in the manner
following:

"A pretty woman—that Miss Crawford, decidedly ladylike—which the other is *not*, however pleasant a companion.
I should as soon think of falling in love with a handsome
bombshell, as with *her*. No knowing when she might
explode. Now if I had met *Miss Crawford* at Newport two
years ago, who knows but affairs might have been different ?
Heigho !" And so Walter Harding went on to his business ;

while Tom Leslie, the member of the party who was
"peckish," accompanied the two girls, who were decidedly
hungry, to that over-gilt and tawdry caricature upon some
of the palace-halls of the Old World, known as "Taylor's
Saloon."

CHAPTER XI.

SOME REFLECTIONS ON COMPARATIVE CHARACTER—OF
HOUSES AS WELL AS MEN—TEMPTATION, AND THE LE-
GENDS OF THE "LURLEY" AND THE "FROZEN HAND"—
A LUNCH AT TAYLOR'S, AND AN ARRANGEMENT.

IN the "great day of final assize," when beneath the one
unerring Eye and Hand all the drosses of life and circumstance shall be melted away and all the films and disfigure-
ments removed from action and intention,—there will be
many things, we have reason to believe, shown in a widely
different light from that in which human eyes have looked
upon them. Human character will surprise the beholders,
if it does not produce the same effect even upon the subject
under examination. Many a poor wretch who has been
stumbling along through life, unfortunate and apparently
guilty, of no seeming use either to himself or the world, will
be found to have filled a place of necessity not suspected—to
have done much good and very little harm—and to have
been acting from motives quite as pure as those that in other
hearts have produced such different effects. Many a " good"
man will be stripped so bare of the garments woven around
him by circumstances or his own self-righteousness, and so
many of his best deeds will be proved to have proceeded from
selfish, interested and unholy motives, that every success and
every word of past approbation will be a reproach, and his
naked soul will stand shivering in the chilling breath of God's
displeasure.

It is not exactly certain that *houses* will come to judgment; but if they do, there will be the same marked difference in the estimation in which many of them have been held by the community surrounding them, and the truth of their influence shown in the "sunlight of the eternal morning." Some miserable tenant-house in Bermondsey or the Swamp, overcrowded with human rats, its atmosphere so noisome that fever floated on every breath and the passer-by from Belgravia or Murray Hill put his perfumed handkerchief to his nostrils to escape the deadly infection,—may be found to have been far less injurious to the neighborhood than the corner-house on Park Lane or the double-front of brown stone within the shadow of Dr. Spring's church on Fifth Avenue. Within the one the miserable occupants may have festered in body and rotted in soul—harming only themselves and the physical atmosphere meanwhile, and victims of the horrible aggregation of poverty in great cities; while within the other a maelstrom of pleasant dissipation has been whirling, to which the victims came in their own carriages with full liveries, the waves as they circled sending up jets of cooling spray and redolent of perfumes from the flowers of sunny lands but continually widening its circle of evil attraction and drawing in those who thenceforth had no power of resistance against the banded demons of wine, of play and of lascivious enjoyment, who lurked beneath the waters, eager for their prey.

The fable of the "Lurline" is the story of human life and temptation; and yet few of the thousands who have read it in the old German legend of the "Lurleiberg" or the charming "Bridal of Belmont" of the author of "Lillian," or who have gazed at it for hours when presented upon the stage in the shape of "Ondine" or the "Naiad Queen,"—have fully realized its significance. To most it has been merely a pretty conceit or an effective spectacle; to the close student it is an absorbing picture of the enthralment of human energies. Sir Huldebrand of Kingstettin is a true as well as a valiant knight, and he has a golden-haired and white-handed ladie-love in the neighboring castle of the Baron of Steinbrunnen. He has a hope, a love, a faith, a duty; and on the day when

he fares forth from Kingstettin and takes his way to the river
bank, he has mirth as well as all these, for Karl, his merry
servant, is beside him.   But the day is hot and sultry, and he
dismounts from his horse and lies down to sleep beside the
Lurleiberg.   He has granted himself rest and indulgence.
Half in his sleep and half in his waking thought he sees the
stream rippling below the banks and circling in pleasant
eddies by rock and mossy edge, while the water-lilies nestle
down their soft cheeks to the lapping water in the sheltered
nooks, and the willows bend down and kiss the stream with
the swaying tips of their hundred fingers, and little gleams
of golden sunshine steal through the branches and touch the
soft ripples here and there with such tints of transparent
light as the pencil of painter never mastered.   Oh, how deli-
ciously sweet and dreamy is that half wakeful feeling of
repose and indulgence !   And then the music rises—gentle
and almost undistinguishable at first from the singing ripple
of the water—then clearer and more distinct, but with still a
tinkling ripple in every cadence, and the name of the listener
insensibly blended.   Flattery has come with indulgence, and
the subtle wine of its intoxication is mounting to his brain.
Then he turns dreamily on his couch of moss, and looks over
the bank into the river.   Above the water white hands are
circling and snowy bosoms are gleaming, and in the midst is
one form of matchless rounded beauty, with a face of angelic
splendor, her eye-lids gemmed with the tear-drops of an
awakened affection, and her waved brown hair caressed by
the tide as it sweeps backward.   All the white hands are
beckoning to him, and all the coral lips are uttering those
low musical words in which his name is blended.   The brain
of the knight grows dizzy—chains of which he only feels a
pleasure in the slight pressure, twine around his limbs.   Voluptuous enjoyment takes the place of energy—he is himself
no longer.   He cannot even laugh—he can only sigh—Karl
has gone chasing some Lurline of his own, far down the
meadow.   Ermengarde, who has been for hours leaning out
of the high window at Steinbrunnen, and looking anxiously
for her expected lover—is nothing to him now.   His promised
aid to Sir Rudolph to-morrow, with helm on brow and

lance in rest, against the invader who threatens the lands
of both with ravage, is nothing to him now. Love and
duty are alike forgotten. The temptation has done its full
work through indolence and indulgence, and the knight is
lost. The brown-haired Lurline is worth all earth and heaven.
Let all the rest go, without a sigh or a regret—be his the mur-
mur of the river, the delicious music embodying his name,
and the beckoning of the white hands towards him! He
does not leap into the water, as some have held: he merely
bends nearer to the verge, then slips down with eager eyes
and outstretched hands; the white arms twine around him;
the music sounds for one moment more sweetly but more
sadly than ever, as the waves close above the pair so unholily
wedded; then the ripples sing on and all is quiet beauty as
before—calm and quiet beauty, as if no tomb had closed above
the energies of a human soul.

Sir Huldebrand may come back again, after a time, as the
legend is fond of making him do. He may even marry the
golden-haired Ermengarde and sire children to heir his lands
and perpetuate his name. But the knight is himself a wreck,
with all his best energies burnt out in those wierd orgies beneath the water; and his bridal vow is a hollow one, for
when he utters it he hears the shriek of the Lurline blending
with the wedding music, and his nightly couch is to be henceforth a torture of unrest—his ride by day a mere hopeless
fleeing from the ghosts of dead pleasures.

Something of the same character is that other wild legend
which has grown into song and drama—sprung from the
Norse branch of the great German mind,—that of the "Ice
Witch" or the "Frozen Hand." Here the Viking Harold is
less wrecked by temptation than by circumstance; but the
result of the enthralment is the same. The ice of the Pole
closes around him with the same fatality as the waters of the
Rhine around his brother and prototype. Surrounded by
the white arms of Hecla in her palace of ice, he ceases to
lament the bride who is awaiting him in the far South; and
he has not even a thought of regret to cast towards his
perished companions and the stout ship that once bore him
so proudly, her brown ribs now bleaching whitely on the

Arctic shore. He too returns, after a long period, but he brings with him the fatal gift of his Northern bride—*a hand of ice.* He may be strong and brave still, as he was when he went away; but he is no longer the peerless and envied warrior. Men look upon him with a ghostly shudder, and women shrink back from his chilling presence. Not even Freja can thaw away all the ice that has gathered in his veins. He may chastise the robber Ruric from the hills, and sleep once more in the warm embrace of Isoldane; but who knows that at some midnight hour the old curse may not return upon him and the hand he stretches in love and fond-ness strike death to the hearts that are dearest? Not the same—changed, changed—as is every man who has once yielded to the great temptation of his existence.

All this, which may be purely irrelevant matter, has grown out of a visit paid by some of the characters in this narration, to a fashionable restaurant and saloon on Broadway, and the belief that in some of those houses temptation is lurking in so insidious and deadly a form that they are doing a thousand times the injury inflicted by the acknowledged haunts of vice. Special allusion may or may not be made to the gorgeous but tawdry room in which the three sat down to discuss their *a la mode* beef, coffee and biscuits. Any one of the fashionable. houses to which ladies habitually resort without male pro-tection, for a noonday lunch when shopping,—may serve as a type of all the rest; and not one of them but may be passed with a shudder, by husbands who wish their wives to remain like Cesar's, not only chaste but above suspicion,— and by fathers who do not desire the peach-bloom too early rubbed off from the innocence of their fair daughters.

At this marble table, where the cloth is being so carefully spread by the white-napkined waiter who has a steaming cluster of dishes on a salver on the table opposite,—there may be a little party, like that of our three friends, dropped in on the most proper of errands—that of merely procuring a bit of lunch in the midst of a day of business, without going home for it or visiting the table d'hote at a hotel; but at the next table and the next there is something different. Here sit a party of three giddy girls, without male protection, innocent enough in their lives and intentions, but boldly exposing their faces to the rude gaze of any of the libertine diners-out who may happen to be at the tables opposite, and returning that gaze, when met, with a smile and a simper that merely means scorn and self-confidence but may be easily construed into a less creditable expression. And at this table, only two removed, discussing a *pate de foix gras* which may or may not have come from Strasburg of the Big Goose Livers, and washing down his edibles with a glass of liqueur that fires the blood like so much molten lava,—sits a bold-faced man, fashionable in dress and perfumed in hair and whiskers, whose gaze is that of the evil eye upon the reputation of any woman, and who has no better occupation than lounging in any place of public resort, to spy out the beauties of female face and figure and the weaknesses in the fortifications that surround female virtue. And here—at one of the opposite row of tables, her cup of coffee and plate of French trifles in pasty just being set down before her—here is a sadder spectacle than either. The wife of a wealthy merchant, yet young, beautiful and attractive, but with a frightened look in her dark eye and a nervous glancing round at the door every time it opens, which too well reveals her story to the close observer. She is waiting for her *lover*—harsh word in that connection, but the true and only one; her lover, whose acquaintance she may have made through unforbidden glances in this very room, and whom she has permitted to approach her, slowly but surely, as the serpent stole upon Eve in Eden, until she has fallen completely into his power, losing honor, self-respect, everything that a true wife most values, and probably supporting the wretch in a course of gambling and dissipation, with money wrung on one pitiable pretext or other from the grudging hand of her betrayed husband.

It is enough!—let the curtain fall. But oh, heart of man, put up the prayer that other and holier lips once uttered: "Lead us not into temptation, but deliver us from evil!" And may not the *houses* indeed come into judgment?

We have no concern whatever with the pleasant small-talk which floated over the little table at Taylor's, from the lips of Tom Leslie and his two female companions; nor is there any

need to pause at this juncture and remark whether the strange
glance of Josephine Harris on being introduced to the young
man on the street, was repeated or returned. The trio seemed
to be a very happy one, Miss Bell Crawford a little starched
at first towards a man who had been flung into her way; so
ambiguously, but rattle-pated Joe firing off occasional
fusillades of odd sayings, and Tom, the prince of *preux
chevaliers*, falling into the position of an old acquaintance
with marvellous rapidity. Their lunch was nearly over,
when the mischievous face of Joe, who had been making
running comments upon some of the people on the other side
of the room, good-naturedly wicked if not complimentary—
lit up with a conceit which set her hazel-gray eyes laughing
away down to the depths of her brain. At the same moment
the quick eyes of Bell Crawford saw that the hand of the
merry girl was rummaging in her pocket, and *her* face became
anxious. Before the latter could speak, however, the hand
of Joe came out with the treasure she had been seeking—a
torn half column, or less, of the *Herald*. The moment Miss
Crawford saw the slip, her anxiety seemed to be redoubled,
and she reached over to Joe, as if to take the paper, with
the words, half-pleading, half-pettish :

" Don't, Joe—pray don't !"

" Oh, but I must !" said the mischievous girl, taking care
that her companion should not reach the slip. " I cannot
think of throwing away such an excellent opportunity. I
say, Mr. Leslie, you are not an unscrupulous destroyer of
female innocence—one of those dreadful fellows we read
about in the books, are you ?"

" Oh, Joe, I am ashamed of you !" said Bell Crawford, and
she lay back in her chair, very near to a fit of the sulks. . .

" Really," said Tom Leslie, blushing a little in spite of
himself, though without knowing precisely why—" really
Miss Harris, I am afraid I am not the best of men, but I hope
I do not deserve any such terrible appellation."

" There, I told you so, Bell, I knew he wasn't !" went on
the wild girl, as if she had been asking a solemn question and
receiving a conclusive answer. " We can trust him—he says

we can, and I am going to put him to the test at once. Suppose, Mr. Leslie, that a couple of distressed damsels—"

"What a ninny you are making of yourself!" put in Miss
Crawford, in a tone not very far from earnest.

"Suppose that a couple of distressed damsels," Josephine
Harris went on, without heeding her in the least, "about to
pass through a gloomy and desolate wood, on the way to an
enchanted castle, should appeal to you to accompany them
and give them the benefit of your courage and your—yes,
your respectability, in the adventure; would you go with
them, even if you were obliged to abandon a game of billiards
and forfeit the smoking of two cigars for that purpose?" and
she threw herself back in her chair, screwed her face into the
expression supposed to belong to a grand inquisitor, and
waited for a reply.

"I would do my devoir like a true knight," said Leslie,
making a mock bow over the table, with his hand on his
heart, "even if I forfeited thereby not only two cigars but
four and the playing of two whole games of billiards."

"Generous knight!" said Joe, still preserving her melo-
dramatic tone, "we trust you—we enlist you into our service, 'for three years or during the war!' Read!" and she
solemnly handed over the slip of paper, on which Leslie perceived the following advertisement, marked around with
black crayon, and under the general head of "Astrology":—

"THE STARS HAVE SAID IT! MADAME ELISE BOUTELL,
from Paris, whom the stars favor and to whom the secrets
of the unknown world are revealed, may be consulted on any of
the great events of life, at No. — Prince Street, near the Bowery,
every day, between 10 A.M. and 6 P.M. Let ignorance be banished, and let the light of the world unknown dawn on the dark-
ened minds. Persons who attempt deception in visiting Madame
Boutell, will find all disguise unavailing; but all confidences are
safe, as strict secrecy is observed."

"Well?" added Leslie, looking up inquiringly, after reading the mysterious announcement.

"Well?" said the mad girl, mimicking him. "Is *that* all
the effect it produces upon you? Do your knees not shake
and does not your hair start up on end when you think of it,
so that your hat—if your hat was not unfortunately hung

upon the hook yonder, would require to be held on by main
force ?"

"How *can* you be so absurd ?" suggested Bell, who really
feared that the pronounced behaviour of her friend might
draw too much attention to their table, as there was indeed
some danger of its doing.

"Bah !" said Joe, "I *couldn't* be absurd ! I was 'never
absurd in my life,' as Sir Hartcourt Courtley says. But Mr.
Leslie !—what have I said ? You look pale—ill !" and the
face of the young girl tamed instantly to an expression of
genuine alarm, not at all unwarranted by the circumstances.
The face of Tom Leslie had indeed undergone a sudden
change. His usual ruddy cheek seemed ghastly white, his
eyes stared glassily, and there was a quick convulsive shiver
running over his frame which did not escape the notice of either
of his two companions. The kind heart of Josephine Harris
at once hit upon a solution for the otherwise strange spectacle. She had said some awkward word—touched some hidden and painful chord connected with past suffering or experience ; and she felt like having her tongue extracted at the
root for the commission of such a blunder.

What *was* the cause of this sudden emotion ? The explanation may not be so difficult to any thoughtful reader of this
story as it was to the two young girls who sought it. Tom
Leslie had merely read over the mendacious advertisement,
at first, with the same indifference given to thousands of corresponding humbugs ; and at the first reading he had not noticed
the place at all. At the second reading, his mind took in the
direction : "No. — Prince Street, near Bowery," and at the
same moment he comprehended the words, "Madame Elise
Boutell, *from Paris.*" Tom Leslie was every thing else than
a coward ; and yet he had shuddered before at the sight and
the memory of the "red woman :" he whitened and shuddered now. What if another meeting with that mysterious
woman was at hand ?—if the scenes of the Rue la Reynie
Ogniard were about to be re-enacted ? The French name
and the words "from Paris," the place, which seemed to him
undoubtedly the same of his adventure with ·Harding—all

made up a presumption of identity that was for the moment overwhelming.

But those who show surprise or emotion quickest are not slowest to recover from its effects. Whatever he felt, nothing more was to be shown the two ladies. Reaching for a glass of ice-water standing upon the table, Leslie drank the whole of it off at a draught, and the electric shock at once restored the tone to his system and brought back the red blood to his face. With a laugh he said :

"I really beg ten thousand pardons for alarming you, but these slight attacks are constitutional, and they need not cause the least fear. That is over, and I am as well as ever. What was it you were saying, Miss Harris ?"

"Thank heaven that you *are* better !" said the kind-hearted girl. "I was really for the instant apprehensive that something I had said might have awakened some painful recollection. I was trying to get you, at that moment, to understand the terrible significance of this advertisement."

"Well," said Leslie, laughing, "what am I to understand ? That you have been testing the skill of this seeress, or that you are about to do so ?"

"There you go !" said Joe Harris. "Now you are on the *other* side of the fence ! Excuse my similes, but I have not always been cooped up in this humdrum city—I occasionally pay visits to the country. A moment ago you grew pale at the name of the mighty Madame Boutell, whose cognomen sounds a good deal like the Yankee 'doo tell !' I admit ; and now you are laughing at her !" The young girl had by this time recovered from her good-natured anxiety and regained her habitual vivacity, and she rattled on to the great edification of her auditors, and happily without attracting any additional notice from the people at the other tables. "Yes, sir, Miss Crawford and myself are about to consult this modest exponent of the mysteries of the stars, though about what we have not the least idea. *I* have not, at least ; have *you*, Bell ?"

"Not the ghost of an idea," was the answer of Miss Crawford.

"Ghost is good, in that connection," rattled on the gay

girl. "You see I have never yet consulted a fortune-teller, and I am afraid I shall soon be too old to do it to advantage. I lost my faith in Santa Claus, a good many years ago, and long before my stocking was too big to hang up; and I cried over the discovery for a fortnight. Suppose I should lose my faith in fortune-telling before I ever had any experience in that direction—wouldn't it be dreadful ?"

"But why this lady in particular ?" asked Leslie, who was at the moment studying a theme which no man knows more about to-day than was known in the days of Aristotle—that of chances and coincidences.

"Oh," said Joe, fumbling in her pocket for other slips, and drawing them out and exhibiting them with great gravity, to the infinite amusement at least of Leslie. "Oh, I have been preparing myself, and found the best. Here is a 'Madame R.,' who has 'just arrived in the city and taken a room at No. 7 Pickle Place.' That would never do, you see. 'Taken a room' is too suggestive of limited accommodations and no carpet on a very dirty stair. Then here is another, in which 'Madame Francena Guessberg' promises to 'give information about absent friends' and to 'show the faces of future husbands.' Most of my friends who are absent I never wish to hear of again; and as to the husbands, I shall see them all soon enough, if not too soon."

"Hem !" said Leslie, though scarcely knowing why he made that comment.

"That is all," continued the wild girl. "All the rest are insignificant or impossible, except—no, here is one who promises to 'call names.' Now if there is any thing in the world that I don't like except when I do it myself, it is 'calling names.' And now see Madame Boutell. There is nothing of the petty or the insignificant about her. She has the 'stars' at command, and is about to open the 'unknown world.' She is the woman, of course ! Knows all about the 'great events' of life. Can't be humbugged, and keeps a secret as a steel-trap holds a rat. And now, will you go with us, and protect us, and—Mr. Harding said you were a newspaper man,—will you take down a full, true and circumstantial accouut of all that occurs ?   That is what I have been trying to get at for this quarter of an hour.   Will you go with us ?"

"You are going to-day, then ?" asked Leslie.

"Miss Harris insisted upon my accompanying her, and I half consented to do so," said Miss Bell Crawford, apologetically.

"Fiddlestick !" said the merry riddle.   "Don't try to beg out of it, Miss Bell !   She sent her carriage home, Mr. Leslie, so that we need not be seen going there with it ; and there we were going, two lovely and unprotected females, when providence raised up a champion in the person of our new friend."

"Who hopes yet to be an *old* friend, and who will go with you, with the greatest pleasure," said Leslie.   "At the same time"—reflecting a moment—"at the same time I must be as prudent about myself, for certain reasons, which I will explain some day if you wish it—as Miss Crawford has been about her carriage.   Oblige me by remaining at the table here and trifling with some creams, chocolate and a few bon-bons, while I leave you for a few minutes—not more than fifteen or twenty.   At the end of that time I shall be ready to accompany you."

Giving the necessary orders and throwing a bill to the waiter, Tom Leslie passed rapidly out into the street and walked quite as rapidly up Broadway, until he turned again down Broome Street, which he had quitted with Harding but a little while before.   Had he *more* to do with the Police ?

11

CHAPTER XII.

FORTUNE-TELLING AND OTHER SUPERSTITIONS—THE EVERY-
DAY OMENS THAT WE HALF BELIEVE—ORIGINS OF THIS
WEAKNESS—FORTUNE-TELLERS OF NEW YORK, BOSTON
AND WASHINGTON.

WHILE Tom Leslie has gone around to Broome Street on
his undeclared errand, and while the ladies are making an
excuse to while away the time until his return, in the discussion of the after-dinner provocatives to indigestion recom-
mended, let us enter a little more closely upon a subject
merely indicated in the foregoing chapter, and then sneered
at by at least one of the conversationists—that of the fortune-telling imposition which so largely prevails, especially
in the great cities, and the general course of human superstition in connection with it.

It may be set down, as a general principle, that every man
is more or less superstitious—that is, impressed with ideas and
omens which go beyond the material world and bid utter defiance to reason. Every woman is certainly so. It is not
less undeniable, meanwhile, that nearly every man and woman denies this fact of their natures and considers the mere
allegation to be an insult. Oftenest from the fear of ridicule,
but sometimes, no doubt, because any discussion of the matter
is deemed improper,—few acknowledge this peculiarity of nature, even to their most intimate friends : some, who must be
aware that they possess it, deny it even to themselves. The
subject is set down as contraband, universally, unless when the
weakness of a third party is to be ridiculed, or a personal freedom from the superstition asserted ; and yet this very silence
and the boasting are both suspicious. No man boasts so much
over his own wealth as he who has little or none ; and no man
is so silent, except under the influence of great excitement, as
he who has a great thought oppressing him or a great fear continually tugging at his heart-strings. The most hopeless dis-
believers in the Divine Being, that can possibly be met, are
those who seldom or never enter into a controversy on the

subject; and the least assured is he who oftenest enters into controversy, perhaps for the purpose of strengthening his own belief. There *are* Captain Barecolts, of course, who go bravely into battle after venting boasts that seem to stamp them as arrant cowards, and who come out of the conflict with stories staggering all human comprehension; but these cases are rare, and they do not go beyond the requisite number of exceptions to justify the rule.

Perhaps the most general of the ordinary superstitions of the country is the indefinable impression that the catching a first sight of the new moon over the right shoulder ensures good fortune in the ensuing month, while a first glance of it over the left is correspondingly unlucky. (It may be said, in a parenthesis, that the fast phrase, "over the left," so prevalent during the past few years, to indicate the reverse of what has just been spoken, has its derivation from the impression that such an untoward sinister glance may neutralize all effort and bring notable misfortune.) Of a hundred men interrogated on this point, ninety-five will assert that they hold no such superstition, and that they have never even thought of the direction in which they first saw the new moon of any particular month. And yet of that ninety-five, the chances are that ninety are in the habit of taking precautions to meet the young crescent in the proper or lucky manner, or of indulging in a slight shudder or feeling of unpleasantness when they realize that they have accidentally blundered into the opposite.

Next in prevalence to this, may be cited the superstition that any pointed article, as a knife, a pin, or a pair of scissors, falling accidentally from the hand and sticking direct in the floor or the carpet, indicates the coming of visitors during the same day, to the house in which the omen occurred. Hundreds and even thousands of housewives, not only the ignorant but the more intelligent, immediately upon witnessing or being informed of such an important event, make preparation, on the part of themselves and their households, if any are felt to be necessary, for the reception of the visitors who are sure to arrive within the time indicated by the omen. Some, but not so many, add to this the superstition that the

involuntary twitching of the eye-lid or itching of the eye-
brow indicates the coming of visitors in the same manner;
and many a projected absence from the house is deferred by
our good ladies; from one or another of these omens and the
impression that by absence at that particular time they may
lose the opportunity of seeing valued friends.

Next in generality, if not even entitled to precedence of the
last, is the superstition that the gift of a knife or any sharp
article of cutlery, is almost certain to produce estrangement
between the giver and the receiver—in other words, to "cut
friendship." Ridiculous as the superstition may appear, there
is scarcely one of either sex who does not pay some respect
to it ; and of one thousand knives that may happen to be
transferred between intimate friends (and lovers) it is safe to
say that not less than nine hundred and ninety have the omen
guarded against by a half playful demand and acceptance of
some small coin in return, giving the transfer some slight
fiction of being a mercantile transaction. The statistics of
how many loves or friendships have really been severed by
non-attention to this important precaution, might be somewhat difficult to compile, and the attempt need not be made
in this connection.

Thousands of musically inclined young ladies have serious
objections to singing before breakfast, quoting, not altogether
jocularly, the proverb that "one who sings before breakfast
will cry [weep] before night," which no doubt had its origin
in a proverb derived from the Orientals, that

> "The bird which singeth in the early morn,
> Ere night by cruel talons will be torn."

Not less unaccountable, and yet impressive, are some of
the superstitions connected with marriage, death, and the departure of friends. A belief very generally prevails that
when a couple enter a church to be married, if the bride steps
at all in advance of the bridegroom, he will be found an unwilling and unfaithful husband ; while if the opposite should
happen to be the order of precedence, even by a few inches,
the marriage tie will prove a happy and long-enduring one.
The belief that the bridal hour should occur during clear

weather, is perhaps a natural one, and derived from well-understood natural laws affecting the physical systems of those entering into such intimate relations; but the superstition goes further and considers sunshine on the bridal day a specific against all the possible ills of matrimonial life. This feeling supplies half of a doggrel couplet which came to us from the Saxons, and which blends marriage and burial somewhat singularly :—

"Happy is the bride that the sun shines on ;
And blessed is the corpse that the rain rains on."

There are thousands of persons who have objections to counting the number of carriages at a funeral, from the superstition that the one who does so will very soon be called to attend a funeral at home ; and the same objection exists to putting on, even for a moment, any portion of a mourning garb worn by another, under the impression that the temporary wearer will in some way be influenced to wear mourning very soon for some lost relative. No doubt fifty other and similar superstitions connected with death and burial might be adduced, even without alluding to those of more frightful import and now very little regarded, which belong more peculiarly to the Eastern world, and which inculcate the leaving open of a window at the moment of death, to allow the unrestrained flight of the passing soul, and reprobate the leaving of any open vessel of water in the vicinity of the death-chamber, in the fear that the disembodied spirit, yet weak and untried of wing, may fall therein and perish !

One more superstition, connected with the departure of friends, must be noted—the more peculiarly as there is a sad beauty in the thought. Very many nervous and excitable people fear to look after those who are going away on long journeys or dangerous enterprises, under the fear that such a look after them may prevent their return. One peculiar instance of the indulgence of this superstition, and its apparent fulfilment, happens to have fallen under notice, during the present struggle. When the President's first call for volunteers was made, among those who responded was one young lad of eighteen, a mere handsome boy in appearance and altogether delicate in constitution, who left a comfortable

position to fulfil what he believed to be a stern duty.   He had
two female cousins, of nearly his own age, and with whom
he had been in close intimacy.   Going away hurriedly, with
little time to bestow on farewells, he called to bid them good-
bye one dark and threatening night.   Some tears of emotion
were shed, and the sad farewell was spoken.   When he
passed down the walk, both the cousins stood without the
door and watched his figure as it grew dimmer and disappeared in the dusk of the distant street.   When they returned
to the cheerfulness of the lighted room, the younger burst
into tears.

"We have doomed him," she said.   "We watched him
when he went away, and looked after him as long as he
could be seen.   He will never come back.   His young life
will fade out and disappear, just as we saw him fading away
in the darkness."

A month later the young soldier was dead ; and something
more than ordinary reasoning will be necessary to persuade
the two cousins—the younger and more impressive, especially—that their gazing after him did not cast an evil omen on
his fate and a blight upon his life.   Another near relative
has since gone away on the same patriotic errand ; but when
the farewells were spoken in the lighted room, the two girls
escaped at once and hid themselves in another apartment, so
that they should not even see him disappear through the
door.   When last heard from,* fever and bullet had yet
spared him ; and what more is needed to make the two
young girls hopelessly superstitious for life, at least in this
one regard ?   They are not the only persons who have seen
and felt that *fading out in the darkness* as an omen ; for the
same observer who once stood on the bluff at Long Branch,
as a heavy night of storm was closing, and saw the " Star of
the West" gradually fade away and disappear into that
threatening storm and darkness—unconscious that she was
to emerge again to play so important a part in the drama of
the nation's degradation,—the same observer saw the same
omen at Niblo's not long ago, when the poor Jewess of Miss

* February 1st, 1863

Bateman's wonderful " Leah" fell back step by step into the crowd, as the curtain was dropping, her last hope withered and her last duty done, and nothing remaining but to " follow on with my people."

And at all such times Proserpine comes back, as she may have cast wistful glances towards the vanishing home of her childhood, when the rude hands of the ravishers were bearing her away from the spot where she was gathering flowers in the vale of Enna; and we think of Orpheus taking that fatal,. wistful last look back at Enrydice, with the thought in his eyes that *could not* give her up even for a moment, when emerging to the outer air from the flames and smoke of Tartarus. Wistful glances back at all we have lost are embodied ; and all these long, agonizing appeals of the eye against that fate of separation which cannot be longer combated with tongue or hand, are made over again for our torture.

It has been said that some persons endeavor to deceive themselves with reference to their holding any belief in omens and auguries. And some of those who by position and education should be lifted above gross errors, are quite as liable as others to this self-deception. Quite a large circle of prominent persons may remember an instance in which a leading Doctor of Divinity, renowned for his strong common-sense as well as beloved for his goodness, was joining in a general conversation on human traits and oddities, when one of the company alluded to popular superstitions and acknowledged that he had one, though only one—that of the " moon over the shoulder." Another confessed to another, and still another to another, while the Doctor " pished" and " pshawed" at each until he made him heartily ashamed of his confession. The man of the lunar tendencies, however, had a habit of bearding lions, clerical as well as other, and he at last turned on the Doctor.

" Do you mean to say that *you* have no superstitions whatever, Doctor ?" he asked.

" None whatever," said the Doctor, confidently.

" You have no confidence in supernatural revelations in any relation of life ?" pursued the questioner.

" None whatever," repeated the Doctor.

"And you never act—try, now, if you please, to remember—
you never act under impression from any omen that does not
appeal to reason, or are made more or less comfortable by
the existence of one? In other words, is there no occurrence
that ever induces you to alter your course of action, when
that occurrence has nothing whatever to do with the object
in view, and when you can give no such explanation to yourself as you would like to give to the outside world, for the
feeling or the change?"

"There is nothing of the kind," replied the Doctor to this
long question. Then he suddenly seemed to remember—
paused, and colored a little as he went on. "I acknowledge
my error, gentlemen," he said. "I *have* a superstition, though
I never before thought of it in the light of one. I am rendered exceedingly uncomfortable, and almost ready to turn
back, if a cat, dog or other animal chances to run across the
way before me, at the moment when I am starting upon any
journey."

The laugh which began to run round the company was po-
litely smothered in compliment to the good Doctor's candor ;
but the fact of a universal superstition of some description or
other was considered to be very prettily established.

But the conversation did not end here ; and one who had
before borne little part in it—a man of some distinction in
literary as well as political life,—was drawn out by what had
occurred, to make a statement with reference to himself which
exhibited another phenomenon in supernaturalist belief—*a
man who not only had a superstition and acknowledged it,
but could give a reason for holding it.*

"Humph !" he said, "some of you have superstitions and
acknowledge them without showing that you have any
grounds for your belief; and the Doctor, who has also a
superstition, does not seem to have been aware of it before.
Now *I* am a believer in the supernatural, and I have had
cause to be so."

"Indeed ! and how ?" asked some member of the company.

"As thus," answered the believer. "And I will tell you
the story as briefly as I can and still make it intelligible,—

from the fact that a severe head-ache is the inevitable penalty of telling it at all. I resided in a country section of a neighboring State, some twenty years ago; and about three miles distant, in another little hamlet of a dozen or two houses, lived the young lady to whom I was engaged to be married. My Sundays were idle ones, and as I was busy most of the week, I generally spent the afternoon of each Sunday, and sometimes the whole of the day, at the house of my expectant bride, whom I will call Gertrude for the occasion. I kept no horse and habitually walked over to the village. I had never ridden over, let it be borne in mind, as that is a point of interest. I very seldom rode anywhere, and Gertrude had never seen me on horseback.

"It happened, as I came out from my place of boarding, one fine Sunday afternoon in mid-winter, that one of the neighbors, who kept a number of fine horses, was bringing a couple of them out for exercise. They were very restive, and he complained that they stood still too much and needed to have the spirit taken out of them a little. I laughingly replied that if he would saddle one, I would do him that favor; and he threw the saddle on a very fast running-mare, and mounted me. Accordingly, and of course from what appeared a mere accident, I rode over to the place of my destination.

"There was a small stable behind the house occupied by the family of my betrothed, across a little garden-lot, and I rode round the house without dismounting, to care for my horse. As I passed the house, I saw Gertrude standing at the door, and looking frightfully ill and pale. I hurried to the stables, threw the saddle from my horse, and returned instantly to the house. Gertrude met me at the door, threw herself into my arms (a demonstration not habitual) and sobbed herself almost into hysterics and insensibility. I succeeded in calming her a little, and she then informed me of the cause of her behavior. She was frightened to death at seeing me come on horseback; and the reason she gave for this was that the night before she had dreamed that I came on horseback—that her brother, a young man in mercantile business a few miles away, also came on horseback (his usual habit)—and

that while her brother and myself were riding rapidly together, I was thrown and his horse dashed out my brains
with his hoofs!

"Here was a pleasant omen, or would have been to a believer in the supernatural; but I belonged to the opposite
extreme. I laughed at Gertrude's fears, and finally succeeded
in driving them away, though with great difficulty, by the information that her brother had gone West the day before and
could not possibly be riding around in this section, seeking
my life with a horse-shoe. She was staggered but no●satis-
fied—I could see that fact in her eye. Still she shook off the
apparent feeling, and we joined the family. Half an hour
after, her brother rode up and stabled his horse—he having
been accidentally prevented leaving for the West as arranged.
At this new confirmation of her fears, very flattering to me
but very inconvenient, Gertrude fell into another fit of frightened hysterics; nothing being said to any of the members
of the family, however. I succeeded in chasing away this
second attack, with a few more kisses and a little less scolding
than before. With the lady again apparently pacified, we
rejoined the company, and the evening passed in music and
conversation. The shadow did not entirely leave the face of
Gertrude, and she watched me continually. For myself, I
had no thought whatever on the subject, except sorrow for
her painful hallucination.

"At about ten o'clock, the brother rose to go for his horse,
and I accompanied him to look after mine but not to go home,
for the "courting" hours—the dearest of all—were yet to
come. At the stable, as he was mounting, we talked of the
speed of his horse and of the one I rode; and he bantered
me to mount and ride with him a mile. There was a splendid
stretch of smooth road for a couple of miles on his way, and
without a moment's thought of Gertrude I threw the saddle
on my horse and rode away with him, the people at the house
being altogether unaware that I had gone farther than to the
stables.

"I have no idea what set us to horse-racing on that Sunday
night; but race we did. Both horses had good foot and the
road was excellent, though the night was dusky. Before we

had gone half a mile we were going at top speed. ·When we reached the end of the hard road he was a little ahead, and I banteringly called to him to ' repeat.' He wheeled at once, and away we went like the wind. From turning behind, I had a little the start, and kept it. Perhaps we were fifty yards from the house, when my mare stepped on a stone, as I suppose, and went down, throwing me clear of the stirrups, up in the air like a rocket, and down on my head like a spile-driver. I of course lay insensible with a crushed skull; and the brother was so near behind and going at such speed that he could not have stopped, even if he had known what was the matter.

" Noise—lights—confusion. Gertrude bending over me in hysteric screams—so they told me afterwards. Part of the hair was gone from one side of my head, dashed off by the foot of the brother's horse, that had just thus narrowly missed dashing out my few brains. That is all, gentlemen. The dream-prophecy was fulfilled within that hair's-breadth (excuse the bad pun), by a succession of circumstances that were not arranged by human motion and could not have been expected from anything in the past; and until some one can explain or reason away the coincidence, I shall not give up my belief that dreams are sometimes revelations."

Perhaps it is idle to enter upon any speculations as to the origin of these superstitions in the human mind; as they may almost be held to be a part of nature, having a corresponding development in all countries and all ages. Some of the worst and most injurious of superstitions—those which involve the supposed presence of the dead, of haunting spectres and evil spirits, destroying the nerves and paralyzing the whole system—unquestionably have much of their origin in the " bug-a-boo" falsehoods told to children by foolish mothers and careless nurses, to frighten them into " being good." Thousands of men as well as women never recover from the effects of these crimes against the credulous faith of childhood—for they are no less. Then there are particular passages in our literature, sacred and profane, which do their share at upholding the belief in the supernatural, espe-cially as connected with the uninspired foretelling of future

events—"fortune-telling." The case of the Witch of Endor
and her invocation of the spirit of Samuel, which is given in
Holy Writ as an actual occurrence and no fable, of course
takes precedence of all others in influence; and the superstitious man who is also a religionist, always has the one un-
answerable reply ready for any one who attempts to reason
away the idea of occult knowledge: "Ah, but the Witch of
Endor: what will you do with *her* ? If the Bible is true—
and you would not like to doubt that—she was a wicked
woman, not susceptible to prophetic influences, and yet she
did foretell the future and bring up the spirits of the dead.
If this was possible then, why not now ?"

From the church we pass to the theatre, and from the
Book of all Books to that which nearest follows it in the sub-
limity of its wisdom—Shakspeare. No one doubts "Hamlet"
much more than the First Book of Samuel, and yet the play
is altogether a falsehood if there is no revelation made to the
Prince of the guilt of his Uncle ; and the spiritual character
of the revelation is not at all affected by the question whether
Hamlet saw or *thought he saw* the ghost of his murdered
father. Again comes "Macbeth," and though we may allow
Banquo's ghost to be altogether a diseased fancy of the
guilty man's brain, yet the whole story of the temptation
is destroyed unless the witches on the blasted heath really
make him true prophecies for false purposes. These sublime fancies appeal to our eyes, and through the eyes to our
beliefs, night after night and year after year; and if they
do not create a superstition in any mind previously clear of
the influence, they at least prevent the disabuse of many a
mind and preserve from ridicule what would else be contemptible.

It was with reference to fortune-telling especially that this
discussion of our predominant superstitions commenced ;
and this indefensibly episodical chapter must close with a
mere suggestion as to the extent to which that imposition is
practised in our leading cities. Very few, it may be suspected, know how prevalent is this superstition among us—
quite equivalent to the gipsy palmistry of the European
countries. Of very late years it has principally become

" spiritualism" and the fortune-tellers are oftener known as
" mediums" than by the older appellation ; and scarcely one
of the impostors but pretends to physic the body as well as
cure the soul ; but the old leaven runs through all, and all
classes have some share in the speculation. Sooty negresses,
up dingy stairs, are consulted by ragged specimens of their
own color, as to the truth of the allegation that too much
familiarity has been exercised by an unauthorized "culled
pusson" towards a certain wife or husband,—or as to the
availability of a certain combination of numbers in a fifty
cent investment at that exciting game known as "policies"
or " 4–11–44," erewhile the peculiar province of that Honorable gentleman who (more or less) wrote " Fort Lafayette."
And, *per contra*, more pretentious witches (the women have
monopolized the trade almost altogether, of late years) are
consulted by fair girls who come in their own carriages, as
to the truth or availability of a lover or the possibility of
recovering lost affections or stolen property. How many of
those seeresses are "mediums" for the worst of communi-
cations, or how many per centum of the habitues of such
places go to eventual ruin, it is not the purpose of this chapter to inquire.

There are three recognized "centres" in the loyal States—
each a city, and supposed to be an enlightened one.) New
York, the commercial, monetary and even military centre;
Boston, the literary and intellectual ; and Washington, the
governmental and diplomatic. Taking up at random the
first three dailies of a certain date, at hand—one from each
of the three cities — the following regular advertisers are
shown, quoting from each of the three "astrology" columns
and omitting the directions.

New York : eleven. No. 1.—"Madame Wilson, a bona-
fide astrologist, that every one can depend on. Tells the
object of your visit as soon as you enter ; tells of the past,
present and future of your life, warns you of danger, and
brings success out of the most perilous undertakings. N. B.
—Celebrated magic charms." No. 2.—"Madame Morrow,
seventh daughter, has foresight to tell how soon and how often
you marry, and all you wish to know, even your thoughts, or

nt pay. Lucky charms free. Her magic image is now in
full operation." No. 3.—"The Gipsey Woman has just arrived. If you wish to know all the secrets of your past and
future life, the knowledge of which will save you years of
sorrow and care, don't fail to consult the palmist." No. 4.—
"Cora A. Seaman, independent clairvoyant, consults on all
subjects, both medical and business; detects diseases of all
kinds and prescribes remedies; gives invaluable advice on all
matters of life." No. 5.—"Madame Ray is the best clairvoyant and astrologist in the city. She tells your very thoughts,
gives lucky numbers, and causes speedy marriages." No. 6.—
"Madame Clifford, the greatest living American clairvoyant.
Detects diseases, prescribes remedies, finds absent friends,
and communes clairvoyantly with persons in the army."
No. 7.—"Madame Estelle, seventh daughter, can be consulted on love, marriage, sickness, losses, business, lucky
numbers and charms. Satisfaction guaranteed." No. 8.—
"Mrs. Addie Banker, medical and business clairvoyant, successfully treats all diseases, consults on business, and gives
invaluable advice on all matters of life." No. 9.—"Who has
not heard of the celebrated Madame Prewster, who can be
consulted with entire satisfaction? She has no equal. She
tells the name of future wife or husband—also that of her
visitor." No. 10.—"The greatest wonder in the world is the
accomplished Madame Byron, from Paris, who can be consulted with the strictest confidence on all affairs of life. Re-
stores drunken and unfaithful husbands; has a secret to make
you beloved by your heart's idol; and brings together those
long separated." No. 11.—"Madame Widger, clairvoyant and
gifted Spanish lady; unveils the mysteries of futurity, love,
marriage, absent friends, sickness; prescribes medicines for
all diseases; tells lucky numbers, property lost or stolen, &c."
Boston: thirteen. No. 1.—"The great astrologer.

> "The road to wedlock would you know,
>   Delay not, but to Baron go.
>   A happy marriage, man or maid,
>   May be secured by Baron's aid.

"He will reveal secrets no living mortal ever knew. No charge

for causing speedy marriages and showing likenesses of friends."
No. 2.—"Astonishing to all ! Madame Wright, the celebrated
astrologist, born with a natural gift to tell all the events of
your life, even your very thoughts and whether you are
married or single; how many times you will marry; will
show the likeness of your present and future husband and
absent friends; will cause speedy marriages; tells the object
of your visit. Her equal is not to be found—has astonished
thousands by her magic power." No. 3.—"Madame F. Gretz-
burg will ensure to whoever addresses her, giving the year of
their birth and their complexion, a correct written delineation
of their character, and a statement of their past, present and
future lives. All questions regarding love, marriage, absent
friends, business, or any subject within the scope of her clear
discerning spiritual vision, will be promptly and definitely
answered * * so far as she with her great and wonderful
prophetic and perceptive powers, can see them." No. 4.
"Prof. A. F. Huse, seer and magnetic physician. The Pro-
fessor's great power of retrovision, his spontaneous and lucid
knowledge of one's present life and affairs, and his keen fore-
casting of one's future career," etc. No. 5.—"Mrs. King will
reveal the mysteries of the past, present and future, and describe absent friends, and is very successful in business matters. Also has an article that causes you good luck in any
undertaking, whether business or love, and can be sent by
mail to any address." No. 6.—"Mrs. Frances, clairvoyant,
describes past, present and forthcoming events, and all kinds
of business and diseases. Has medicines," etc. No. 7.—
"Prof. Lyster, astrologer and botanic physician." No. 8.—
"Madame Wilder, the world-renowned fortune-teller and independent clairvoyant * * * is prepared to reveal the
mysteries of the past, present and future." No. 9.—"Madame
Roussell, independent clairvoyant, is prepared to reveal the
mysteries of the past, present and future." No. 10.—"Madame
Jerome Nurtnay, the celebrated Canadian seeress and natural
clairvoyant, * * will reveal the present and future." (This
one clairvoyant, it will be observed, has no *past*.) No. 11.—
"Mrs. Yah, clairvoyant and healing medium * * will examine and heal the sick, and also reveal business affairs,

describe absent friends, and call names. Has been very successful in recovering stolen property." No. 12.—"Madame
Cousin Cannon, the only world-renowned fortune-teller and
independent clairvoyant," etc. No. 13. — "Madame Mont
* * would like to be patronized by her friends and the
public, on the past, present and future events."

Washington : nine. No. 1.—"Madame Ross, doctress and
astrologist. Was born with a natural gift—was never known
to fail. She can tell your very thoughts, cause speedy marriages, and bring together those long separated." No. 2.—
"Mrs. L. Smith, a most excellent test and healing medium * *
sees your living as well as deceased friends, gets names, reads
the future." No. 3.—(Here we have the first male name, as
well as apparently the most dangerously powerful of all).
"Mons. Herbonne, from Paris. Clairvoyant, seer and fortune-teller. Reads the future as well as the past, and has
infallible charms. Can cast the horoscope of any soldier
about going into battle, and foretell his fate to a certainty."
No. 4.—"Madame Bushe, powerful clairvoyant and influ
encing medium. Has secrets for the obtaining of places desired under government, and love-philters for those who have
been unfortunate in their attachments." Nos. 5, 6, 7, 8 and
9 differing not materially from those before cited as able to
read the past, present and future, re-join the parted and influence the whole future life.

And here, as by this time Tom Leslie must certainly have
accomplished his business in Broome Street, and Joe Harris
and Bell Crawford sipped and eaten themselves into an indigestion at Taylor's—this examination of a subject little
understood must cease, to allow the three to carry out their
projected folly. But really how much have superior education and increasing intelligence done to clear away the grossest
of impositions and to discourage the most audacious experi-
ments upon public patience ? And yet—what shall be said
of the facts—uncolored and undeniable facts—narrated in a
subsequent chapter ?

CHAPTER XIII.

TEN MINUTES AT A COSTUMER'S—HOW TOM LESLIE GREW SUD-
DENLY OLD—JOE HARRIS' SPECULATION ON "THOSE EYES"
—ANOTHER SURPRISE, AND WHAT FOLLOWED.

MR. TOM LESLIE'S visit was *not* to the Police headquarters
in Broome Street, albeit he turned down that street from
Broadway when he reached it after leaving the two ladies at
Taylor's.   He took the other or upper side of the street, and
stopped immediately opposite the Police building, at a
two-story brick house whereon appeared the name of "R.
Williams" in gilt letters, and a little lower, "Ball Costumer,"
and in the two first floor windows of which, over a basement
set apart for the use of persons in need of bad servants and
servants in search of worse places—appeared such a collection of distorted human faces that a general execution by
the guillotine seemed to have been going on, with all the
heads hung up against the glass to dry.   The ghastly faces
were, in fact, those of papier-maché masks, waiting for customers desirous of a certain amount of personal disfigurement, whether on the stage or in the masked ball; and behind one row of them could be seen the glitter of an imitation coat of mail which looked very much like the real article
at a distance, but would have been of about as much use to
keep out sword-point or lance-head in the tourneys of the
olden time, as so much cobweb or blotting paper.

Within the inner door of the costumer's, which Leslie entered hurriedly, might have been gathered the spoils of all
ages and all kingdoms, taking tinsel for gold and stuff for
brocade.   The robes and mantles of queens hung suspended
from the walls, blended here and there with suits of beaded
and fringed Indian leather, odd coats and trousers for ex-
aggerated Jonathans, and diamonded garments of motley for
clowns.   Around on the floor, on two sides of the apartment,
lay heaps of garments of all incongruous descriptions, from
the court dress of King Charles' time to the tow and home-
spun of the Southern darkey, as if just tumbled over for
12

examination. A few stage swords and spears and two or
three suits of armor of suspicious likeness to block-tin, occupied one of the back corners ; while suspended from pegs
and arranged upon shelves were false beards, wigs and eyebrows, preposterous noses, Indian head-dresses of feathers,
hats of Italian bandits wreathed with greasy ribbons, and
crowns and coronets of all apparent values, from that flashing
with light which Isabella might have worn when all the gold
and gems of Columbus' new world lay at her disposal, to the
thin band of gold with one gem in the centre of the front,
which some virgin princess might modestly have blushed
under on her wedding day. Through the half-open door
leading to the adjoining apartment in the rear, still other
treasures of costume run mad were discoverable ; until the
thought was likely to strike the observer that " R. Williams,
Costumer," had been the happy recipient of all the cast-off
clothes, hirsute as well as sartorial, dropped by half a dozen
generations ranging from king to clod-hopper.

A short, dark-whiskered, sallow man came forward as
Leslie entered, addressing him by name, with an inquiry
after his wishes.

" I want a disguise," said Leslie—" particularly a disguise
of the face, and one that can deceive the sharpest of eyes."

The costumer looked at his face for a moment. " I can
make you up," he said, " so that your best friend—or what
is of more difficulty, the woman who loved you best or hated
you worst—wouldn't know you."

" That is it," said Leslie. " Now be quick, like a good
fellow, for I have only five minutes."

" You will not need to change your pants, I think," said
the costumer. " Throw off your coat—here is one that will
button close and hide your vest, and I think you will find it
about your size. Yours is a gray—this is a dark brown and
rather a genteel garment, and will suit the gray pants."

Leslie threw off his coat and put on the brown substitute,
which fitted him very respectably.

" That is enough in the way of clothes, I should think,"
remarked the costumer, unless you should be dodging a *very*
sharp woman, or one of Kennedy's men."

"It *is* a sharp woman I am trying to dodge," said Leslie, with a laugh, "but I think she will know very little about my clothes. The face—the face is the thing! Make me up so that you don't know me—so that I won't know myself—so that my wife, if I had one, would scream for a policeman if I attempted to kiss her."

"Yes, the face—that is what we are coming to," replied the costumer. "You have a moustache already. That we cannot very well cut off, I suppose."

"Not if I know it!" graphically but somewhat inelegantly said Tom, who had one of his many prides hidden away somewhere in the flowing sweep of that ornament to the upper lip.

"Then we must gray it!" said the costumer. "No objection to looking a little older?"

"Make me as old as Dr. Parr or old Galen's head, if you like," was the answer. "Only be quick, for the sauciest and best-looking girl in New York is waiting for me."

"To run away and be married? eh?" asked the costumer, as he went to a shelf and took down a cup of some preparation very like paint, and with it a brush. "None of my business, though! Hold still, and never mind the smell. It will be dry in two minutes, and water will not touch it, but you can clean it out at once with turpentine." He applied the mixture to Leslie's moustache, the member over it being drawn up considerably at times as if the bouquet of one of Hackley's summer gutters was rising; but in less than two minutes, as the costumer had said, the smell ceased, the mixture was dry, and Tom Leslie had a moustache grayish-white enough to have belonged to Sulpizio.

"Beautiful!" said the costumer, handing the subject a small mirror from the wall. "The hair and beard directly. Now for a complexion old enough to suit such a facial ornament." In a moment, he had a small cup of brown paint, with a camel's-hair brush, and was operating on Leslie's forehead and cheeks, artistically throwing in a few wrinkles on the former and neatly executed crows-feet under the eyes, in water-colors that dried as soon as applied. Leslie, by the aid of a glass, saw himself getting old, a little more plainly

than most of us recognize the ravages made on our faces by
time.

"By George!" he said. "Stop!—hold on!—don't make
those crows-feet any plainer, or I shall begin to get weak in
the back and shaky in the knees, and you will need to supply me with a cane."

"They will come off easier than the next ones painted
there, probably!" commented the philosophical costumer, as
he finished painting up his human sign. "And now for the
finishing stroke!" He stepped to a drawer, took out a gray
full-bottom beard, fitted it neatly to the chin, clasped the
springs back of the ears, added to it a gray wig, made easy-
fitting by the short hair on the head, and once more handed
Leslie the glass.

The young man looked. The last vestige of youth had de-
parted, and he appeared as he might have expected to do
thirty years later when he had touched sixty and gone on
downward.

"Capital!" he said—"capital! If any man, or woman,
knows me behind this disguise, there is some reason beyond
nature for their doing so. There—throw me a hat—anything unlike my own—for I have already remained too long.
I will see you again some time this evening." Handing the
costumer a bill, with the air of one who had taken such accommodations before and knew what they cost, Leslie put
on a respectable looking speckled Leghorn hat brought from
the back room, took one more glance at his metamorphosis in
the glass, and passed hurriedly out into the street and down
Broadway towards Taylor's.

To return to that place for a few moments, after Tom Leslie had left it and before he was again heard from.

Josephine Harris sat for perhaps five minutes after the
chocolate was brought, toying with the spoon and the cup, a
little consciously red in face, and saying never a word—an
amount of reticence quite as unusual for her, as ice in summer. Bell Crawford made two or three remarks, and she
answered them with "Ah!" and "Humph!" till the other
pouted a little sullenly and said no more.

At length the wayward girl shoved aside her cup, stopped

uibbling a bon-bon, planted one elbow on the table, leaned her chin on her hand, and looked her companion full in the face with a comic earnestness that was very laughable.

"Bell," she said, "I am gone!"

"Gone?" asked the other. "What do you mean?"

"Sent for—done up—wilted—caved in—and any other descriptive words that may happen to be in the language!" was the reply.

"What ails you? Are you crazy?" was the not unnatural inquiry of Bell.

"Crazy? No!" answered the wild girl. "I wonder if I ever shall be!" and for the instant her eyes were very sad, as if some painful thought had been touched. But the instant after sunshine broke into them again, as she said, making a motion of her hand towards the door:—

"That's he!"

Bell Crawford looked, but did not see any one, and the fact rather added to her impression that Miss Josey had suddenly taken leave of her senses. "Who's he? I don't see him!" she replied.

"Pshaw! how stupid you are!" said Josey, pettishly. "See here. Let me tell you something. Do you remember one day, five or six weeks ago, when I came into your house a little in a hurry, with a bunch of violets for Dick?"

"Yes," said Bell, "I remember it, by the fact that you nearly pulled off the bell-handle because the door was not opened quick enough."

"Right," said Joe, as if she had been complimented by the observation. "That's me. If Betty doesn't answer the bell a little quicker, some of these times, you will find that piece of silver-plating at a junk-shop, sold for old iron. Well, do you happen to remember what I told you and Dick on that occasion?"

"Oh, good gracious, no!" exclaimed Bell provokingly. "Surely you can't expect me to keep any account of what you say in the course of a month. Stop, though—I do remember something. You said, I believe, that coming up Madison Avenue you found the bunch of violets carrying a small boy—or the other way; and that at the same time you found a hat—wasn't it a hat?"

"Bah!" said Joe. "You have kept hold of the wrong end of the story, of course. I said that just as I met the small boy with the violets and their perfume began to set me crazy and make me think of being out in the country among the laughing brooks and the singing birds and the—yes, the cows and the chickens—that just then some one else met the small boy and the violets. That was the proprietor of the eyes, and if it had not been for that outrageous hat I should have had a full view of them. As it was, they nearly spoiled my peace of mind altogether, and I have been sighing ever since —Heigho!—haven't you heard me sighing all around in odd corners?"

"What a goose!" was the complimentary reply of Bell. "If you *have* sighed, the sound was very much like that of loud talking and laughter. But what has all that to do with to-day, and why were you pointing towards the door?"

"Why, you ninny," cried Joe, in response to the "goose" compliment just passed—"that man who has just left us— that man who is coming back in a moment!—is the owner of the eyes; and those eyes are my destiny!"

"Pshaw!" said Bell, "I did not see anything remarkable about the eyes, or the man."

"Didn't you, now!" said Josephine, with the least bit in the world of pique in her voice. "Well, that is the fault of *your* eyes, and not of *his*. I tell you those eyes are my destiny—I feel it and know it. I have not seen a pair before in a long while, that looked as if they could laugh and make love at the same time, and still have a little lightning in reserve for somebody they hated. Mr. Tom Leslie—well, it is a rather pretty name, and I think I must take him."

"For shame, Joe!" said Miss Bell, her propriety really shocked at the idea of a young girl declaring herself, even in jest, in love with a man who had said nothing to justify the preference.

"Yes, I suppose it is all wrong!" said Joe, between a sigh and a laugh. "You know I have been doing wrong things all my life, and anything else would not be natural.

Do you remember, Bell," and her dark eyes had an expression of demure fun in them that was irresistibly droll—"do you remember how I left all my trunks unlocked and my room door open, at the Philadelphia hotel when we were stopping there one winter on our way from Washington,—and how I left my purse on the bureau in my room and grabbed a gentleman by the arm in the street, accusing him of picking my pocket ?"

"I do remember," said Bell, a little with the air of a very proper Mentor who was not in the habit of making corresponding blunders. "And I should think, Joe, that now that you are a little older you would be a little more careful !"

"Yes, I daresay you do," answered Miss Josey, "but you know that I am myself and nobody else. I should stagnate and die in a week, if I was either one of those 'wealthy curled darlings' kept in exact position by the possession of too many thousands, or so hemmed by more confined worldly circumstances that I dared not take one step without stopping to consider the consequences. Hang propriety !—I hate propriety ! Now you have it, and you may eat it with that last wafer !"

"How you do run on !" merely remarked Bell, who probably enjoyed the wild girl's conversation quite as much as she was capable of enjoying anything.

"Yes," said Joe, "and I should like to know any reason for stopping, at least before our impressed beau comes back. Has he gone off to make arrangements with the fortune-teller, I wonder, so as to play a trick upon us when we get there ?"

"Eh," said Bell, a little startled, "could such a trick be possible !"

"Very possible, my dear !" said Joe. "I'll warrant such things have been done, and my gentleman looks just mischievous enough. But no—he would not dare do such a thing, for he could see with half an eye that if he did I should one day pay him for it !"

"If you ever had a chance !" remarked Bell with some approach to a sneer.

"Oh," said Joe. "Trust me for that ! Didn't I just tell

you that I had half made up my mind to take him? and if I
should, you know, I should have plenty of time to bring him
into the proper subjection."

."How do you know but he may be married?" asked Bell,
who had a little more forethought than Miss Joe in certain·
directions.

"Humph!" said Joe, ."that *would* be awkward, especially··
as I am not quite ready, yet, for an elopement and the sub-·
sequent flattering paragraphs in the papers, about 'the beautiful and accomplished Miss J. H.' having left for Europe on
the last steamer from· Boston, in company with 'the popular
journalist but sad Lothario, Mr. T. L., who has left an
interesting wife and two children to deplore the departure
of the husband and father from the paths of rectitude.' "

"Well, you *are* incorrigible!" laughed Miss Crawford,·
fairly carried away by the irresistible current of the wild·
girl's humor. "How can you talk so flippantly of things so·
deplorable?".

"I scarcely know, myself!" was the answer. "But there·
is really a dash of romance about such things,. which almost
makes them endurable. Poor Mrs. Brannan made a mess
of it, to be sure, coming out at last with a ruined character
and the widow of a man several ranks lower in the army
than the husband from whom she had run away; but was
there not something chivalrous in Wyman coming back at
once at the breaking out of the war, and sending an offer to
the man he had injured, to afford him any satisfaction he
might think proper to demand?"

"And was there not something sublimely cutting," asked
Bell, "in the reply of General Brannan that he demanded no
satisfaction whatever, as Colonel Wyman had only relieved
him of a woman unworthy of his love or confidence?"

"Yes, that *was* a little lowering to the dignity of the woman, if she had any left," said Joe. "But the Kearney elopement—was not *that* romantic without any drawback? There
was something of the wicked old Paladin, that rattle-heads
like myself cannot help admiring, in the one-armed man
whose other limb slept in an honored grave in Mexico ·
invading the charmed circle of New York moneyed-respecta

bility, carrying off the daughter of one of its first lawyers and
an ex-Collector—then submitting to a divorce, marrying the
woman who had trusted all to his honor, and plunging into
the fights of Magenta and Solferino with the same spirit
which had led him into the thick of the conflicts at Chapul-
tepec and the Garita de Belen. Poor Wyman has already
expiated his errors with his life, but I do hope that Kearney
may carry his remaining arm through this miserable war and
live to be so honored that even his one great fault may be
forgotten!"

The young girl's eyes flashed, her cheeks were flushed,
and any one who looked upon her at that moment would have
believed her almost brave enough for an Amazon and more
than a little warped in her perceptions of what constituted
the right and the wrong of domestic relations. How little,
meanwhile, they would have known her! Ninety-nine out
of one hundred of the women unwilling to confess that they
had ever read a page of the Wyman or the Kearney scandal, and saying "hush!" and "tut! tut!" to any one who
pretended to make the least defence of either—would have
been found infinitely more approachable for any purpose of
actual wrong or vice, than rattling, out-spoken and irrepressi-
ble Joe Harris!

Wyman was dead, as she had said—having expiated, with
his life, so much as could be expiated of all past wrong, and
having partially hidden the memory of his crime by his brave
offer of satisfaction to the wronged husband and his unflinch-
ing conduct before the enemies of his country in battle. But
how little she thought, at the moment of speaking, that the
bullet was already billeted for the breast of Kearney, and that
he was to fall, but a few weeks after, a sacrifice to his own rash-
ness and the incapacity of others! Does war indeed have a
mission beyond the national good or evil for which it is in-
stituted? And are its missiles of death and the diseases to
which its exposures give rise, especially commissioned to repay past crimes and by-gone errors? Not so, inevitably!—
or many a worthless incapable and many a dishonest trader
in his country's blood and treasure would before this have
bitten the dust,—and Baker, Lyon, Lander, Winthrop and

fifty other prominent martyrs to the cause of the Union
would yet have been alive and battling for the right!

Suddenly, the conversation between Josephine Harris and
Bell Crawford came to a conclusion, and the former sprung
to her feet with a frightened and angry "ough!" while the
latter leaned back in her chair in a state of stupefied vexation
not easy to describe. The cause of this excitement may be
briefly given. Both at the same instant discovered a face
thrust down to the level of their own and immediately between them, with a familiarity most inexcusable in a stranger.
Yet the face was certainly that of an entire stranger—a respectably dressed elderly man, with full gray hair and beard,
and holding a speckled Leghorn hat in his hand.

"Ough! get out! who are you and what do you want
here?" broke out the excited girl, with a propensity, meanwhile, to repay this second impudence of the day by such a
sound boxing of the ears as would make the event one to be
remembered; while Miss Crawford took a rather more practical view of the matter, with the single word "Impertinence!" and a supplementary call of "Waiter!"

"Ladies! ladies! what is the matter?" asked the elderly
intruder, as he saw the movements of the two girls, and the
waiter hurrying up with his towel over his arm, in obedience to the call.

"Anything wanted, Miss?" asked the waiter.

"Yes," said Miss Bell Crawford. "Take that man away
from this table. He must be either a wretch or a madman,
to intrude in this way where he is not known or wanted."

"Yes," echoed Joe, remembering the scene in the street,
only an hour or two before—"take him away, and if you can
find any one to do it, have him caned soundly."

"Come, sir, you must go to another table—these ladies are
strangers and complain of you," said the waiter, taking the
strange man by the arm, and disposed to relieve two ladies
from impertinence, though not, as suggested, to lose a cus-
tomer for the house.

"Why, ladies, this treatment is really very strange!" said
the man complained of, all gravity and surprise. "Just as
if I was really a stranger—just as if—"

But here he was broken in upon by Joe Harris absolutely screaming with laughter and dropping into her chair as abruptly as she had quitted it the moment before.

"Well?" queried Bell; and "Well?" though he did not give the query words, looked the puzzled waiter.

"Oh! oh! oh! that is too good!" broke out the laughing girl. "Oh! oh! oh! why don't you recognize him, Bell? That is Mr. Leslie!"

Whether Miss Joe had recognized him by the voice, the second time he spoke, or whether something in the undisguiseable eyes (were her own the keen eyes of love, already awakened, that saw more clearly than others could do?) had betrayed him—certain it was that the masquerade was over, so far as she was concerned, and our friend Tom Leslie stood fully discovered. The waiter saw that his interference was no longer needed, and moved away at once; and Bell Crawford, at length fully aware of the trick, joined less noisily in the laugh which convulsed her friend.

"And what does the masquerade mean?" finally asked the soberer of the two girls, as they were leaving the saloon, —while the other, who wished to know much worse, was considerably more ashamed to ask.

"Humph!" answered Tom Leslie. "You have a right to ask, ladies, but if you will excuse me I should prefer not to answer until the visit is paid. You will remember that I told you I had a reason something like your own for leaving the carriage; and if for the present you will accept the explanation that I wish to test the accuracy of the fortune-teller without her being at all indebted to any observation of my face or any possible previous recollection of me, I shall be your debtor to the extent of a full explanation afterwards, should you think proper to demand it."

It is not impossible that Joe Harris, who had just been congratulating herself upon a promenade with a man not only good-looking but comparatively *young*, may have had her personal objections to the even temporary substitution of sixty-five or seventy; but if so, her red lip only pouted a little, and she said nothing more on the subject as the three

took their way up Broadway and down Prince Street to the
place where all the secrets of the past, present and future
were to be revealed.

---◆--◆--◆---

CHAPTER XIV.

NECROMANCY IN A THUNDER-STORM—A VERY IMPROPER
"JOINING OF HANDS"—BELL CRAWFORD'S EYES, AND OTHER
EYES—TWO PICTURES IN THE DUSSELDORF—A THUNDER-
CLAP AND A SHRIEK—THE RED WOMAN WITHOUT A MASK.

IT was perhaps four o'clock in the afternoon when the trio
of fortune-seekers reached the door that had been designated
by the advertisement as No. — Prince Street; and the fiery
heat that had been pouring down during all the earlier part
of the day was somewhat moderated by heavy clouds rising
in the West and skimming half the upper sky, indicating a
thunder-storm rapidly approaching.   Perhaps Tom Leslie
thought, as he approached the door sacred to the sublime
mysteries of humbug, of the appropriateness of thunder in
the heavens and lightning playing down on the beaten earth
—provided he *should* find the mysterious woman of the Rue
la Reynie Ogniard, who had succeeded in giving to his frank
and bold spirit the only shock it had ever received from the
powers of the supernatural world.   Perhaps he felt that for
whatever was to come—melancholy jest or terrible earnest—
the bursting roar of the warring elements would be a fitting
accompaniment, to lend it a little dignity in the one event and
to distract the overstrained attention in the other.

Perhaps he was even a little theatrical in his fancies, and
remembered the crashes of sheet-iron thunder and the blinding blaze of the gunpowder lightning, that always accompanied the shot-cylinder rain when Macbeth was seeking the
weird sisters for the second time—when the fearful incantations of "Der Freischutz" were about to be commenced—or

when the ever-ready demon was invoked by Faust, the first
printer-devil. If he had any of these fancies he was in a fair
way of being accommodated; for casting a glance up at the
heavens as they approached the house, he saw that the obscurity was becoming still denser; and more than once, above
the rumble of the carts and omnibuses that made Broadway
one wide earthquake of subterranean noises, he caught a far-
off booming that he knew to be the thunder of the advancing
storm, already playing its fearful overture among the mountains of Pennsylvania.

His companions were too much absorbed by the novelty
of their errand, and a little expressed apprehension on the
part of Bell that if the rain came on and the carriage should
not be ready at the exact moment when it was wanted, her
costly summer drapery might run a chance of being wetted
and disordered,—to make any close examination of the outside
of the building at the door of which Leslie rang; and indeed
they had not the same reason for remarking any peculiarities.
Leslie saw that it was certainly the same at which Harding
and himself had stood two nights before—that the tree (his
tree, for had he not "hugged" it?—and who shall dare, in
this proper age, to "hug" what is not his own?)—that the
tree stood in the relation he remembered, to the window—and
that at that window the same white curtain was visible,
though not swept back, and now covering all the sash completely. He almost thought that he could distinguish the flag
in the pavement on which he must have struck the hardest
when tumbling down from the tree, and his vivid imagination
would not have been much surprised to see a slight dint there,
such as may be made on a tin pot or a stove-pipe by the
iconoclastic hammer in the hand of an exuberant four-year-
old.

On one of the lintels of the door, as he had not noticed on
the previous visit, was a narrow strip of black japanned tin,
with "Madame Elise Boutell" in small bronze letters, of
that back-slope writing only made by French painters, and
which can only be met with, ordinarily, in the French cities
or those of the adjacent German provinces. It seems unlikely that any particular attention should have been paid to

the latter unimportant detail at that moment; but the detail
was really *not* an unimportant one. Among the half-working
amusements of his idle hours in youth, Leslie had indulged
in a little amateur sign-painting, and he boasted that he
could distinguish one of the cities of the Union from any
other, by the styles of the signs alone, if he should be set
down blindfold in the commercial centre, and then allowed
the use of his eyes. In the present instance, by the use of
his quick faculty of observation, he saw that the lettering of
the sign was no American imitation, but really French. The
deductions were that it had been done in Paris—that it had
been used there—that "Madame Elise Boutell" had used it
for the same purpose there. Was not here a corroboration
of the theory of the Rue la Reynie Ogniard ?

All these observations, of course, had been made very
briefly—in the little time necessary for Bell Crawford finally
to congratulate herself that the ribbons of her hat would at
least be sheltered by the house for a time, and for Joe Harris
to remark what a dirty and tumble-down precinct Prince
Street seemed to be, altogether. By this time, the ring was
answered and the door opened by a neatly dressed negro
girl, who seemed to have none of the peculiarities of the
race except its color, and of whom Leslie asked :

"Madame Boutell ? Can we see her ?"

"If Monsieur and Mesdames will have the goodness to
step into this room," was the reply of the servant, opening
the door of the parlor, "Madame Boutell will have the
honor of receiving them in a few moments."

"Aha !" said Leslie to himself, as they entered the room,
the door closed and the negro-girl disappeared. "Aha !
' Monsieur' and ' Mesdames,' besides being marvellously correct in her speech and polite enough for a French dancing
master ! All this looks more and more suspicious."

"Nothing so very terrible here," remarked Josephine Harris, at once addressing her attention to some excellent prints,
commonly framed, hanging on the wall. "Some of these
pictures are very nice, and as I could throw away the frames,
I should not much mind hooking them if I had a good opportunity."

"But the piano is shockingly out of tune," remarked Bell, who had immediately commenced a listless kind of assault on that ill-used indispensable of all rooms in which people are expected to wait.

"Bell, for conscience sake leave that piano alone! You have nearly murdered the one at home, and I do not see why you should be the enemy of the whole race!" was the complimentary reply of Josephine, which caused Bell, with a little pout on her lip, to leave the piano and commence tap-. ping the cheap bronzes on the mantel with the end of her parasol, by way of discovering whether they were metal or plaster.

Just then there were steps in the hall, the outer door opened, and Joe, running suddenly to the window, was enabled to catch a glimpse through the blinds, of a gentleman and a lady passing down the steps from the door and walking hurriedly towards Broadway. The next moment the door from the hall opened, and the negro girl, stepping within, said:

"Madame Boutell will have the honor to receive Monsieur and Mesdames, if they will be so good as to ascend the stairs."

"Now for it," said Joe, touching Leslie's arm with a little bit of shudder, real or affected, and speaking in a tone so low that it seemed designed only for his ear and flattered that male person's vanity amazingly. "Now for it!—I have never been anywhere near the infernal regions before, to my knowledge, and you must take care of us!"

"I will *try*—Miss Harris—may I not say Josephine?" was the reply of Leslie, who, though he had said very little in that direction, kept his eyes pretty closely on the wild female counterpart of himself, and was really getting on somewhat rapidly towards an entanglement.

The apartment into which the seekers after information (or *no* information) were ushered, was reached by ascending an old-fashioned stair, through a hall not very well lighted, even in a summer afternoon; and when they entered it they found it to be one of two, divided by a red curtain which dropped to the floor and supplied the place of a door. No necromantic appliances were visible in the room; and with the exception of a table, three or four chairs and a carpet more or less worn, it was without articles of use or ornament. Motioning the party to chairs, which only Bell accepted, the negro attendant said :

"Will Monsieur and the ladies enter Madame's private room together, or singly ? Madame does not often receive more than one at once, but will do so for this distinguished company, if they wish ?"

"Ahem !" said Leslie, involuntarily pulling up his collar at the words "distinguished company," while "Good gracious !—how did they know that *we* were coming ?" was the exclamation of Joe, to Bell, *sotto voce.*

"Oh, let us all go in together," said Bell, who probably had less suspicion of a secret that could possibly be awkward of disclosure, in her own breast, than either of her companions.

"No, I think not," said Joe. "You may have nothing to conceal, Bell, but I have—lots of things ; and though I may be willing to have the French woman drain me dry, like a pump, I do not know that I shall offer *you* the same privilege."

"No, on the whole, decidedly not," said Leslie. "Of course, ladies, there is really nothing for the most timid to fear ; and even if there were, the two others will be in the room immediately adjoining. Decidedly, if you are both willing, each had better tempt fate alone."

"And who will go in first, then ?" asked Bell.

"Humph !" said Joe, "there *is* a grave question. The decrees of fate must not be tampered with, and the wrong one going in first might send those 'stars' on which the witch depends, into most alarming collision."

"Easily arranged," said Leslie, drawing a handful of coin from his pocket, handing one of the pieces to each of the girls, and retaining one himself. "As fate is the deity to be consulted, let fate take care of her own. The one who happens to hold the piece of oldest date shall take the first chance, and the others will follow according to the same rule. I have settled more than one important question of my life in this manner, and I have an idea that they have been settled quite as satisfactorily as they could have been by any exercise of judgment."

"Eighteen hundred and fifty-two," said Bell, looking at the date on her coin. "Eighteen hundred and fifty-seven," said Joe, paying the same attention to the one she held. And "Eighteen hundred and sixty-one—only last year!" said Leslie, jingling the coins in his hand and then dropping them back into his pocket,—from which (*par parenthese*) they were so soon and so effectually to disappear, with all others of their kind, in the turning of exchanges against us and the general derangement of the currency of the country.

"You are first, Bell, you see!" said Joe, "and I hope you will be able to take the fiery edge off the teeth of the dragon before I get in to him."

"And *I* am the last, you perceive!" said Leslie. "The last, as I always have been where women were concerned—too late, and of course unsuccessful."

There may have been no positive reason for the slight flush which crossed the face of Josephine Harris at that moment, or for the conscious look of pleasure that danced for an instant in her eyes; and yet there may have been a thought of true happiness at the assurance which the last words of Leslie conveyed, that he was an unmarried man and had been, so far, near enough heart-whole for all practical purposes. If the latter should even have been true, she need not have flushed a second time at recognizing the feeling in herself; for most certainly those apparently light words of Tom Leslie had been, so to speak, shot at her, with a determined intention of feeling ground to be afterwards trodden.

"Madame is waiting your pleasure," said the negro girl, who had remained standing near the curtain all this while, but too far distant to catch many of the words passing between the three visitors, which had all been uttered in a low tone.

"Ah, yes, we have kept her waiting too long, perhaps," said Leslie, "and who knows but the fates may be the more unkind to us for the neglect of their priestess." He was really not very well at his ease, but somewhat anxious to appear so, as all very bashful people can fully understand,

13

when they remember the efforts they have sometimes made
to appear the most impudent men in creation. Tom Leslie
was not in the slightest degree bashful, and so the comparison
fails in that regard ; but he was more than a little nervous at
the certainty which he felt of once more meeting the "red
woman," and for that reason he wished to seem the man with
no nerves whatever.

"It is my turn—I will go in," said Bell Crawford, rising
from her chair and following the negro attendant within the
curtain, which only parted a little to admit her and then swept
down again to the floor, giving no glimpse to the two out-
siders of what might be within.

The sky had now grown perceptibly darker, though it was
still some hours to night; and at the moment when Bell
Crawford entered the inner room of the sorceress the gathering thunder-storm burst in fury. The thunder was not as
yet peculiarly heavy, and the flashes of lightning had often
been surpassed in vividness; but the rain poured down in
torrents and the gust of wind, which swept through the streets
set windows rattling and doors and shutters banging at a rate
which promised work for the carpenters. The two windows
of the room looked out upon the street, though through closed
blinds ; and whether intentionally or inadvertently, the two
in waiting drew two chairs to one of the windows, very near
together, and sat there, watching the dashing rain and listening to the storm. Had there been any possibility of hearing
the words spoken in the adjoining room, that possibility would
now have been entirely destroyed by the noise of the storm ;
and whatever of curiosity either may have felt for the result
of Bell's adventure, was rendered inefficient for the time.
Meanwhile, something else was working of quite as much
consequence.

Chances and accidents are very curious things ; and those
who have no belief in a Supreme Being who brings about
great results by apparently insignificant agencies, must have
a very difficult time of it, in reconciling the incongruous and
the inadequate. Holmes, the merriest and wisest of social
philosophers (when he does not run mad on the human-snake
theory, as he has done in "Elsie Venner") very prettily illus-

trates the opposite, as to how the agency which moves the
great may also perform the little, in

"The force that wheels the planets round delights in spinning tops,
And that young earthquake t'other day was great on shaking
props;"

but the opposite may be illustrated more easily, and is certainly illustrated much oftener. Not only may

"A broken girth decide a nation's fate,"

in battle; but a gnawing insignificant rat may sink a ship,
and one contemptible traitor be able to disseminate poison
enough to destroy a republic; while the question of whether
Bobby does or does not take his top with him to school to-
day, may decide whether he does or does not wander off to
the neighboring pond to be drowned; and Smith's being seen
to step into a billiard-room may decide the question of credit
against him in the Bank discount-committee, and send him to
the commercial wall, a bankrupt. That glance of unnecessary
and unladylike scorn which Lady Flora yesterday cast upon
a beggar-woman who accidently brushed against her costly
robes on Broadway, may have lost her a rich husband, who
would otherwise have been deceived until after marriage, as
to her real character; and the involuntary act of courtesy of
John Hawkins, stooping down to pick up the dropped umbrella of a common woman with a baby and two bundles, in
a passenger-car, may make him a friend for life, worth more
than all he has won by twenty-five years of hard-working
industry and honesty.

In this point of view there are no "little things;" and
probably he is best prepared for all the exigencies of coming
life, who is ready to be the least surprised at finding a
dwarfed shrub growing up from an acorn, and a mighty tree
springing from the proverbial "grain of mustard seed."

Not to be prolix on this subject—let us remember one
capital illustration—that of the clown and his two pieces of
fireworks. No matter in what pantomime the scene occurs,
as it may do for any. The clown approaches the door of a

dealer in fireworks, finds no one on duty in the shop, enters, and
comes out laden with pyrotechnic spoils. He takes a small
rocket, fires it, and is knocked down, frightened and stunned
by the unexpectedly-heavy explosion. But he recovers directly, and determines to try the experiment over again.
There is one immense rocket among the collection he has
brought out—one almost as long as himself and apparently
capable of holding half a barrel of explosive material. He
shakes his head knowingly to the audience, indicative of the
fact that _this_ is something immense and that he is going to
be very careful about it. He sticks it up in the very middle
of the stage, secures a light at the end of a long pole, and
touches it off with great fear and trembling. The explosion
which follows is exactly that of one Chinese fire-cracker;
and the comically disappointed face which the clown turns to
the audience is precisely the same that each individual of that
audience is continually turning to another audience surrounding him, when the great and small rockets of his daily life go
off with such disproportionate effect.

Perhaps it was chance that not only produced the previous
circumstances of that day, but so ordered that Bell Crawford
should be the first to vacate the outer room, leaving that extraordinary couple alone together. Perhaps it was chance
that led them to take seats beside each other at the window,
when they might so easily have found room to sit with some
distance between them. Perhaps it was chance that made
the lightning flash in long lines of blinding light across the
sky, and sent the thunder booming and crashing above the
roofs of the houses, producing that indefinable feeling that
needed companionship—that "huddling together" which even
the terrible beasts of the East Indian jungles show in the
midst of the fearful tornadoes of that region. Perhaps it was
chance that, after a moment or two of silence, induced Tom
Leslie, without well knowing why he did it, to lay his open
palm on his knee, and to look for a moment with a glance of
inquiry, full in the eyes of the young girl who sat at his
right, as if to say : "There is my open hand—we have known
each other but a little while—dare you lay _your_ hand in it ?"
Perhaps it was chance that made the young girl return the

steady glance—then drop her eyes with so sad a look that
tears might easily have been trembling under the long lashes,
—color a little on cheek and brow, as if some tint of the sunrise flush had for a moment rested upon her face—then slowly
reach over her right hand and let it drop and nestle into the
one ready to receive it. Perhaps all these things were chance:
well, let them be so set down—such "chances" are worth
something in life, to those who know how to embrace them!
What have we here? Two persons who had spoken to
each other for the first time, only a few hours before, and who
had since held marvellously little conversation, now sitting
hand in hand, their soft palms pressed close together, and
every pulse of the mental and physical natures of both thrill-
ing at the touch! Exceedingly improper!—exceedingly hurried!—exceedingly indelicate! Modesty, where were you
about this time? If we have gone so fast already, how fast
may we go by-and-bye? Alas, they are living people whom
we have before us—not cherubim and seraphim; and they do
as they please, and act very humanly, in spite of every care
we can take of their morals. They have not said one word
of love to each other, it is true; but the mischief seems to
have been done. Nothing may have been said, in the way
of a promise of marriage, capable of being taken hold of by
the keenest lawyer who pleads in the Brown-Stone building;
but we are not sure that ever tongue spoke to ear, or ever
lip kissed back to lip, so true and enduring a betrothal as has
sometimes been signed in the meeting of two palms, when
not a word had been spoken and when neither of the pair
had one rational thought of the future.

Suddenly and without warning the curtain between the two
rooms moved. How quickly those two hands drew apart from
each other, as if some act of guilt had been doing! If any
additional proof was wanting, of something clandestine (and
of course improper!) between the parties, here it was certainly supplied. People never attempt to deceive, who have
not been playing tricks. Well-regulated and candid people,
who do everything by rule, never start and blush at any awkward contretemps, never have any concealments, but tell
everything to the outer world. Privacy is a crime—all sly

people are reprobates. Wicked Tom and erring Joe!—what
a gulf of perdition they were sinking into without knowing it !

The curtain not only moved but was drawn aside, and out
of it stepped Bell Crawford. She walked slowly and deliberately, like one in deep thought, and without a word
crossed the room towards the point where her two friends
were sitting. Something in her face brought them both to
their feet. What was that something ? She had been absent
from them for perhaps ten minutes—certainly not more than
a quarter of an hour; and yet change enough had passed
over her, to have marked the passage of ten twelve-months.
The face looked older, perhaps sadder, more like that of her
brother, and yet less querulous, more womanly, better and
more loveable. Something seemed to have stirred the depths
of her nature, of which only the surface had been before exposed to view. The revelation was better than the index.
She was capable of generous things at that moment, of which
she had been utterly incapable the hour before. It was probable that she could never again dash all over town in the search
for a yard of ribbon of a particular color : her next search
was likely to be a much more serious one.

The first glance at her face, and the marvellous change there
exhibited, wrought in so short a time, not only puzzled but
alarmed Josephine Harris. She could not see where and in
what feature lay the change, any more than she could realize
what could have been powerful enough to produce it. Tom
Leslie may have been quite as much alarmed ; but his older
years and wider experience, conjoined with the feelings with
which he had come to that house, made it impossible that he
should be so much puzzled. He saw at once that the marked
change was in the *eyes.* In their depths (he had before remarked them, that day, as indicating a nature a little weak,
purposeless and not prone to self-examination)—in their
depths, clear enough now, there lay a dark, sombre, but not
unpleasing shadow, such as only shows itself in eyes that
have been turned *inward.* We usually say of a man whose
eyes show the same expression : " That man has studied
much," or, " he has suffered much," or, " he is a *spiritualist.*"

By the latter expression, we mean that he looks more or less beneath the surface of events that meet him in the world—that he is more or less a student of the spiritual in mentality, and of the supernatural in cause and effect. Such eyes do not stare, they merely gaze. When they look at you, they look at something else through you and behind you, of which you may or may not be a part.

Let it be said here, the occasion being a most inviting one for this species of digression,—that the painter who can succeed in transferring to canvas that expression of *seeing more than is presented to the physical eye*, has achieved a triumph over great difficulties. Frequent visitors to the old Dusseldorf Gallery, now so sadly disrupted and its treasures scattered through twenty private galleries where they can only be visible to the eyes of a favored few,—will remember two instances, perhaps by the same painter, of the eye being thus made to reveal the inner thought and a life beyond that passing at the moment. The first and most notable is in the "Charles the Second fleeing from the Battle of Worcester." The king and two nobles are in the immediate foreground, in flight, while far away the sun is going down in a red glare behind the smoke of battle, the lurid flames of the burning town, and the royal standard just fluttering down from the battlements of a castle lost by the royal arms at the very close of Cromwell's "crowning mercy." Through the smoke of the middle distance can be dimly seen dusky forms in flight, or in the last hopeless conflict. Each of the nobles at the side of the fugitive king is heavily armed, with sword in hand, mounted on heavy, galloping horses, going at high speed; and each is looking out anxiously, with head turned aside as he flies, for any danger which may menace—not himself, but the sovereign. Charles Stuart, riding between them, is mounted upon a dark, high-stepping, pure-blooded English horse. He wears the peaked hat of the time, and his long hair—that which afterward became so notorious in the masks and orgies of Whitehall, and in the prosecution of his amours in the purlieus of the capital—floats out in wild dishevelment from his shoulders. He is dressed in the dark velvet short cloak, and broad, pointed collar peculiar to pic-

tures of himself and his unfortunate father; he shows no
weapon, and is leaning ungracefully forward, as if outstrip-
ping the hard-trotting speed of his horse. But the true interest of this figure, and of the whole picture, is concentrated in the eyes. Those sad, dark eyes, steady and immovable in their fixed gaze, reveal whole pages of history
and whole years of suffering. The fugitive king is not thinking of his flight, of any dangers that may beset him, of the
companions at his side, or even of where he shall lay his
perilled head in the night that is coming. Those eyes have
shut away the physical and the real, and through the mists of
the future they are trying to read the great question of *fate!*
Worcester is lost, and with it a kingdom : is he to be henceforth a crownless king and a hunted fugitive, or has the future its compensations ? This is what the fixed and glassy
eyes are saying to every beholder, and there is not one who
does not answer the question with a mental response forced
by that mute appeal of suffering thought: "The king shall
have his own again !"
.The second picture lately in the same collection, is much
smaller, and commands less attention ; but it tells another
story of the same great struggle between King and Parlia
ment, through the agency of the same feature. A wounded
cavalier, accompanied by one of his retainers, also wounded,
is being forced along on foot, evidently to imprisonment, by
one of Cromwell's Ironsides and a long-faced, high-hatted
Puritan cavalry-man, both on horseback, and a third on foot,
with musquetoon on shoulder. The cavalier's garments are
red and blood-stained, and there is a bloody handkerchief
binding his brow, and telling how, when his house was surprised and his dependants slaughtered, he himself fought till
he was struck down, bound and overpowered, still hurling
defiance at his enemies and their cause, until his anger and
disdain grew to the terrible height of silence and he said no
more. He strides sullenly along, looking neither to the right
nor the left; and the triumphant captors behind him know
nothing of the story that is told in his face. The eyes fixed
and steady in the shadow of the bloody bandage, tell nothing
of the pain of his wound or the tension of the cords which

are binding his crossed wrists. In their intense depth, which really seems to convey the impression of looking through forty feet of the still but dangerous waters of Lake George and seeing the glimmering of the golden sand beneath,—we read of a burned house and an outraged family, and we see a prophecy written there, that if his mounted guards could read, they would set spurs and flee away like the wind—a calm, silent, but irrevocable prophecy: "I can bear all this, for my time is coming! Not a man of all these will live, not a roof-tree that shelters them but will be in ashes, when I take my revenge!" Not a gazer but knows, through those marvellous eyes alone, that the day is coming when he *will* have his revenge, and that the subject of pity is the victorious Roundhead instead of the wounded and captive cavalier!

Not all this, of course, was expressed in the eyes of Bell Crawford as she stood before her two companions under the circumstances just detailed; but it scarcely needed a second glance to tell the keen man of the world that the eyes and the brain beneath them had both been taught something before unknown. He thought what might possibly have been the expression of his own eyes, on a night so many times before alluded to, could he but have seen them as did others; and if he had before held one lingering doubt of the personality of the woman whose presence she had just quitted, that doubt would have remained no longer. It *was* the "red woman," beyond a question. For just one moment another thought crossed his mind, founded upon that "union of hands" so lately consummated. Should he permit *her* to be subjected to the same influences?.. And yet, why not? The good within her could not be injured, either by sorcery or super-knowledge—either by the assumption or the possession on the part of the seeress, of information beyond that of ordinary mortality and altogether out of its pale. He *would* permit her to undergo the same influences, even as in a few moments he would submit to them himself.

Josephine Harris, in the time consumed by all these reflections running through the mind of Leslie, had not yet recovered from her surprise at the altered expression on the face of her friend—an expression, oddly enough, that pleased her better than any she had ever before observed there, and yet frightened her correspondingly.

"Dear Bell," she said, anxiously, and using a word of endearment that had been very rare between them, spite of their extreme intimacy.—"What has happened? What have you seen? Are you sick? Your eyes frighten me—they seem so sad and earnest!"

"Do they?" said Bell, forcing a smile that was really sad enough, but better became her face than many expressions that had before passed over it. "Well, Josey, to tell you the truth, I have seen some strange things, of which I will tell you at another time; and I have been thinking very deeply. Nothing more."

"You have seen nothing frightful—dreadful—terrible?" the young girl asked, with an unmistakable expression of anxiety upon her face.

"Nothing terrible, though something very strange," was the reply of Bell. "Nothing that you need fear."

"Oh, I am not afraid!" answered Joe, with an assumption of bravery that she probably felt to be a sham all the while. "I believe it is my turn now. Dear me, how heavy that thunder is! Try and amuse yourselves, good people, while I 'follow in the footsteps of my illustrious predecessor'!" and with an affectation of gaiety that was a little transparent, she obeyed the summons of the black girl who at that moment made her appearance again outside the curtain, and followed her within.

Bell Crawford dropped into one of the chairs that stood by the window, and leaned her head upon her hand, in an attitude of deep thought. Leslie did not attempt to speak to her at that moment, either aware that such a course could only be painful to her, or too much absorbed in the remembrance of the other who had just passed within the curtain, to wish to do so. He walked the floor, from one side to the other of the room, the sound of his heel falling somewhat heavily even on the carpeted floor, and his head thrown forward in such a position that when he threw his glance on a level with his line of vision it came out from under his bent

brows. The rain seemed to beat heavier and heavier outside, and dashed against the windows with such force as to
threaten to beat them in; and successive discharges of thunder, accompanied with constant flashes of fierce lightning,
crashed and rumbled among the house-tops and seemed to be
at times actually booming through the room, immediately
over their heads.

In this way some fifteen minutes passed, seeming almost
so many hours to the young man, whatever they may have
appeared to the young girl who sat by the window, so absorbed by her own thoughts that she scarcely heard the muttering thunder or saw the blinding flashes of the lightning.

Suddenly there was a louder and fiercer crash of thunder
than any that had preceded it—a crash of that peculiar sharp-
ness indicating that it must have struck the very house in
which they heard it; and this accompanied by one of those
terribly intense flashes of lightning which seemed to sear the
eyeballs and play in blue flame through the air of the room,
—then followed by a heavy dull rumbling shock and boom
like that of a thousand pieces of artillery fired at once, rocking the building to its foundation and threatening to send it
tumbling in ruins on their heads. Tom Leslie involuntarily
put his hands to his eyes, to shut out the flash, and Bell
Crawford, at last startled, sprung from her chair; but both
were worse startled, the very second after, by a long, loud,
piercing shriek, in the voice of Josephine Harris, that burst
from the inner room and seemed like some cry extorted by
mortal pain or unendurable terror.

Both rushed towards the curtain, at once, but Leslie in advance—both with the impression that some dreadful catastrophe connected with the lightning must have occurred.
But just as Leslie laid his hand upon the curtain to draw it
aside, it was dashed open from within, and Josephine Harris
literally flung herself through it, still shrieking and in that
deadly mortal terror which threatens the reason. She seemed
about to fall, and Tom Leslie stretched out his arms to receive
her. She half fell into them, then rolled, nearer than described
any other motion, into those of Bell Crawford; and almost
before Leslie could quite realize what had occurred, she lay

with her head in Bell's lap, the extremity of her terror over, uttering no word, but sobbing and moaning like a little child that had been too severely dealt with and broken down under the blow.

Tom Leslie's hand, it has been said, was on the curtain, to remove it. He released it for the instant, to look after the welfare of the frightened girl; but when he saw her lying in Bell's lap another feeling became paramount even to his anxiety for her safety, and he grasped the curtain again and dashed through into the inner room.

As he had expected, the red woman of the Rue la Reynie Ogniard stood before him, presenting the same magnificent° outline of face and the same ghastly redness of complexion that she had shown at such a distance of time and place. In her hand was a white wand, glittering like silver, with some bright and flashing colorless stone at the end. Her dress, as he then remembered, had been red when he saw her in Paris, and no relief to her ghastly color had been shown, except in the mass of dark hair sweeping down her shoulders. Now her tall and stately form was wrapped in black, against which her cloud of dark hair was unnoticed. Leslie had not observed, at any time during the absence of either of the two girls, any odor of smoke or any appearance of it creeping out from the curtain into the room; but now, as he looked, he saw white wreaths of vapor circling near the ceiling and fading away there; and he realized at once, with the memory of the past in mind, what had been the form in which the images were presented, producing so startling an effect on both.

At the moment when he entered, the black girl was just disappearing through what appeared to be a small door opening out of the room upon the landing of the stairs, and ordinarily concealed by the sweeping drapery of dark cloth that was looped around the entire apartment. Whether the attendant was carrying away any of the properties that might have been used in the late jugglery, he had, of course, no means of judging. The sorceress herself, at the moment when he broke in upon her, was apparently advancing from the little table at which she had been standing, partially

within the sweep of the hangings, towards the dividing curtain. At sight of the intruder she stopped suddenly and
drew her tall form to its full height, while such a flash of
anger appeared to dart from her keen eyes as would have
produced a sensible effect on any man less used to varying
sensations than the cosmopolitan journalist.

"What do you want?" she asked, and the words came
from her lips with the same short hissing tone that he so well
remembered. creating the impression that there must be a
serpent hidden somewhere in the throat and hissing through
what would otherwise be the voice.

"What sorcery have you practised upon that poor girl, to
drive her into this state of distraction, red fiend?" was the
answering question, bold enough in seeming, though Tom
Leslie, asked in regard to the matter to-day, would undoubtedly acknowledge that he had felt far less tremor when under
the heaviest play of the Russian cannon at Inkermann, than
when throwing this sharp taunt into the teeth of the sorceress.

"Nothing but what you have seen and endured!" was the
reply, made in the same tone as before. "I have shown
them the truth, and the truth is terrible. It is murder and
ruin in their own households—it is battle and death around
those they love—it is desolation and destruction to the land!
Go!—those who cannot witness my power without blenching,
should never seek me; and you blench like those sick girls—
I have seen you blench before?"

"Seen me?" echoed Leslie.

"Seen you!" was the fierce reply of the sorceress. "Fool!
do you think I cannot penerate that thin disguise—that old
man's hair and those false wrinkles? You were younger-
looking, eighteen months since, in another land where the
eagle screams less but tears its enemies more deeply with its
talons!"

"I was," answered Leslie, carried beyond himself. "I remember the Rue la Reynie Ogniard, and I acknowledge your
fearful power, though I know not if it comes from heaven or
hell! But tell me—who are you, so magnificently beautiful,
and yet so—so—" and here (a rare thing for him,) the voice
of Tom Leslie faltered.

"So horribly hideous, you would say," broke in the sor
ceress. "Stay I you have said one word that touches the
woman within me. You have recognized my beauty as well
as my terror. Look for one instant at what no mortal eye
has seen for years or may ever see again I Look I"

Tom Leslie started, nay, staggered—for no other word can
express the motion—back towards the door, infinitely more
surprised than he had been on the night of his first adventure with the sorceress. She held something in her hand,
but that could only be seen afterwards : for the moment his
eyes could only behold that marvellous face. If the, Sons of
God when they intermarried with the beautiful daughters of
clay, left any descendants behind them, certainly that face
must have belonged to one of the number. No longer
ghastly red, but almost marble white, with the hue of health
yet mantling beneath the wondrous transparent skin, and every
line and curve of beauty such as would make the sculptor drop
his chisel in despair—with a lip that might have belonged to
Juno and a brow that should have been set beneath the hel-
met of Athena—with the glorious dark eye fringed with long
sweeping lashes and the wealth of the dark brown hair
swept back in masses of rippled and tangled shadow that
caught and lost the eye continually,—what a perfect vision
of high-born beauty was that face, the patent of nobility
coming direct from heaven !

And what was that which she held in her hand, and the removal of which had produced so wonderful a transformation ?
One of those masks of dark red golden wire, so fine as to be
almost impalpable, and wrought by fingers of such cunning
skill that while it concealed the natural skin of the face, every
lineament and even every sweep and dimple was copied, as
if the moulder had been working in wax—the eye looking
through as naturally as in the ordinary face, and even the
very play of the lips permitted. That strange red light
which had seemed to permeate the whole face and affect even
the eyes, had merely been the red metallic glitter of the gold,
leaving little work for the imagination to complete a picture
fascinating as unnatural.

"Great God !—can such beauty be real ?" broke out Les;

lie, when he had gazed for one instant on the splendid vision
before him. "Matchless, peerless, glorious woman! Let
me come nearer! Let me look longer on God's master-
work, if I even die at the sight !"

Here was the faithful lover of Josephine Harris half an
hour before,—and in what a situation! Oh man, man, what
an eye for miscellaneous beauty is that with which your sex
is gifted! All Mormons at heart, it is to be feared, however
a more self-denying canon may be observed perforce! It is
not certain that Tom Leslie would have run away with his
new divinity, had the chance been offered at that moment;
and it is not certain that he would *not* have done so. Very
fortunately, the opportunity was wanting. Very fortunately,
too, the storm had not yet ceased altogether, and the two
ladies in the other room were likely to be too busy in restoring and being restored, to hear very clearly what was going
on within.

"Back !" said the sharp voice of the sorceress, at the im-
passioned tone of the last words and that clasping of the
hands which told that the subject might be kneeling the next
moment. "Back! No nearer, on your life! I have not
the power of life and death, but I may have the power of
happiness and misery. Go!—or wish that you had done so,
till the very day you die !"

Her arm was stretched out with a queenly gesture, at once
of warning and command. Tom Leslie obeyed, with such an
effort as one sometimes makes in a forced arousing from sleep.
He took one more glance at the motionless face and form, then
dashed through the curtain and let it fall behind him. Joe
Harris had partially recovered from her excitement, and sat
beside Bell, with her face on the latter's shoulder. She roused
herself and even attempted a laugh with some success, when
the voice of Leslie was heard; and if for one instant the alle
giance of the young man had wavered in the presence of the
unnatural and the overwhelming, there was something in that
bright, clear, good face, only temporarily shadowed by her
late excitement, calculated to restore him at once to thought
and to truth.

With the heavy crash of thunder which had accompanied

if it had not caused the fright of the young girl, the storm
seemed to have culminated and spent itself; and by this time
the rain had nearly ceased. Not a word passed between the
three as to what had occurred to either—any conversation 'on
that subject was naturally reserved for another place and a
later hour. The black girl came out again from behind the
curtain and received with a "Thank you, Monsieur!" and a
curtsey the half eagle which dropped into her hand. Leslie
left the ladies alone for a moment, ran down to the door and
found a carriage; and in a few moments, without further
adventure, the three were on their way up-town, the journalist
to return again to his evening avocations, after accompanying
the two, whose disordered nerves he scarcely yet dared trust
alone, to their place of destination.

If during that ride the hand of Josephine Harris, a little
hot and feverish from late excitement, accidentally fell again
into his own and rested there as if it rather liked the position
—whose business was it, except their own?

CHAPTER XV.

A Peep at Camp Lyon and the Two Hundredth Regiment—Discipline and the Dice-Box—How Seven Hundred Men Can Be Squeezed into Three.

"I am going to West Falls again in a few days—that is, if
we do not get orders for Washington," Colonel Egbert Crawford said, speaking to his cousin, a few chapters back, as may
be remembered. By which he meant, of course, if he meant
anything, that the Two Hundredth Regiment, with the raising of which he had been charged by Major-General Governor
Morgan, was in a high state of discipline as well as fully up
to the maximum in numbers, and burning to go down to the
field of carnage and revenge the deaths of those foully slaughtered by rebel hands

t may be interesting to know exactly what *was* the condition of the Two Hundredth Regiment, at that exact time—
how many it numbered—what was its proficiency in drill—
what was the appearance of the camp at which it was quartered—and how laboriously Colonel Crawford was engaged
in bringing it up to the highest standard of perfection for
citizen soldiery. For this purpose, it will be well to look in
at the encampment, with the eyes of some persons from the
city who visited it on Sunday the 29th of June—the very day
on which McClellan, from sheer lack of troops, abandoned
the White House, necessarily destroying so much valuable
property, losing for the time the last hope of the capture of
Richmond, and falling back on the line of the James River.

The Two Hundredth Regiment lay at "Camp Lyon," (as
it may be designated for the purposes of this chronicle)—a
locality on Long Island, a few miles eastward from the City
Hall of Brooklyn, and easily accessible by one of the lines of
horse-cars running from Fulton Ferry. It had been some two
months established ; recruiting for the regiment was said to
be going on very rapidly ; "only a few more men wanted" was
the burden of the song sung in the advertising columns of the
morning papers ; rations for some seven hundred men were
continually furnished for it, by the Quartermaster's Department ; the Colonel made flattering reports of it every day or
two, to the higher military authorities in the city, and at least
once a week to the still higher authorities at Albany ; and a
political Brigadier-General was reported to have gone down
and reviewed it, once or twice, coming back eminently satisfied
with its numbers, discipline and performances.

The visitors from the city, who, having no other connection
whatever with the progress of this story, may be fobbed off
with the very ordinary names of Smith and Brown,—reached
the camp at about four o'clock on that Sunday afternoon,
having waited until that late hour in the day for the purpose
of avoiding the noon-tide heat, and being anxious to be present at the evening drill, which was supposed to take place
in the neighborhood of six o'clock. An acquaintance of
theirs, an officer in the Two Hundredth, one Lieutenant
Woodruff, had several times invited them to "run down to

14

camp and see him before he went away," promising to do the
honors of the encampment in the best manner compatible
with the duties of a "fellow busy all the time, you know."

Alighting from the vehicle, Smith and Brown found the
camp stretching before them, scarcely so picturesque as they
had anticipated, but with enough of the military air about
its green sod and conical tents, to make it rather varied and
pleasing to a couple of "cits" who had not looked upon the
extended army pageant around Washington, or seen anything more of war than could be observed in a turn-out of
the First Division on the Fourth of July.   On a broad level,
stretching back for a quarter of a mile from the railroad-
track, and terminating in a strip of noble oak woods, the
tents of the encampment were pitched, forty or fifty in number, not too white and cleanly-looking, even at a distance,
and decidedly dingy and yellow when brought to a nearer
view.   Some attempt had been made at forming them into
lines, with regular alleys between ; the hospital-tent at some
distance in the rear, distinguished by a yellow flag hanging
listlessly from a pole in front ; and the Colonel's large round
tent or marquee prominent in the centre, a small American
flag before it, doing its best to wave in the slight sea air that
came in over the Long Island hills.   Groups of soldiers,
variously disposed, dotted the space between the tents or sat
at the doors, chatting with male or female civilians, or their
own wives and daughters, who had run down to see them as
an amusement for Sunday afternoon ; while sentinels paced
backward and forward along certain lines and offered an uncertain amount of inconvenience to those who wished to
traverse the camp-grounds in one direction or another.

Smith and Brown, looking for Woodruff and finding it a
matter of some difficulty to discover him, paced up and down
among the tents, wherever the sentinels permitted, looking in
at the doors of those canvas cottages and observing the humors
which denoted that the occupants had been the possessors
of plenty of time for other purposes than drill, however proficient they might have become in that military necessity.
Scarcely one of the alleys between the rows of tents but had
its street-name, stuck up on a piece of chalked or charcoaled

board at the entrance—from the ambitious "Broadway" to
the aristocratic "Fifth Avenue" and the doubtful "Mercer
Street." Many of the tents bore equally significant inscrip-
tion, from the "City Hall" (where some scion of an alderman
probably made his warlike abode), to the "Astor House", and
the St. Nicholas" (where perhaps some depreciated son of
snobbery was known to have his quarters), and the "Hotel
de Coffee and Cakes," suggestive of inmates from the less
pretentious precincts of the city. Within the tents, as Smith
and Brown took the liberty of looking in, a variety of spectacles were discovered. Straw seemed to be an almost universal commodity—quite as indispensable there as in pig-
pens or railroad-cars, and next to straw, perhaps battered
trunks and very cheap pine tables predominated. Greasy
kettles and dishes could be discovered just under the flap of
the tent, in many instances; and here and there a tent would
be passed, emitting odors of rancid grease, stale tobacco and
personal foulness, not at all appetizing to visitors unfamiliar
with the gutters of Mackerelville or the hold of a ship in the
horse-latitudes.

In some of the tents the men were asleep on the tables, in
others on the trunks, in still others on the straw. In a few
Smith and Brown saw soldiers drinking; in others, in positions suggestive of being very drunk, had they found them
elsewhere than in a well-regulated camp; in still others
playing cards for pennies, furtively behind the flaps of the
tent or openly in the vicinity of the door. They caught
fragments of broad oaths from a few, and snatches of obscene
stories from a few others; and taken altogether, the impression of the Two Hundredth being in a high state of
discipline or a very excellent sanitary condition, was not
strongly forced upon their minds. This impression was not
strengthened, when, being directed by one of the sentries to
the hospital-tent as a place where they might be likely at that
moment to find Lieutenant Woodruff,—they failed to discover
him there, but did not fail to discover one corporal keeping
guard in that sanitary domicil, so drunk that he was asleep
and so drunkenly abusive when they woke him that they

were glad to permit him to fall back again into his beastly
slumber.

At length they found Lieutenant Woodruff, who had just
returned from escorting another party of friends to the cars,
on their way back to town. He seemed glad to see them,
though not enthusiastic in his demonstrations—invited them
to the tent in which he messed with some brother officers—
and they took that direction for a rest after their hot promenade.

Somewhat to the apparent mortification of Woodruff, when
they reached the tent none of the brother officers to whom he
had promised to introduce his friends, were to be found ; but
they had left their traces behind them. Two or three empty
bottles and as many uncleaned glasses lay about the table,
and the remains of spilt liquor wetted and stained the boards
of the seats, while a very dirty pack of cards, half on the
table and the remainder on the ground, showed that the
officers were not only a little unscrupulous as to the character
of their Sunday amusements, but equally indifferent as to the
cleanliness of the tools with which they performed the arduous labors of old-sledge, euchre and division-loo. Woodruff
cleared away the debris from the table, and flung it into one
corner with some petulance which did not escape the notice
of his visitors. Finally part of a box of bad cigars was introduced, and among the fumes engendered by those indispensable " weeds," a little conversation followed.

" Well, when do you get off ?" asked Smith, who had been
very anxious to come on that Sunday, instead of waiting for
the next, under the impression that the regiment might move
at any time and thus deprive them of the visit. He had been
led to suppose so, partially from conversations with Woodruff
in the city, and partially by the statements in the newspapers,
before alluded to, made with reference to this and other
" favorite regiments."

" Get off !" answered Woodruff, with no concealment of
the vexation in his tone. "Humph ! well, I think we shall
need to get *on* a little faster, before we get off at all !"

" Not full yet, eh ?" asked Brown.

" Not *exactly*," was the answer of the Lieutenant, with a

satirical emphasis on the second word which indicated that some other would have been quite as well in place.

"Why, I thought you were!" said Smith. "The papers had you up to seven hundred some time ago, and with all your big posters and advertisements and the large bounties offered, you ought to be bringing them in very rapidly.".

"Yes, I suppose so!" answered Woodruff. "We *ought* to do a good many things in this world, that we do not find it convenient to do. We *ought* to have been full, and off to Washington, a month ago, and would have been, if there had been any management."

"Why you speak as if you were discouraged and dissatisfied," said Brown, "and not at all as you talked to us when in the city a few days ago."

"No, probably not," answered the Lieutenant. "Well, the fact is, boys, that I have been lying to you like—(and here he used a very hard word not necessary to be recorded.) We have *all* been lying; but to you, at least, I mean to make a clean breast of it. I did not suppose you would come down, and while you kept at a distance I thought we might as well keep up a good reputation. Now that you are here, you have not half an eye if you do not know that 'Camp Lyon' is a humbug, and that there is no discipline or anything else in it that *should* be here. I am going to get out of it, if I can with any honor."

"What is the matter?" asked Smith, very much disappointed, and very much discouraged at the key which the situation of Camp Lyon seemed to offer to the corresponding situation of many others of the crack recruiting stations depended upon for filling up the reduced ranks of the army.

"What is the matter? Everything!" said Woodruff, fairly launched out in an exposure of the abuses of the recruiting service, for which he had not before had a fair and *safe* opportunity. "Half the men are good for nothing, and almost all the officers worse. We could get along with worthless *men*, and perhaps make soldiers of them, if we only had officers worth their salt. Field or line, there is not one in three that knows when a 'shoulder-arms' is correctly made; and there is no more attempt at either study or practice than

there would be if we were a hunting party encamped in the
Northern woods. Commissions have been issued to anybody
supposed to possess some political influence ; and subordinate
commissions have been promised by the higher officers to
any one who offered to bring in a certain number of rap-
scallions or pay down a certain sum of money. Those who
are not drunken, are lazy ; and the men know about as much
of wholesome discipline as a hog knows of holy-water. I
have tried to do a little better with some of the squads of my
own company; but I think that complaints have been made
that I 'overworked' the men, and I have fallen into decidedly
bad odor with the good people up at the big house yonder."

"And who are *they?*" asked Brown, wofully ignorant of
the details of recruiting in 1862. "And what are they doing
up at the 'big house,' as you call it ?"

"Eh? you haven't been in there, have you?" said Woodruff. "Come along then, and see. Of course you know that
I must refer to our gallant Colonel and the other leading
officers at the head of the regiment; and of course you are
not so green as not to know that the big house beyond the
railroad track, there, is a tavern. Come along and let us see
what Colonel Crawford and the rest of them happen to be
doing; and by the time that is over we shall have our
'evening parade,' which you must certainly see before you go
home."

Escorted by the Lieutenant, the two citizens took their
way to the "big house"—a hotel standing on the north side
of the railroad track and very near it—a wooden building of
two stories, with a piazza in front and at the east end, and
flanked by a row of horse-sheds indicating that there was
some dependence made upon the patronage of fast drivers
stopping there on race days or when trotting was peculiarly
good on the pike or the plank. Before the house paced two
sentries, with muskets at the shoulder, though what they were
guarding was not so clear, as every one passed who wished
to do so, whether in uniform or citizen's dress. Behind the
corner of the piazza, eastward, an officer was leaning back in
his chair against the clap-boards, with his hat over his eyes
and apparently asleep ; and a few feet from him a sergeant,

distinguishable by three dingy stripes on his arm that should have been laid upon his back, was toying, not too decently, with a woman whose looks and manners both proclaimed her one of the " necessary evils" of a modern community.

" Do they allow such actions as that—right here in public, and in the very presence of the officers ?" asked Smith, whose education had possibly been a little neglected in some other particulars, as Brown's had been in the details of the military profession.

" Guess so !" was the significant reply of Woodruff. " Come up stairs !" and the party passed on. As they did so, they looked through a door to the left, and saw a bar of unplaned boards extending the whole length of a spacious room, with half a dozen attendants behind it and as many beer kegs and whiskey decanters pouring out their contents. Mingled with here and there a civilian, the whole front of the bar was full of soldiers, all apparently drinking, and drinking again, and drinking yet again, nibbling cheese, crackers and smoked-beef meanwhile, apparently to keep up the necessary thirst. "Fire and fall back !" seemed to be a military axiom not always observed by the rank and file of the Two Hundredth, as many of them kept their places and went on with their guzzling, with a determination worthy of a much better cause. But it was occasionally observed, after all, for there were a few who had been overcome by the heat of the bibu-latory conflict, and who had relapsed into partial helpless-ness in chairs around the walls; and there were others who began to stagger and talk thickly at the counter, growing obscure and maudlin in their oaths, and shaking hands alto-gether too often, indicating the sleepy stage as very soon to follow.

As the two friends and their conductor passed up-stairs, they noticed two officers in somewhat loud conversation, not far from the landing and near the door of a side-room, on the handle of the door of which one of them held his hand a por-tion of the time. Without any effort, some of the words of their conversation could easily be heard; and Smith and Brown, who had no more than the average of that creditable delicacy which hears nothing intended only for other ears;

caught some words which will bear setting down here as
affording an additional clue to the state of discipline.

"That," said Woodruff, giving Smith a nudge as they
came to the head of the stairs, speaking in a low tone, and
pointing to the taller of the two men, who stood with his
side-face presented at the moment,—"that is Colonel Crawford; and the other, the shorter man, is Captain Lowndes,
who has been recruiting for the regiment at the Park. If I
was in better odor with the Colonel, I would introduce you;
but come on."

Smith and Jones did *not* "come on" at the instant, and
what they caught from the two officers was the following:

"Not *one* in a week?" asked the Colonel, in a tone min-
gling surprise and anger. "Not one?" D—n it!"

"I am sorry to say, not one," was the reply of Captain
Lowndes. "They nearly all sing the same tune, however."

"Well, it won't do for *us*, you know!" said the Colonel.
"Another review, and by some officer who was not a d—d
lawyer blockhead, might be awkward!" Colonel Crawford
either forgot, at that moment, that he had any connection
with the legal profession, or he chose to ignore the fact; and
it is not to be supposed that his subordinate reminded him
of it. "We must have a paragraph in the —— to-morrow
morning," he went on, naming an influential daily, "giving
the regiment another 'blow.' If it does not get us any
recruits, it will at least make the thing look better at Albany.
Hum—where's Dalton?"

"The Adjutant went to Boston yesterday," was the response of Lowndes. "Said he had business, though as he
had a girl with him when he stepped on board the boat, I
suspect his business was rather personal."

"D—n him!" muttered the Colonel, between his teeth.
Then louder, to Lowndes: "I thought I told you to request
him, if you saw him, not to leave the city again without permission from *me!* It seems you *have* seen him; and why
were my orders not obeyed?" The Colonel spoke now with
great dignity, and drew himself up so that the eagles on his
shoulder-straps were at least half an inch higher than when
he was squatted down into easy position

"Your orders *were* obeyed," answered the Captain. "I *did* tell him."

"And what did he say?" asked the Colonel, lifting his eyebrows with some appearance of interest.

"He said," replied the Captain, enunciating his words very clearly, as if he had no objection to their producing their full weight on his superior—"That Colonel Egbert Crawford might go to h—ll, and he would go to Boston."

"Did he?—d—n him!" said the Colonel, who seemed to have a small bottle of profanity lately uncorked, or one that he certainly was not in the habit of uncorking in the presence of those on whom he wished to produce a different impression.

"Yes he did," answered the Captain. "He said a little more. Perhaps you would like to have *that*, while I am at it?"

"That?—yes, out with the whole of it!" spoke the Colonel, with another oath which need not be recorded here as any additional seasoning.

"He took occasion to remark, where the lady who was with him could hear it," Lowndes went on—"that he didn't care a d—n for you, and that you dare not make a complaint against him at Albany, a bit more than you dare jump into a place that is even hotter than the weather is here to-day."

"Did he—the infernal hound!" broke out the Colonel, his dark brows literally corrugated with rage. "I'll teach him whether I *dare* or not, before I am forty-eight hours older!" But either there *was* something behind the curtain, or Colonel Egbert Crawford was a man of most angelic temper, for the moment after he broke out into a laugh that was not of the most musical order, and said: "Oh, well—Dalton is a pretty good fellow, after all, and perhaps the next Adjutant would be a worse one for the regiment."

With these words Colonel Egbert Crawford passed into the side room by the door of which he had been standing, while Captain Lowndes touched his hat to him very slightly and went on to the larger room towards which the others were proceeding. As the Colonel swung back the door, Smith caught a very quick glance within, and saw a table, with bottles, a pack of cards, a couple of dice-boxes, and four or five persons seated, lounging and smoking. The party appeared

to him as if they might have been interrupted in a little harmless Sunday afternoon amusement, and as if they were only
waiting for the return of the Colonel to the room, to renew
that amusement in a very pleasant and effective manner. That
impression was not removed by his hearing, after he had passed
through the open door into the other room, a suspicious sound,
like the rattling of dice and another sound very like the chink-
ing of coin, proceeding from the smaller apartment.

Smith and Brown found very little in the officers' room,
dignified by the name of "regimental head-quarters," demanding particular record. There were two red pine tables set together and forming a counter, behind which the regimental
officers were supposed to be located; and on the end of the
tables nearest the front of the house was a small desk, with
pigeon-holes, at which, by the same fiction, the Adjutant was
supposed to be always sitting, performing the arduous duties
of his office. Supported by nails in the ceiling were two flag-
staffs, their butts shaped to fit the muzzles of short rifles, and
from the upper end of each depending one of the "guidons"
of the regiment, gorgeously blue in color and lettered in shaded
gold—understood to be the gift of certain ladies who properly
appreciated the talents and devotion of the officers and the
hopeful prospects of the regiment under formation. Behind
the tables was a mantel; and on it stood two decanters
partially filled with liquor, a plate of crackers and another of
cheese. A Lieutenant was seated at the Adjutant's desk, engaged in filling up blank leaves-of-absence for each in turn, of
a disorderly crowd of twenty or thirty soldiers who pressed
forward from the door to receive them. Two or three of this
crowd presented former leaves, to have them extended. One
of these was refused, the Lieutenant laboring under some sort
of impression that a private who had been three weeks under
enlistment, and absent all that time on leave, would not
become very proficient in drill unless he spent at least one
week at the encampment before marching. The wronged
man did not appear to take the refusal very much to heart,
however: he merely remarked to one of the others, loud enough
for the Lieutenant to have heard if he had been very observant,
that "he didn't care two cusses for the leave: he would go off

when he liked and stay as long as he liked, and he should like to see anybody smart enough to stop him."

At the mantel, taking a quiet drink with half a dozen civilian friends who had been admitted behind the tables, stood a tall, soldierly-looking man, pointed out by Woodruff as Lieut. Colonel Burns. Unaccountably, he wore no straps on the shoulder, his blue blouse looking as if it was thrown on for use instead of show, and his whole demeanor that of a man who, if opportunity should only be given him, would be a soldier. He had his sword-belts at the waist, however, and also wore his sword, as if he had some indefinite idea that something would thereby be gained in an *appearance* of efficiency for the regiment.

" Have you seen almost enough ?" asked Lieutenant Woodruff, of the two citizens.

" Quite enough !" said both in a breath

" Well, time is just up," said the Lieutenant. " And in good time comes the drum-beat for evening parade. Come along, and see what it is like. I must leave you, but you can see the display without me."

A couple of snare-drums were rattling somewhere among the tents, and the shrill notes of a light infantry bugle sounded. Lieut. Colonel Burns buckled his sword belts a little tighter and straightened himself to a soldierly bearing, as he left the room with his friends. A sergeant took down the guidons, and all, except the one Lieutenant at the desk and two or three soldiers who did not consider the call as of sufficient consequence, followed them down to the parade-ground in front of the camp. Col. Egbert Crawford seemed to be like the two or three soldiers named, and not to consider the call of consequence enough to demand any attention on his part ; for he did not, at least during the stay of Smith and Brown, emerge from the privacy of the inner room or make any movement to superintend the "dress parade."

That "dress parade" completed the experience of Smith and Brown ; and it completed, at the same time, their knowledge of the numbers and efficiency of the Two Hundredth Regiment that was "almost ready to march." In squads of from ten to twenty-five, the soldiers gathered from their

slovenly tents, until the observers could count something
more than two hundred. Then by squads and afterwards in
what was intended as a "regimental formation," they went
through a series of marchings, countermarchings and facings,
with about the proficiency which would be shown by the
same number of entirely raw recruits, and with the same
proportion of the most obvious blunderings that used to be
exhibited by the "slab-companies" at the "general trainings"
or "general musters" in the country sections, when a lamentable caricature upon military spirit was kept up, in the years
following the War of 1812.

Not a musket was to be seen in the hands of one of these
men, except the few sentries. They "had not been furnished," as the explanation was sure to be given afterwards
when the regiment was discovered to be an undisciplined
mob! They would probably not be "furnished" until just at
the moment when the regiment should be forced to move, and
then they would be put into hands liable to be called on to
use them in battle within a week—those hands knowing no
more of the management of the deadly instrument of modern
warfare, than so many Sioux or South Sea Islanders might
have known of watch-making or extracting the cube-root.

And yet with these men, and in this manner, the armies of
the republic were being recruited ; and on the deeds in arms
wrought by these men, possibly in the very first conflict into
which they were rushed like huddled sheep, the eyes of the
military nations of Europe were to be turned with anxious
interest. They were to fight, too, against a race of men to
whom deadly weapons had been familiar from childhood, and
who would consequently make soldiers, to the full extent of
their capability, with one-half the training which was to
these Northern men an absolute necessity ! Is it any wonder
that we have occasionally met with a Bull Run or a Second
Field of Manassas, with this shameful waste of our opportunities and our war-material?

Smith and Brown left "Camp Lyon," before the comple-
tion of the "dress parade," with a dim consciousness of being
painfully disenchanted in a very important particular.

"Do you know, Smith," said Brown, as they were rolling

along in the car, homeward—"that I doubt whether there are three hundred men in that regiment, absentees and all—instead of seven hundred as the papers report?"

"Humph," said Smith, "it seems to be all a humbug together! But I wonder what becomes of the extra pay issued to seven hundred men, when there are only three hundred entitled to receive it? And I wonder what becomes of all the extra rations that are drawn for them every day? Somebody must be making something out of it—eh? I wonder if there are any more regiments in the same condition?"

"Probably!" said Brown. Whereupon the two citizens fell into a very deep and silent train of thought, leaving us no additional speech to record.

Other people than Smith, at about that time, felt like propounding the same queries as to the disposition of extra pay and rations. Some of those queries, which *have* been propounded, have not yet been answered. When they are, if that happy period ever arrives, we may know something more of the channels and sluices through which the wealth of the richest nation on the globe has ebbed away, leaving such inconsiderable results to show for the expenditure.

And yet Colonel Egbert Crawford, visiting the city two hours afterwards, and dropping in at two or three favorite resorts of men who talked horse, war and politics, on his way to the house of his cousin,—bore himself bravely under his weight of uniform, and more than once threw in a pardonable boast over the services he was rendering the country, the sacrifices he was making, and the rapid growth and efficiency of the Two Hundredth Regiment.

"All brass is not fashioned and moulded in foundries, where men do swelter like to those standing in the flames of the fiery furnace," says an old writer, Arnold of Thorndean, "but much of it doth become shaped in the human countenance."

CHAPTER XVI.

Two Modes of Writing Romances—More of the Up-town
Mystery—A Watch, an Escape, and a Police Post
Mortem on a Vacant House.

The question may have been asked, before this point in
narration, by some of those who have been induced to follow
the progress of this story—What has become of some of the
prominent characters first introduced, Dexter Ralston, the
stalwart Virginian, and the girl Kate, who seemed at that
time to be so closely identified with the movements of the
"red woman." The curiosity is a natural one, whether
there really was such a secret of disloyalty, hidden away
either in the house on Prince Street or that on East 5—, as
justified Tom Leslie and Walter Harding in their long ride
at midnight and their subsequent interview with Police-
Superintendent Kennedy. To some extent this question can
be answered, at this point; but there will still remain some
mysteries unexplainable until the end of this narration, and
even some impossible to elucidate until the close of the war
and the re-union of Northern and Southern society on the
old basis, makes it possible to reveal all that may have
occurred during the conflict.

There are two modes in which romances can be written.
The first, and perhaps the more popular, is that in which no
bound whatever is set by either probability or conscience—in
which the narrator assumes to know what never could be
known except to an omniscient being, and to describe such
circumstances as never could have occurred in any world
under the same general regulations as our own. To this
writer, no doors are barred, and from him the secret of no
heart can be hidden. He has no difficulty whatever in re-
tracing the path of history, back to the days of Michael Paleo-
logus or Timour the Tartar, and describing the viands set
upon their tables and the thoughts that may have entered
their brains; while in events of the present day he finds no
more trouble in describing circumstantially the last moments

of a traveller dying alone at the North Pole or in the midst of the most trackless waste of Sahara. The manner in which he became possessed of the facts narrated, is held to be a matter of very little consequence; and if he lacks the opportunity of calling other witnesses or surrounding circumstances to corroborate him, he at least is removed from the fear of any authoritative contradiction. The reader, of course, would sometimes be grateful for a little insight into what is so impenetrably hidden; and if the links binding the narrator to his subject were made a little plainer to the naked eye, perhaps more general satisfaction might be given. When, for instance, in the "Legend of the Terrible Tower," Sir Bronzeface the Implacable is shown as threatening the Lady Charmengarde with the most cruel tortures his slighted love and growing hate can devise—when the very words of that atrocious monster are set down as carefully as if they had been taken from his lips by the rapid pencil of the stenographer—and when in the context we learn that in the midst of his threatenings, the thousand barrels of gunpowder secretly stored in another part of the castle for the purpose of arming a million of retainers to make a deadly onslaught on the stronghold of his hated rival the Lord of Hardcheek, suddenly takes fire, and the castle, with both the interlocutors and all others who could possibly be present, is seen hurled into infinitesimal fragments,—there is some unavoidable curiosity in the mind of the reader, at this juncture, to know precisely how these very words and actions became known to the narrator, as well as how the gunpowder was manufactured in the year of grace nine hundred and eighty-four.

For corresponding knowledge of events in the actual present, the believers in clairvoyance may be able to offer some explanation; but, unfortunately or the reverse, the believers in effective clairvoyance are in a very meagre minority; and the world will cling a little tenaciously to the belief that what cannot be seen, heard, or otherwise realized by the recognized natural senses, cannot be definitely ascertained. Let it not be for one moment supposed, meanwhile, that romances constructed on such bases will be less popular than those which have more reason and probability at the bottom; for the ma-

jority of novel-readers desire to be frightened, mystified or
idly amused; and perhaps that writer who makes *thought* a
condition of reading and understanding what he writes, com-
mits the most silly of crimes against his own pocket and
reputation.

The other mode in which romances can be written, is that
in which the writer only details that which he has enjoyed an
opportunity to know, embodying with them such speculations
and reflections as seem legitimately to grow out of the subject. This mode is unquestionably an unprofitable one to
employ; but unfortunately this narration can be conducted
on no other. Actual events and conversations *only* are
given, and no speculations as to *what might have been* can be
indulged. It might have been very easy to depict a disloyal
or "secesh" household in this city, and a club of fashionable
people with pro-slavery sympathies, meeting periodically, with
grips, signs and passwords, and exercising an injurious influence on the National cause by holding clandestine correspondence with rebels in the revolted States. That such households have existed in this city during the entire struggle, and
that such combinations of disloyal men have been doing their
worst to cripple the government and distract the nation, no
rational man doubts for a moment. But *no loyal citizen has
been admitted behind the curtain, in either of the supposable
instances.* No one could have been, and still remained loyal,
without making such public revelations in the interest of
patriotism, that any pretended *private* revelation must necessarily have become a farce. No one, especially, would have
held any such secret for months, and then divulged it in the
ambiguous mode of a romance, while arbitrary arrests and
unexplained imprisonments were making the once free States
of the Old Union a second Venice. Suspicious circumstances
have been observed, and suspicious persons put under watch;
but if anything more than mere suspicion has been reached,
the disloyal persons themselves, and the government, are the
only parties who possess the information.

All this, to say that the materials for this narration have
not been gathered from disloyal sources or found in disloyal
company, and that, as a consequence, it does not enter within

doors closed to true men, by any magic key of the mind or the imagination. And if any mystery suggested, from that cause remains even partially unsolved, truth and loyalty, and not a desire for mystification, must supply the explanation.

And now to detail, very briefly, what is further known of the house on East 5— Street, and its occupation

It has already been related that Superintendent Kennedy, in spite of his slighting replies to the two young men, did not really undervalue their information, and that two vigilant detectives, with assistants, were entrusted with the duty of watching the two houses. "L—— and another good man", had been ordered to take charge of the house on East 5— Street, and they entered upon their duties at once. Not as ordinary policemen, of course, for such a plan would necessarily have defeated any chance of successful observation. It was as a very modest private gentleman, elderly, with a cane and a slight limp, that L—— managed to lounge by the house repeatedly within the space of an hour; while his assistant, dressed in the clothes of a glass-mender, and with a box of the proper cut strapped on his back, haunted that street and invited business with a cry which the boys irreverently designated "glass pudding!" During the two hours thus spent, no person entered or left the house, nor was there a sign of life at any of the windows,—though what eyes may really have been watching from those closed blinds, it is quite impossible to say. Enough that they kept their watch closely until the coming on of the same heavy thunder-storm which burst upon the visitors to the sorceress in Prince Street; and that when the first drops of that shower were falling, conceiving themselves very unlikely to be repaid for a thorough wetting, they temporarily withdrew to the Station-house, or, as the act would now be expressed, "raised the blockade" for a very limited period.

Within five minutes after their departure, and when the wind and the rain had fairly begun to play together at rough gymnastics in the street, there was evidence that eyes probably *had* been observing the elderly gentleman with the limp, walking past the house a little too frequently. At all events, a man of tall figure, wrapped in an oil-skin coat, and

15

with a round black hat and umbrella, emerged from the front
door and dashed rapidly up the street. He was gone but a
few minutes, and returned in the very height of the storm, in
a carriage which drew up at the door. Perhaps ten minutes
more, and some of the neighbors, who had been observing
these singular movements, saw the same tall man, with an
elderly lady and two younger ones, come out and enter the
carriage, which, after taking on two large trunks, drove away
at ordinary speed. The conclusion to which these good
people came, was that the party were obliged to go out in
the storm for the purpose of catching one of the late evening
trains out of the city; and they may have been very nearly
correct in the conjecture.

The storm passed over, and the summer evening came on.
The two detectives came back to their places, varying their
disguises for the evening. The house seemed all quiet, as
before, and L—— came to the conclusion that there was either
no one within or that the inmates were disposed to lie very
close, as they did not even open the front windows to admit
the clear evening air, cooled by the shower, or to look at the
splendid sunset sky. So time passed on until nine o'clock,
when the two detectives agreed to adopt the "ride-and-tie"
principle—one keeping strict watch until midnight and the
other until morning. This arrangement was duly carried out;
and L——, who had taken the turn till midnight, again resumed his place at six o'clock. All was quiet—no one had
entered or left the house, and L—— became thoroughly satisfied that it must be unoccupied. He might have haunted the
house in one disguise or another, retaining the same correct
opinion, until doomsday, had not one of the neighboring
houses contained one of those inquisitive gentlemen (sometimes depreciatingly called "meddlers") who can never be
content without knowing the business of all others, better than
their own.

This person, partially an invalid, and much confined to the
house and to very short walks in the neighborhood,—had observed the surveillance of the day before, still continued that
morning; and he had also observed the episode of the carriage
in the midst of the thunder-storm, of which the officer was as

yet happily oblivious. Putting all the appearances together, he concluded that there had been some accusation, a watch and an escape; and about nine o'clock that morning he strolled out to the sidewalk; accosted the detective; informed him, with a knowing wink of the eye, that he understood the whole matter; and finished by advising him that "the birds had flown," and of the particular time when they took wing. As appendiary matter, he also informed the detective that the house was a furnished one belonging to a wealthy grocer who had just gone to Europe with his family—that it had been rented for a few weeks past to some very odd people—and that he had wondered at their being no attention paid to it before, as he was satisfied it was a receptacle for stolen goods.

To say that L—— was surprised at the first part of this intelligence, would be to say nothing; to say that he was mortified and enraged at being obliged to make such a report to the Superintendent, would be to put the case very mildly; and to say that he felt like amputating the head of a large-sized nail with his teeth, would only being doing justice to his feelings at this juncture.

The communicative neighbor finally informed him that he doubted whether the house was fastened, from the suddenness of the departure the day before; and on the hint the detective acted. The front door was found to be secured, but only by the latch-key bolt; and the area door was entirely unfastened. They entered and explored the house. It was a neatly furnished modern building, with everything in its place and nothing to mark any hasty departure of occupants, except a dinner-table left setting in the dining-room, with food on the plates and evidence that the meal had been left unfinished.

No clothing or other articles that could have belonged to the late inmates had been left behind, except half a dozen books, one of which was Simms' "History of South Carolina," another a copy of that odd jumble of short sketches published three or four years ago by Miss Martha Haines Butt, and a third one of Marion Harland's novels—"The Hidden Path." Part of a letter was found, the signature gone and all one side burned off, as if it had been used in lighting a cigar or a gas-burner, but still showing the date; "Richmond, Va.,

C. S. A., May 28th, 1862," and apparently written by a young officer in the Confederate army to his sister in this city. No other traces were found, though these were quite enough to increase the chagrin of the detectives, in the knowledge that they had allowed persons to escape who certainly must have been in correspondence with the rebel capital; and with this the crest-fallen L—— and his subordinate prepared to make their report to a superior not much in the habit of excusing failure or making allowance for extenuating circumstances.

It is to be believed that the inquisitive and communicative neighbor enjoyed the best night's rest he had known for a twelvemonth, on the night following, after this conference with a couple of detectives and this peep into a house that had really excited his curiosity. It is doubtful, meanwhile, whether the grocer landlord, informed by his agent, by the next mail, of the exodus of his tenants without liquidation, saw the matter in so enjoyable a light.

Of course, with the fugitives given some fifteen hours start and the use of modern railroad facilities, any thought of pursuit would have been folly, even had there been any conclusive data upon which to found proceedings for their apprehension. And with such meagre and unsatisfactory results closed that portion of the supposed secession mystery—at least for the time. After events showed that the "red woman" disappeared from Prince Street on the same night, whether in company with her former acquaintances or alone. What after-glimpses were caught of any of the other persons concerned, will be shown at a later period of this narration.

CHAPTER XVII.

LOOKING FOR JOHN CRAWFORD, OF DURYEA'S ZOUAVES—THE MORNING OF THE FIRST OF JULY—MCCLELLAN AND HIS GENERALS—THE FIRST BATTLE OF MALVERN—VICTORY IN RETREAT.

IT will be remembered that Richard Crawford, lying help-lessly on his sofa and murmuring over the bodily disability which at once entailed idleness and suffering, made it one of the grounds of comparisons injurious to himself, that his brother John was on service in Virginia with the Advance Guard—better known, perhaps, as "Duryea's Zouaves"—that gallant corps designated by the rebels as the "red-legged devils," and spoken of by every European officer who has seen their action in battle, as the equals of any body of regulars of any service in the world. The claims of business alone had prevented his being in the ranks of that regiment, if in no higher position, when they marched down Broadway on their departure in the summer of 1861, receiving the merited compliment of being the finest-looking body of men, as to physique and probable endurance, that had ever passed over that procession-trodden pavement, and headed by a gallant officer (Colonel, now General, Abram Duryea) who had been so largely instrumental in making the Seventh Regiment famous for drill, discipline and readiness for any service.

John Crawford, a younger brother of Richard (his *only* brother, in fact—the whole living family being comprised in Richard, Isabella and John) had left his lucrative employment as a confidential dry-goods clerk, in one of the largest down-town establishments, and joined the Advance Guard. He had participated in nearly or quite all the battles shared in by that lucky corps, from Big Bethel, where they performed the wonderful feat of re-forming under fire in the space of four minutes, after having been thrown into complete disorder by the discharge from an ambuscade of artillery,—to the severe conflicts of the Peninsula, in McClellan's advance upon Richmond; and only once had he been wounded, ever slightly.

He seemed to bear a charmed life; and there was something
in the rollick and dash of his letters home, always full charged
with the very sense of bravery and physical enjoyment, well
calculated to arouse the feeling; if not the envy, of a brother
quite as patriotic and probably quite as brave as himself, but
kept back by circumstances and afterwards by ill-health from
participating in the same glorious conflicts.   No matter
whether he described the carnage of the turning point in a
day of battle; an hour beside a wounded soldier in the
hospital, talking of home and friends; or one of the chicken-
and-pig-foraging expeditions for which the Zouaves have been
almost as famous as for their fighting,—through all these shone
the spirit of the gay, rattling, contented soldier, who might
have sat for a portrait, any day, of Paddy Murphy, in the
"Happy Man," making his baggage-wagon, commissariat and
camp-chest of a one-headed drum, ready to fall in love with
the first neat pair of ankles that peeped from beneath a well-
kept petticoat, a little regardless of any proprietorship in the
same ankles, other than that vested in the actual owner, and
splendidly indifferent as to either the time or the mode of his
death, whenever that death should become a matter of necessity.

    The letters of such soldiers as these are the best recruit-
ing-sergeants that can be sent abroad among any people;
just as the letters of whining, lugubrious or dissatisfied men,
who have gone into war without expecting any of its dangers
or discomforts—who are satisfied with no fare less luxurious
than that served up at Delmonico's or the Maison Dorée,
and who protest against any sleeping which is not done upon
spring-mattresses strown with rose-leaves,—cannot do otherwise than discourage and unnerve the whole immediate community in which they fall.   Whether the growlers through
the press and in general society, have done most to discourage and demoralize the army, or whether the grumblers in
the army have wrought more effectually in discouraging enlistments and weakening the national cause, certain it is that
the two evil influences have worked together, and that those
who have displayed the contrary spirit are entitled to full
redit from the whole loyal community.

John Crawford, the Zouave, has not yet made his appear
ance upon the scene; but it will now become necessary to
turn attention to events and incidents in which he was engaged, and to discover what influence his action may have
produced on the after events of this story. In this change
of scene, too, we pass away for the time from the outside actions and influences of the war—the examination of recruiting
officers, their camps and their Broadway parades, with the
domestic and social entanglements in which they were involved by the struggle,—to the theatre of the war itself
and the sights and sounds involved in one of the deadliest
conflicts that ever shook the earth with the thunder created
by the blood-shedding descendants of Cain.

It is with the battle of Malvern Hill that we have to do—
a battle as yet misunderstood and underrated by many who
think themselves thoroughly conversant with the events of the
war—one of those marvellous *victories in retreat* which often
more fully than successes in advance illustrate the genius of
those who achieve them. When the history of the War for the
Union comes to be written at a later day, and when the petty
jealousies and misunderstandings are discarded which now
embarrass all contemporary records,—it is scarcely to be
doubted that the battle of Malvern Hill will be set down as
the most terrible conflict ever known on this continent; the
most splendid artillery duel of any country or any age; a
crowning test of indomitable bravery on the part of both
loyalists and rebels; and a brilliant victory for the Union
cause, which saved an army, crowned the reputation of its
young General, and averted a series of evils which could not
have failed to culminate in the fall of Washington and the
virtual destruction of the last hope of the republic.

The events which had immediately preceded Malvern Hill
are too fresh in the minds of the people to need any extended
recapitulation. McClellan, deprived of his last hope for the
immediate capture of Richmond, by the unexpected strength
shown by the Confederates in front and the withdrawal of
McDowell under the orders of the government, when within
ten miles of effecting a junction with him;—McClellan, his
forces sadly thinned by the labors and the diseases incident to

the long delay amid the swamps of the Chickahominy ; Mc-
Clellan, driven at last from the possibility of even holding his
position, by the arrival at Richmond of a large proportion of
the rebel army driven from Corinth by Halleck, and by the
movement of Jackson with a body of forty thousand men to
take his right wing in flank ;—McClellan had abandoned the
White House on the Pamunkey River, on Sunday the twenty-
ninth of June, after the terrific conflict of the Friday previous,
burning the White House itself and immense quantities of
stores and supplies that could not be transported, and was now
falling back on the line of the James River, where he could
meet the protection of the Union gunboats and safely await
the slow coming of those reinforcements with the aid of which
he yet made no doubt of being able to take the rebel capital.

To McClellan's army this movement, accompanied with so
much haste and such extensive destruction of valuables, necessarily looked more like a disastrous retreat after defeat than
it was in reality ; and the consequence was such a depression
of spirits in many of the corps, as could only have been prevented growing into demoralization by the confidence that
every officer and every soldier yet felt in the young commander.   To the rebels, knowing the country better than the
loyal troops, the movement appeared nearer what it really
was, a successful escape from overwhelming difficulties, to a
better and more secure position, from which an offensive movement might again be made at an early day, threatening their
capital beyond a hope of defence.   To them, a prize long
watched and supposed to be securely entrapped, was after all
escaping to a place of safety ; and every Confederate officer
and soldier seemed to feel that the Union army must not be
allowed to gain the line of the James as an army, if any series
of desperate and continued attacks could suffice to destroy it.
Never, perhaps, was greater bravery or more indefatigable
energy shown in pursuing a beaten but dangerous foe, than
was shown on this occasion by Hill, Longstreet and Jackson ;
and never, certainly, was the doggedly dangerous defence of
the tiger slowly retreating to his jungle, more splendidly
shown than by McClellan, Hooker, Sumner, Keyes, Heintzelman and the other Union commanders.   The conflict of Mon-

day th; thirtieth June, at White Oak Swamp, had brought no substantial benefit to the Confederate arms, nor had it in any considerable degree weakened the Union forces ; and on the night of that day it became evident to the commanders of both armies that if Tuesday the first of July should pass without a substantial victory gained by the Confederates, the Union troops would gain the shelter of the James and the gunboats, and the rebel advance be checked effectually.

It was upon the two armies in this position that the night of Monday closed down ; and it was upon the two armies with their positions very little changed, that the morning broke on Tuesday, giving light for the double battle, of a whole day's duration, hereafter to be known as that of Malvern Hill.*

Nature has no sympathy with bloodshed and but little with suffering ; and it is only when a God puts off mortal ex istence that the earth is racked with the thunders and the earthquakes of Calvary. The birds sing as sweetly and the sun shines as brightly as usual, on the day when we lay in the earth all that was mortal of one dearer to us than sunshine or bird-music ; and the moon does not turn red· or veil her light, even in the presence of midnight murder. : If the skies weep rain upon Waterloo, it does not fall because the powers in heaven are making lamentation over the slaughter so soon to be accomplished, but because the crops of the Flemish farmers have called up to the skies for moisture.

The sun peeps lovingly down even on many a battle-field, and it kisses the tips of bayonets soon to be wet with the blood of brothers and the blades of swords that are to be hacked and hammered in deadly conflict, just as it might glint upon the polished barrel of the sportsman or flash from

---

* For the close and accurate description of this battle, the correctness of the technical terms employed, the ground occupied, and some of the very language used,—the writer in this place begs to make his acknowledgments to Mr William H. White, soldier and scholar, a Lieutenant in the Ninth Infantry in the campaign against the city of Mexico, and author of the popular "Sketches of the Mexican War" which have supplied our literature with some of the finest battle-pieces in the language.

the diamond aigrette of the lady riding forth on her white
palfrey to catch the breath of early morning. And how man,
with the capacity of thought, shrinks and shrivels within
himself when he marks the eternity of the course of nature
and the very silent scorn bestowed upon him when he is committing crimes or displaying heroisms that make all *his* little
world one overwhelming convulsion! It was the reply of
an officer of undaunted bravery, when asked what was the
predominant feeling in his mind when he headed the for-
lorn-hope in one of the desperate assaults that preceded the
taking of the City of Mexico: "I think I heard the singing
of the birds in the trees, more distinctly than anything else,
and I felt a little vexed that they seemed to care nothing
about the terrible scrape we were pitching into." And something of the same dissatisfaction, though more tinged with
melancholy, has been felt by many who stood beside the closing grave and heard the same bird-music making harsh discord with the rumbling of the clods falling on the lid of the
coffin, and who saw the pleasant sunshine tinging the very
sods that were in a few moments to form an impassable bar-
rier between the beloved dead and the miserable living.

Nature smiled upon the field of Malvern, on the morning
of the First of July, however the powers that wheel the
courses of the sun may have frowned behind their battlements at the sacrifice of life then beginning and the fearful
passions then being called into more active exertion. A
slight mist lay over wood and river, in the very early morning, but the first beams of the sun dispelled it, and the picturesque Virginia landscape was exposed to full view, with its
long stretches of hill and plain, its river glimmering in the
distance, its patches of corn and tobacco, its scattered and
unthrifty farm-houses flanked with their negro quarters, and
its long lines of white and sun-baked roads.

At that point on the direct road from Charles City to
Richmond, and about four miles from Malvern Hill in a
North-west direction, such a scene was presented, half an
hour after sunrise, as has seldom been looked upon by mortal
eye. The increasing light brought more and more plainly to
view the retreating march of the Union forces—unmistakably

a retreat and yet quite as unmistakably no panic. Interminable lines of wagons, whose length and number no one can estimate who has not seen a formidable army on the march, rolled on slowly over the white roads, raising clouds of impalpable dust that rose no higher than the wheels and then settled again without obscuring the view. Battery after battery of rifled Parrots, smooth-bores, howitzers and monster siege-guns, rumbled leisurely along the uneven way. Long lines of jaded cavalry tramped wearily and stiffly, the horses with drooping heads and the riders with listless attitudes and loose seats in their saddles which denoted the very extremity of fatigue and exhaustion. Streams of limping, footsore stragglers and slightly-wounded soldiers flanked the roads on either side, trudging along beside the ambulances in which their worse-wounded companions were being carried forward. Mixed in with these were unshorn Confederate prisoners; teamsters whose mules and wagons lay at various points between the Chickahominy and Turkey Bend; and ruined sutlers whose precious captured stores were now giving aid and comfort to the appreciative stomachs of the hungry rebels. The Provost-Marshal's Guard and fatigue-party of Colonel Porter brought up the rear—picking up stragglers; blowing up ammunition that had been left by the way; burning feed and forage; smashing barrels of liquids, of which the apparent wanton waste on the ground would at any other time have almost produced a revolt in the ranks; bending the barrels and throwing into the swamp, of muskets dropped by dead and exhausted soldiers; breaking up and burning abandoned wagons, and destroying knapsacks, blankets, and all such other articles that could be of any possible use to an enemy, as had been left behind by the regiments that had passed on to the James River.

The position at which our point of view is taken, and through which these streams of wagons, guns, horses and men were passing with the appearance of a retreat and yet with the steady regularity of an ordinary march, formed the camping-ground of Genl. Fitz-John Porter's command, lately the right wing but now the rear of the army of the Potomac. The shattered remnants of the corps of that indomitable Gene-

ral, who after services of the first bravery and importance,
was so soon afterwards to be placed in an ambiguous position
before the country and dismissed from a service which he had
illustrated rather than disgraced,—together with portions of
those of Sumner, Heintzelman and Keyes, made up his present
command and the rear-guard of the army, holding this point
on the Richmond and Charles City road. And whatever may
have been the merits of other commands embraced in that still
vast army, in that of General Porter was certainly included
some of the best regulars yet spared to the service, and some
of the bravest and most efficient volunteer regiments that were
ever suddenly formed from the ranks of civil life, to defend the
honor of any country. To them the often-misapplied phrase,
"war-worn veterans," could now be applied without mockery,
for the men and their encampment furniture looked alike worn
and jaded, and it was only by their regularity and evident discipline that they could be recognized for what they really were
—the most reliable soldiers in the army, and men well worthy
of the trust confided to them, of defending the threatened rear
and breaking any sudden assault of a foe flushed with success.
Those men who stood upon guard at various points of the
hasty encampment, may have been faded and ragged in uniform, the arms they bore may have shown hard usage, and
their discolored tents showed little of the "pomp and circumstance of glorious war;" but they had full warrant for all this
in past services, for not a storm in all the long campaign that
they had not breasted, and not a battle of all the long line on
the Peninsula in which they had not sown the soil of freedom
with sacred seed from their thinned ranks.

A bloodless military pageant may be a splendid spectacle,
and hearts may beat high and eyes grow bright when the
steady footfall of our "household troops" is heard on Broadway, and they file by with rich music, flashing banners and
the proud consciousness of a strength that would be terrible
if asserted; but what are such feelings to those with which
the truly patriotic look upon those who have lost all their glow
and gilding in the "baptism of fire," and acquired that sacred
squalor springing from active and dangerous service? The
faded coat and cap and the dingy accoutrements are badges

of honor, worth a thousand of those new, bright, untried, and incapable of telling or suggesting any heroic story. And if the ranks of a regiment of such men are thin, there is a glorious shadow standing in every vacant place once filled by a gallant soldier; and a voice rings out which gives the same reply to the inquiry after the absent ones, that was so long given in the armies of Napoleon's time to the roll-call which pronounced the name of La Tour d'Auvergne, the "First Soldier of France"—"dead on the field of honor!" Think of it, lady of the agricultural and ornithological bonnet and the irreproachable silks, when the next time in a city railroad car two "soldiers" sit down beside you, and one is a spruce, natty-whiskered, good-looking member of a pet regiment of the N. G. S. N. Y. or the N. Y. S. M., going down to an evening drill and a supper of oysters after it, and the other a hard-featured and weather-beaten discharged soldier from our Southern battle-fields, lame or otherwise, in faded uniform and a shirt not too suggestive of plentiful washerwomen,—think of this, and if you smile bewitchingly upon the one, as is your nature, when he apologizes for accidentally creasing your dress,—do not gather up your robes with too much contempt, from contact with the stained garments of the other, who has outraged your *amor propre* by taking a place beside you; for though you may be merely shunning contact with a vulgar ruffian or a coward who has deserted his colors in the hour of need—you *may* be insulting a *hero*.

Outlying pickets had of course been thrown out from General Porter's force, now posted to keep the advancing rebels at bay until the still immense trains of stores and ammunition could be conveyed to Harrison's Landing, and the siege-guns and field-batteries placed in position at Malvern Hill and other points guarding the new base. McClellan had evidently calculated upon making the last and effectual stand at Malvern Hill, and the rebels had quite as evidently calculated upon his doing so if allowed to reach it; and on the issue of the struggle in that neighborhood was to depend the question whether the Union forces were to be driven pell-mell into the James River, surrender or hold their own and repulse their assailants. Sudden attacks and attempts at surprise

were naturally expected by the rear-guard at any moment;
and against these usual and unusual precautions had been
taken, which would have satisfied old Frederick himself—that
hard-headed old soldier who dreaded nothing in war but an
attack by surprise.

The nature of the country in the neighborhood as well as
indeed along the whole line from the Chickahominy to the
James, abounding as it did in woods and swamps, made it
impossible to form extended lines of battle even at the spot
where successful defence and the holding of a certain position
appeared to be the most necessary. Many regiments had not
even room to deploy more than half the length of their proper
fronts; and the full strength of the command could not possibly be brought to bear against an attacking foe, distributed
as it was in knots for miles across the country.

These natural obstacles, meanwhile, were not disadvan-
tageous to the rebels. Their superior knowledge of the section, with its numerous minor swamp-roads, forest-paths and
approaches necessarily unknown to the Union forces, gave
them immense advantages, such as they had not been slow to
improve, in corresponding circumstances, during the whole
of the preceding campaign. Aware of these facts, a night
attack on Monday might have been expected by the Federal
officers, and the men had slept on their arms in anticipation
of it. But White Oak Swamp had been too severe a trial of
courage and energy; they were not disposed to attack again
before receiving more of the reinforcements steadily pouring
onward from Richmond; and as a consequence the wearied
troops had been allowed to pass the night without disturbance, and they had even overhauled the remains of rations
remaining in their haversacks and made their scanty and un-
savory breakfasts, long before the expected hostile cloud burst
upon them.

It was nearly nine o'clock in the morning when some of the
scouts of Smith's brigade came in and announced the enemy
advancing in force. In a moment after, the rattling rolls of
drums and the brazen notes of bugles resounded among the
bivouacs; and with the regimental and national colors planted
at prominent points before arranged, the regiments formed ⸜

upon them and took up the positions assigned. Some of the brigades were hidden in the cornfields adjoining the encampment; some were drawn up along the lines of fences, affording little protection, but obscuring knowledge of the field by an enemy attempting to reconnoitre from a distance; several regiments were thrown into the woods right and left; and a considerable portion of the command awaited the attack on open ground, without other protection than God, the justice of their cause, and their own valor. Kern's Pennsylvania Battery, Martin's Massachusetts, and Carlisle's and Tidball's Regular Batteries, were on the ground. They moved up nearer the front than they had before been lying, the Regular Batteries in the main road and upon an eminence to the right. Kern took position near the edge of the swamp on the left; and Martin found post in a wheat-field to the right. Several brigades of infantry were also thrown well in advance, though not in range of the artillery; and so prepared, the Union troops awaited what they felt was to be a decisive conflict.

Gradually the " crack! crack! crack!" of a scattering fire of small-arms, which had been heard for a quarter of an hour to the westward, came nearer and nearer, as the pickets were driven in, contesting their ground stubbornly as they fell back. On came the Confederates, slowly at first and afterwards with more rapidity, throwing out clouds of skirmishers, in the rear of which the main body marched in such formations as the nature of the ground permitted. Whenever they deployed in line of battle, instead of the customary arrangement of a single line of two ranks, they formed in three lines " closed *en masse*," thus making their front six ranks deep. This disposition of course was calculated to give increased weight in a bayonet charge, and indeed to make it well nigh irresistible; but besides the fact that the solid formation would render the execution of artillery among them much more destructive, in the event of a repulse it would be almost impossible to rally them, as the different regiments would necessarily lack space in which to manœuvre, the lines inevitably mix up in an inextricable mass, and the whole body become a disorganized mob. Some of the rebel divisions

were formed in column, either of division or company, all
closed up at half distance.

It was a matter of remark to the Union officers who saw
the advance of the Confederate forces on that day—the most
formidable advance, perhaps, that they have made during any
battle of the war,—that there were no flashing and showy
uniforms, and that but few flags were seen. The same
remark had before been made during other conflicts of the
Peninsular campaign, and the contrast thus presented to the
gaudy and careless dressing of many of the Union troops,
seemed one to reflect credit on the Confederate prudence at
the expense of that quality on which they had so prided
themselves—their *chivalry.* Except as the sun shone on the
sloping musket-barrels and bristling bayonets, there were
few brilliant objects in all that formidable array, on which
the sharp-shooters of the Federal army could readily fix as
targets. Few bright buttons flashed on uniforms, even of
officers, and shoulder-straps were so uncommon as to make it
difficult to distinguish an officer (even a field or staff officer,
if not on horseback) from a private. Our own forces, throughout the war, have probably been needlessly reckless in this
regard; and there is no doubt that the brilliant uniforms,
particularly of the various Zouave corps, have often made
them more easily distinguishable and added to their losses
when fighting at long range. But the truly brave man is not
apt to consider the consequences to his own safety, of wearing a dress or carrying an insignia which he would otherwise
bear with propriety and with pride. It was an inviting
mark which Henri of Navarre offered to the foe at Ivry, in
the white plume with which he led on his followers; and
Murat, when he made those desperate charges to which
reference has before been made during the progress of this
narration, must have known that his flashing silks, his
feathers and embroidery, put his life much more in danger
than that of an officer less conspicuously clad; but neither
the foe of the League nor the brother-in-law of Napoleon
remembered the danger when the glory was to be won and
the great object of the soldier accomplished. Perhaps that
duellist may be pardoned by those who look on, when he

carefully removes from his person every mark that could furnish a target to his enemy, but he is no more than pardoned; and if there is one redeeming trait in the detestable character of the duellist, it is to be found in that ready exposure of his life to the chances of *fate* and *skill*, which does not stop to calculate a button or measure the narrowest line of aim which can be presented to an adversary. Straitened circumstances and the want of many of the appliances of luxury, may have had something to do with the lack of personal display on the part of the Confederates, more especially the officers, throughout the struggle; but a long time will elapse before the non-chivalrous "Yankees" whom they have despised, will cease to believe that commendable anxiety for personal safety has lain at the bottom of the self-denial.

The fire of the rebel skirmishers, in this advance, was met promptly by those of the Union army, and so sharply that the former were soon driven back pell-mell on the main body. The Federal sharpshooters, taking advantage of every tree, rock or knoll, frequently overlapping their flanks, kept up a continual and most destructive fire on the steadily advancing lines and columns. The Confederates came on in excellent order, their dingy lines sometimes bulging to the front, then occasionally bending rearwards,—now the left wing curving forward, and then the right swaying in an opposite direction. But these trifling deviations from mathematical lines were always quickly corrected, and the "dress" of their long fronts was really so good as to give evidence of continued and careful drill on the part of the men and much ability on that of the officers.

A heavy gray-clad body of rebels advanced in soldierly style until they came within two hundred yards of the position occupied by Couch's division, which was lying down in the weeds and partially screened by them. A blast of bugles —a roll of drums—a few sharp words of command; and up rose the before-dormant mass to their feet. A scorching, withering fire of small-arms, delivered by companies from left to right, and with the greatest deliberation, was sent directly into the faces of the advancing rebels—such a close and deadly fire as seems almost as impossible to advance against

16

as against the lightnings of heaven. They halted, wavered,
and gave signs of confusion ; but they were soon restored to
order and again came on. Again one of those close and terrible volleys was poured into them, thinning the ranks and
encumbering every step with dead ; and again they halted
and wavered. This time they deployed in line of battle and
commenced a fierce fire on the opposing divisions, accompanied by yells peculiar to themselves—such as no other
civilized troops in the world have ever uttered—not a hurrah,
a cheer, or even a roar, but a *shriek* as dissonant as the
Indian war-whoop, and more terrible.

On the right and on the left the enemy came hurrying up,
their columns at a double quick. But they were met and
brought to a stand at every point. Their artillery, ordered to
the front, dashed up by batteries, took positions, unlimbered
and opened savagely. The Union batteries, already posted,
commenced their splendid practice. Sheet after sheet of
deadly flame burst from one side and the other of the combatants ; the rattling crack of the volleys of firearms became
blended with the heavy metallic ring and sullen boom of the
artillery ; and the first battle of Malvern Hill—that which was
to decide the approach to the main position—was now fairly
begun.

From various and hitherto unknown paths through the
woods and marshes, the gray-clads came on in swarms, every
moment adding to the formidable character of the attack, the
evident numbers of the assailants, and the certainty that the
struggle was to be a close and terrible one. But the gathering thousands were fiercely met by the blue-clad veterans of
the Union, and repeatedly driven back in confusion. Let this
be recorded, from the personal knowledge of sharers in that
combat—whatever after-history may choose to consider authority on the subject,—that *the Federal troops never permanently yielded one foot of ground during the fight,* how
ever worn-out with fatigue, embarrassed by a cramped position, outnumbered and at one time half-surrounded.

It has before been said that the Battle of Malvern Hill was
one of the most magnificent artillery duels known to the
history of war ; and though the most splendid effects of that

terrible arm were shown at a later period, when the whole range of McClellan's heavy pieces came into play, yet even now the effects were such as to have satisfied the very Moloch of destructive war. The play of the Union regular batteries was beautiful, (if such a term can be applied to that which defaces the beauty of God's handiwork, in however holy a cause.) Every shot could be seen to tear open the dense masses of the enemy in wide spaces, through which the white background could be distinctly seen until they were closed again by almost superhuman efforts. The volunteer batteries seemed little behind in their practice—their solid shot and bursting shell falling in a perpetual shower, and making fearful havoc alternately in the solid masses of the rebels and among the gunners of their artillery.

When the Confederates opened with their batteries, General Porter, accompanied by a part of his staff, was occupying the upper slope of an eminence to the right, from which a tolerably good view of the battle-ground could be obtained. It was not one of those points "from which all the details of the fight could be taken in at a glance," according to the phraseology of many of the graphic describers of modern battles; for no such spot has ever been known, in the neighborhood of any extensive conflict, since the use of artillery covered every field with smoke and destroyed the romantic opportunities for observation which existed in the days of the lance and the cross-bow. But it was the very best position for a general oversight of the field, attainable under the circumstances; and that it was within easy range of the enemy's missiles was demonstrated by one of the very first shot, which struck a tree immediately behind the General, shattering it to pieces and severely wounding one of the aid-de-camps with the flying splinters.

It is impossible to describe, in such form that it can be realized by the reader, this fiercest of battle-fields for the two hours which followed the first attack. Many men felt it, and of those who live to tell the tale, all will remember it; but it may be said that no man saw it. The canvas best depicting it would be deprived of all the essentials of a picture, and merely made a chaos of destruction, with here the glint of a gun and

there the flash of a sabre ; here a momentary view of a black
piece of heavy artillery, and there a head, an arm and a leg
of one of the combatants ; here a puff of smoke, and there a
volley of belching flame—but all indistinct, terrible and in-
describable.   Solid shot, conical shell and spherical case went
humming, hurtling and howling through the air, blotting out
rebels and slaying loyalists.   The leaden messengers of the
sharp-shooters went shrieking to their living targets, killing,
crippling and intimidating ; buck, ball and Minie bullets missed
and made their marks ; and the rattling volleys of companies
and platoons became at length blended in one general and
irregular burst of all destructive sounds known to modern
warfare.

The Union ranks were of course sadly thinned by the murderous discharges from those of the rebels, even if their own
fire was so effective.   The odds in point of numbers and weight
of fire was heavily against them, and they knew it.   The pres-
tige of success was not theirs, for though the enemy had been
beaten in almost every trial of arms since the first landing on
the Peninsula, yet the irresistible force of circumstances (and
what the world will always believe *blunders*) had prevented
their reaping the fruits of those repeated victories, and the
great object of the expedition—Richmond—had been daily
receding and was now apparently out of reach.   The brilliant
flank movement which McClellan was executing, seemed to
them to be a simple retreat which was to take the remains of
the Army of the Potomac to the James River for the purpose
of an immediate embarkation and abandonment of the campaign.   Men less heroic would have grown disheartened
and struck feebly in the midst of so many causes of discouragement ; and the able review of the Campaign on the Peninsula, by a true man and a soldier, the Prince de Joinville,
shows that even with his past knowledge of their bravery and
endurance *he* would not have been surprised to see the spirit
of the whole army sinking under sufferings, wrongs and disasters.   Perhaps such would have been the case, had they
had less confidence in their leaders ; but while that existed
there could be nothing like demoralization ; and if there has
ever been a day since that time, when the same noble body

of men and the others who have been joined with or replaced them, have displayed that hopeless deterioration of efficiency as an army, the fault has lain in their being led by men in whom they lacked confidence and men who lacked confidence in themselves! Up to this time no such misfortune had fallen upon them. They had learned to suffer and endure, but they had not yet learned to be permanently defeated. Sumner, Franklin, Kearney, Heintzelman, Keyes and Fitz-John Porter, but above all McClellan, possessed their undivided confidence; and whenever, at any point of the retreat towards the James, either of those great chiefs had appeared in their midst or ridden along their battle-thinned ranks—renewed hope and energy had been always evinced by the heartiest acclamations. Particularly, it has been said, was this the case with McClellan. His extraordinary popularity has been more than once incidentally adverted to, in the course of this narration; and if it has been so, the cause is not to be found in either partisan spirit or man-worship on the part of the writer, but in the unavoidable necessity of echoing what "everybody says." "Little Mac" was then, he is to-day,* the most popular soldier of the age, whether the country has or has not anything to show for the confidence long reposed in him by the government and the immense bodies of troops at one time placed at his disposal. No general since Napoleon has ever so gained the love of his soldiers or so inspired them with confidence in his will and ability to *take care of them* and *to accomplish what he was set to do, if not interfered with.* Their favorite reply to any suspicion of danger to any corps, was: "Little Mac will take care of us!" and to any doubt of the success of the campaign: "Little Mac knows what he is about!" Blind confidence, perhaps!—but such confidence, or something approaching it, must be commanded by personal qualities, or great operations in war can never be accomplished. At no time during the Peninsular campaign has the commanding General so fully commanded the confidence of the soldiers, as during all those severe battles afterwards to be known as the Seven Days. His calm and collected action

* February 16th, 1863.

had been of the very character to inspire that confidence, and
could not have wrought more effectually to that end had it
had no other purpose. Some men, jubilant and light-hearted
when all their plans are progressing favorably, permit their
words to become few and their manner sombre and abstracted
when difficulties thicken, creating fear and distrust in the
minds of those around them, even when they themselves have
not lost confidence and are only absorbed in thought. McClellan, always a silent man, displayed the very opposite. One
of his staff officers said of him on that terrible Friday afternoon of the first conflict, when the result certainly seemed a
most threatening one for the Union arms : "Little Mac seems
to have woke up,! I have not seen him look so happy before,
since he received the news of McDowell's falling back on
Washington." And there had not been wanting those to cir-
culate throughout the army his confident and self-possessed
action on the morning before—that of White Oak Swamp,
when he sat on horseback at the cross-roads, with aid-de-
camps dashing up with unfavorable reports, and heads of
divisions a little embarrassed if not dispirited around him.
"Gentlemen, take it easy ! Only obey me, and I will bring
you out of all this without the loss of a man or a gun, God
willing !"

Such words had been like the pause of the Bruce to cut his
armor-strap when flying before the English enemy—they had
inspirited the whole command. He had remained, too, the
whole of Monday, in the neighborhood of the White Oak
Swamp, personally superintending everything and hastening
the passage of the immense trains onward towards the James.
Nothing had seemed to discourage him, and no exposure in
the terrible heat had seemed to fatigue him beyond endurance.
All these facts had crept out to every division of the army,
as they will do through the subtle and unaccountable tele-
graphism of comrade-ry ; and when regiment after regiment
heard of the incident since made memorable by De Joinville,
of his rising from his momentary rest on the piazza of a house
near White Oak and going out with a smile to prevent his
soldiers picking and eating the cherries belonging to his pretty
hostess, they had burst out into laughs and cheers more com-

plimentary to.the young General's pluck than his devotion to
Nelly Marcy, and fancied that he might have been engaged
in picking other cherries for himself, that grew on red lips
instead of on the tree !

Such were the influences which combatted those otherwise
so unfavorable, kept up their spirits even when they could
see nothing but defeat and discouragement in every movement, and made every blow they struck at the advancing
enemy more deadly than the last. Such were the influences
peculiarly active on this day when they were so much needed,
and which inspired the army-corps of Fitz-John Porter for
the memorable blow struck in the first battle of Malvern.
The rebel South will long mourn for its lost children, perished in that sanguinary conflict and in the wider and more
destructive but not fiercer one which was so soon to follow at
Malvern Hill itself.

CHAPTER XVIII.

MORE OF THE FIRST BATTLE OF MALVERN—A PAUSE—
THE ATTACKS ON THE MAIN POSITION—REPULSE AFTER
REPULSE—VICTORY—STRANGE INCIDENTS OF THE LAST
HOUR OF THE BATTLE.

STILL the battle went on—that ferocious attack which
seemed to have the desperation of defence, and that steady
defence which appeared to have the assured confidence of an
attack. The smoke gathered rapidly, rolled away at times,
then settled in dense masses, shutting out portions of the
battle-field and whole divisions of either army from view,
and concealing the movements of either belligerent from the
other until lifted in the occasional lulls of the fiery storm or
wafted away by the lazy breeze which came sluggishly over
from the James River marshes. Men fell thickly, crushed, mangled and dead, or so terribly wounded by shot or shell that

life could be henceforth nothing more than one long, helpless agony. Slightly wounded soldiers went limping to the rear, seeking surgical aid; while badly wounded men were eagerly caught up and borne off the field by their "comrades in battle," or by white-livered recreants, anxious to desert their braver companions and place themselves in safety. A certain percentage of such craven-hearted libels on humanity—let it be said here—are always to be found in every army and on every battle-field, dusky backgrounds against which brave men show the brighter, and ever ready to take advantage of any circumstance that will help them to the rear. In the armies of the older and more warlike nations of Europe, where the reins of discipline are much more tightly drawn than in our own, such skulking is prevented by regularly-organized ambulance-parties and by the prompt shooting down of any officer or soldier, not wounded, who dares to leave the ranks without orders. Even in our own service, a Taylor is occasionally found, fighting such a desperate battle as that of the Bad Axe against the Indians, and posting a line of his most reliable troops in the rear, with orders to make short work of the skulkers. Such discipline as this—an enemy in front and an equally dangerous body of friends behind, is generally found efficacious even for the weakest knees; and but few hours of such experience are necessary to produce a marked change in the steadiness of any corps under fire.

Noon now approached, and the battle had raged for more than two hours, without any intermission except the occasional lulls when batteries were limbered up and dragged off at a gallop to new positions, and when regiments deployed in line or closed in column, making evolutions to the flanks, or movements to the front. Attacks had been fiercely made on every portion of the Union lines by the maddened rebels—maddened, as was afterwards discovered, by the gunpowdered whiskey in their canteens; and they had been quite as fiercely repulsed by the loyal troops, who neither needed nor received any such stimulus. This defence had been materially assisted, and the Federal troops enabled to gain ground at every repulse of the rebels, by the arrival of several regiments of infantry and two of his best batteries, sent in haste by McClellan from his main position at Malvern Hill, so soon as the roar of artillery announced that the fight had fairly begun with the rear-guard.

A little before meridian, the musket fire of the enemy slackened perceptibly, while their artillery, operating against the Union left, seemed to redouble its fury. This change was at once made known to Porter, who as quickly divined the intention of Longstreet. This was to engage all attention with the Federal left, while several of his divisions, passing rapidly through roadways and obscure paths in the woods known only to the native Virginians, were to take the right wing in flank. Porter immediately directed counter movements to meet them—movements admirably calculated and as admirably executed. Burns, with his own and two other brigades, moved rapidly to the right and deployed in line opposite the edge of the white oaks from which the rebels must emerge to make their attack. Four batteries went up at a trot and took position where they were masked by a fringe of bushes and some patches of tall corn. From this point the artillery could concentrate a terrible fire of grape, canister and short-fuse shell upon any part of the opposite woods from which the enemy might make their appearance. The infantry were ordered to lie down, and were concealed from view by clumps of trees, corn and underbrush. This repelling force was not kept long in suspense, and it was evident that the movement had not been made a moment too soon for safety. Suddenly from the shadow of the white-oaks, out came the Confederates by regiments, without tap of drum or bugle-call, pouring from the various openings in double-quick time, and by the right and left flanks. They filed rapidly right and left until the woods were cleared; then by a halt and face-to-the-front they were brought quickly into line of battle. A halt of very brief space to align and close up ranks, and they were ordered forward to the attack. On they came, in close order and with long swaying lines, exulting in the prospect of a successful issue to their bold movement, and so confident that they would take the Federal flank and rear by complete surprise, that silence was no longer

felt to be necessary and yells and shouts of triumph were
beginning to burst from one portion and another of their
line. Still on they came, and not a shot had been fired on
either side since they emerged from the woods. Their left
was thrown forward in advance of the centre and right, as if
seeking to surround the positions supposed to be held by the
Federal troops They were even allowed to advance within
pistol-shot of some portions of the ambuscade, before the
trap laid for them was sprung.

Then what a change !—like that when the thunder-storm,
long gathering but still silent, breaks at once into desolating
fury. It seemed as if at one and the same instant the four Union
batteries opened, and a terrible concentrating storm of flame
and projectiles leaped from the muzzles of twenty-four pieces
of artillery and burst upon their centre with devastating effect.
In an instant after, the infantry sprung to their feet, and a
sheet of fire burst from right to left, one deadly and irresistible shower of lead sweeping through the rebel ranks that
had so little expected such a reception. They hesitated—
halted—recoiled. Before they could recover from the awful
shock, volley after volley was poured into their wavering lines,
and they could not again be brought forward. On the instant
when their discomfiture was clearly perceived, a charge was
ordered against them. The Union men dashed forward, glad
to have that order at last, and breaking into ringing cheers—
the first in which they had indulged that day. The rebels
could not stand a moment before that impetuous onset, but
broke and ran for the cover of the white-oaks, leaving the
ground of the conflict almost impassable with the terrible piles
of their dead and wounded.

A general advance of our lines was now ordered, and the
command was obeyed with alacrity. The rebel front, weakened by the withdrawal of so many troops for the grand flanking movement, gave way before they could be reached with
the steel ; and their three-deep lines became mixed up in the
most hopeless disorder. Kearney's division made a gallant
charge, in this movement, Sickles' Excelsior Brigade once
more evidencing that splendid steadiness with the bayonet
which had been so conspicuous at Williamsburgh and Fair

Oaks. General Heintzelman joined in this brilliant advance, his tall form and blue blouse conspicuous as he rode rapidly along the lines, speaking words of cheer and steadying the men who did not need urging forward.

The Union batteries had meanwhile kept up their terrible fire, while those of the enemy were silenced one after another and drawn off with the recoiling troops, with the exception of one battery, which maintained its fire with invincible obstinacy. It was felt that this battery must be taken or silenced. A stream of men in dingy French blue were seen to leap forward, and it was known that the Excelsior boys were making a dash at the battery. The gunners saw the movement, began to limber up their pieces and succeeded in galloping away with four of them. But the two remaining guns could not be handled quickly enough, and the Excelsiors took them with a rush and a cheer, and in such excellent spirits that one of them was the moment after sitting astride of each gun and waving his cap in token of victory. The battle-flag of one of the Georgia regiments, and three hundred prisoners, were also captured in this gallant dash, which effectually showed how little the spirits of the Army of the Potomac had been damped by recent misfortunes. General Heintzelman lost his horse by the last fire of one of the captured pieces, and at the same time received a wound in the arm—fortunately not serious. The repulse of the rebels was now complete. Longstreet was compelled to "retire" and not by any means in "good order," leaving the field with its dead and wounded, and many arms and other trophies, in the possession of the Federal forces.

Of course this success could not be followed up, the object of the battle having been to secure an uninterrupted line of march to the James River. And of course the Union generals were well aware that while the rebels possessed any remaining strength, they would not give up their cherished object of crippling or destroying the main body before it could reach the shelter of the river and the gun-boats. Fresh troops would be brought up; and but little time would be allowed the Federal troops to recover from the fatigue and excitement of that arduous morning. The rebel plan evidently was to

give the Federal forces no rest—to precipitate fresh masses of
their own troops continually upon them, when weary and
exhausted with previous fighting; and when they were at
last fairly worn out and incapable of further exertion, to
"gobble them up" (to use an expressive, though not elegant
phrase) or destroy them in detail and at leisure. The theory
was admirable, and both brain and heart were necessary to
prevent its being carried out in successful practice.

The Federal dead were buried on the field where they had
so bravely fallen; the wounded were sent on to Harrison's
Landing; the slaughtered rebels were left to the tender care
of their approaching comrades; the prisoners were gathered
together and put properly under guard; and then the army-
corps of General Fitz-John Porter fell back under previous
orders to the strong position of Malvern Hill proper, where
McClellan was certain he would at once be attacked by the
rebels in force, its possession being the most important point
in their plan of action, and its triumphant retention one of the
most important in his own.

The first battle of Malvern was ended; but the curtain was
soon to rise on a still more fearful scene of slaughter and one
yet more uneven in its character as regarded the losses of
the Union army and the rebels.

The main position occupied by McClellan was a splendid
one for defence; and, thanks to what De Joinville calls the
"happy foresight of the General, who, notwithstanding all
the hindrances presented by the nature of the soil to his
numerous artillery, had spared no pains to bring it with
him"—the preparations for holding that position were magnificently adequate. The extreme right flank was comparatively narrow, and as it was a point liable to a determined
attack, strong earth-works had been hastily thrown up entirely across it, and it had been further protected by a thick,
impenetrable mass of abattis, the materials for which were so
plentifully furnished by the Virginia woods and in the con-
struction of which the quasi-mechanical army was rapidly
efficient. The left was protected by the James River and
the terror-inspiring gun-boats. In front the hill sloped
gently down to the Charles City and Richmond road, and

other points by which the enemy must debouch to begin the attack. On this natural plateau not less than three hundred pieces of artillery—a number fabulous in any preceding strug-gle-in the history of the world—were placed in battery; so arranged that they would not interfere with the fire of the infantry along the natural glacis up which the assailants would be obliged to advance unsheltered. In the skirts of the woods lying beyond the foot of the hills, long lines of rifle-pits had been dug—these, and the woods beyond, occu-pied by a brigade of Maine and Wisconsin infantry and a por-tion of Berdan's celebrated regiment, to act as sharp-shooters. The sun was sinking rapidly westward in the direction of Richmond—that coveted capital of Secessia, for the pos-session of which so much blood and treasure had been unavailingly expended; the trees, which for so many hours had afforded no shelter from the blinding blaze, except imme-diately beneath their spreading branches and dust-dimmed leaves, began to cast long shadows eastward; and the fervent heat began to be more sensibly tempered by the breeze creep-ing in from the placid James. Still the Union troops were resting on their arms, weary but undaunted, awaiting the approach of the Confederates, then (at five o'clock) reported as advancing to the attack. The line was formed as follows: the remnants of Porter's and Sumner's corps on the right; Franklin and Heintzelman in the centre; and Couch's divi-sion of Keyes' corps on the left. In position, on the left, were two New York batteries, Robertson's United States battery of six pieces, Allen's Massachusetts and Kern's Penn-sylvania batteries. Griffin's United States battery, Weeden's Rhode Island, and three from New York, held positions in the centre. On the right were Tidball's, Weed's and Car-lisle's regular batteries, a German battery of twenty-four pounders, a battery belonging to the Pennsylvania reserve, and one New York battery—in all about eighty pieces.

Within a few minutes of five the signal officers at the various stations waved their telegraphic bunting, announcing the approach of the rebels under Magruder, and immediately afterwards they appeared in sight, in large dense masses reaching apparently quite across the country to the West,

North-west and West-south-west,—with cavalry on either
flank and artillery thickly scattered at various points, all
along their line. Stretching away from the foot of Malvern
Hill, in the hostile direction, lay a large open space known
as Carter's Field—a field destined that day to be more thickly
sown with dead than almost any historic spot on the globe
except some portions of the field of Waterloo or that of
Grokow. It was a mile long by three quarters of a mile in
breadth, enclosed by thick woods on the three distant sides,
while that towards the Hill was open. On the two sides
flanking the enemy's approach our sharp-shooters were principally concealed. Entirely across Carter's Field stretched
the rebel line, while in depth their columns extended so far
back that the eye of the signal officer lost them in a wavering
line far away in the thick woods extending beyond the scene
of the morning's battle.

The Union forces rose up wearily but steadily, and awaited
the approach of the Confederate host, known to be at least
twice or thrice their own number, and led on by that sanguinary commander otherwise described by a writer who accompanied him through all his battles in the United States service
and thoroughly knows his habits of speech and action,*—as
" the flowery and ever-thirsty John Bankhead Magruder—
the pet of *Newport* and the petter of *old wine.*" The rebels
moved forward in good order ; slowly at first, and then, as if
spurred on irresistibly from behind in all parts of the field,
the whole dingy-gray mass broke from the " common time"
step into that " dog-trot" known in the tactics of the present
day as the " double-quick." At the same moment they broke
into those shrieks of horrible dissonance, remarked in the
fight of the morning, rising even above the din of the opening
artillery, and more resembling the whoops of the copper-
skinned warriors of the renegade Albert Pike, than soldiers
of what is called a Christian nation, led on by a commander
believing himself the very " pink of chivalry."

Gallantly, it must be owned by all who saw the movement,
did the gray-clads spring forward to the encounter, rushing

---

* White—" Mexican War Sketches."

over the field at an accelerating speed which soon increased to a full run. Then and not till then again burst the deadly storm of defence. From the Federal lines across the hill there belched murderous blasts of grape and canister into their front, and from the rifle-pits and woods went shrieking showers of rifle shots and Minié balls into their flanks, the two terrible influences almost sweeping them away like leaves caught by the gale. They fell by hundreds at a discharge, encumbering the ground and leaving wide gaps in their ranks; yet still their dense columns closed again and dashed resolutely up, until more than two-thirds the distance across Carter's Field was accomplished. Here the carnage, from the combined effects of artillery and small-arms at short range, became absolutely terrible among the rebels—such a spectacle as even loyal soldiers, gazing at it, could not but feel to be a species of wholesale murder for which the cause could no more than give excuse. The bones in the rebel regiments seemed to be crushed like window-glass in a hail-storm; masses of gory pulp that had but a few moments before been men, began to form an absolute coating for the ground; and the fierce yells of attack had become awfully commingled with the shrieks of those mangled beyond endurance and dying in agony. It was too much for human bravery to withstand—probably no troops in the world would have stood longer under that withering fire, than the brave but misguided tools of the secession heresy. Their lines began to waver with a ricketty, swaying motion, to and fro, as if the whole body was one man and he was exhausted and tottering; then there was a movement to the "right about," and the whole head of the column sought hasty shelter under the friendly woods in the rear, from which they had so lately debouched.

A terrific artillery-duel proper was now commenced, and kept up for more than an hour, the Confederates showing no disposition to renew the attack, and the Federal forces contented to hold them at bay under circumstances in which the balance of damage by artillery must be so largely in their own favor. Then came a sudden lull in the storm, during which the Confederates made preparations to capture the

flanking rifle-pits of the Federals, which had annoyed them
so severely in the charge. Several desperate attempts were
made upon them in quick succession, and they were taken and
retaken repeatedly. In the end, however, they were permanently held by the defenders, whose stubborn pluck, aided by
the enfilading fire of the advanced batteries, proved more than
a match for the determined bravery of the attacking forces.

On the summit of Malvern Hill, and nearly in the middle
of the plateau formed by the whole eminence, stands a red
brick mansion-house, quaintly built, antique and sombre.
The house is of two stories, long and low. Solemn shade-
trees surround it; and corn and wheat fields stretch away
from the Virginia fences of its spacious yard, down the slope
of the hill and across the lowland to the margin of the James.
In time of peace, this old house boasted a most charming
situation, and the view from the verandah was one of the very
finest in the country, taking in at a glance the long line of
the winding river for many miles in either direction, and
looking up the river, the high range of bluffs on the other
side/ on which has been erected that serious obstacle to an
advance on Richmond by water—Fort Darling. At the
eastern end of the mansion stand the inevitable "negro-
quarters," now empty and deserted, and with nothing about
them to remind one of their former dusky denizens, except
that unmistakable odor which supplies an obvious parody on
Moore's aroma of the roses in the broken vase. Opposite the
west end of the house is a deep, roof-covered well; and
around this crowds of the wounded and thirsty Union soldiers
were continually gathered during the fight, drinking in, as fast
as permitted, that sweetest as well as freest of Nature's bless-
ings—water.

On the west gable of this mansion, on the afternoon of the
battle, a signal-officer was stationed, with his ten-foot staff
and odd-shaped parti-colored yard of muslin, and his field-
glass. His view extended far in the direction of Richmond,
taking in the various camps of Wise's Legion, Jackson's and
Huger's divisions, and others of the rebel forces; while river-
wards his eye could easily reach, with the aid of the glass and
when the smoke of the field did not arise too thickly, the famed

Drury's Bluff and the redoubtable Fort Darling itself, still frowning defiance at the threatening little Monitor.

The failure to take the rifle-pits had been followed by a second lull, betokening, to the experienced soldier, fresh rebel preparations for an attack in another quarter. Suddenly, when the sun was just sending the last of its rays through the murky clouds of the battle-field, as if in indication that the eye of heaven had not wholly deserted the brotherhood of Cain,—the Federal signal-officers in the distance waved their flags, and other signal-officers in the vicinity repeated their motions. These pantomimic exhibitions, mysterious to the unpractised eye, told to the officers in command, that the Confederates, strongly reinforced by the fresh troops of Jackson and Huger, and their troops inspired by fresh draughts of the maddening gunpowdered whiskey, were being marshalled for another and final attack upon the Federal position.

, But a few moments elapsed before the roar of the Confederate batteries gave proof that this warning had not been in vain. Every piece they could bring to bear sent its missiles of death hurtling into the Union lines, the next charge to be made under cover of that cannonade. But probably even they had not calculated upon such a reply as was given by the artillery of McClellan. Never before, since war became a science of butchery, did so many pieces thunder at once upon the devoted ranks of any attacking force. Never before were the very peals of the artillery of heaven so terribly rivalled. Only a portion of the Union guns had before been brought into play : now nearly the whole three hundred belched forth their deadly defiance in crashing and booming repetitions. Those who heard the sound will never forget it ; nor will many of them live to hear that sound repeated. Far away among the mountains, a hundred and fifty miles distant, the boom of that terrible cannonade was heard, announcing the conflict to loyalist and rebel who had no other means of knowing that it was in progress. At times the firm earth shook with the continued reverberations, as if an earthquake was passing ; and combatants even stood still in the very face of the deadliest danger, under a momentary impression that some fearful convulsion of nature must be in progress and that the

17

sinking sun must be going down on the last day of a crumbling earth.

The rebel artillery was skilfully managed, and their range proved to be excellent; while the management and effect of the Union guns can only be described by one word—magnificent. The superior weight and management of the Federal metal was manifest from one fact if no other—the continual limbering up and changing positions of the rebel pieces, to escape the deadly aim of artillerymen who have probably never been excelled in any service. The only historian who has as yet dealt with the events of that great day,* says that it was "madness for the Confederates to rush against such obstacles," and that during the entire day, owing to the weight and superior management of the Federal artillery, they fought "without for a single moment having a chance of success." And yet this was the artillery of an army, and this was the army itself, spoken of by detractors as "defeated" and "demoralized," and utterly incapable of further offensive movements against Richmond, however rested and reinforced!

Under cover of the smoke of this fire, the mighty hosts of Huger, Jackson and Magruder advanced to the second general assault. Onward they rushed, and, emerging from the sulphurous clouds, rolled forward in heavy columns. They presented a still more imposing front than at the first attack, stretching more than half a mile across the fatal Carter's Field, with scarce a break or an interval in its entire length. On they pressed—steadily, resolutely, desperately—pausing an instant to pour in their fire, and then forward again at quick step. The advance was met with belching volumes from rifles, muskets and batteries, sending such storms of "leaden rain and iron hail" as no body of men on earth could hope to withstand, and joining with the shrieks and shouts of the combatants and the dying, to create such a din as might well have given the impression that the chains of Pandemonium were unloosed and all the lost replying to the thunders of heaven with screams of blasphemy and desperation.

At this moment, too, a new element of terror and de-

* De Joinville.

struction broke suddenly into the conflict. As if the powers
of the air had indeed begun to take part in the struggle,
fiery meteors fell out of the air, from a direction not commanded by the Federal batteries—fiery meteors before which
whole ranks of men seemed like stubble before the scythe.
One of them would fall hissing through the air, burst with a
horrible explosion, and the moment after nothing would re
main of the ranks of rebels within thirty or forty feet of it,
but a mass of shattered and mangled fragments, limbs torn
from limbs and heads from bodies. At first the rebels could
not understand the meaning of this new and awful visita-
tion; and even the Union troops were not for the time aware
what new power had come to their aid, destroying more of
the enemy at a blow than their heaviest and best-served batteries. But the signal officer on the gable of the old mansion on Malvern Hill saw, and soon communicated the fact
to the officers in command—that the gun-boats Galena and
Aroostook (not the Monitor, as has been sometimes reported),
had steamed up from their anchorage at Curl's Neck, two
miles below, and opened furious broadsides of shell from their
heavy rifled guns. These shells were the terrible missiles
working that untold destruction in the rebel ranks; and the
horrors and dangers of the fight to them must have been intensely aggravated by these fiery monsters that came tearing
and shrieking through the forest and exploded with concus-
sions that shook the earth like discharges from whole batteries. Only after the battle was over could the ravages
made by this agency be fully appreciated, from the effects
produced on natural objects lying in the line of their course.
In many places, avenues rods long and many feet in width,
were cut through the tree-tops and branches; and in not a
few instances, great trees, three and four feet in diameter,
were burst open from branch to root, split to shreds and scattered in splinters in all directions.

Panting, swearing, whooping and bleeding, the Confederate
lines had been pushed on, until they had reached a point
nearly as far in advance as in the former attack. But here,
beneath the storm of canister, case-shot and grape-shot,
solid-shot, shell and musketry, human endurance failed and

even the madness of intoxication grew useless. The hurricane of metal was too deadly for mortal man to withstand.
No efforts could urge them further forward; and finding it
impossible to run to the end that gauntlet of iron and lead,
they once more wavered and broke, faced about and sought
the shelter of the woods, leaving Carter's Field burdened with
its second terrible harvest of death for that day—the dead in
actual heaps and winrows, and the wounded one mere struggling, writhing and groaning mass.

But why repeat the story that has no variety except in
horror? Again and again, with fresh troops flung every
time to the front, that mad attempt to carry Malvern Hill
was repeated and repulsed. An attack—a repulse; and
each time with added but never-varied slaughter. The con-
sumption of raw spirits among the rebel ranks must have
been enormous during the day; for every rebel canteen found
on the field had been filled with that maddening compound,
with or without the fiendish addition of the sulphur and ni-
tre of gunpowder. Their attacks were like the rolling of
billows toward a beach: their waves of battle swept up with
raging fierceness, but broke and receded at every dash; and,
like the waves when the tide is fast ebbing, the surging lines
broke farther off at each advance. The attack on Malvern
Hill had failed—at what a fearful expenditure of valor and
courage on the part of the Union troops, only those who
participated can ever know;—and at what a cost of life to
the rebels, only that Eye which looked down from a greater
height than that of the signal-officer on the gable of the old
mansion, could have power to measure!

During the last of these rebel attacks, the gun-boats were
signalled to cease firing, lest their shells might prove equally
fatal to friends and foes; and the Union forces were ordered
to prepare for an advance, as Porter had determined to act,
temporarily at least, on the offensive, and thus crown the
events of a day which had been virtually one of splendid victory for the Union arms. Just when the rebels were halting
and wavering under the effects of the renewed artillery fire
poured out to meet them, Burns', Meagher's, Dana's and
French's brigades, of the right, were ordered to charge. The

order did not come too soon for the brave fellows who had been chafing like caged lions at the necessity of fighting all day on the defensive. Right gallantly and with ringing cheers did they spring forward, until within a hundred yards of the enemy, when they halted and sent a scorching fire of musketry directly into their faces. Couch's division on the left had been thrown forward almost at the same moment, and the order was obeyed with equal alacrity and effect. Then the whole line was ordered to advance, and away they went with ringing shouts, like so many confined school-boys suddenly let out for an hour's play, but going, alas!—to a game of "ball" that entailed death on many of the players.

The brave Irishmen of Meagher were already in the advance, blazing and chopping away with that indomitable good humor which seems to be the normal condition of the Hibernian when fairly launched into his darling fight. In this general advance Duryea's blue, red and baggy Zouaves led the way, as they had done in many a fight before, and always with success,—dashing savagely on the foe with ear-splitting shouts peculiar to themselves, and borrowed from the well-known war-cry of the corresponding regiments in the French service. The long Federal line of bristling steel pushed on at double-quick with irresistible force; and it was only for an instant that any portion of the Confederate line stood to meet it. At last discouraged and appalled—perhaps as much by the appearance and the war-cry of the never-defeated Zouaves as by any other agency that could have been brought to bear upon them,—they first wavered in front, then grew unsteady in the main body, and at last broke and fled in confusion and indecent haste, seeking once more the shelter of the woods from which they were no more to emerge as an attacking party.

The Federal troops were not allowed to follow them to the woods, night falling and the commander being indisposed to allow his exhausted troops any further exertion. The rebels left, in this last attack, several dismounted pieces of artillery, many blown-up caissons, and thousands of small arms, besides a thousand unhurt prisoners and a field literally covered with dead and wounded. The battle of Malvern Hill was over, though the rebel artillery continued to belch at intervals until

after ten o'clock at night, the Federal advanced batteries replying to every fire. At length, and when the still summer
night had thus far fallen on the late scene of conflict, the last
rebel shot was sullenly fired, the last response was made by
the Federal gunners, and the long conflict ceased. The baffled
and beaten rebels, who had certainly fought with bravery and
determination worthy of a better cause, fell back behind the
sheltering woods and commenced their final retreat towards
Richmond, having received at last a satisfactory taste of the
quality yet remaining in the outnumbered, harrassed, but
never-discouraged and ever-dangerous Army of the Potomac.

Owing to the fact that this battle was so largely an artillery-
duel, as has before been remarked, the opportunities for the
display or observation of personal bravery were comparatively limited, and mostly confined to a short period towards
the close of the battle. That the Union troops would have
shown the same personal dash and daring throughout, had
the plan of the General in command made hand-to-hand fighting advisable—was fully proved by the short conflict which
closed the day. In that short period occupied by the advance of the two wings and afterwards of the main body,
two or three incidents occurred, which some of the combatants will yet remember when their attention is thus called to
them, and without which this battle-picture, necessarily very
defective, and aiming much more at truth than sensation,
would be found almost destitute of details

In the first advance, no less than three color-bearers, carrying the same flag of one of the regiments of Meagher's Irish
brigade, were shot down within less than five minutes. When
the third fell, a Lieutenant in the color-company of the same
regiment, who had not many months before deserted the mock
combats of the stage for the sanguinary fights of actual warfare, concluded to try *his* success at carrying the dangerous
bunting. He seized the staff and held it, himself untouched,
for several minutes, while bullets were actually riddling the
flag. At the end of that time a stalwart Irishman, finding his
rifle-barrel heated and the ramrod jammed in attempting to
load, made two or three ineffectual jerks at the rod, found
that it was impossible to remove it ; then grasped the weapon

by the muzzle, whirled it half a dozen times around his head, bringing the butt down in each instance with crushing force, on the head of a foe ; and finally, giving it another and longer whirl, with a wild " Whooruh !" that might have originated among the bogs of Connaught, sent it whirling among the enemy with such force that it literally plowed its way through them and left a perceptible track of fallen foemen. " Be the Hill of Howth !" roared Paddy, when he had completed this exploit. " It's meself hasn't the bit of a muskit left to fight wid at all at all ! Here, Captain !" to the Lieutenant holding the flag, " it's meself should be houldin' that, and not you !" and at the word he grasped the staff out of the officer's hands and plunged still farther forward among the enemy with it, than it had before been carried by either of the bearers, coming out of the fight at last without a scratch.

At very nearly the same time, and at the point in the rebel front assailed by Meagher's brigade, another scene was presented, perhaps unexampled in the history of war. A Georgia regiment (Georgia has sent out some of the very best and most determined fighters of the whole rebel army) was in the front and immediately opposed to the jolly New York Irishmen. The evening being a hot one, most of the Irish boys had prepared themselves for the charge by throwing off knapsacks, coats, and even hats, so as to "fight asier." Their habit of doing this, by the way, in hot weather and in the excitement of battle, has not only cost the government a round sum for new clothing and equipments, but given many opportunities to the Confederates for boasting of a victory when they had won nothing of the kind. They have regarded the thrown-away coats and knapsacks as evidence of a panic and a rout, when the fact is that they have only evidenced Paddy's desire, quoted above, to "fight asy."

In the present instance, Capt. S——, a young Irishman, of Meagher's Brigade, a fire-boy and a gymnast, was surrounded by a knot of his fellows, and they were making good progress in driving back the Georgia regiment, when the Captain encountered the Major of the Georgians. Whether something in the eye of each defied the other, will perhaps never be known ; but certain it is that Captain S—— sprung

for a single combat with the Major, and that the Major, quite
as willing, sprung forward with a corresponding intention. A
few passes were made with the sword by each, and then both
seemed to forget the use of the weapon. In half a minute
swords were dropped, and the two combatants were clenched,
pounding away with their *fists!* Something after the manner
of the armies of old time when two great warriors met single-
handed, the combatants on both sides seemed to stand still for
the moment and look on at this singular struggle—this novelty
in deadly war. Captain S—— was the heavier man, but the
Georgia Major the nimbler, and they seemed very well matched
The Confederates were giving way on either side, and the
Georgia regiment must necessarily retreat decidedly in a moment. The effort of Captain S—— accordingly seemed to be
directed to first "knocking" the Major "out of time," and
then making a captive of him ; while probably the Major had
no fancy for that termination of the affair. At length the
rush came from behind and on either side, and the whole
group were irresistibly borne backward. Some of the Georgia
soldiers grasped the Major from behind, and attempted to
drag him off. Some of the Irishmen rushed forward to assist
in holding him. In a minute more, not two men, but dozens,
were engaged in a fist-fight, not a weapon being used. Directly Captain S—— managed to get in a blow under the
chin of the Major, and in the neighborhood of the gullet, which
sent him backwards nearly insensible. As he fell he kicked
with mechanical force, and the kick striking the Captain in the
lower abdomen, "doubled him up" effectually. The Georgians were still laboring to save their commander from capture, and Captain S—— and his men to take him, or *as much
as they could of him.* The *finale* was that the Georgia Major
was lugged off and rescued by his men, and that Captain
S——, clinging to him with the proverbial Kilkenny tenacity,
succeeded in dragging off him his coat, sword and belts, and
revolver,—leaving the foe very much in the condition of his
own men—that of shirt and trowsers.

It is a somewhat pitiful conclusion to this little reminiscence
of S——'s odd adventure, that the next morning, in his tent,
showing the captured weapons to one of his comrades, the

revolver went off accidentally and blew the Captain's left arm
to fragments! Such are the chances of war—a soldier
escaping unhurt amid a very rain of destroying missiles, and
meeting wounds and disablement from a trifling accident in a
moment of fancied security!

The third incident of that day, and still more notable than
either of the others, occurred on the left while the incidents
previously recorded were taking place on the right and in the
centre. When Couch's division were just advancing to the
attack and at the very moment when the conflict began to grow
close and deadly, some of the men in the front, and the rebels
as well, witnessed a spectacle equally startling and unexplainable. A figure in white burst suddenly through from the Union
rear to the front, prostrating a dozen men with the irresistible
rapidity of the movement; and then it sprung into the very thick
of the rebels and commenced its most singular and primitive warfare. Of the hundreds who unavoidably saw the apparition (for
apparition it certainly seemed) not one will ever forget it or
remember it without a shudder. The figure was that of a very
tall man, evidently of immense natural strength, with a face
shrunk to skeleton thinness and terrible staring eyes rendered
more fearful by the heavy red beard and long matted hair. It
was dressed in what appeared to be white trousers, but barefoot; and its upper clothing seemed to be a shirt beneath and
a loose flowing white robe hanging from the shoulders. In its
hand this terrible figure carried a club of green sapling oak,
heavily knotted at the end, about five feet in length, two inches
in diameter at the butt and tapering to where it was grasped
at the lower end. A more effective weapon in close combat
could not be devised; and with this weapon, and with fierce
yells that seemed like those emanating from the throat of an
infuriate madman, this strange combatant began laying about
him in the rebel ranks, crushing heads, breaking arms, and
killing and disabling scores of armed men. No sword could
reach him, and no bullet appeared to strike him, though dozens
of the rebels discharged muskets and even revolvers at him,
at close range, when it began to be apparent on which side he
was fighting. Up went that mighty flail, and down it came
again on the heads of the human tares of rebeldom who so

needed threshing out in the very garner of wrath. More than one of the Union men in the vicinity of the strange spectacle, who happened to have been classic readers in other days, gazing at the white figure and its terrible prowess, thought of Castor and Pollux and the apparitions in white which decided the battle on the shore of Lake Regillus, when the Thirty Cities warred against Rome. But there was nothing of the supernatural in this figure ; for after a few moments of wonderful immunity in the midst of that plunging fire, and after a destruction of life which seemed really wonderful to be accomplished by one single man,—fate withdrew the shield which had been interposed before him. The great club was full uplifted in the air, when the combatants saw him suddenly waver and stagger, then saw the deadly weapon drop, a stream of spouting blood from the wounded breast gush over the white garment, and that tall figure and ghastly face sink downward to the earth, one last long yell, wilder and more fearful than any that had preceded it, sounding the signal of his death, and the battle again going on over the trampled body.

It was not until hours after that the mystery of the white figure was fully explained. The poor fellow had been a soldier of one of the Western regiments, ill with fever, and sent on to Harrison's Landing with the first of the troops who reached the James. In his delirium he had no doubt heard the booming of the cannon in the morning attack, and gathered the impression that a battle must be going on and that *he* should not be absent. He had managed, by some means, to elude the guards and the few hospital nurses yet spared to the army ; had escaped from the temporary hospital, barefoot and clothed only in his white drawers, shirt, and a sheet thrown around his shoulders ; had made his way, unseen, through the woods and over the marshes lying between Harrison's Landing and Malvern ; had provided himself probably by means of his still remaining jack-knife, with that singular but fatal weapon of offence ; and then, nerved with fictitious strength by his fever and the sights and sounds of battle raging before him, he had rushed into the conflict as before described, dying a death more noble than the lingering decay of fever, after working such destruction among the rebel ranks as he might never have been able to do in the pride of his health and manhood.

And here this extended picture of one of the most important battles ever yet fought on this continent, must close, except so far as in side-issues connected with it may happen to be involved some of the persons more intimately concerned in the progress of this relation.

CHAPTER XIX.

JOHN CRAWFORD THE ZOUAVE, AND BOB WEBSTER, DITTO—
BUSH-FIGHTING, WITH VARIOUS RESULTS—THE BURNING
HOUSE AND A STRANGE DEATH-SCENE—JOHN CRAWFORD
BECOMES A MAN OF FAMILY.

IT has not yet been our fortune to happen upon John Crawford the Zouave, in the search for whom we have stumbled upon Malvern Hill and its fearful panorama of bloodshed. As a member of the Advance Guard, he was not likely to be absent from the fierce charge made by his corps at the close of that day ; and he was not. It is at the very moment of the conclusion of that charge, that the quest becomes successful.

John Crawford participated in that general advance, in the front rank of the Zouaves, in high health and spirits, and yelling quite as loudly and discordantly as any of his companions. This was not his first adventure with the bayonet, for he had gone unwounded through the determined charges of his corps, with the same deadly weapon, at Williamsburgh and Fair Oaks ; and he had grown to have confidence in himself and in any body of men that used the modern footman's lance with the due ferocity. Though five years younger than his brother Richard, John Crawford looked older than he did even in his sickness ; for the exposures of a year had browned his round and ruddy face, if it had not dimmed the

brightness of his blue eye; and the heavy waved brown
hair and moustache in which he retained so prominent a
characteristic of his Gaelic ancestry of a hundred years before, added materially to the appearance of manly maturity.
Were it a *preux chevalier* sitting under this verbal lens for
his photograph, there might be difficulty in proceeding farther in this description; for though your knight of old seems
to have been splendidly oblivious as to the needs of clean linen,
and able to wear one surcoat and one suit of armor for any
length of time without becoming repugnant to the nose of
his lady when brought into the opportunity for an embrace,
—yet the heroes of this day have sore need of occasional aid
from the washerwoman, and even the tailor becomes necessary for the replenishing of worn-out and faded garments.
John Crawford the Zouave—the truth must be told—though
he showed very little shirt, showed that little in an unclean
condition; and the baggy red of his trousers and the hanging blue of his jacket, both looked shabby and discolored.
Not much more could be said in favor of the white and yellow
turban with the dirty white tassel hanging behind, ostensibly
worn on his head but really drooping on the back part of it,
quite as much as were the ladies' bonnets two or three years
ago when the suggestion was made that they "should be
carried behind them in a spoon." And yet this soiled and
uncombed man was a soldier—every inch a soldier—and had
in him all the materials for the making of a hero.

We have said that John Crawford was in good health and
spirits, after sharing with the army in all its battles, fatigues
and privations. He was so, not alone because the corps was
somewhat better managed and cared for than many of the
others, but because he was a sober man and one physically
well-educated. He did not heat his blood for fever, and de-
bilitate his system for exposure, by the use of liquor whenever he could reach it; and having been a member of the
Seventh before he joined the Zouaves, and a habitue of the
Gymnasium so much affected by the members of that regiment, he had acquired some capacity of bearing fatigue before
entering upon that soldier-life which of all demands the most
unrelaxing endurance.

A picture very little different from that just presented, though taller and lanker in figure, was to be found in Bob Webster, John Crawford's comrade and file-closer, who went into the charge that evening at his side. A little less hardy, more of a giant in strength, and with a ruddy tinge on the end of his long nose, that had been acquired by more years and more whiskey than confessed to by Crawford—such was the only difference observable in the two men of the dirty white turbans and the discolored uniforms, who went into battle together.

The point of the enemy's front at which the Zouaves struck, in the charge, was considerably to the right of the Union centre (the enemy's left) and very near to the edge of the wood bounding Carter's Field on the North. The company to which the two comrades belonged had the extreme right; (the post of honor), and they were consequently, when the charge had penetrated so far that the rebels began to give way, almost in the edge of the woods. Some of the men in a South Carolina regiment, the enemy's extreme left, seemed to fight like fiends, supported by a battery of the same State that it became necessary to capture. This was finally swept; and the South Carolinians at last gave way, falling back into the woods, now beginning to grow dark, but firing from behind trees as they retired. Too much excited to heed the recall just then sounded, a dozen or two of the Zouaves, remembering their unexpended ammunition, tried their hand for the time at bush-fighting, with more or less success. Some of them were shot down, but others succeeded in killing or capturing the peculiar fugitives of whom they started in chase. Crawford and Webster had so far succeeded in keeping together, and neither had received even a scratch.

One of the rebels, conspicuous by the fact that he had lost or thrown off his coat and was consequently in "Irish uniform," had been especially followed by half a dozen of the Zouaves, as he fell back farther and farther into the woods, dodging and firing from behind trees, and proving that he must have come from one of the hill regions of the Palmetto State, where the hunting of wild beasts yet keeps the woodman in train for a soldier. Not less than three of the

Zouaves had paid for their tenacity with their lives, by she a
sent from that single long-rifle. Crawford and Webster,
fancying that they bore charmed lives, still kept on the chase,
catching glimpses through the dusk, of the rebel's shirt, as it
dodged in and out behind the trees. In this manner they
had penetrated perhaps a quarter of a mile into the woods,
the sounds of the battle growing more and more indistinct
behind them, when a broad light burst up through the trees
to the North, shining redly through boles and branches and
indicating a fire in the immediate neighborhood.

"What is that?" said Webster, his attention momentarily
distracted from the rebel whom he had seen dodging behind
a tree but a moment before.

"A fire of some kind," said Crawford, looking in the same
direction   "From its size, it may be a burning house."

"Humph! though it is hot enough without, I shouldn't
mind being at one more fire!" said Webster, who, like most
New Yorkers of a certain age, had once in his time "rur
wid der masheen."

"But where is that gentleman from the South?" asked
Crawford. "He may give us a pop directly—look out!"

"The no-coated devil!" said Webster. "He was dodging
behind that big oak a moment ago. I think I see the edge
of his shirt—yes!"

He *did* see the tip of the Southerner's shirt, and some one
else *felt* him; for at that instant "crack!" went the long
rifle, and John Crawford gave vent to an "Ough!" that par-
took of the mingled characters of an oath and a yell, staggering
up against the nearest tree at the same moment, with a rifle-
bullet through his left fore-arm, and feeling that sentiment of
disgust at the stomach which is inseparable from the forcible
entrance of any substance into the human body, in the shape
of a wound.

"Hallo, Jack!   Eh, you did it, did you?—d—n you!"
sputtered Webster, as he heard the report and saw the effect.
Of course the first part of his remark was addressed to his
comrade, and the last to the rebel, who had made such a capital shot that he allowed too much of his figure to be exposed
while making his survey.   In an instant, Webster's piece

was drawn up, and a second "crack!" rang out through the trees.

"Ten to one I hit him!" cried Webster. "For the first time I got a fair view of one side of his dirty white shirt. But how badly are you hurt, Jack? Where are you hit?"

"Hurt a good deal, but not seriously, I think," answered Crawford, a little faintly. "He hit me here in the left arm, below the elbow. I think the bullet went through, and may-be the bone is broken."

"Too bad! tut! tut!" said his brother Zouave. "Never mind—I will bind it up in a moment. Do you think you can lean against that tree and keep from fainting until I run and see whether my little joker went in the right direction?"

"Nary faint!" said Crawford, making a strong effort to overcome the pain he was suffering. "Go ahead, Bob, and hurry!"

Webster did hurry, and Crawford had scarcely more than time to enjoy half-a-dozen exquisite throbs of agony and ob-serve that the light through the trees, Northward, was grow-ing brighter and brighter, when he came running back, very jubilant.

"Dead as the deadest kind of a herring!" he said. "Didn't hit him where I meant to, but it answered. Bored him right through the skull, and he lies there, hugging the root of the tree he was so fond of."

"Well, I am glad of that, at all events!" answered Craw-ford. Men, even of the best hearts and warmest natures, change terribly in times of war and among the influences of the camp and the battle-field. The man who by nature could only have said "Thank God!" at some benefit rendered to his kind or some dispensation of Providence by which the lives of his perilled fellow-men have been preserved—easily learns to be thankful for the explosion of a magazine or the sinking of a ship by which hundreds of men have been sent suddenly into eternity, those men being *his enemies.*

"But come—let us see what kind of a nick you have got!" said Webster, examining the arm, with some skill once ac-quired in a doctor's shop to which run-over and fainted peo-ple were sometimes brought for sudden assistance. "No,

the bones are not broken—all right! Here, let me bind it
up with my handkerchief and put my scarf-belt around your
neck for a sling." He proceeded to make these dispositions,
with speed and dexterity, and in a moment after Crawford
felt the sickening pain subsiding and the slight faintness
leaving him

"Humph! that is better—it scarcely hurts at all now,"
he said. "Thank you, Bob—or Doctor Bob, I ought to call
you."

"Well, call me anything you like, except a coward or a
humbug!" answered Webster. "And now, old fellow, think
you are strong enough to get back to the Hill ?"

"Yes, but I am not going there!" said John Crawford.
"Don't you see how bright that fire through the trees is
getting? In this hot weather nobody builds a camp-fire of
that size, and I think there must be a house burning. If you
say so, we will take a tour in that direction."

"Anywhere with *you*," said Webster. "But," he added,
careful for his wounded companion though not for himself,
"suppose it should be a burning house, with rebels around,
and you with your lame arm."

"Oh, Bob, we'll take the chances," said the wounded
Zouave. "My impression is that they have had enough of
Little Mac for one day, and got out of this, and that you
killed about the last one of them. At all events, we'll take
the chances—come on!"

Bob Webster had been in the habit of following his file-
leader, and he did so in this instance. The two struck across
the woods in the direction of the fire, their path through the
trees and under-growth being made an easy one by the light
it cast. A few hundred yards brought them to the edge of
the wood, at a narrow place where a spur of the Malvern
Hill made a sudden curve Southward and broke into the timber. As they approached the edge of the clear space, they
saw that a house was indeed on fire, the flames now licking
through the roof and enveloping the chimneys, while all the
lower portion seemed burned to a shell. The house, which
stood at the foot of the hill, appeared to have been of fair
size, and surrounded on three sides with carefully cultivated

grounds, now marred and desolated alike by the foot of the invader and the defender.

Climbing a broken fence that lay between the wood and the cultivated ground, the two soldiers drew nearer to the burning house, which strangely enough showed no person moving around the flames, and no indication that it was not burning in utter loneliness. Such things as traps and decoys had been heard of by the comrades, however, as they had been heard of by every soldier subjected to the tricks of the Confederates; and they were not too certain that enemies might not lie concealed in the neighborhood, waiting to pick off any Union soldier discerned in the light of the fire. On this account, Webster, who had re-loaded his rifle, carried it ready for instant use, while Crawford carried his in the unwounded hand, at half-cock, and ready to make some kind of an attempt, in the event of danger, to use it as a pistol. These precautions seemed to be all superfluous, for as they came still nearer to the burning house, now almost ready to fall into a heap of blazing and smouldering ruins, no voice was heard and no sign of life was visible.

" Nobody there," said Webster.

" Nobody *living*, at least, in or about that shanty !" was the reply of Crawford. " The people are either burned, saved, or there have been none there."

" One of the three—yes—I should say so !" replied Webster to this self-evident proposition.

"And as there seems nothing to be done, in the way of putting out the fire, saving anybody or killing anybody, suppose we go back to the Hill ?" said Crawford.

" Not yet," answered Webster. "We have not yet been on the other side of the house. Perhaps there may be out-buildings on that side, that have not yet taken fire; and if there is no one living in the house, there may be cattle or hogs roasting in the enclosures."

" Very well said, Bob," said Crawford. " Let us see the other side of the house." And the two soldiers advanced as near as was comfortable to the blazing building, for that purpose. It had not yet fallen, though every board had dropped away, and every timber was a thin line of fire, fast charring

18

to coals. The house had evidently been that of a person of
some condition, though of perhaps no remarkable wealth. It
had been of two stories, with a piazza in front and a neat little yard showing a few flower-shrubs, a bordering of fruit-
trees at the sides of the enclosure, and two medium-sized
Lombardy poplar trees at the gate. No negro-quarter was
visible, or any evidence that the "peculiar institution" had
formed any part of the domestic policy of the occupants.

Just as the companions approached the gate and stood observing these particulars, the demon of fire obtained his last
triumph over the material of the building. The snapping
and crackling of the flames increased for a moment, and the
forked tongues seemed licking closer and closer around the
doomed pile; then there was a sudden change—the arched
rafters sunk away—the slight shock disturbed what had yet
remained of the frame-work—and the instant after, with a
loud rumbling crash, the whole building went down into a
heap of ruins, one high burst of flame shooting up skyward as
a signal that the destruction had been accomplished, and
showers of sparks following it, like a burst of fire-works at
some grand celebration. With the fall, the broad light of the
fire over the surrounding fields and on the neighboring woods
died away, and there only remained a great heap of burning
timbers, smouldering coals and embers, giving scarcely more
light than an ordinary watch-fire.

But the peculiar interest of that scene did not die out with
the fall of the building: on the contrary, it was at that moment that it began to assume proportions more easily recognized. For mingled with the crash of the fall there seemed
to be the sharp, shrill, terrible scream of a human voice in
agony ; and the very instant after that scream was repeated,
so distinctly that it drove the blood from the cheeks of both
the soldiers at the gate.

"My God ! did you hear that ?" said Crawford.

"Didn't I !" answered Webster. "I wish I hadn't ! Jack,
do you know, there must have been somebody in the house
after all, burning to death ; and that scream, when the building fell, was the wind-up of a life !"

"It must have been so, and we have been standing here,

doing nothing, when aid might have been given !" said Crawford, in self-reproach, and forgetting how little a man with
one arm can do in the way of carrying out people from a
burning building. "Yet no—stop ! No, Bob, that scream
was not the last of the person's life, for didn't you notice, we
heard it *twice*, and the last time after the house had fallen in ?
After that house fell, no one inside of it ever screamed, and
so—"

"And so," said Webster, interrupting, "there is somebody,
not in the house, who screamed ? That is what you mean,
and by Jupiter, Jack, you are right !"

"Now we *must* look the other side of the house," said
Crawford. "Some poor creature, badly burned, may have
crawled out from the flames and be lying there in agony."

So there might have been, truly ! And what a strange
riddle is human nature, even on that other side—mercy ! We
but a little while ago considered the ease with which a man
born with the warmest aspirations for human good, might become eager for the destruction of life, when that life belonged
to a foeman : let the opposite spectacle be considered, of a
man who had just been plunging into the thick of a hand-to-
hand fight, estimating human heads as of no more value than
cocoa-nuts, and human lives as something to be taken without
a shudder or a pang of compunction,—a few minutes afterwards speaking of a "poor creature" whose life might be
threatened by fire, and speaking of that "poor creature" with
all the tenderness of a mother or a lover ! And is this inconsistent? No—it is consistent to the last degree. The
brave man is the pitiful man ; and while he may consider a
hecatomb necessary for a cause, he regards one life sacrificed
unnecessarily, as *murder*. "Who needlessly sets foot upon a
worm, is all unfit to live !" says one of the old poet-philoso-
phers. And are worms therefore never to be trodden upon ?
Not so, by any means ! The adverbial adjective "needlessly"
explains the broad distinction. Not one worm, even the
creeping, crawling and disgusting caterpillar, for cruelty or
even for neglect : millions of worms, whether caterpillar or
human worm of the dust, for a sacred cause and a great
duty !

"Yes, come on around the house. The heat is not so great now, and we *must* see if there is anything living here," was the reply of Webster to the last suggestion of Crawford; and they at once followed the yard as closely round as the burning ruins would permit. They heard no repetition of the sound; nor could they see any sign of human life. Behind the house, hillward, stood a small barn and stables, while a wood-shed and some other small outbuildings stood on the eastern side of the enclosure. These had been nearly connected with the house by board fences, and in two places those fences had taken fire and threatened to carry the flames to the other buildings. But the evening had been calm, and the fire had not run many yards along the fences before it became extinguished for want of compelling wind and quick fuel.

A proposition from Webster that they should search the outbuildings for the source of the cry, was negatived by Crawford, who thought it very likely, after all his previous confidence, that some of the Confederate troops, who had certainly held the woods at one time during the day, might be located in the barn—not dangerous, perhaps, if undisturbed, but very likely to be troublesome if two soldiers, one with one arm and both on a very blind errand, should go stumbling about in the dark too miscellaneously.

"Well," said Webster, "no doubt you are right, Jack, as you almost always are. In that case we have nothing to do but to get back to camp and look a little more closely after that shivered arm of yours, for there is certainly no one near the edge of the fire."

"Hark!" said Crawford, as they started to retrace their steps around the house, and move away. They were within a few steps of what appeared to be a wood-shed, standing on the east side of the enclosure, and some forty or fifty feet from the house. "Hark!"

"Well, what is it? I heard nothing!" said Webster, who had been listening exclusively for another shriek.

"Well, *I* heard something, and it was a groan!" said Crawford.

"Oh Lord!" exclaimed the not-very-reverent Webster.

"What next, I wonder? Awhile ago we had shrieks: now we have groans! I wonder if this place is haunted—just a little?"

"Hark! there it was again!" said Crawford. "It *was* a groan, and not very far from us, either!"

"In that case," said Webster, "as it is incumbent upon two members of the Advance Guard not to come all this distance for nothing, we shall be under the necessity of hunting out the groan. Ah!" and the speaker paused a moment. "By Jupiter it *is* a groan. I heard it myself that time. It is here, under this shed!"

The long legs of Webster at once made a movement in that direction, followed by the shorter and more symmetrical ones of Crawford. They reached the door of the wood-house, opening towards the burned mansion. The door was unclosed, and they could look within. Just as they reached the door both heard another groan—quite sufficient to satisfy them that they were not in error as to the place from which the sound had proceeded. A faint red light from the fallen embers of the burning house shone within the rough shed from the narrow door—scarce enough, at first, to make objects distinctly visible; but as they gazed the eyes grew accustomed to the dim light and they could distinctly trace what the building contained. They stepped slowly within, no motion from the occupants giving indication that their presence was known; and this is what they saw—dimly, but clearly enough for the purposes of recognition.

On a straw pallet lay an old man, thin-faced and hollow-eyed, his scanty white hair streaming backward on the end of the pallet, which had been turned up to form a pillow. Over him and reaching from his feet to his breast, was drawn a sheet, and on that sheet lay one of his thin, wrinkled and nerveless hands. His eyes were shut, and he might have appeared to be asleep, but that ever and anon there broke from him one of those low but distinct groans indicative of severe inward pain, which had startled the two Zouaves. But the old man was not the most singular or the most painful feature of this spectacle. Beside him on the ground, kneeling, and rocking backward and forward with that pecu-

culiar motion so indicative of intense and hopeless grief when
used by some of the European peasantry, was a young girl—
apparently very young, very small and very girlish, though
there was something about her which even in that dim light
gave the impression that she was not a little girl, but a
woman.

So much the two soldiers saw, while neither of the occupants
of the shed seemed to be aware of their presence; but Webster, an intensely practical man and more fertile in resources
than overflowing with delicacy, was not quite satisfied with
the view obtained, and instantly determined to improve it.

"Wait here—I am going for a light," he said, and stepping
hastily from the door he ran to the burning embers of the
house, caught the end of a piece of pine scantling of which
the other was in full blaze, and in a moment more entered the
door of the shed, his novel torch throwing an odd, ghastly
light upon all the objects within the little building. Then
and not till then did the intruders become aware that they
stood face to face with one who was dying, in the old man
on the pallet,—and with a woman of a rare and almost
startling order of beauty, in the young girl who knelt beside him. Her form, as they could see, even in her kneeling position, was almost childish in the shortness of its
stature and the petite mould of her limbs; and yet there
was nothing thin or attenuated about her, and the epithet "fragile" could not have been applied to her with
half the justice of that very opposite word, "willowy." Her
face was infantile in the smallness of the features, in their
perfect round, and in the expression of helpless placidity
which seemed to lie upon it. But those features were yet
classical in outline, and the mouth, especially, was very sweet
and budding. The open eyes were blue as heaven; and the
hair, of which there was a great wealth, loosed from all restraint and sweeping back on her shoulders, was of that delicate and almost impalpable blonde so seldom met (even among
the English, who arrogate to themselves the purest blonde hair
in the world) and so universally admired—nay, almost worshipped.

It is not to be supposed that so long a time was necessary

for the two Zouaves to catch the particulars here set down, as would be indicated by the length of the description itself; and certainly no such length of time was allowed them without interruption. It was now evident that neither the dying man nor the young girl had before been aware of the entrance of the strangers; but as Webster entered with his torch of pine, the sudden light startled both. The old man's eyes did not unclose, but the young girl's looked around with a startled glance; she rose to her feet, clasped her hands imploringly, while so sad and beseeching an expression rested upon her face, that she might have been the discarded Peri pleading for her lost place in heaven,—and said:

" Go away, please! Grandfather is dying. Don't disturb him—please don't!"

" My poor girl, we do not mean to disturb him, or you," said Crawford, advancing a little way towards the side of the pallet, and throwing into his voice all its native sympathy and kindness. " We are friends."

" Marion, who is that?" asked the old man, feebly. He had before shown that his eyes were affected by the light, and made a motion to rise, which brought the young girl at once to her knees again beside him, with her hand and arm affectionately round his head.

" I do not know, grandpa! They are soldiers—two soldiers."

" Tell them to go away—ask them to go away, and let me die in peace!" said the old man, his voice still feeble, and his utterance difficult as before.

" I have asked them, grandpa, and they will not go," said the young girl, her tones, strangely enough, even in characterizing what she must have felt to be an outrage, expressing no feeling of anger, but soft and low as flute notes of the lower register.

" We do not wish to intrude. We will go away," said Crawford.

"Ah!" said the old man, a perceptible shadow passing over his face, "that was the voice of a *gentleman!* Ask him who he is, Marion. But he must be a rebel," and the old man went on, his voice falling still lower as if he was speaking to himself. "He must be a rebel, for McClellan has been beaten and driven back. They have been fighting all day, and I know the end—I know the end."

"We are *not* rebels," said Crawford, who had caught the last words, whether intended or not even for the grand-daughter's ear. "I hope you will not fear us. I am John Crawford, private in Duryea's Zouaves, of McClellan's army; and this is Robert Webster, private in the same regiment."

"Union men? Men faithful to the country and the old flag?" asked the old man, a gleam of delight passing over his wasted features. "Here, quick, quick, Marion, raise me up."

The young girl tried to obey, but her scant strength was insufficient even to raise the thin form of the old man. Robert Webster stepped forward to assist her, and as the old man was raised knelt down behind and supported the head and upper body in a half-sitting position. Though the eyes had remained closed before, they opened now, to confront Crawford—poor old, dim, lack-lustre eyes, that yet seemed to have one burning spark in the centre.

"You say that you are a Union soldier. Will you swear it?" he asked, in the same low, solemn tones.

"I do solemnly swear, in the presence of Almighty God," said John Crawford, lifting his hand to heaven, remembering some portions of the oath so commonly administered in our courts of justice, and adding on some words not commonly used in the same connection, "that I am a true and loyal soldier in the service of the United States, and the enemy of all rebels and traitors! Amen!"

"Thank God!" said the old man, solemnly. "If I cannot die with the old flag over me, I can at least have the company of those who uphold it! Give me your hand. What!" as the young soldier came closer. "You are wounded. You have been in the battle to-day. You are defeated and a fugitive?"

"No!" said the Zouave, with a world of triumph in his tone, and giving his uninjured hand at the same time. "I am wounded, but McClellan and Fitz-John Porter have to-day flogged the rebels out of their boots at Malvern Hill, and the Union army is safe!"

"Thank God! oh, thank God!" said the old man, reverently. "Marion, lay me back, I am faint." He did not seem to be aware that Webster was assisting to hold him up, or that any one was in the place except Crawford and his grand-daughter. His request was obeyed, and he was laid down again on the pallet; but the excitement of the last few minutes had perceptibly weakened him, and he was evidently failing fast. "Marion, it hurts me to talk—a little. Tell the gentleman, for he is a gentleman, I know—who we are and how we came to be here."

"This is my grandfather," the young girl said, still on her knees by the pallet, and evidencing in her calm and childlike tone no surprise at the request, and no agitation in relating what must have pained her so terribly under the circumstances. "His name is Chester Hobart. We belong to a good family, and they say that we are related to the English Earls of Buckinghamshire. My father was Charles Hampden Hobart. He was an officer in the navy, and was drowned when I was quite a little girl." Crawford did not notice, then, but remembered afterwards, that in this strange relation she said nothing of another parent who seemed likewise to be dead—her *mother*. "My grandfather and myself lived in the house, here. We had black servants, but they have all gone away. We did not have any negro quarter—the servants lived in one part of the house. My grandfather has been very ill —so ill that I thought he would die. He is very fond of the Union—*I* do not know anything about politics. He was better a little; but the house took fire awhile ago, and I could scarcely help him out. I got out the straw mattress and a sheet, and I could get out nothing more. I am afraid my poor grandfather is very ill, now; perhaps he is dying. I thought he was dying a little while ago, and I screamed—I could not help it. That is all, grandfather, is it not? oh, grandfather! grandfather!" and the poor girl, for the first time broken down, fell forward on the straw pallet, buried her face near the old man's head, and sobbed like an over-tasked child.

"Poor girl!" said John Crawford. He did not mean to speak aloud, but he did so, and the dying man heard him.

"Young man," he said, "you took an oath just now. Will you take another, to make an old man die happier?"

"I will!" answered the young man, bending close to him. He was too much exhausted, now, to raise his head any more.

"You say that the Union troops have won the fight to-day?"

"I do say so. We have repulsed the rebel attacks every time; and the last repulse was a rout. They are defeated."

"You believe that you can reach the Union camp in safety?"

"I have no doubt of it," answered the Zouave.

"Then swear to me, with the same uplifted hand you used awhile ago, that you will remove my grand-daughter, Marion Hobart, to the North—out of this den of secession. She has money in a Bank in New York, enough to make her comfortable—I put it there three years ago, thinking such a time as this might come. Swear to me that you will find her a home with some honest family, and that you will neither do harm to her yourself nor permit it to approach her if you can shelter her from it. Swear it by the Ever-Living God."

"I swear!" said the young soldier, lifting his hand solemnly.

The old man lay still on his pillow, a strange and awful shadow stealing over his face. His grand-daughter had raised her head, and she saw it, though the torch had burned low and there was little but the red light of the fire glimmering into the building. She buried her face once more in the pallet, threw her arms around the old man's form, and sobbed,

"Grandfather! oh, grandfather!"

"Hark! did I not hear cannon again? Are you *sure* the Union troops have won the victory?" came from the closing lips. "You are a soldier and a gentleman. You said your name was Craw—Crawford. A good old name. Never mind me—take care of Marion. Marion—Ma—." He was silent, and silent forever, except as the dumb lips may be hereafter opened!

Marion Hobart saw the lower jaw fall and the open eyes put on that ghastly appearance which is the seal of the triumph of death: and she knew, without a word from either of her companions, that he was dead. The soldiers saw that she comprehended all that had occurred, and expected that she would shriek again and throw herself wildly on the body. She did not—she merely clasped her hands and looked on the body with such a pitiful gaze of fixed sorrow that Crawford could not bear it and turned away his eyes, while Webster found sudden and unexplained necessity for blowing his long nose.

Suddenly, and before a word had been spoken by either of the soldiers, a new thought came to the young girl and a terrible look of fear and sorrow swept over her face.

"It is night and we cannot bury him!" she said, her voice broken and agonized. "How can I leave him unburied? Gentlemen—gentlemen—how can I leave my poor grandfather unburied?"

"He shall not remain unburied!" said Crawford, instantly and earnestly.

"He should not, Miss, if I had to make a ground-hog of myself and dig his grave with my own hands!" put in Webster, who had scarcely spoken before during all the sad scene.

"Oh thank you!—thank you both!" she began—then suddenly pausing, she said : "But how—I do not understand— it is night, and we have nothing—"

"In half an hour we will be at camp, God willing," answered Crawford, "and Colonel Warren will send a guard of soldiers to watch the body until morning and then to bury it with all honor. Do you understand, Miss Hobart?"

"I do," answered the young girl, her sad calmness returning at once. "You are both very good and kind, and may God bless you. You want to go? We must go, I suppose; and we can do poor grandfather no good now by staying. Good-bye, grandfather—poor grandfather! I shall never see you again, and you do not see me, even now! Good-bye! oh, grandfather, grandfather! I am so lonesome! so lonesome!"

For one moment she threw herself forward on the pallet and embraced the body of the old man, in uncontrollable sorrow, while both the two Zouaves found themselves shedding tears very inappropriate for the evening of a day of battle.

Then she rose to her feet, put her fingers to her eyes as if pressing out the moisture that had gathered unbidden under the lids, and said :

"Shall we go ? I am ready."

Reverently, Crawford drew the sheet over the face of the corpse, hiding it forever from the eyes of the bereaved grand-daughter as it was so soon to be hidden from the eyes of all the living; and then the doubly-orphaned girl and her new-found friends took their way from the scene of death. She was dressed only in light delaine and had neither shawl nor bonnet ; but the night air was not too cool, and Webster wrapped his Zouave jacket around the slight form, while Crawford supplied her with his handkerchief as a covering for her head. They took their way at once from the house, now little more than a heap of darkening coals,—and struck south-eastward over the spur of the hill and through that portion of the woods least likely to retain any ambushed rebels, towards the quarters on Malvern. The sounds of battle had almost entirely ceased, it being now some ten o'clock in the evening ; and only occasionally the boom of a cannon half a mile away to the south-westward showed that the opposing forces yet remained near each other. The thick smoke which had shrouded all the country during the day, had almost all rolled away, the young moon had disappeared in the west, and the stars looked down as clearly and beautifully as if no such things as war and death could exist in a world gazed upon by such pure eyes.

Scarcely a word was spoken by either, during the short walk to the top of Malvern Hill. The young girl leaned upon the uninjured arm of John Crawford, with a touching confidence and trust, an occasional convulsion of grief shaking her frame and an occasional sob breaking from her ; while Bob Webster acted as scout and guide, carrying both rifles, and perhaps not the more on that account prepared to repel any sudden danger. But no such danger came. The rebels had indeed retired, and the various corps of the Union army had been gathered in to their respective quarters, preparatory to the march to Harrison's Landing, which was to be pursued at daylight. Not all of them, however. It was well that the course of Crawford and his companions did not lie across Carter's Field; for if it had done so, they must have seen hundreds of lanterns moving about, and hundreds of dark figures moving and toiling—the fatigue-parties burying the Union dead and planting the soil of the Old Dominion with more of that martyr seed which may yet spring up to the redemption of the land and the glory of the nation. This would have been a sad and harrowing sight for the young girl, after so lately leaving her last relative to be made a prey for worms; and fortunately she was spared it.

Perhaps half an hour after leaving the burned house, the Zouaves and their charge reached the bivouac of the Advance Guard, half way down the slope towards Carter's Field. The loss of the corps had been but trifling, in spite of their furious charge; and though tired and hungry, those who had not dropped down in their places to sleep, were merry and jubilant. The Union forces had won one last great victory in defeat, and they knew it and knew that the army was safe. Crawford had ever been a favorite with his corps, respected by the men and even petted by the officers; and he was recognized with shouts of welcome by many, as he made his way, with his charge on his arm, towards the Colonel's tent.

"Hallo, old fellow! Safe eh, after all!" cried one who recognized him; while another said: "Thought you had gone to Richmond, without waiting for the rest of us!" and another, but in a lower tone that perhaps Marion Hobart did not hear: "I say, Jack, where the deuce did you pick up a petticoat, and a white one at that?"

Colonel Warren received the young Zouave, and heard his story, paying all respect to the young girl under his protection. He at once promised, at Crawford's request, that a file of soldiers should go down to the burned house and perform the rites of burial before the corps left the hill; whereupon the face of the young girl more fully repaid him by its expression of true gratitude, than did even her words of sad thankfulness. There are men who have called Colonel Warren not only a martinet but a man devoid of feeling: let

his action on this occasion prove how little those know him
who speak of him thus coldly.

"Some of the wagons are leaving for the Landing just
now," he said to Crawford, after the latter had explained the
nature of his wound and briefly told the story of the protection he had promised the young girl, which he would have
no difficulty in finding for her in the company of his brother
and sister. "Some of the wagons are going down now.
You are of no use here, and you had as well take the lady
down at once. Make her as comfortable as you can in one
of the wagons. The ride is only a short one; and perhaps
you may be able to find a berth for her on board one of the
boats at the Landing. Stay, Crawford, a despatch-boat will
be going down to Monroe in the morning. You are a faithful fellow and a good soldier. I will see to it, in the morning, that you have a furlough for a month. I think we shall
do nothing more for a month, and you may need that time to
get a new arm. Take Miss Hobart at once to New York,
and place her with your sister. That is all—now look for a
place in one of the wagons. Good night—I will see about
the rest before the boat leaves."

Crawford's warm "God bless you, Colonel!" was more
softly, but not less earnestly echoed by the "I thank you, sir,
very much. You are very good and kind!" of the young
girl; and the two left the tent to follow out the directions of
the officer. Bob Webster, unwounded, was already with his
companions, picking up what he could find left in the way of
rations, and telling over, for the sixth time already, the adventures of the night.

Not to linger upon what no longer needs particular description, let it be said in a word that Crawford succeeded in se-
curing transportation for the young girl and himself to Harrison's Landing; that they reached that return terminus of
the campaign against Richmond, a little after midnight; that
a place was found on board one of the boats at the Landing,
for Miss Hobart, under the kind care of the colored chambermaid; that Colonel Warren kept his promise and procured the
wounded Zouave, (whose arm had been examined by one of
the surgeons, and found to be badly torn and lacerated, though

none of the bones were broken), his furlough for a month "or
until recovered;" that they went down the next day on the
despatch boat to Fortress Monroe, whence General Wool at
once sent them on to Washington; and that on the evening
of-the Fourth of July they reached the city of New York, and
John Crawford had the pleasure of placing his sacred charge
under the protection of his brother, whom he found yet so
sadly an invalid,—and of his sister, who received her with a
warmer and more considerate kindness than he had ever before known her to exhibit towards any living object.

CHAPTER XX.

JUDGE OWEN AND HIS DOMESTIC DISCIPLINE—TWO CRIMINALS
AT THE BAR, WITH A SPECIAL EDICT FOLLOWING—A ROW AT
WALLACK'S, AND ONE MORE RECOGNITION.

IT has again been unavoidable, in following the fortunes of
other characters connected with this narration, to lose sight of
those who have prominently figured in the mansion of Judge
Owen—the Judge himself, his wife, his daughter Emily, Aunt
Martha, and the two lovers who fought over that very pretty
little bone as if they had been dogs and she a tit-bit of very
different description. But it is one of the first principles of
conducting the successful march of an army, that no stragglers
should be allowed to lag too far behind, lest a sudden onslaught
upon them might cause a panic extending to all the other portions of the force. Let the Judge and his family, then, be
kept up as nearly as possible to the march of the main body;
and especially let not pretty Emily Owen and her mischievous
printer-lover be lost from the ranks by any contingency.

Aunt Martha saw farther into futurity than her niece, when
she decided that the row between Frank Wallace and Colonel
John Boadley Bancker, if it came to the Judge's ears, would
be likely to make affairs much worse instead of better; and

Emily and she had some serious conversation over the prospect, that night of the street accident, after both the rivals had
gone,—which did not tend to make the young girl go to her
white pillow with the most blissful of anticipations. The
younger lady thought it doubtful whether the matter need
come to the knowledge of her father at all, as she did not believe that the Colonel would so far bemean himself as to make
a complaint to the father of the young girl he was pursuing, of
the advantages which another suitor might possess over him in
the mind of the girl herself. Aunt Martha, who had seen somewhat more than her niece of the world and its meanness, did
not consider the Colonel too proud to take such a course, if
he believed himself likely to gain by it; and besides—she remembered, what her niece did not, that they were by no means
alone in the house when the little affair occurred. Servants
—those important personages, who in modern days keep the
houses and permit their masters and mistresses, on the pay-
ment of a round sum per week, to live in the house with them
—those ubiquitous personages, who seem to have the faculty
of being precisely where they are not wanted, when any family trouble is to be ventilated,—servants were in the house
at the time, and there was no guaranty whatever that they
had not been sufficiently near to hear every awkward word
that had been spoken.

The good Aunt felt that she had the more cause to be
apprehensive in the latter direction, from some observations
that she had accidentally made a few weeks before. Not
long after the coming into the house of Miss Hetty, cook
and kitchen girl, (she is certainly entitled to the prefix of
"Miss," at least once, from the fact of her holding her head
a little higher than any member of the family) a little after
her advent, we say, Aunt Martha happened one evening to
pass through the lower hall, in list slippers, and accidentally
became aware that two persons were talking in a very low
tone, just within the door of the dining-room. Perhaps it
may have been accidentally, but possibly on purpose, that
she took one glance through the crack of the door, herself unobserved, and noticed that the talkers were Judge
Owen and Hetty. The tone was certainly confidential, and

the two stood very near together. Had Mrs. Martha West not been aware of certain points in her brother's character which would make a criminal flirtation with a servant-girl in his own house impossible, she might have drawn the conclusion that some impropriety of that kind was on foot. As it was, she became satisfied that some of her previous suspicions were correct, and that Judge Owen, who habitually went to the intelligence-offices and selected the servants when any change became necessary, was capable of the ineffable meanness of bribing his domestics to play the spy on his own household and detail all the occurrences to him! Where the estimable man had picked up that particular meanness, she had no idea, nor is this a place in which to hazard a suggestion. If it was so, it might be suggested that the practice of hearing and allowing weight to spy testimony, caught through key-holes and the cracks of doors, or picked up by lounging at people's elbows on sidewalks and in bar-rooms, had possibly some connection with the application of the same system to his own household.

Perhaps there may be persons upright and straight-forward enough themselves, and unsuspicious enough of the vices and meannesses of others, to doubt whether such things as those just hinted at, exist in the great city. To such it might not be amiss to say, that there are operations of this character, in what is called "respectable society," so much worse than the mere procured espionage of servants, that they make that atrocity almost endurable. Fancy the husband of a second wife keeping his eldest daughter by a former marriage, herself a married woman, in the same house with his wife, with orders to keep that wife constantly in view, to watch her when she receives company, dog her when she goes out, and dole out to her the necessaries for the family from closets, chests and cupboards of which she [the daughter] keeps the keys! Fancy these things, and the wife submitting to them, perforce! And then understand, what is the humiliating truth, that the lady subjected to these practices is a most beautiful and accomplished favorite, delighting thousands by her public appearances, envied by all, and supposed to be rolling in wealth and revelling in comfort!

19

Not long ago there was a story going the rounds of the
press, of some spicy sporting operations in England, in which
one trainer and jockey threw one of his creatures, in the disguise of a stable-boy, into the stables of another, to watch the
appearance and action of his horses, to overhear what he
could of the conversation of the trainer, to discover for what
cups and matches they were about to be entered, and to make
weekly reports to him, through letters pretendedly addressed
to the boy's "mother," so that he could take advantage of
the knowledge so unfairly attained, in making up his betting-
book.   By a mere accident the trainer discovered what kind
of an emissary of the enemy was quartered in his stables,
and instead of kicking him out he merely *gave him plenty to
report.*   He managed to have the boy overhear all sorts of
manufactured conversations, rode his horses unfairly on the
training-course, stuffed him with false reports of the matches
for which they were entered, and, in short, gave him such
budgets to send home to his master, that the latter grew
completely mystified, bet on the losing chances instead of the
winning ones, and lost about twenty thousand pounds, which
went into the pocket of the intended victim.   The story is a
good one, and for the honor of humanity ought to be true.

Not many years ago a jealous old husband in this city, who
had fallen into the misfortune of a young and handsome wife,
grew jealous of her without the least cause, and descended
to the execrable meanness of putting one of the chamber-maids
under pay to play the detective and report to him what letters her mistress received and all the "goings on" in the
house.   Biddy was not quite keen enough for her new position, and the bright eyes of the young wife were not long in
discovering that she was watched and dogged !   What did
the outraged wife ?   Send the vixen packing, bag and baggage, with a boxed ear for a parting present, as she might'
have done with all propriety ?   Not at all—she retained her
and kept her own discovery a secret, merely adopting the
same plan as our friend the trainer, and giving her *something
to tell.*   The wife fortunately had half a dozen male cousins,
living at a distance, and as many female friends, living near.
Between these two corps of assistants she managed to receive

such letters, accidentally dropped for the servant-girl to finger, and received such clandestine visits when her husband was absent and at suspicious hours, as left no doubt whatever in the mind of a *reasonable* man like the husband, that she must be terribly false to her marital vows. The catastrophe of all this need not be given : it was final enough, in all conscience, and sent the husband down town one day with a dim consciousness that he had made himself the greatest fool since Adam, and that an early burial would not be so great a calamity after all !

Unfortunately Judge Owen, of this writing, had no such sharp-witted and reckless opponent, and his meanness was left to work itself out in a natural manner. Aunt Martha's apprehensions were not idle, as was proved very soon after. The Judge and his wife returned from their little trip up the Hudson, on the second day after their departure ; and within three hours after their arrival, before the Judge had been absent from the house a moment and before Colonel Boadley Bancker could by any means have managed to see him, the storm of paternal wrath and indignation burst on the devoted heads for which it was intended.

The gas had just been lighted on the floor below, and Aunt Martha and Emily were seated enjoying the summer twilight in the front-room of the latter, up-stairs, when the stentorian voice of the Judge was heard bawling from the hall :

"Martha—Emily—come down here a moment !".

"There it is ! there is trouble ahead ! I knew it !" said Aunt Martha.

"He *cannot* have heard anything about it, vet," said the niece.

"He *has*, I am sure of it !" answered the Aunt. "We may as well go down and take the thunder-storm, at once, as have it hanging over us for a month."

"Oh, Aunt, I cannot endure to have Papa scold, when he is in one of his terrible humors," said the frightened girl. "I have done nothing, that I know of ; but you don't know what rough words he says to me sometimes, and I have been almost afraid that he would strike me with that heavy hand ! I believe I should *die* if he did."

"No, child, you would not *die*, I think," said the more practical Aunt, "but something might occur for which your father would one day be quïte as sorry,—your last particle of love and respect for him might die, and that would be sadder than the death of many bodies. But come, Emily; we shall be called again in a moment."

Aunt and niece descended the stairs to the parlor, the latter trembling like a leaf in the wind and the former in a strange flutter that was part trepidation and part indignation. They found affairs in the parlor in a very promising condition, as the aunt had suspected. Judge Owen was too angry to sit in his large chair, as he would have liked to do, and receive the culprits with judicial dignity. He was walking the floor, with his hands behind his back and every indication of very stormy weather on his countenance. He looked bigger and more burly than ever, and less than ever like what the brother and father should have been, to the two who entered. Mrs. Owen sat in a rocking-chair, swaying backward and forward, with her hand to her eyes and very much the appearance of a whipped child who had been set down in that chair with orders to be "good." It was not supposable that the Judge had been whipping her, physically; but he had unquestionably been "getting his hand in" for the exercise that was to come, by reading her a severe lecture upon everything that she had done and everything she had *not* done, since the day they were married.

"So then!" he broke out, the moment the culprits appeared in view. "This is the kind of order you keep in my house— *my* house!" and he emphasized the possessive pronoun so severely that the poor little word must have had a hard time of it among his strong front teeth.

Emily, as yet, replied nothing. But Aunt Martha said:

"Well really, brother, I do not see that the house is in very bad order! Perhaps that rocker is a little out of place, and the *etagere*—"

"D—n it, woman, I am not talking of the furniture, and you know it!" thundered the Judge.

"William Owen!" said Aunt Martha, who had not gone through fifty or a hundred such conflicts without deriving some controversial profit from them—"I do not choose to be sworn at, in *your* house or the house of any other man. If you were a gentleman, you would not be guilty of the outrage."

Emily trembled. Here was Jupiter plucked by the beard, and called hard names to his face, by one of the mere underlings of his dominions! William Owen not a gentleman! *Judge* Owen not a gentleman! Could human presumption go farther? What would be the end of this?

"I will swear as I like, and when I like!" said the Judge, after a pause of an instant. But he did not swear again immediately, and not at all again at his sister, during the whole interview, it was noticeable. Brutality is not best met by brutality; but it is a mistake to suppose that it is best met by abject submission. What it needs, as its master and corrective, is *dignified firmness*.

"So this is the way, is it," the Judge went on. "The moment my back is turned, my house is full of low characters, and quarrelling and fighting become the order of the day."

"When did all this occur?" asked Aunt Martha, innocently.

"The very evening I left!" thundered the Judge.

"And how have you found it all out, so soon?" queried his sister, looking him very calmly in the eyes.

It may be a libel, for which an action would lie, to say that Judge Owen blushed at this home-thrust. He certainly reddened, but that may have been with anger—not shame.

"How do I know it? What business is that of yours, woman? It is enough to say that I *do* know it, and that I will break all that sort of thing up, or I will break half a dozen heads!" This was a favorite simile of the Judge's, because it brought in the word "break" twice, in such an effective manner. "Well, Miss Emily Owen, what have you to say to all this?" It may be libel, again, to say that the Judge was sheering off his vessel from a battery that worried him, to engage one that seemed comparatively helpless; but really the whole thing bore that appearance.

"I, father? I have nothing to say," returned the daughter, "and for that reason I have not said anything."

"You do not deny, then," thundered the Judge, his voice

rising higher because he had a younger, lower-voiced and less
formidable antagonist, "that on the very night I went away
there was low company in this house, and that—"

Perhaps Emily Owen had never presumed to interrupt her
father half a dozen times during her life, but we have before
seen that she *could* do so, even wickedly, when fully aroused,
and the temptation to do so in the present instance was overpowering. Besides, she had just caught a lesson from her
aunt, in the "*womanly* art of self-defence," the muscular development for which lies in the tongue.

"Do you call Colonel Bancker low company, father?"

"Colonel Bancker? No, girl! Colonel Bancker is a gentleman and a soldier," replied the Judge. "I am speaking of
that low, contemptible scoundrel, Wallace."

"And *he* has been in the habit of coming here with your
consent, papa," answered the daughter, "and so I do not
know how we were to blame for receiving the visits of people
when you were gone, whom you were in the habit of receiving
when you were at home."

"Hush, child! Hush, Emily!" Mrs. Owen felt it necessary to say at this moment. She had not before spoken a
word, but she may have felt that that incarnation of reason
and dignity, her husband, was "taking damage" at the hands
of very ordinary mortals. "Hush, child—do not bandy words
with your father."

"No, miss, do not bandy words with *me!*" roared the Judge,
put exactly upon the right track, from which he had before
strayed a little, by the words of his wife. "*I* am master in
this house, as I mean to let you know!" Humble Judge!—
he *had* let them know it, long before, quite as much as lay in
his power. "I will not allow myself to be run over in this
manner, any longer!" Ponderous and self-sacrificing Judge!
—apart from the fact that no one in that house had ever tried
the experiment, what a vehicle it would have been that could
"run over" that man without danger from the encounter!
And now gathering strength and force as well as anger, as he
rolled down the mountain of denunciation, he went on: "I
have called you down, both of you, and you especially, Emily,
to make a final settlement with you! I have told you before

that you should marry Colonel John Boadley Bancker, and I
need not tell you again, for by G— you *shall!* And now I
tell you something more. If you ever permit that d—d low-
lived, miserable, contemptible puppy, whom you call Frank
Wallace, to cross the door-step of this house again, I will
break every bone in his infernal carcase; and when he goes
into the street, you go with him! Do you hear ?"

"Yes, father, I hear," said his daughter.

"Yes, we both hear, as I suppose you intended it for both
of us," said his sister.

"I intended it for *everybody!*" roared the Judge. "Now
let us see whether you obey or not! Come, Mrs. Owen, is
supper ready ?"

Probably the Judge supposed that he had supplied both
the others with quite as much supper as they needed, as he did
not extend the invitation to either. He certainly had done
so: they were both "full," in one sense of the word if not in
the other. His daughter was "full" of trouble and anxiety;
and Aunt Martha was "full" of a more dangerous feeling—
outraged pride and indignation.

"Poor Frank!—he cannot come to the house any more!"
said the young girl, when they had left the parlor. "What
shall I do? Aunt—Aunt—don't scold me, but I *love him.*
That is the truth; and don't *you* scold me, but help me if you
can."

"Until this hour, Emily," said the aunt, gravely, and taking
the hand of her niece kindly in her own, "I had simply been
determined that you should not be forced into a marriage with
Colonel Bancker, if I could prevent it. Within this half hour
I have made up my mind to go farther. I know that you
love Frank Wallace; I believe him to be a good man, and I
know him to be a brave one; and now you shall marry him,
if any aid *I* can offer will help you to that end!"

"Aunt! Aunt! dear, good, kind Aunt!" cried the young
girl, throwing herself into the widow's arms and giving her
such a hug and such a storm of kisses as would have made
Frank Wallace whistle "Hail Columbia" and "Abraham's
Daughter" for forty-eight hours in succession.

Such was the radical effect, towards carrying out his de-

termination in regard to each of the two rivals, produced by
Judge Owen's ultimatum. He was not the first man, and he
probably will not be the last, to pour the drop too much into
the bucket of endurance and add that last feather to the load
which weighs down the camel of patience. Something more
of the "effect" will be seen in this immediate connection.

Judge Owen had occasion to attend a political caucus, at
one of the down-town hotels, early in the evening of the
second day from that on which the collision with his sister
and daughter had occurred ; and he consequently did not go
home to dinner when his court adjourned. He dined at the
hotel where the caucus took place, and afterwards strolled up
Broadway, airing his portly figure, and intending to take the
Third-Avenue cars at Astor Place or Fourteenth Street.
When he came opposite Wallack's Theatre, at about nine
o'clock, the lights shone brightly before the door, the placards
announcing the "Returned Volunteer" and "Mischievous
Annie" looked tempting, and as Judge Owen had an eye for
the drama and was officially marked "D. H." on the book at
the gate, he concluded to see the balance of the performance.

He passed in. Florence was just indulging in that terrible
war-dance of jealousy which follows the supposed discovery
of the fact that the wife of Bill Williams has taken up with
a Picaninny, and the laughter and applause were uproarious.
The Judge found some acquaintances in the lobby, and chatted with them while he watched the piece and while waiting
for the next.

Finally another friend, a family acquaintance, came up the
aisle, from the orchestra-seats, probably on his way to those
pleasant lower regions in which refreshment to the inner man
is dispensed. As he shook hands with the Judge, he said :

"Ah, Judge, I did not know that you were here. I saw
your daughter, just now, down in the orchestra, but I am
sure she did not come in with you."

"My daughter !" said the Judge, surprised, "I think you
must be mistaken. "Mrs. Owen did not speak of coming to
the theatre this evening."

"Oh," said the acquaintance, "Mrs. Owen is not here. I
should have seen her if she had been. Your daughter came

in with a young man, and they are sitting together down there in the second row from the front."

"You do not know the young man?" asked the Judge, on whom the compound noun for some cause produced an unpleasant effect.

"No," answered the acquaintance, "I do not know him. He is a rather good-looking young fellow, short, with brown curly hair, and a moustache, and dressed in light-gray. No doubt you know him by the description."

Judge Owen *did* know him by the description, but too well! That short good-looking young man with the curly hair, the moustache and the light-gray clothes, was as certainly the man he had forbidden his house and the company of his daughter, as his own name was Owen and his dignity a judicial one!

Here was an outrage!—witness it ye fathers whose daughters do not always obey your high behests. Here was a call for the exercise of the highest qualities of authority!—bear witness to that, all you good people who have at one time or another dragged your wives out of churches because you did not like the ritual, or who have dragged them *into* churches because suitors armed with money-bags or aristocratic names or political influence, stood within and beckoned! Here was a necessity for proving what Judge Owen had only a day or two before so loudly asserted—his ascendency in his own household. Here was an opportunity to show to the public that Judge Owen, arbiter of the legal destinies of his fellow-men when they did not range beyond a certain insignificant number of dollars, was at once a Solon and a Draco in his own domestic relations. Great men *will* develope themselves at some period or other in their lives, however they may previously have been kept back by adverse circumstances; and Judge Owen had never yet enjoyed the opportunity of showing half his mighty energies. Armed with the double power of a parent and the law, he felt that he could combat anything—even a young and delicate woman : gifted with a rigid sense of right which rose above all personal considerations, he felt that to that right he could sacri-

fice anything—even the privacy and sanctity of his domestic
relations.

The great men of old had done something in that way:
Brutus had laid his son, without a tear or a groan, on the
altar of his country; Virginius had slain his daughter when
her perilled honor demanded that violent deed; and only
half a century before his own time, Napoleon had given up a
beloved Empress and married a royal nobody, for the sake of
preserving the dynasty that his people so demanded. It only
remained for William Owen, Judge, to emulate those great
examples and drag his daughter out of the theatre!

It may have been that Judge Owen did not think of quite
all those great examples, as he walked broadly and pompously
down the aisle, disturbing the audience just when the curtain
was rising on the second piece; but he certainly bore himself
as if he remembered all of them and a few hundreds more.
Anxious spectators looked at him as he came down, speculating painfully whether he was likely to take his seat in front
of *them*, and calculating what would be their chances of seeing in that event. But the Judge was not going to sit down
—no! At the gate he encountered a momentary obstruction,
in the shape of the usher who loooked after the orchestra
tickets; but he swept him away as a spring freshet might
carry away a bundle of obstructing sedge, by a majestic wave
of the hand and the information that he was merely going
down there for a moment on business.

Then he strode on down the aisle, unobserved as yet by
the lovers. who sat in the seat next the front and within three
or four places of the end of the row, enjoying the dramatic
entertainment and each others' company about equally. Perhaps they sat a very little closer together than they might
have done had there been no parental objection in the way;
and under the folds of Emily's dark mantilla, which lay upon
her lap, there may have been two hands clasped together.
Let the young and the loving, whose province it is to make
such follies half the material of their lives, decide whether
affairs were likely to be exactly in the shape suggested,—as
also, whether at any time during the evening, when it had
become necessary for Frank Wallace to make a remark to

his companion, he had or had not leaned down his lips so close to her ear as almost to kiss its pink pendant.

The first intimation had by the absorbed lovers that the paternal bomb was bursting in the neighborhood, was conveyed by the Judge halting at the end of their row, leaning over the two or three people between, without any apology, stretching out his arm, and saying in his loud, coarse voice:

"Miss Emily Owen, you are wanted at home."

The blood flew to the face of the young girl in an instant, though it was the blood of anxiety and not of shame, and she asked:

"Is any one ill—hurt?—My mother—"

"Your mother is well, and there is no one sick at home,' said the Judge, determined that his lesson to his daughter should not be balked by any one of the audience thinking him less a brute than he was. "But I find you here in improper company and against my orders; and I command you to leave that man and come home with me instantly."

Decided sensation in the orchestra-seats, and even on the stage, where Mrs. Florence paused in the middle of one of her most effective Yankeeisms, to know what caused the interruption. Sensation in a good many fingers, that they would like to be applied violently to the ears of the man who could speak in that manner to so sweet-looking a girl, no matter under what provocation. A few hisses and cries of "Hush-h-h!" "Hush-h-h!" Poor Emily had sunk back in her chair, the moment her anxiety was relieved by mortification, merely saying in a pleading voice, as if to disarm her tyrant:

"Oh, father!"

Frank Wallace, meanwhile, had sprung to his feet, the moment the opprobrious epithet was applied to him; and though he distinctly saw that the intruder was the puissant Judge Owen, Emily's father, and large enough, physically, to eat him for lunch—he was on the point of springing across the intervening space and giving him a taste of his gymnastic quality. This would have been terribly improper, no doubt, towards a man much older than himself, and the father of the girl he yet hoped one day to make his wife; but the specta-

tors, had he done so, and could they have known all the facts
of the case, would have been much more likely to forgive him
than the miserable hound (now a miserable secessionist—thank
Heaven for his choice !) who bore a military title to his name,
a few years ago, and sat still in one of the theatres of this city,
without daring to lift a hand in opposition, while the just-
married wife by his side was brutally caned by her millionaire
father for daring to marry *him!* High temper may be dangerous, and the rough hand something to be avoided and re-
probated ; but there is something worse in the extreme opposite, and humanity worse sickens at the sight of an abject
poltroon, than at any other worthless fungus that springs as
an excrescence from God's footstool.

All the saints be praised for these little women ! They
are, after all, the balance-wheels of life, and the whole machinery would run riot and go to destruction without them.
They bring us to ourselves, often, and so save us *from* ourselves. When they advise peace and patience, they are generally right, for at such times violence is seldom politic.
Frank Wallace would probably have carried out his violent
first intention, but for the hand of Emily which dropped upon
his arm almost before he had risen, and the soft voice which
spoke in his ear, very hurriedly :

"Don't, Frank, for *my* sake ! Let me go, and sit still.
You shall see me again in a day or two. *I'll* pay Pa for this !"

Very much consoled by these words, and especially by the
last clause, Frank Wallace resumed his seat, merely indulging
in a remark which was heard by many around him, and which
may or may not have been heard by the person at whom it
was aimed :

"Bah ! you big brute !"

A little suppressed clapping of hands in the neighborhood,
which the actors probably thought intended for themselves,
but which certainly was not. Meanwhile Emily Owen, dropping her hand by some kind of unexplainable intuition to the
very spot where Frank's was lying, gave it a quick squeeze,
then stumbled gracefully over the legs of the persons sitting
between her and the aisle, and followed her father. As she
passed two or three steps up the aisle, the Judge leading

pompously, and the gate-keeper calculating the chances of being able to crush him by accidentally letting the iron gate slam to against his legs,—she encountered a recognition that was almost an adventure. A young girl who sat in the next to the end seat of the back-row of the orchestra, leaned over the gentleman outside and caught her hand, saying :

"Emily Owen—I know it is ! Do you not remember me ?"

"Josephine Harris ! How glad I am to see you !" was the reply of Emily, the moment her eyes fairly took in the face and figure before her.

"I could not see your face before, and did not know that you were here. How long it is since I saw you !—ever since I left Rutgers, and you were still hammering away there !" said Josephine Harris, who was indeed the other, having come down to Wallack's with a party of friends, for the evening, and who had not before had a chance to recognize her old friend and school-fellow at the Rutgers Institute.

"Come and see me. Papa is in a hurry, and I cannot wait," said Emily, doubtful whether her friend had or had not observed the preceding movements. "I have not time for a card—look in the Directory and send me yours. Good night !" and in a moment she was gone, following the Judge to that mental slaughter involved in riding home with him in his present mood, and leaving the performance to pass on again as if no interruption had occurred.

As may be supposed, Frank Wallace was something of an "object of interest" for the small remainder of the evening ; but he had no acquaintances in the neighborhood, and not much remark was ventured. One man behind him, indeed, leaned over and said : "Lost your girl, eh ?" but Frank's "Ya-a-s !" was so broad and discouraging for any further questions, that the inquiry was not pursued. Most men, under similar circumstances, would have left the theatre at once, to avoid observation and to hide annoyance : he did not, and he may have acted wisely or unwisely in that course of conduct.

Josephine Harris *had* observed the preceding movements on the part of Judge Owen, and it was through recognition of his figure that she looked after and recognized Emily.

Had the latter been left quietly sitting beside her lover, her
schoolmate would probably not have seen her face, they
would have left the theatre without recognition of each other,
and Judge Owen's house might have escaped a very early
visit destined to work important changes in the relations of
residents and visitors. The puissant and pompous Judge
had effected two *coups d'etat* within as many days. The one
had driven Aunt Martha fairly over into the ranks of the
enemy: had the second introduced Joe Harris, an electric
wire full charged with destruction, into the immediate vicinity of his domestic magazine?

CHAPTER XXI.

ANOTHER SCENE AT THE CRAWFORDS'—JOE HARRIS PLAY-
ING THE DETECTIVE, WITH MUSICAL ACCOMPANIMENTS—
A STRANGE CONVERSATION, AND A STRANGE VISIT TO A
STRANGE DOCTOR.

SOME chapters back in this narration, we saw Colonel Egbert Crawford playing volunteer physician to his invalid
cousin Richard, and applying a certain bandage more or less
suspicious in its character, while Josephine Harris held a
very ambiguous position behind the parlor-door and drew
certain deductions not complimentary to the character or intentions of the gallant Colonel. To take up the dropped
thread of relation at that point—the Colonel left in a few
moments afterwards, and Joe, from her position in the room
up-stairs, watched his departure. By that time, the fearful
agitation which had at first oppressed her, had somewhat
moderated, and she was much more capable than before of
thinking with clearness and acting with decision. "A perfect
little fool" in many of her first confidences (as some of her
friends paid her the doubtful compliment of calling her), Josephine Harris had yet a vein of distrust in her character,

not difficult to touch; and when that vein was touched there was not "poppy or mandragora" enough in the world to lull to sleep her suspicions, until they were either proved true or fairly exploded.

Frank and generous natures will sometimes discern more clearly than subtle and designing ones, just as the naked eye will sometimes take in particulars in any scene more readily than when assisted by the glass. The power of discernment may be aided, in some degree, by the fact that they are not guarded against as some are because they bear the look or reputation of being dangerous. Many a man has taken off the outer garb of his soul and gone in his mental shirt-sleeves (so to speak) from the impression on his mind that he was in the company of the confiding and the unobservant; and many a bad man has found detection and ruin in the experiment.

Josephine Harris had seen something in the eyes of Colonel Egbert Crawford, when directed towards his invalid cousin, which said: "I hate you, and I would put you out of the way if I could!" She had remarked the terrible agitation of Richard Crawford when she made her random observation to that effect. Now she had overheard enough to put her in possession of the conflict of interests; and she had at the same time witnessed the application to the body of the invalid, of a preparation that was expressly ordered to be kept from the knowledge of the physician. Taking all these things together, and jumping at a conclusion with a rash haste which such people will sometimes exhibit—away down in the depths of her mind she whispered the word "poison!" She might never have thought of the existence of an outward poison dangerous to human life, but she had read Mrs. Ann S. Stephens' touching story of "The Pillow of Roses," and remembered how the life of the first lover of Mary Stuart had been sacrificed by the introduction of a deadly bane into the silken pillow—the very gift of love on which he so confidingly laid his head. Might not this be something of the same kind—a murderous practice unknown to the great body of people, and yet in the knowledge of some peculiarly instructed? What more likely than that a lawyer whose line of business

led him into the company of criminals and made him acquainted with their secret confessions, should have arrived at
a knowledge so dangerous and resolved to apply it for his
own benefit and the removal of a rival?

Such were the reflections of Josephine Harris, when her
blood had a little cooled down from the terrible fever of fright
and anxiety into which she had been thrown at the first discovery; and how nearly right she was in the most important
particular—the fact of an attempted poisoning by outward
application—all will recognize who remember the interview
between the lawyer and the Obi woman of Thomas Street,
with the *dark paste* which he brought away with him as the
result of that visit.

At all events, the young girl felt that she had seen enough
to remove any doubt of the propriety of making farther. researches, and to do away with any shame that she had originally felt in playing the part of a spy and listener. Ardent
natures like hers may possibly be blamed for adopting so
readily the maxim that "the end justifies the means," and for
plunging so determinedly into what cannot be considered their
own business; but let those blame them who will, the good
they accomplish may well be made a set-off for any evil they
unwittingly cause; and the parable of the man who "fell among
thieves," and the heartless wretches who "passed by on the
other side," should make us a little slow in blaming the "good
Samaritans" who work so enthusiastically even if uninvited
and unskilfully.

The plain English of all which is, that Josephine Harris
had determined to fathom the whole of the mystery lying between Richard Crawford and his cousin, no matter what deceptions she might be called upon to pursue in carrying out
her plan, or what amount of time and trouble might be necessary for that purpose. She might have applied the rules of
Egbert Crawford's own profession to him, in expressing this
determination, and said that enough had been proved against
the suspected person, to put him on his trial before a fair and
impartial jury—that jury being herself in the first instance.
Herself and herself only. For once Joe Harris determined to
suppress her propensity for talking everywhere and to every-

body, and to admit no confidant whatever into a knowledge of her suspicions. What else she intended to do, will in due time develop itself in action.

As a first step, she smoothed down her face with her hands, under some kind of impression that she could in that way remove the redness from her cheeks and the startled look from her eyes. Then she ran into Bell's chamber, assuming all the nonchalance she could pick up on the way, to ascertain whether that young lady was likely to remain away from the parlor for a brief period longer. She found her very busy among a miscellaneous heap of dresses and millinery (this was before the visit to the sorceress, which gave her something else to think about—let it be remembered,) and in that occupation she was safe to remain for an indefinite period. No visitors coming in, then, she was likely to have the field below-stairs to herself for a short time at least, and that time must be used vigorously.

She ran lightly down-stairs and into the empty parlor. There was no sound whatever coming out of the little room of the invalid—he was no doubt still alone. With the same care which she had before taken, she stepped to the glass doors, slid them apart as before, and looked through. Richard Crawford was yet lying on the sofa, and he was *buttoning up his vest.* A very simple and natural movement, and one not at all noticeable under ordinary circumstances; but to Josephine Harris, at that moment, it seemed very significant. There *was* poison; that poison lay in the bandage; he *had* suspected his cousin, allowed him to change and replace that bandage, and the moment he believed himself alone and unobserved, had *taken it off!* To say that Joe Harris's eyes sparkled at this proof of her suspicions, would be quite insufficient—they flashed, danced and radiated with delight, in such a manner as made it very fortunate for the peace of mind of the whole male sex that she happened to be alone.

Richard Crawford had taken off that bandage, and that bandage must come into her possession at once, while the preparation was fresh. But how was it to be obtained? Where had he put it? From the fact that he had been

20

re-arranging his clothes while yet in a recumbent position,
the chances seemed to be that he had taken off the bandage,
if at all, without getting up, and that he then had it somewhere about him, intending to lock it up or put it away
when he rose to go to the bed-room.   He was very neat in
his personal habits, as well as somewhat nervous in disposition; and on the score of cleanliness he was not likely to
have put it into one of his pockets, while if he indeed felt it
to be poison he would have been quite as unlikely to retain it
so near his person.   Joe felt that if removed, that bandage
must be somewhere about the sofa.   How to get it, even
then?   He would not be at all likely to go to bed, leaving it
there; besides, she wanted it *at once!*   He must be got suddenly out of the room, and he was too weak and suffering to
remove often or on small provocation.   The piano!—ah, yes,
she would try the piano !

Joe's musical performances were always pyrotechnic; except on particular occasions when the sad soul that underlay
the merriment came uppermost, and then they were mournful
enough to tempt suicide.   To say that she knew nothing
about music, would be untrue of any one taught at the same
trouble and expense; but to say that she understood it, taking
the knowledge of other people as a standard, would be equally
incorrect.   When studying music under an excellent teacher,
it had been found impossible to confine her to any set rules,
and quite as impossible to make her execute her lessons properly.   When she should have been performing that routine
duty, her eolian piano at home was half the time turned into
a banjo or a harp, tinkling a serenade, or into an organ, playing some ponderous old anthem or sobbing out some dirge
of a broken heart.   These were all well enough, in their way,
but they were not studying the piano.   As a result, she
could produce all those effects upon the instrument, that no
one else would ever have thought of attempting; the only
penalty being, that what any one else could have done, she
could not do at all.   This did not suit some people, but it
suited Miss Joe, exactly; and as she was pleased, perhaps
no one else had a right to complain.   If any one *did* complain he or she was likely to be at once treated to one of

the lugubrious compositions before mentioned, producing the "dumps" for a month after.

On this occasion Joe threw open the lid of the piano with such dexterity as to tangle the cover inextricably with the lid, set up the stool with a whirl, and dashed into the midst of a composition that might have been conceived by a mad musician and wailed out on an instrument possessed, like Paganini's fiddle, one night when the demons of the storm were playing at hide-and-seek among the Hartz Mountains of Germany. It went from the top to the bottom of the scale, in such moanings, and wailings, and sobbings, intermingled with such fiendish dashes of exultation and laughter, that the nerves of a strong man might have been thrown into permanent disorder by it, while those of a sick one could not do otherwise than suffer the most exquisite torture.

"I think that will do!" said Miss Joe to herself, pausing for an instant and then going on again. She was right, for at the next partial pause she heard the voice of Dick Crawford, from the back-room, yelling out with more energy than the man himself had before thought that he possessed:

"Sto-o-o-op!".

She did stop—ran to the sliding-doors and opened them at once, to find Crawford sitting upon the sofa, with his hands to both ears.

"Eh? what's the matter, Dick? Does the music disturb you?" she asked, as naturally as if she had not before been aware of the fact.

"Disturb me? It *murders* me—you know it does, you torment!" was the reply of Crawford.

"I am so sorry," said Joe, with the least perceptible pout on her lip. "I suppose that I must go home, then, and play."

"No," said Crawford, who had no idea of being guilty of the ungallantry of driving a lady out of his house, especially dear, delicious, tormenting Joe. "No, don't go home. But if you must play, why not play something Christian and respectable—something that a man can listen to without gritting his teeth and stopping his ears more than half the time?"

"Well, that *is* complimentary!" sighed Josey. "Just when I was doing the very best that I could! Besides, I

wasn't playing for *you*. You were not in the room, but stuck
away off there in a corner. I'll tell you what I will do, Mr.
Dick Crawford. Let me help you out here to a sofa in *this*
room—the air will not hurt you, but do you good,—and I
promise to play for you the very tunes you wish. If not—"

"Oh, you need not mention the alternative," said Crawford, remembering the preceding performance and afraid of a
repetition. "Come here, give me your arm, and I *will* come
out for a few minutes."

"Bravo!" thought wild Joe, but she did not say it. Very
gently and tenderly she assisted the invalid from his sofa and
to a standing position, and then quite as tenderly through the
door and to the sofa that stood nearly opposite the piano.
Then she ran back and *closed the sliding-doors* again, for fear,
as she said, that there might be too much draught of air on
the invalid. So far, so good! Richard Crawford had been
coaxed out of his room and into the parlor that he scarcely
entered once a month. What next?

"Play me a wreath of Scottish melodies," said Crawford,
with the feeling of the old blood coming up within him.
"And be sure that you throw in 'Roy's Wife' and 'Annie
Laurie.' Will you?—That's a good girl?". Dick spoke more
cheerfully than had been his late habit, and settled himself
to an easy position on the sofa with more the air of a man
ready to enjoy, than he had for some time manifested.

"Has there been an incubus suddenly lifted from his
breast?" Joe Harris asked herself, noticing the change.

If there was anything that she really *could* play on the
piano, her forte lay in those very Scottish airs, which she
certainly rendered with exquisite feeling and with skill enough
for the moderate demands of that class of music. And on
this occasion she felt bound to exert herself, to repay the ob-
ligation of Crawford's coming out to hear her, though her
brain was all in a whirl for fear something might occur to
drive the patient back into his room, and her fingers, as they
touched the white keys, itched to be busying themselves about
the cushions of the invalid's sofa. For a few moments, while
"Within a Mile of Edinboro' Town," "Roy's Wife," "Charlie
is My Darling." "Bonnie Doon" and half a dozen others of

the Scottish wreath were dripping from her fingers, and
while Richard Crawford was enjoying his favorite music better than he had before enjoyed anything for many a week,—
for this few moments Joe Harris was nonplussed. How should
she get out of the room? Oh! Suddenly she remembered
that there was some music on one of the tables up-stairs, and
she acted upon that excuse for absence.

"Oh, Dick, please lie still a moment. There is a piece up-
stairs that I must bring down and play for you. I know you
will like it. One of Gottschalk's—'Las Ojos Criollos.'" She
had caught sight of that composition lying at the top of the
heap of music near her, and without being observed by Crawford she caught the sheet, rolled it up in her hand, and was
out of the room in a moment.

"Tut! tut! what a pity that that girl *never* can be still a
moment and do exactly what any one asks her to do !" was
the mental comment of that gentleman as her flying skirts
disappeared through the door.

Of course Josephine Harris did not go up stairs. She had
no real errand whatever in that direction. There was a door
opening from Richard's little bed-room, adjoining his study,
into the hall; and her hope was to find that door unlocked.
If not, some other excuse must be made to get into his room,
to invent which she must play a few more tunes, and run a
little more risk of being interrupted. She stepped very lightly
to the door, with a repetition of that cat-step which seemed
that day suddenly to have come to her. She turned the knob
—it *was* unlocked—it opened. One dart through the other
door and to the sofa. The cushion was a moveable one, as
she knew, and very likely to be made a temporary hiding-place
for any small article, by one lying upon it. She lifted the
edge of the cushion, her heart beating at trip-hammers again,
and her whole being almost as much excited as it had been
half an hour before. Human life is full of blunders, but happily there are some movements that are *not* blunders; and this
was one of them. A small, round roll of linen, three or four
inches wide, was stuck a little distance under the edge. She
drew it out, hastily unrolled it until she saw that a dark
plaster lay in the middle, then, with a "Whew!" of triumph,

quite as hastily rolled it up again and thrust it into her pocket. Half a minute more, and she had softly ascended a dozen steps of the stairs, and descended again with plenty of noise, springing down with a decided bump on the landing. Then she burst into the parlor with her *piece of music*, and sat down once more to the piano.

"Excuse my running away, Dick. Haven't been long— have I?"

"No, not very long," answered Crawford, whose impressions of Joe's steadiness were not enthusiastic. "You know I should not have been surprised if you had not come back in a week."

"Fie! fie! Dick Crawford! I have half a mind not to play for you at all, after that insult." But she did attempt to play, and to play "Las Ojos Criollos." If she ever could have played that most brilliant and difficult of all Gottschalk's pieces, which was very doubtful, she certainly was not capable of doing it when her fingers were in such a tremor, and with the mysterious package in her pocket; and though it may be an ungallant and improper thing to say of a lady's performance, she "made a mess of it."

"Pshaw!" she said, as naturally as if really vexed. "That piece is very difficult. I thought that I had mastered it, a dozen times, yet here it is bothering me again. Never mind! —I know what I *can* play—something that you like, or if you do not, you should!" And very much to Crawford's delight, for she did not often sing, though she frequently *hummed,—* she broke out with voice and instrument into that finest, though worst-hackneyed, of modern love-ballads—"Ever of Thee." There are unaccountable fancies, in music as well as in personal regard, and one piece will sometimes make itself the very key-note of a human heart, without being in itself so pre-eminently beautiful as to command that distinction. Crawford had before many times heard Josephine Harris humming that air, or touching it lightly on the keys of the piano, but he had never before heard her *sing* it. Before half of the first stanza was finished, he knew that it supplied to her a need in music that all the compositions of all the great masters would fail to fill; and before she had finished the last, he believed that some painful secret of her young life must be bound up in it. He was the more painfully confirmed in that belief, when he saw her rise from the piano the moment after she had concluded the song, and dash her hand to her eyes with the unmistakeable gesture of wiping away a tear.

"Joe—dear Joe," he said, "come here a moment."

She crossed the room at once and stood beside him. He held out his hand to her, and she took it as a sister might have taken that of a dearly beloved brother. There was nothing of heat or tremor in the touch, though there was everything of kindness. Absorbed in something else, both had for the moment forgotten the feeling before predominant—Crawford his sickness and crippled condition, and Joe Harris her anxieties and her plans with reference to him.

"Josephine Harris," he said, very kindly, almost tenderly, "answer me one question, as candidly as it is asked. Will you?"

"You could not ask me an improper question," she replied, "and so I could have no reason for refusing to answer you. I will."

"You have been singing 'Ever of Thee,'" he went on. "Your whole heart was in it when you sung, and when you stopped your voice was broken and your eyes were full of tears. Tell me—is there a sad secret of your life connected with that song? Consider me your brother, and do not be afraid or ashamed to answer me."

"Richard Crawford, I do consider you as a brother," the young girl replied—"a dear brother, in whom I would confide as in one of my own blood. I mean to prove to you, some day, what a true sister I am. I am neither afraid or ashamed to answer your question. I have no grief or sad memory connected with 'Ever of Thee,' any more than with any other sadly beautiful piece of music with words of the same character."

"Indeed!—I thought otherwise!" said Crawford, with something of disappointment in his tone. "And yet it moves your light heart very strangely."

"It does," said Josephine Harris. "I never sing it or hear

it sung without the tears gathering in my eyes, even if they do not fall."

"And you can give no reason for this peculiar feeling?"

"Oh yes," answered the young girl, "though no doubt you ..ill laugh at my reason when you hear it."

"I think not," said Crawford. "Tell me."

"You think me very gay and merry," said Josephine. "So I am, but I suppose that I have something deeper in my nature, that 'crops out' occasionally, as the geologists say. I suppose that I am a visionary in some respects and among my visions is a love worthily fixed and fully returned. So few seem to find this, that I fear I shall miss it—either miss it altogether or find it too late. The thought is a sad one, and that song seems insensibly to blend with it. When I am singing 'Ever of Thee,' I am singing to my ideal love that may be escaping beyond the reach of my fingers forever."

True woman of the golden heart!—God in heaven grant that to you and such as you this vision may be no dim un-reality! God grant you true hearts against which your own may beat, and faithful arms upon which you may lean when the day of your probation is accomplished! And failing this fruition, the same God of love and peace grant you a truer and more enduring union with hearts that pulsate truly to your own, in that land where the sad wail of "Too Late!" is never heard and where no binding link fetters the limbs or galls the spirit!

"I understand you now," said Richard Crawford. "And yet yours is a strange fancy and would be a dangerous one in many minds. But you are a brave girl, I believe, and that makes all the difference. Besides, you have health and strength, and most of the time high spirits. An invalid—a miserable cripple like myself, housed and shut away, can scarcely hope to understand or appreciate anything that comes freshly in out of God's sunshine!" The old sad and repining spirit had once more come over Richard Crawford, perhaps invoked by something in the young girl's words; and she saw the shadow almost as soon as he felt it. From that moment she was the rattle-pate again, and he caught no more glimpses into the sanctuary of her inner heart. He was to catch no more, forever; for the next time they spoke together in private was after certain events already related had occurred—after her hand had lain in another, in so significant a pressure that no time or change could ever take away the tingle of the blood which it communicated—after her eyes began to open on a new phase of destiny—and after "Ever of Thee" ceased to be a sad abstraction.

Just now she rattled on, as she assisted the invalid back to his room, endeavoring to rouse his once-more sinking spirits, with all her old gayety and abandon.

"You call me brave, do you?" she said. "Dick Crawford, if I was not a little ashamed of you for allowing yourself to have these fits of low spirits, I would tell you something to prove how 'brave' I am! Well, I *will* tell you, because I know that it is exceedingly improper and I ought not to do so. Two or three weeks ago, spending an evening at Mrs. R——'s, her daughters showed me a suit of clothes belonging to a stripling brother, just gone away to the war. One of them bantered me to put on the suit and go down-stairs among the gentlemen. I thought it would be a good joke, and I tried it. The girls said that I made a very handsome boy—hem! and I suppose that I did. At all events, I went down-stairs and opened the parlor-door, bold as a sheep, when—what do you think happened? Why, I thought, all at once, that all the clothes were sticking tight to my limbs; and when one of the gentlemen came towards me, I grabbed the cloth from the centre-table for a cloak, and played hob with some Bohemian glassware and a few Parian ornaments, finishing by skedaddling up-stairs a good deal more rapidly than I came down. Was not *there* 'courage' for you?"

"No want of it, certainly," said Crawford, who had been laughing a little, spite of his low spirits, at the naivete of the relation. "It was modesty and not want of personal courage that drove you out of that very funny position."

"Think so?" said the wild girl. "Then as I *am* a coward and mean to be known for what I am, I must tell you another story. A few weeks ago I went into a menagerie, and

one of the lions made a rush at the bars of his cage—probably because he saw *me*. There was about as much danger
of his getting out, I suppose, as there would have been of
my doing so in the same circumstances; but of course I made
a fool of myself, got frightened, yelled, and had all the visitors
in the menagerie looking at me. How was *that?* No want
of courage? Eh?"

"That," said Richard Crawford, sententiously, "that was
the *woman.*"

"Humph!" said Joe, as she once more assisted the invalid
to dispose himself comfortably on his usual couch. "Now
you will not agree to my estimate of *myself,* perhaps you will
think better of my estimate of *you.*"

"Perhaps so," said Crawford. "Try me."

"Well, then, I have been watching you half the afternoon,
and I have made up my mind about you more nearly than
ever before."

"And what am I?" asked Crawford, with just a dash of
impatience in his tone.

"A hypochondriac!" said Joe. "You are a little sick,
and you think yourself much worse. You look better and
feel better within the last hour—"

"Eh, what?" said the invalid, startled apparently by some
sudden thought connected with the words.

"I say that you look better and feel better, within the last
hour, than you have done for weeks. You are getting better,
and you have neither the honesty to acknowledge it or the
grace to thank God for it! Dick Crawford, if you ever die
—and I suppose you will, some time—you will commit suicide by taking an over-dose of low spirits!"

How flippantly the wild girl spoke!—and yet she was
right, and Dick Crawford felt that she was right. The supplying cause of his malady removed, such a lecture, from
such ready lips, was precisely the thing that he needed, to
break up the habit of despondency—the habit of *enjoying and
nursing suffering* (that phrase may express the fact as well
as another) which settles so often like a murky cloud upon
the minds of those who have been kept for weeks or months
as confirmed invalids, after lives of previous activity. She

was right, too, as to the suicide of low spirits. The red
devils of Pandemonium may be terrible, fresh from the flames
of the pit; but they are nothing to their brothers in blue,
who people the air, overcloud the eyes and set up torture-
chambers in the brain. Bunyan, in that ever-living "Pilgrim's
Progress," paints no tyrant so terrible as "Giant Despair,"
and no obstruction to the way so fatally impassable as the
" Slough of Despond." And we have never read over the
sorrowful conclusion of the "Bride of Lammermoor" without believing that the young master of Ravenswood, on that
sombre November morning, sunk the sooner and the more
fatally in the quicksands of the Kelpie's Flow, from the
weight of the leaden heart he carried in his bosom.

Suddenly, and before Richard Crawford had quite decided
how to answer her last remark, Josephine Harris said, as if
the thought had only that instant come to her :

" Oh, Dick, I am going to ask a favor, in return for my
good opinion. The carriage is in, I believe. May I ring for
it, for an hour ?"

" Certainly," said Crawford. Josephine rung the bell, and
the order was given.'

" It is dusk, you see," said the young girl, apologetically,
"and I must go down the Avenue before I go home. Many
thanks. Be a good boy and take care of yourself, till I see
you again. John will set me down at home when my little
errand is over. Good night !" and her kiss fell warm and soft
upon his forehead—a sister's kiss, pure and unimpassioned,
even if there was no tie of blood between them.

Bell Crawford came down stairs and sat by her brother's
side when she heard the carriage roll away with her friend.
And whither did that carriage roll ? Richard Crawford had
no idea that Joe's "little errand" could possibly have any connection with himself; and yet it had—a most intimate and
important connection, as will be perceived.

The coachman, at her request, drove out to Fifth Avenue,
then down that avenue to Tenth Street, where he opened the
door and set her down, receiving orders to wait there for her
return. The young girl tripped up from the corner, a few
doors on the left hand side, past a church, and entered the

front-yard railing of one of two or three unpretending three-
story brick-houses standing together.   It was now past dusk
and the street-lamps were lighted; and looking in at the
basement windows of this house, Joe saw that no curtains
were drawn, that the gas was burning within, over a table
and under a shade; and that at the table sat a man with head
bent down and fingers busy at some kind of mechanical con-
trivance.

    "That will do," she muttered to herself.   "The Doctor *is*
in, as I believed he might be at this hour, and I shall have no
occasion to disturb the people up-stairs."

    Passing under the steps she reached the closed door, and
instead of ringing, banged half a dozen times against the
panels with her hand, very slowly and tragically, as the
ghost in "Don Giovanni" might ask to be admitted, provided
it had any occasion for using the door.   Immediately there
was a shuffle inside, and directly the door opened and a tall
figure stood in the doorway.   There was enough light from
the street-lamp to make the young girl's face and figure pretty
plainly visible, and the moment he saw her the occupant said :

    "I thought so—mischief !   I thought I knew that knock !
No one else ever takes such liberties with my office-door.
What do you want now ?   But come in, before you forget
it !" and seizing both her hands with a playful gesture, he
dragged her within the door, closed it, pulled her through
the side-door into the front basement which formed the office,
drew up a clumsy cushioned operating-chair near the table,
sat her down in it, then cast himself into a chair immediately
in front of her, threw one leg over the other and his hands
behind his head, and said :

    "Now I am resigned and prepared.   Out with it !"

    Had Josephine Harris not been familiar with the place and
its occupant, as it was quite evident that she *was*, she would
have looked twice at the one and several times at the other.
That little basement-room was not only the office in which
Doctor LaTurque received professional calls, but it was also
the sanctum in which were prepared most of the oddly-
trenchant articles in the *Scimetar*, a quarterly medical and
critical publication with a habit cutting as its name and a

reputation dangerous enough to suit the most sensational
fancy. Few persons connected with the practice of medicine
in or about the great city, who had not first or last suffered
some incision from the trenchant blade of the *Scimetar*,
wielded by the wiry arm of the Doctor; and few humbugs
but he had pricked and exposed, by the same means or in
personal conversation, while he was himself the greatest
humbug of all. Others habitually humbugged others: he
humbugged himself, or tried to do so, insisting to himself that
he was a hard man, an iron man, a brute, a skeptic, and
everything that was ugly and detestable; while in fact he had
the warm heart of an unspoiled child, and a faith in everything good, that was really part of his being—all combined
with the vigor of the experienced surgeon and the close study
of the untiring student. He used hard words—rough ones,
sometimes, and tried to make himself believe that they were
the emanations of a hard disposition; while every rough
word was really made under protest from his nature, and few
men on the whole earth were more ready to do an act of
genuine kindness. It is not for us to say that there was not
some intentional affectation of singularity underlying his
manner; for he evidently loved notice if not notoriety; and
other means than the white coat and disarranged trowsers of
the Tribune Philosopher have sometimes been adopted to secure the same end.

Certainly Dr. LaTurque was not remarkably choice in the
style of his "den," if he *had* handsomely furnished apart-
ments in the house above, and if his windows *did* look out
on Fifth Avenue. The ceilings were low, the walls plain,
the furniture was very common, and yet a little odd, as became the place. The floor was oil-clothed; a table covered
with dark cloth stood in the middle of the room; an old-
fashioned secretary, with books piled on either end, stood
against the wall on the right as the visitor entered, with a
globe half hidden behind it; on the wall opposite hung the
print of a muscular Apollo (muscular, because it was drawn
anatomically, with no flesh covering the integuments); on
either end of the mantel stood a small statue; in the centre
was an impudent placard of bronze on japanned tin, an-

nouncing that no complimentary visits could possibly be received in that room, while the occupant, if there, was ready
to falsify the announcement at any moment; on a small table
between the windows, under a glass globe, lay the cast in
plaster of a marvellously handsome male Italian face; two or
three small pictures, commonly framed, hung over secretary
and mantel; in the corner between the mantel and the window stood a stuffed eagle on a low table covered with the
suggestive appliances of a fractured leg; and just behind it,
on a bit of rug, nestled a disabled pigeon from his pet flock
on the roof, that had come down, with excellent judgment, to
be nursed and tended by the surgeon.

In the midst of this odd assemblage Dr. LaTurque was himself not by any means the least remarkable object. He was certainly a singular-looking man, and had a fancy (or pretended
to have a fancy) that he was a very homely one. He was not
so, however, to any eye of taste—only striking. In figure
he was tall and rather thin, but the same epithet we have
applied to his arm may be used for the whole man—*wiry*.
He seemed capable of strong nervous effort and of great endurance; and one could see that something more than fifty
years had not diminished the locomotive will or power. In
the too large and too aquiline nose (literally a beak)—in the
iron-gray moustache, imperial, and heavy brown hair—in the
thin cheeks and keen gray eye,—there was a marvellous reminder of the portraits of Louis Napoleon, and at the same
time another and a stronger suggestion. There is no close
observer of physiognomy but has remarked bird, beast and
even reptile reproduced in the faces of different men—one
being a human lion, another a human bear, a third a human
hyena, and still a fourth a human serpent. It scarcely seemed
that it could have been by chance that the gray eagle stood
stuffed in the corner; for the observer just as naturally detected the eagle in that human face, as he could ever have
detected either of the others named, in different physiog-
nomies, and the dead bird seemed the *totem* of the living
man.

" Well, battle and murder and sudden death !" said the medical Laurence Boythorn, when he had forced the young girl

down into a seat. "What is it you want? Who is married or dead, or whom do you intend to kill, or what is it?"

"Are you sober?" asked the young girl, looking into his eyes very gravely.

"Why, you impudent demon in petticoats!" said the Doctor, with a great appearance of indignation. "What do you mean? You know that I am never otherwise than sober."

"From the effects of liquor, of course not," was the reply. "But your hot head, like mine, has the capacity of becoming intoxicated sometimes without any thanks to liquor; and I want to know whether you are cool and clear, or whether you have been puzzling over some bad case, or talking with some man with a stupid skull, until your head is all muddled?"

"Clear as one of the mountain springs that you are some day going with me to see," said the Doctor. "Now out with it."

"Well," said Joe, "I know that you hate chemistry, but in spite of that you *must* give me a little chemical judgment. I want you to tell me," and she took out the surreptitiously-obtained roll of linen, unrolled it and laid it upon the table, under the full light of the burner—"I want you to tell me what is that dark substance which looks like black paste, whether it is animal, vegetable, or mineral, and what you think its properties."

"And after I *do* tell you, if I can," said the Doctor, eyeing the suspicious-looking mass, "I suppose that I am to be told why you wish to know?"

"Not one word," said Joe. "At least, not at present. All your reward is to be the honor of conversing with *me* on the subject."

"Bravo, Empress; I rather like *that!*" said the Doctor, who *did* like it, nevertheless, to judge by the jolly expression of his face. "You are a refreshing young woman, and some day I expect to see you stretch out your arm with imperial dignity and clear off all the pigmies from the face of the earth with a 'Go away, small people! I have had enough of you! You may leave!'"

"Very likely," said Joe. "But meanwhile I have not ·

quite done with *you*. Please examine that stuff, for I am in
a hurry."

"As usual !" commented the Doctor, going on to smell, in-
spect, and even taste the dark compound on the cloth.

" Take care !" cried the young girl, in alarm, when she saw
him apply his tongue to the substance.

" Pshaw !" said the Doctor. " Don't be alarmed. I am so
full of dangerous ingredients myself, that the most virulent of
poisons could not produce any effect on me."

" I should not like to see you trust it too far—that is, not
if I cared for you !" said the lady, as if *she* had been the chemist and he the neophyte.

"Well," said the Doctor, after a moment's pause and a still
closer inspection, "you will give me no particulars, and so I
shall give *you* none. I suppose the main fact is what you
want to know. The substance is a little dried, and consequently it has lost some of its aroma. But my impression is
that it is a very powerful vegetable poison, compounded from
certain simples that grow along running streams in the
tropics, and especially in some of the West Indies."

" I thought so !" said Joe, almost involuntarily, and an unmistakeable gleam of pleasure lighting up her face. "But
would that poison produce any effect if applied outwardly ?"

" I should think so," replied the Doctor, "though, as you say,
I hate chemistry. I should think that substance, applied to
any vital part of the body, and kept there continuously, would
produce racking pains and weakness, and be very likely to
result in a disease resembling inflammatory rheumatism, or
possibly paralysis, and death."

" Thank you—thank you a dozen times," said Joe, springing up and grasping the Doctor very warmly by the hand.
"You do not know how much good you may be doing by
this examination ; but you *shall* know, sometime—I will tell
you all about it. And now good-night !" rolling up the package and putting it back into her pocket. " My time is up,
Mother will be worried about me, and I have a borrowed carriage waiting at the corner."

"Allow me to see you to it," said the Doctor, rising with
quick courtesy.

"No farther than the gate, for the world," said the young girl. "For certain reasons, which you shall know some time, I must not be seen in your company to-night, even by the coachman."

She tripped away instantly, the Doctor accompanying her to the gate,—and rolled away homeward at once. What a day that had been to her! And in what a whirl was her brain when she reflected on all she had discovered and tried to arrange in her own mind the details of what she yet felt it necessary to do! It was within forty-eight hours after, and when her mind had not become at all calmed from the thoughts of the crime surrounding her and those she loved, that the visit to the sorceress was made, as before recorded. How much of additional information she may really have expected to gain from the sorceress, it is impossible to say,—or whether this matter of the attempted poisoning was really the matter which sent her to that questionable fountain of intelligence; but it is not at all strange that she should have blended the terrors of the real and the imaginary together, and been powerfully impressed by the events of that day which marked so important an era in her existence.

It may be said here, that two days after the events just narrated, when Bell accompanied her to the sorceress, she did not see Richard Crawford. Thereafter, for many days, she did not visit the house at all, for reasons that will soon make themselves manifest; and consequently the awkwardness of any meeting with the invalid, which might have involved questions she did not care to answer at that moment, was avoided. Joe Harris felt that for once in her life she had a "mission"—something to do, and to do in her own way; and until that work was done, or she had utterly failed in the attempt, she did not mean to let that chattering tongue of hers say one word that could give a clue to her thoughts or intentions. We shall see, presently, how nearly and in what manner her plans were carried out.

21

CHAPTER XXII.

A LITTLE ARRANGEMENT BETWEEN TOM LESLIE AND JOE
HARRIS—UP THE HUDSON-RIVER ROAD—A DETENTION
AND A RECOGNITION—GOING TO WEST FALLS, AND A PEEP
AT THE HALSTEAD HOMESTEAD.

THERE are some things too sacred to be pryed into, and
there are some things too difficult to make any progress in
that attempt, even when the effort is made with the most determined will. Both these conditions will to some extent
apply to the intimacy between Tom Leslie and Josephine
Harris, which commenced on a day we well remember, and
which may not close until their joint destiny is accomplished.
The very next day after that adventure, he called at the house
of Mrs. Harris, was introduced to her with great empresse-
ment by her daughter, and received by her with great cordiality. The good lady, whom we have no intention whatever of describing, was a splendid specimen of the widowed
matron in comfortable circumstances, with just enough threads
of silver shining amid her dark hair, to make her matron-
hood sacred and all the more loveable. That she, who was
not always pleased with a new-comer, chanced to like him
from the first, completed the vanquishment of the journalist,
if that object had not before been entirely accomplished; and
within an hour after setting foot within that comfortable little
home the young man felt that it had become dearer to him
than any other building of bricks and mortar into which he
had ever entered.

So of the confidence which at once began to exist between
the two lovers. Yes—let the word be set down—lovers.
When Josephine Harris accompanied Tom Leslie to the door,
on the night of his first visit to her at home, he held out his
arms to her, without a word, and she nestled into them in the
same silence, and returned the first kiss he pressed upon her
lips. Thenceforth their lips, we may believe, belonged exclusively to neither, but had a divided interest. What matter,

thereafter, how many times they were pressed together, or how long that pressure lingered? What matter how many words they spoke, or what formed the burden of those words? They had accidentally touched, when drifting down the stream of life, and who should thenceforth have power to separate them? A month before, Tom Leslie, who had had fifty flirtations or less, would have laughed at the idea of being "in love," with what seemed like a life-passion; and even three days before Josephine Harris would have considered such an event, on her part, not undesirable, but simply impossible. So much for what we know, to-day, of that which is to exist to-morrow, even in the "best-regulated families!"

It was on the third visit paid to the house by Leslie, that Josephine communicated to him her intention to be absent from the city for a week or ten days, visiting some friends in one of the country sections reached by the New York Central Railroad; after which she was again to return to the city and accompany her mother, late in July, on her annual pilgrimage to the Ocean House at Newport. She would leave for the north on one of the first days of July—perhaps the Third or the Fourth. Strangely enough, Leslie had arranged to go to Niagara for a few days, at about the same time, and he suddenly found it a matter of no consequence - that he should go by the Erie Road, as he had at first intended. Subsequent inquiries proved that the young girl would go unattended, and leave the railroad at Utica, taking stage for the short remainder of her journey. Leslie felt it almost a matter of inexcusable impudence, after so short an acquaintance, to ask the favor of timing his journey by hers and being her escort so far as Utica; but he dared the risk, as he had dared many a risk before, from things quite as deadly as woman's eyes; and he did *not* meet even one objection or expression of embarrassment. Josephine Harris accepted his escort as freely as offered, and seemed rather pleased than otherwise! How absurd, and in fact how improper! She should have blushed, simpered, and hinted that she would be very much pleased with his escort—but—so short an acquaintance – all her friends would know it—what would people say?—etc., etc. Joe Harris did not un-

derstand all these things, exactly ; but the next woman would
have acted out that role to perfection.

Not to linger over these details, Mamma Harris not object-
ing, they left the city of New York by the five o'clock train
on the Hudson River Railroad, on the evening of the Fourth
of July, just when the city was sweltering in its most deadly
heat and all ablaze with patriotic fireworks.   Leslie had certain patrio-political engagements which occupied him until
after noon on that day, rendering it impossible to leave by
the morning train.   Leaving by that at five o'clock, they
would connect with the train on the New York Central leaving Albany at midnight, and reach Utica very early in the
morning.   There Josephine would be set down, while Leslie, after seeing to her stage accommodation, would whirl onward with the train, for Niagara.

The connection between love and railroad-riding may not
be obvious to all ; and there are some, no doubt, who think
the flying speed of the modern conveyance terribly unromantic.   But there are others who know of nothing more
thoroughly pleasant than lounging back easily in the cushioned
seat of a railway-carriage, with *the one* close beside, with
one hand in reach at any moment, the one face ready to reply
in smiles to the look of pleasure given, and the one head
ready to repose upon the shoulder when night comes on or
the continued motion of the train brings on drowsiness.   Of
the latter class were both Tom Leslie and Joe Harris, both
of whom had travelled much, though very differently, and
neither of whom had ever before experienced the luxury of
the one peculiar companionship.   They may ride far and see
Nature in her most wonderful phases, in other days ; but it
is doubtful whether either will ever experience a greater
pleasure than that of sitting by the side of the other, on that
July afternoon, conscious that they were *together*, and of
very little else, but dimly aware, too, that they were sweeping away from the hot and dusty city, with its thousands of
sweltering inhabitants, and flying through green woods,
among towering hills and beside flashing waters.

It is not more true that "man proposes but God disposes,"
of any other series of events in life than railroad connections.

That Albany express-train on the Hudson-River Road, dashed merrily on for the Highlands, meeting excursion-trains passing backwards and forwards between the various towns on the line, all decked with flags and evergreens, and the passengers in all waving flags and shouting out their patriotic merriment. Already the Highlands of the Hudson were rising close before them, with the westering sun sinking low and casting broad shadows from their tops over the quiet river,—when suddenly, a little below Peekskill, the train came to a halt, without any station appearing in view.

"What is the matter?" asked some of the passengers, after the halt had been prolonged a few minutes. "Have we met with any accident?" asked others when that halt was longer protracted; and "Are we *never* going to get on?" asked all parties together, when the delay lengthened to more than half an hour and there appeared to be no signs of starting.

Finally, when more than the half hour had elapsed, a brakeman satisfied the eager inquiries of the passengers by the information that a coal-schooner had attempted to pass through the draw-bridge half a mile above Peekskill, when the tide was too far spent—that she had managed to get aground in the draw-bridge, immediately across the track—and that, consequently, no train could possibly pass until the tide rose again and released the unfortunate boat, well along towards midnight! Here was a pleasant predicament, especially for those who, like our travellers, had connections to make at Albany for the North and West; and yet, to their credit be it said, that particular couple bore the delay with wonderful equanimity! It is just possible that both remembered that they would be together a few hours longer on account of the accident, and that they were prepared to endure even a longer forced companionship!

At last the train moved on, but slowly, through the village of Peekskill, and reached the little creek, under the very edge of the Highlands, where the accident had occurred. The scene was certainly a picturesque one, with the grounded boat, the swung draw-bridge, the men laboring to lighter-off the vessel by unloading the coal, the passengers crowding and swarming from the cars, the setting sun over the noble head-

lands to the West, and the placid river coming out from the
dark shadow of the Highlands and sweeping grandly down to
Haverstraw Bay.

It had been arranged that all the passengers by the up-
train should disembark and cross the long bridge over the
estuary, on the narrow strips of plank temporarily laid down
for that purpose, so as to be ready to take the next down-
train from Albany, the moment it arrived, and go back with
it;—while the passengers by the down-train would cross in
the same manner and run back with the up-train towards
New York;—thus saving what would otherwise be hours of
additional detention.   Then streamed across those planks a
most picturesque line of pedestrians, sturdy men and timid
women, each a little afraid of so narrow a footing over the
water, some of the women nervous and screaming a little,
and some of the men quite as cowardly but much more
ashamed to acknowledge the feeling.   The novelty of the
picture was materially added to, meanwhile, by the fact that
nearly every male passenger was loaded like a pack-horse
with baggage, and the ladies with shawls, parasols and bundles,—and that all, when they reached the neck of land at
the end of the bridge, squatted down miscellaneously on the
dry grass and among the wood and timber, like so many
Arabs making a noon encampment.

"Oh, isn't this jolly!" exclaimed Joe Harris, as Tom Leslie
was leading her over the line of plank, when they were about
half way across, and when, from the instability of a part of
the structure, there seemed a fair prospect of taking a duck
in the river.

"Bravo, little girl!" said Tom Leslie, in reply.   "That is
the way to take detention and disappointment in travelling;
and after that expression I would bet on you for ascending
Mont Blanc or living on a raft."   Such little events, to close
observers, sometimes furnish keys to the capabilities of
whole characters.

"You compliment me," said the young girl, "but there is
really nothing to compliment me about.   I am not enduring,
but enjoying.   Look out!—there I go!   No I don't!" as she
partially lost her balance and then recovered it.   "Why we

should have lost all this, but for the accident; and probably nothing in our whole ride could have compensated it."

"It is indeed a striking scene," said Leslie, his quick appreciation of the beautiful actively brought into play, as they landed safely on the sward at the end of the bridge. "See the dusky shadows creeping over the Highlands, yonder, and their still duskier shadows in the still water. See the orange and pink of the sunset sky, reaching half way to the zenith, and that quarter moon dividing the sunset colors from the dark blue beyond, like a sentinel. Then see that steamboat creeping close in under the shadow of the land, as if she was trying to steal by unobserved. And then yonder, that smelting furnace perched on one of the hills, throwing out its gleams of molten metal, with their glowing reflection in the little creek. And last, not least, Peekskill lying across the cove yonder, with its Independence flags still flying, those untimely rockets going up, boats with singing parties putting off from the shore, and the music of the band coming over the water just softly enough to make an undertone for the feeling of the place and the hour."

"It is indeed a picture worth remembering," said Josephine, "and the more so after you have so graphically described it." But suddenly, and without any perceptible reason, at that moment the young girl pulled away from his arm, on which she had been leaning, flung down the light veil of her bonnet, stepped away a few paces, and turned her face towards the river. Leslie looked around to see what could have caused the movement, but saw nothing except a few of the last passengers leaving the planks, and among them a military officer in full colonel's uniform, whose face he did not recognize. He saw that the officer passed on, farther up the railroad-track; and the moment after, slightly turning her head, but very warily, the young girl appeared to be beckoning to him. He stepped towards her at once, and turning her head once more towards the river and the western skies, she said:

"Excuse my strange behaviour; I know that you will do so when you understand my reasons—no, you cannot understand them all, at least just now—but part of them. I

dare not turn around my head, for fear of being recognized.
You saw an officer coming off the bridge just now. Did you
know him ?"

"No, I did not," answered Leslie, and it must be confessed
that he wished to add, though he did not do so, "But what
the deuce is the mystery in *your* young life, that you are
obliged to shun recognition in this manner?"

Josephine Harris, from the position in which she stood,
could not clearly see his face, and she was consequently spared
his look of surprise, almost of pain, which was momentary.
The instant after, she asked:

"Is he here still ? Is he close by us ?"

"No," said Leslie, looking around, "he has passed up the
track some distance. But tell me—what *can* be the matter ?"

"I know you must think it odd," said the young girl, turning her face around towards Leslie, now that she knew the
officer was not near them. "Not only odd, but a little suspicious. But a few words will explain all that it is either necessary or proper for me to say in this place. Keep an eye
on that man, please, and if you see him coming this way again,
let me know. That officer is Colonel Egbert Crawford, of
whom you may have heard."

"I think I have heard the name, through the newspapers.
Getting up a bogus regiment, or something of that kind, isn't
he ?" asked Leslie. "Any relation to Miss Bell, who accompanied us the other day on that—that expedition ?"

"Which you regard as among the most foolish things of
your life ? Eh, Mr. Leslie ?" asked Joe, with a little mischief
in her tone.

"Which I regard as one of the most fortunate events in my
whole existence," said the young journalist, managing to touch
her hand at the same time. She appeared to understand the
words and the gesture, and went on with the explanation that
had been interrupted.

"He is a cousin of Miss Bell Crawford, and very intimate
in the family. I have met him very often, and he would recognize me in a moment if he should see my face. If he
should do so, probably the great object of my visit to the
North would be prevented."

"And that is—" began Leslie.

"Precisely what I cannot tell you, until I know more of the matter myself, because I have no right to take liberties with the characters of others. Would you have thought me so prudent?" concluded the young girl.

"I do not now need to learn for the first time," answered Leslie, "that those whom the world calls 'rattle-brains'—and I am sure they call *you* one,—have sometimes plenty of forethought and a good deal of prudence."

"Thank you," said Josephine, and no doubt she did thank him, from her soul. For the rarest flattery is of course the sweetest, and poor wild Joe was in the habit of being oftener complimented for any thing else rather than that terrible quality "forethought."

"But I may tell you," the young girl resumed, "that I have very grave suspicions of that man's honesty, in some of his dealings with the Crawfords, who are my very dear friends; and I am going to unsex myself, I suppose, in your mind, by acknowledging that I am playing the part of a detective, *en amateur*, for a few days."

"Not a particle unsexed," said Leslie, rubbing a match on his boot-sole and preparing to desecrate the sweet air of evening with cigar-smoke. "Go on, please."

"Well," said Joe, "if I do not mistake, Col. Egbert Crawford and myself are going to the very same place—at least to houses not a quarter of a mile apart; and if he should know of my presence in the neighborhood all my researches might be blocked. Do you see?"

"I see," said Leslie, though how he *could* see through that cloud of cigar-smoke, was a little unaccountable.

"That is why I turned away and dropped my veil," the young girl went on. "And now I am under the necessity of troubling you a little more than I intended. You must look out, for me, that we do not get into the same car, and afterwards you may have a good deal more of trouble to keep us apart May I tax you so far?"

"I think so," answered Leslie. "Hark!"

Through the hills above them there swept down a rumble, a roar, and a rattle, growing deeper every moment.

"Clear the track, there," cried Leslie, loud enough to be heard by all the hundreds of passengers. "The down-train is coming!"

In an instant the train from Albany broke into sight from the woods above, and came thundering down, barely giving the passengers who had been lounging on the track, time to drag themselves and their baggage out of the way. It was now growing dusk, but the train stopped upon the bridge without accident; and in a few moments the down passengers were unloaded and transferred, those going up were on board, and the long line moved back again, the locomotive in the rear and pushing all the cars backwards like a gigantic wheelbarrow.

Leslie had taken Miss Harris' hint at once, and kept his eye on the Colonel when the embarkation was being made. He saw him step on board one of the rear cars, and himself and his companion took places farther forward, so that any danger of recognition was past for the time.

There was nothing of incident in the night-ride which followed, demanding description in these pages, except that Leslie found a pleasure he had not anticipated, in Miss Josey's growing drowsy and making a pillow of him eventually. There have been heavier burdens than that he bore; and what with the soft breath playing so near his cheek in the innocence of slumber—the light form around which he was obliged to clasp his arm (as a matter of duty—to keep her from slipping from the seat, of course!)—the dashes through dusky woods and the glimpses of the moonlit river,—what with all these and the pleasant company of a heart that had never yet known what it was to be desponding, Tom Leslie managed to enjoy the latter portion of the ride to Albany, amazingly. At one o'clock he woke up the pleasant burden on his arm, and half an hour after, Josephine Harris was cradled in soft slumbers at the Delavan, in Albany, while Tom Leslie, a very human description of guardian angel, was watching over her slumbers from his sleepless pillow in another wing of the building.

Corresponding precautions to those of the evening were taken in the morning, when the travellers took the cars of the ventral Road, for Utica and their separation; but in that instance they seemed to be superfluous. Whether Colonel Egbert Crawford disdained to pursue his route at that early hour in the morning, or whether he had one more favorable report to make at the Adjutant-General's office, of the condition of the Two Hundredth Regiment, detaining him in Albany for another train,—certain it is that he did not make his appearance, and that the "amateur detective" and her companion were free to choose any of the cars of the train. A rapid-ride through the Mohawk Valley, with the quiet river of the same name ever at their side, and the Erie Canal continually in view, with its pleasant reminder of the extent and the wealth of the Empire State,—and before their morning's conversation was half finished (for what check or bound is there to the invaluable nothings of two lovers who have not yet recovered from the novelty of their first impressions?) they dashed up to the station at Utica and alighted for dinner at the American.

It is no matter, here, what arrangements had been made between the two for their subsequent meeting and correspondence; it is enough to know that no fetter has yet been forged by any Tubal Cain of them all, strong enough to hold apart those who choose to single out each other from the world. Tom Leslie and Josephine Harris were to meet again, and at an early day; and with that understanding both were reasonably well content—the male member of the combination because he had no option, and the female member because she really had such a multitude of benevolent plans in her busy brain that she had no time to be otherwise.

Before Josephine Harris had finished her capital dinner at the American, and ceased trifling with those magnificent strawberries, the finest of any season within memory, (that young person was favored with a most unromantic appetite, and often managed to astonish those who had the pleasure of paying her bills at a restaurant dinner or supper)—before all this was accomplished, and before the bell had rung, calling the passengers for the Northward to resume their seats on the train, Leslie had succeeded in discovering the whereabouts of the proper stage for the remainder of Miss Josey's

journey, and making the necessary arrangements for her
baggage and her personal accommodation. This done, and
his mind at rest on that particular point, the bell rung, the
two made a hurried farewell, in which a warm pressure of
the hand served (for propriety's sake) in the place of a parting kiss understood ; and Leslie sprung into his car and was
whirled away Northward towards the Mecca of American
summer-tourists ; while the young girl went up to "do"
Utica in a bird's-eye view from the window of her room,
and to await the four o'clock that was to bear her away in
the lumbering stage to West Falls. Perhaps Tom Leslie
felt at that moment that he would have been glad of any
excuse or any shadow of invitation to accompany her to that
rustic paradise, instead of going away alone to any paradise
named in Bible or Koran ; and perhaps Joe Harris had the
faintest suspicion of a heavy and lonely feeling at her heart,
at parting with the "eyes" and the merry brain that lay behind them, so suddenly flung as an element into her own
existence.

Henceforward, for the present, the business of this narration only requires that the course of Miss Josephine Harris
shall be traced, leaving the "other half" of her incomplete
"pair of scissors" to be picked up hereafter.

No one who has ever travelled among the mountains or
through any of the Northern hill-sections, needs any description of the heavy lumbering "Concord coach" in which the
young girl and her stage-companions were slowly dragged up
Genesee Street, Utica, by four horses of lymphatic temperament, on that sultry July afternoon with occasional sprinkles
of shower thrown in to make it endurable. They are all
alike—those heavy coaches—except as to paint and uphol
stery, wherever we meet them,—whether they drag us up
the Cattskills, bear us over from Moreau to Lake George,
dash down with us through the gorges of the White Mountains, or jog us heavily along the rough roads that thread the
Alleghanies. The same half cord of wood in each of the
curved bodies—the same complication of sole-leather in the
swinging jacks which serve in the place of springs—the same
cumbrous weight of wheel, suggesting that a mill may have

gone out on its travels, locomoted on its running-gear And yet there is no conveyance so safe or so easy for the mountain; and some of us have enjoyed pleasant hours lounging back upon those polished leather cushions within, or shouting out enthusiastic admiration of scenery from the pokerish seats on the top.

It is a pleasant ride, at any season of the year—that from Utica over the range of hills which lies westward, to the Oneida Valley which nestles down a few miles beyond. And it was especially pleasant and enjoyable, that afternoon, with the cloud-shadows playing over the yet uncut wheat-fields, and the glints of sunlight falling on the roofs and gables of cozy-looking farmsteads bordering the road on either hand or peeping out from behind clumps of woods in the distance. The opened back-curtains of the coach gave a delicious view, when they had surmounted the height, of Utica lying on the slope below, stretching downwards towards the Mohawk and the Canal, with its clustering domes and spires and the melancholy Lunatic Asylum overlooking all from the North-west. And a view not less pleasant opened before, of the long stretch of valley lying in the distance, bounded on either side by a continuous range of hills rising up with an almost even slope, crowned with woods and diversified with the divisions of cultivated fields, and here and there a glint of water, showing where the silver Sauquoit, most laboriously taxed of all minor streams except those of the Naugatuck and Housatonic Valleys, wound its busy way down to the Mohawk.

And when the eye tired of resting upon these, it could find variety in studying the Welsh contour and primitive aspect of many of the Oneida countrymen passing upon the road—the clumsy contrivances of a hundred years ago, on which the gathered loads of hay were going homeward from some of the out-lands—and the long, low wagons on which great pyramids of boxes of cheese, the staple of the section, were being slowly dragged towards Utica and a market.

But fair Oneida showed that war was in the land, removed though it might be from the great centres of recruiting operations. Joe Harris had noticed that a recruiting tent for

McQuade's gallant Fourteenth stood in the middle of Genesee
Street, only a little way above the hotels; with drums beating and flags and placards exhibited ; and even in the fields
she saw traces of the effort to answer the President's last
demand for troops. Where on the visits of previous years
she had seen only men toiling in the sunshine, many women
were laboring now, and the change was significant. The
homes of Oneida had already given of their best and bravest
to the cause of the nation, and still the Moloch of war demanded more !—more, ever and continually more !

There was a reminder of the war, too, within the coach,
and a reminder of the mode in which the recruiting service
was being conducted. On one of the front seats sat a fine-
looking young man, bright-eyed and keen-faced, in the
shoddy uniform of a private. His conversation was at once
that of a patriot and a gentleman ; and it did not require
many moments of unavoidable listening for the young girl to
discover that he was well educated. Further conversation
between himself and other passengers who seemed to know
and respect him, showed that he had abandoned his studies
in a leading institution, to answer the call of the country—
that mathematics and military science had formed a considerable part of his studies—that he had had some hopes, when he
enlisted, of obtaining the grade of a subaltern officer, when
he should succeed in procuring sufficient enlistments—that
by his personal efforts and fervid eloquence he had already
succeeded in enlisting more than fifty men for the regiment
with which he was connected, and was then on his way to
another section of the county to make further efforts in the
same direction—and that he was still a "full private," with
a certainty of rising no higher, because he had neither money
nor political influence to put him forward. So that this
young patriot and soldier, who showed the power and energy
of his nature in every glance of his eye and every word he
spoke, was to be kept in the lowest position known to the
service, and commanded by men who had never heard of
a book on military science or tactics, a week before, but who
could buy commissions or command a certain number of votes
at a town-meeting ! Josephine Harris had studied the cur-

rent history of the time, enough to know and recognize the picture set before her, and to say, silently and between her set teeth:

"Oh, I wish I was only a man, to start out with a horsewhip and lash these incapables until they howled!"

Six o'clock, and the stage went rumbling and swaying into the little village of West Falls, which it is hoped that no matter-of-fact reader will attempt to find on the map of Oneida, albeit it has a veritable existence there under another name. It was a cozy little spot, nestled down into the valley of a small stream, half creek and half river, that formed a cataract in the neighborhood and gave it the name. Factories clustered along the stream, making the idle water labor for the benefit of man, and within them whirred the spindle of the cotton or wool spinner and clanked the hammer of the worker in iron and steel. The village itself lay partly in the valley, along the east margin of the stream, and partly climbing the slight range of hills that bounded it still farther eastward. A wilderness of shade-trees bordered the main street and seemed to cluster around every house on the narrow lanes that branched from it, presenting a cool and refreshing picture in the hot summer afternoon, and suggesting rosy-cheeked lasses, breezy halls and bed-rooms, real milk instead of the manufactured article, and all the other pleasant things traditionally supposed to belong to summer in the country.

Up the long shady street, then down a wide bye-street that branched to the left under the very edge of the hills, and the accommodating stage set the city girl down at the gate of a neat-looking story-and-a-half house, buried in trees and bowered in summer flowers, unvisited by her for the previous three years, but before that time the scene of many an hour of quiet rustic enjoyment. For reasons best known to herself, Josephine Harris had chosen not to advise her hostess of her intended visit, but she had no fears that it could possibly find her "not at home," and indeed before the clanking steps of the coach were well let down, the new-comer had been recognized from the house, and a young girl came flying down the pathway to the gate. This was Susan Halstead, her cousin, three years younger than herself, petite in figure,

brown-haired and round-faced, with the curls flying loose
over her shoulders and her childish mouth all puckered with
pleasure at once more seeing and embracing "Cousin Joe."

The stage rolled away, the luggage found its way inside
the white gate, and Josephine was soon in the arms of her
matronly-looking Aunt Betsey, her mother's sister and the
country type of the family as Mrs. Harris herself supplied
that representing the city. Much taller in figure than her
daughter, a little deaf and with many threads of silver shining
in her dark hair, but with the kindest face and the merriest
laugh in the world, Mrs. Betsey Halstead furnished a pleasant
specimen of those moderately-circumstanced Lady Bountifuls
of the country and the country village, who always have a
spare bed for the wayfarer, always a cup of milk and a slice
of fresh bread for the weak and the needy, and always an
unalloyed enjoyment in the coming of "company," i.e., visitors.

It need scarcely be said that the coming of merry Joe
was a pleasure as well as a surprise, that she was over-
whelmed with welcomes as well as questions, that aunt and
cousin and the tidy "help" all vied in the effort to "put away
her things," and that in five minutes the city girl was more
pleasantly flustered than she would have been on entering a
fashionable ball at Irving Hall or attending the first hop of
the season at Newport. Pleasantly flustered—that is, she did
not quite know whether her head was on or off her shoulders,
and yet she knew that she was for the time in a quiet little
haven of country rest from the noise and whirl of the great
city, very pleasant to contemplate.

"And you did not write us a word about your coming?"
said Aunt Betsey, interrogatively, when the bonnet had been
laid off, the dust brushed away, and the second kiss of meeting exchanged.

"Not a word, Aunt," was the young girl's reply. "You
know that I never do things like other people. I knew that
you would be at home—knew that you would be glad to see
me—did not know that I was coming, myself, until a day or
two ago—and do not think that I should have written, if I
had, when it was so much easier to bring the information
myself."

"Still the same rattle-brain!" said Aunt Betsey, shaking her head with that peculiar gesture which really implies admiration of a prodigy. "So mother is still in the city, is she? Why did not she come along?"

"Yes?" echoed Susan. "Why didn't she come along? Did you come all the way alone?"

"No," answered Josey, with the least little bit of hesitation in her answer, and the tiniest flush creeping up on her face, that neither of the others had the tact to see. "There were some friends of mine going on to Niagara, and so I had company all the way to Utica, and they set me down there." Sly Joe!—why did she use the plural number,—"friends," and "they"? Why will people, even those belonging to the most irreproachable classes of society, indulge in these little fibs upon occasion?

"Oh, Cousin Joe," said Susy, "you do not know what a nice little room we have for you, up-stairs. The vines have climbed up and half covered the window, and a robin has built its nest in one of the branches of the big apple-tree, that hangs so close to it. Little robie will wake you early in the morning, I'll be bound—none of the late lying in bed that they say you all practice in the great city!"

"No, you rose-bud!" exclaimed Joe. "I will get up as early as any of you, especially as I have not come out here to be idle, but to *work*. But where is Uncle?—I have not seen *him* yet?"

"Your Uncle Halstead," said Aunt Betsey, with a shade of sorrow momentarily crossing her kindly face. "Oh, I suppose you did not know it! Your Uncle has gone to the war, with the rest of them. There have a great many gone from Oneida—scarcely a family that does not miss one member at least. Some of them will not come back, I suppose; and some may. God shelter and keep your Uncle! It was a little hard to part with him, after being together nearly all the time for so many years; but he felt that he must go, and he knew his duty best."

"And you so cheerful about it that I did not even know till now that he was gone!" said Joe, with surprise.

"Why yes," said her Aunt. "If *they* have a duty to fight
22

for the country we have a duty to be patient while they ar i
gone and do the best we can with what they leave behind
them !"

Bravely and truly said, wife of the Oneida soldier ! If the
battles of the Union are lost, half the fault will lie with the
women who have preferred their own ease and the content-
ment of their own affections, to the peril of their native land ;
and if those battles are won, no small share of the credit will
be due to those true-hearted descendants of Molly Starke,
who have emulated the self-sacrificing spirit of the women of
old Rome and sent off the husbands they loved and the sons
upon whom they leaned, to win their love and confidence over
again on the battle-field, or to die for the worshipped flag and
the perilled nation !

"God shelter and keep him, indeed !" responded the young
girl. "And he will, without a doubt." No one could exactly
understand why it should be so, in conjunction with the dash
and freedom of her character ; but hidden away somewhere
among the dark glossy hair was a bump of Veneration that
recognized the Supreme Being with the most filial love and
trust—and in the heart there was a corresponding throb of
gratitude, confidence and childlike dependence.

"But what have you got, out-of-doors ?" she asked, changing
her manner again to that of one who had no thought beyond
the present. "I have not quite forgotten how the old yard
looks, with the smoke-house close to the back door, and the
barn at the other end. Got any pigs and chickens ? And
how's your cat ?"

"The cat is well," said Susan, gravely—"that is, as well
as could be expected. She has quite a family. We have lots
of chickens—you must have seen some of them in the front
yard as you came in. And pigs—a pen full of them, but a
little too big to suit you. They are too heavy and dirty to
take in your arms, and all the curl is gone out of their tails."

"So sorry !" said Miss Josey, with the most melancholy
of pouts on her lip, and with a funny reminder or Laura
Keene when she uses the same expression to the discarded
Pomander in "Peg Woffington."

"But we have something else that you will like," Susy

continued, determined to atone for any disappointment in the
pigs and their terminations. "We have got a calf—a nice
red-and-white spotted calf, only about a week old."

"Oh, that is the thing!" cried the merry girl. "We will
go at once and have a look at the calf. Does it hook?"

"Hook?—you stupid thing!" laughed Susy. "Why it is
only a week old, I tell you; and of course it hasn't any horns.
But come along!" and down from a convenient peg she pulled
a couple of sun-bonnets, her mother's and her own, sticking
one on the gypsy head of Josey and the other on her own
refractory curls. "But stop—we have something else that
you have not thought of"—and she pulled down the head of
her cousin and whispered in her ear.

"Cherries! oh good gracious!" absolutely yelled the young
lady. "Quick—get me some boy's-trousers and a step-ladder!
No, you needn't mind the trousers, as long as it is only you,
Susy, who is going to help me pick; but the step-ladder—
don't forget the step-ladder!" and away she went, flying out
of the house, her hand in that of Susan, and the whole movement more suggestive than anything else, of two young colts
turned out in a clover-field for a summer-day frolic.

Five minutes afterwards, a subterranean observer, could
such a person have been possible, would have seen Miss Josey
most unromantically astride of a limb, half way up the big
Tartarean cherry tree overhanging the smoke-house, appro-
priating those pulpy little purple globes at a most luxurious
rate, and staining her cherry lips and her white fingers very
nearly of the same color. Susy stood below, laughing and
clapping her hands at mad Joseph's position, and eating, by
way of sympathy, the few clusters thrown down to her by
the busy fingers.

But we cannot linger upon this picture, pleasant as it is—
nor yet upon the adventures of Josey among the pigs, chickens,
cats, with the calf (which managed to "butt" her over, even
if it could not "hook"), and among all and singular the be-
longings and appliances connected with that cozy little retreat
in the country village. Then what a supper followed, with
the flaky white tea-biscuit made by Aunt Betsey's own hands,
with the fresh cream equally divided between the cherries and

the strawberries, and the scent of the roses stolen by the slight evening breeze and thrown in at the windows. Then an hour of moonlight, but only an hour, for the young girl was wearied out by the changes of scene that had kept her excited during the day, and the broken rest of the night before. Long hours earlier than Tom Leslie heard the whistle of his train, braking-up at Suspension Bridge, Josephine was nestling among the white sheets and cool pillows of her pleasant chamber, nodded at by the vines at the window and just lovingly kissed by one glint of the moon that stole in upon her privacy—sleeping such a sleep as wealth and power turn wearily upon their pillows and pray for without hope.

CHAPTER XXIII.

JOSEPHINE HARRIS IN SEARCH OF INFORMATION—A BIG FIB FOR A GOOD END—MARY CRAWFORD WITH HER EYES SHUT, AND WITH THE SAME EYES OPENED—A BOMB-SHELL FOR COLONEL EGBERT CRAWFORD.

PLEASANT though those hours in the little homestead at West Falls may have been, they must be passed rapidly over, except as each bore some event connected with the progress of this story.

When Josephine Harris woke next morning with the birds singing Sunday matins under her window, all the fogs and mists of merriment and country enjoyment seemed for the time to have rolled away from her brain, and the prime object of her visit to West Falls came prominently into her mind. In order to effect it, it was necessary that her aunt and cousin should both be taken somewhat into her confidence ; and she had no fear of any evil result from this, as their location at a distance from the city would prevent any ill effects even from an unguarded word. Whatever these confidences were to be, however, there was no occasion to make them with any great

suddenness; and in her character of an "amateur detective"
she naturally preferred to make what discoveries might be
possible, before explaining her motives for making the inquiries.

Accordingly, when breakfast and the Sunday-"morning
work" had been dispatched, she pulled little Susy away from
the house, under the pretence of taking a "swing" in the
popular abomination of that name, suspended between two of
the trees in the back-yard. Seated side by side on the board
seat between the ropes, and with their arms clasping each
other's waists, the two girls fell into a conversation which
was very soon led by Josephine into the direction she wished.
Not, however, until she had propitiated the demon of mischief
within her, by making an onslaught upon a daguerreotype
which she had found in one of the drawers of the bureau in
her room during an imprudent "rummage" before breakfast.
A few sly hits at the appearance of the face there depicted,
brought a sudden flush to the face of little Susy; and not
long elapsed before they elicited the information, given through
deeper and warmer blushes, that she was under an engagement of marriage to the young man whose portrait was thus
made a hidden treasure—that he was an engineer on a distant
railroad, who could only make his visits to West Falls at intervals of a month or two—and that they were to be married
sometime during the ensuing year, if life and health would
permit. Simple Susy!—what a pity that she could not have
been informed of some of the events in the life of her cousin
which had occurred during the previous few days—especially
of the "friends" who had accompanied her to Utica! In
that case it is just possible that the blushes might have been
duplicated, though no corresponding confidence could have
been elicited, for the best of all reasons. As it was, Susan
had nothing to do but to pour out the one life-secret of her
innocent heart, receiving nothing in return but a peal or two
of merry laughter and a final assurance that "he would do,"
and that "he was not so *very* homely and awkward, after
all!"

When she had reduced her cousin to that state of defence-
lessness and subserviency, Pussy Harris (as we have before

had occasion to call her) suspended amusement, went into business, and commenced her round of enquiries.

A quarter of a mile away, in full sight of the grounds in the neighborhood of the barn, from its elevated position near the top of a gently-swelling knoll, a little separated from the main chain of hills that stretched away eastward—stood a large two-story farm-house, a little old and Dutch in its appearance, but thrifty-looking and suggesting that the man who made it a residence was the owner of many broad acres. This appearance was very much added to by the size and extent of the barns and out-houses; and the impression of age and stability was enhanced by the fine old trees which surrounded the yards and added so much to the pleasantness of the situation. From her old memory of the place, and of conversations during previous visits when she had no interest whatever in the inmates, Josephine Harris had an impression that this house was the abode of the Crawfords; and it was upon that supposition that she began her enquiries.

"Let me see—I almost forget," she said, pausing in their swing, and with the air of one trying very hard to remember—"Who was it that used to live in the big house yonder on the hill? Thompson? Johnson? What was the name?"

"The big house? oh, Crawford—the Crawfords live there," answered Susan, very innocently.

"Oh, yes, the name was Crawford," said Joe. "Let me see—there was an old man—"

"Yes, old John Crawford," so Susan supplied the missing name.

"And he had one daughter—only one daughter, and only one child, I think," said Josephine, working her features into a terrible semblance of trying to recollect something in the past, that had almost escaped her.

"Why yes, he had only one child, Mary," said Susan, evincing a little surprise. "But I did not know that you ever met her, so as to take any interest in her."

"Humph! well, I never did meet her, except at church," said the city girl, evasively. "But you were pretty young, then, and you would scarcely have remembered it if I had. I remember thinking that the old house must be a nice place for living in the country, and I thought of it again this morning. Is the old man living still?"

Less unsophisticated persons than little Susan Halstead might have been led into pursuing a subject of village gossip, by so specious a trap as that set by Josephine; and it is not strange that she fell at once into the line of conversation that the other desired.

"Yes, old Mr. Crawford is still living," said Susy, "and that is about all that can be said. He is old and very feeble, and they have been expecting him to die any day for the past three or four months. And that is not all—as you seem to have known something about Mary, I do not care if I tell you. There is serious trouble in that house, Cousin Josey!"

"Trouble?" echoed the young girl "Indeed! why what is the matter?"

"It is a long story," said Susan, "but perhaps I can tell it without using many words. You know that the Crawfords are richer than most of us here—they say that the old man is *very* rich—and so they belong to the aristocracy and do not associate with everybody. Mary is older than myself, a year or two, but we were at school together. We have not had much intimacy since, but a little, in spite of the difference in our circumstances. Mary is a dear, good soul, and not a bit proud, though the family are proud as Lucifer. Well, she used to come here once in awhile, and she made me come over there, though I always felt out of place in the big house. She was as gay and merry, then, as could be, and seemed always happy and light-hearted. She used to think a great deal of Mother, apparently; and once, two years ago, when Mother was very sick, she came down two or three times a day and brought her everything nice that she could think of. Lately she has not come here at all, and as she is richer than I, I am too proud to put myself in her way."

"Did nothing occur between you, to make any change in her behavior towards you?" asked the female lawyer.

"Nothing at all," answered little Susy. "I suppose that some of her fine acquaintances told her that she must not visit people poorer than herself, and that may have made the difference."

"But this is not the 'trouble' you spoke of, is it ?" asked the young girl, who did not by any means intend to allow the cross-examination to fall through at this point.

"Oh, not at all," said the unsuspicious Susan. "I was coming to that directly. There was a cousin of Mary's, Richard, from New York, who used to come up here very often. I sometimes saw them together, and then it was that she looked so gay and happy. I am sure that they loved each other, and every one thought that some day they would be married. Of course I have never heard any of these things from *her*, and perhaps I ought not to talk about them; but you know such things will creep out. Well, Richard Crawford does not come up here any more. They say that he has been leading a dreadful life, drinking and going into bad places, until he is all broken down and a miserable cripple. There is another cousin, a Colonel, who comes up here now, and he and Mary go out together sometimes. The Crawfords are notorious for trying to keep all their property in the family ; and so, as the other has proved so bad, probably *this* cousin and Mary may be married. But she looks like a ghost when I meet her, at church or when she is riding out ; and I know that she is unhappy Perhaps she loves the poor young man still, bad as he is. Don't you think that is possible, cousin Joe ? And may that not be what ails her ?"

"Why yes, you dear little soul, I should think very likely !" said the city girl, leaning down her head on her hand and trying to still the throbbing of her temples. What a revelation was here, from lips so innocent and evidently so truthful ! And how the whole story tallied with what she had heard in her ambush and conjectured from other circumstances ! She was on the right scent, beyond a question—but here came her difficulty,—how to cut this knot of villainy, even now that it lay plainly before her ! This was the question that labored through the young girl's brain and bent down her head on her hand. And yet it must be done, whatever the difficulty. Courage, Joseph Harris !—there never was a difficult thing, either in wickedness or benevolence, that a woman could not master when she once fairly set about it !

"It is indeed a sad story that you have been telling," she

said, "an l it interests me more and more in the family and especially in Mary. I wish I could see her and talk to her for half an hour." She had gathered all the information that she had any right to expect, and now came the necessary confidence. "What would you say now, Susy, if I could put back some of the light into Miss Mary Crawford's eyes?"

" You?" and the country girl looked at her as if a pair of horns had suddenly sprouted from under the dark hair.

"Yes, I!" echoed the "amateur detective."

"I don't see how you can do it, especially as you do not know these people or anything much about them," said Susan. "But indeed I should be very much pleased if you could, and I should—yes, I should just think you a witch!"

"Well," said Josephine, "suppose then that I had known something about these people for a long time, and that I had come up to West Falls not only to see my dear aunt and cousin, but to serve them in a way that they knew nothing about—would you and your mother keep the secret and help me?"

The wondering eyes looked at her more wonderingly still, but they seemed to see that the speaker was not jesting, and some of those country people have a faith in the abilities of people from the "big city," not always justified.

"Certainly I would," said Susy, "and I am sure that mother would do anything to serve Mary. But what is it all, Cousin Joe?"

"That is what I am just going to tell you, or at least a part of it," said Josephine. "In one word, all these stories about Richard Crawford are *lies*. He is a good, true-hearted young man, as can be found in the world. I know him very well, and visit him and his sister every day or two—sometimes, when I am very idle, every day. I love him as I would my own brother, if I had one."

"Not *better* than a brother, eh, cousin Josey?" asked the country girl, with a funny glance out of the corners of her eyes.

"Oh, no," said Joe, laughing. "Not *better* than a brother or I should scarcely be trying to make matters right between him and Mary Crawford."

"No, I suppose you would not—I didn't think of that,"
said Susy. "And so you know them, and you know *him*,
and he is a good man, is he? Why, cousin Josey, where did
all these stories come from, then?"

"Humph!" said the city girl, "we may find all that out
by-and-bye. It is enough to say that they are not true, and
that I *know* them not to be true. If I find that I am right
in my suspicions of their origin, I will tell you: if not, you
will be the better for not knowing."

"And what are you going to do?" asked the proprietor of
the unmanageable curls and the wondering eyes.

"I scarcely know yet, myself," said the schemer. "It
seems certain that no time is to be lost. You say that old
Mr. Crawford may die any day. Now, Susy, it is my belief
that if he should die to-day, as matters are arranged Mary
and all the property would go—well, I cannot tell you where,
but where you would not like to see them."

"Indeed you frighten me, cousin!" said Susy.

"I suppose so, answered Josephine. "But now—see
here! I think I ought to see Mary Crawford this very day,
and without any one at the big house knowing that I am
at West Falls or that she has any communication with this
house. How can that be managed?"

"Indeed I do not see how it can be managed at all!" said
the country girl, with a very hopeless look at her pleasant
face.

"Indeed it *must!*" said Miss Josey, who was only confirmed
in the determination by the supposed difficulty.

"I do not see how it can," repeated Susy. "You cannot go
there, of course, without being seen, and I do not know of any
way to get her *here*."

"But that is the thing," persisted Josephine. "She must
be got *here*, in some way or another. Pshaw! I don't see
how it is to be done, but it *must* be done. We might set fire
to the house, and that would probably bring her over, but then
it would bring all the other people from the house, and then
your mother might have some objections."

"I should think very likely she *would!*" said Susy, with

another wondering look around at the female torpedo who was thus exploding in West Falls.

"Stop! I have it!" cried the wild girl, a flash of triumph passing over her face. "Run into the house, Susy, and ask your mother to come out here. Your 'help' must not hear what is said."

Susy ran into the house on her errand, stopping once, as she turned the corner, to look around and satisfy herself whether Cousin Joe had not escaped from some lunatic asylum. While she was gone, Joe sat in the swing alone and did some energetic thinking; but twice, before the old lady came, she endorsed her plan with: "Yes, that will do. That *must* do!"

Directly Aunt Betsey came out to the swing, her arms floured to the elbows, having been interrupted in the midst of the divine mysteries of moulding cherry-dumplings, for the Sunday dinner. But she did not look the less amiable and good-natured for the interruption, as many good housewives might have done.

"Aunt," said Josephine, grasping her by the hand, in spite of the flour. "Aunt, I want you to do a good and benevolent action, at once."

"Well, I will try, my child!" said the good woman. "That is, if it *is* a good action that you want me to do. But you know, Josey, that you are a bit of a rattle-brain."

"Yes, well, I think that I may have heard that observation before," said Miss Josey. "However, I can live through it. Aunt, I will tell you *why*, by-and-bye when there is more time, —but I have a reason, that may be one of life and death, for what I ask. I want you to believe in the weight of my reasons at once, and to help me get Mary Crawford from the big house yonder, over *here*, immediately."

"Why, she does not come here now-a-days; and what can you want of her?" asked Aunt Betsey.

"There you go, Aunt!" said Joe. "You are not doing what I asked you to do. I tell you there are reasons why I must see Mary Crawford to-day, and with no one, outside of this house, knowing that I do so."

"She is right, Mother," said Susan. "She has told me

what she means, and she ought to see her at once. Do help
her—pray do !" These dear little innocent people who are
happy in their own love-affairs, have a marvellous faculty of
falling into the needs of others, and God bless them for it !

"But how ?" asked Aunt Betsey.

"Oh," I don't know," said Susan. "Cousin Josey knows."

"I only know one plan to get her here without suspicion,"
said Josephine. "To do that we must tell a falsehood, but
only for an hour "

"Oh, I cannot tell a falsehood," said the conscientious
matron.

"Yes you can, or you can let *us* tell it," said the incorrigi
ble. "Susy tells me that when you were sick, two years
ago, Mary Crawford came to see you very often."

"She did, and she was a very kind nurse—Heaven bless
her, even if she *does not* come to see us any more !" said the
old lady.

"If she thought you sick, she would come again, I think,"
said Josephine. "Once here, my word for it that she would
not be angry, but thank you, when she heard all that I have
to tell her "

"I do not like it, my child !" said the straightforward woman.

But what can a kind-hearted old lady do, with two
young ones and one a model of her sex, tugging at her apron-
strings ? In five minutes more, without at all understanding
what was to be done or why it should be done, Aunt Betsey
had given her consent to take part in what was probably one
of the first falsehoods of her life. In ten minutes more, one
of the boys who had already dressed himself for church, was
on his way to the Crawford mansion, with a sealed note in
the school-girl hand-writing of Susan, written under the
dictation of Josephine, and reading as follows :

SUNDAY, July 6th, (morning).

Dear Miss Crawford :—

Please pardon the liberty I take. Mother is very ill, and we
should be very grateful if you would say nothing to any one else
about this note and come over to the house *immediately.*

Very respectfully your friend,

SUSAN HALSTEAD.

No call is so irresistible as that which appeals to the sympathy of a true woman ; and no crime is so unpardonable as
that which trifles with such sympathy. Less than half an
hour had elapsed, and Aunt Betsey, a little ashamed and a
good deal frightened at what had been done, had gone up-
stairs to escape the possibility of first meeting the young girl
if she should come,—when Josephine, looking impatiently
out of the window at the road leading down from the hill
towards the centre of the village, saw a young lady coming
down the path at the side of the road and approaching the
gate. The figure was short and rather slight, dressed in
some light summer-material, wearing one of the light jockey
hats of the time, and sheltered from the hot morning sun by a
parasol of dimensions too large to be fashionable. There was
no reason why some other young lady should not be walking
the foot-path at that time, especially as church-hour was approaching ; but Josephine Harris had an indefinite impression
that it was Mary Crawford, and that a trial was approaching,
more severe than any to which she had ever before subjected
herself. Susy was close at her side, and as the figure approached, Josephine called her attention to it.

"Yes," said Susy, looking out of the window for only one
instant, "that *is* Mary Crawford, and she is coming here."

To say that Josephine Harris's heart was beating quickly,
and that there was such a confused rumbling in her head as
that which forms part of the stage-fright to an actress or the
first embarrassment to a public speaker before a large audience—would only be stating the simple truth. She had certainly been doing a bold act—even a rash one,—meddling in
the business of another, with the best intentions, it was true,
but under circumstances very liable to be misunderstood. If
things should not be as she had understood them to be, at
the Crawford mansion, or if she should fail in convincing
Miss Crawford of the truth of the statements she was ready
to make, nothing could be more painful than the position in
which she would herself remain, and nothing more injurious
than the predicament in which she would have placed her
aunt and cousin. All this she realized, and for one moment
she felt like running up-stairs with her aunt, and hiding her-

self between two of the thickest feather-beds, in spite of the
heat of the season. But, courage once more, Joe Harris!
The playing of detective *en amateur* is not always a sinecure
or a pleasant labor; but if it succeeds—aye, if it succeeds
—why then!

By the time these reflections had fairly passed through her
mind, the figure of Miss Crawford had entered the gate and
was coming up to the porch.

"Go into the back room, Susan," said the city girl. "You
will not know how to receive her. I must do it."

Instantly Susan glided through the back door, and shut it,
and Josephine Harris was alone in her singular position.
At the same moment Miss Crawford tapped at the closed
front door, and Josephine at once opened it to admit her.

Mary Crawford had been a charmingly-pretty country-
girl—that Joe Harris saw at a glance, the moment her eye
took in the whole contour; and she did not for a moment
wonder that Richard should have been fond of her or that
his cousin should have used all *honorable* means to supplant
him. More of what she had been than what she was, the
observer saw. No change, except age, could take away the
charm from the rich chestnut auburn (is there not such a
color?) of her hair; and her face could never be other than a
pleasant and a *good* one. But the hazel eyes looked as if
they had been more accustomed to filling with tears than any
one knew besides the owner; the handsomely rounded cheeks
looked almost as sallow as they might have done from long
sickness; the full, girlish mouth had a pinched and pained
expression; and though she was dressed richly and with
excellent taste, for a mere call in the country, there was
something about her small figure which showed that it had
once been fuller and rounder, and that she had fallen into
lassitude and comparative lifelessness.

"I had a note from Miss Halstead, saying that her mother
was ill," said Miss Crawford, recognizing a stranger's face as
the door was opened.

"Yes," said Josephine. "Miss Mary Crawford, I pre-
sume? Pray come in."

"Where *is* Mrs. Halstead?" asked the visitor, perhaps a

little surprised that she should not at least have been received by one of the family.

"Pray walk into this room a moment and lay off your bonnet," said Josephine, opening the door into the cool, shaded parlor which adjoined the sitting-room, drawing her in and shutting the door. Perhaps Miss Crawford saw something strange, too, in this or in the young girl's manner, for her eyes ranged around the room and then alighted upon her companion, with a little wonder expressed in them. Josephine Harris saw and marked the expression; and she was too much excited, herself, not to satisfy that wonder very quickly.

"Pray sit down, Miss Crawford," she said, drawing a large cushioned rocker near one of the windows.

"But Mrs. Halstead?" again asked the other. "Is she not *very* sick?"

"I have never had the pleasure of seeing you before this moment, Miss Crawford," said Josephine, her voice much thicker and huskier than she had ever before known it to be—"but I am going to ask you to do me a very great favor?"

"I do not understand you, Miss ——," said the visitor.

"Of course not," said the temporary hostess. "I am such an odd jumble that nobody understands me, at first. But let me hope that I may make myself fully understood directly."

"May I ask your name, Miss ——?" again said the young girl, inquiringly.

"Certainly, you have a perfect right to my name," said Josephine. "I am called Josephine Harris, and I am a niece of Mrs. Halstead."

"Oh," said Mary Crawford; but whether she uttered the word in recognition or in depreciation, the other had no means of guessing.

"I said that I was going to ask a great favor of you," said the city girl, going on. "It is that you will remain in this room while I say some very strange things to you, and that you will try not to be hurt or angry with me until I have done."

"This *is* certainly very strange," said Mary Crawford. "What can I think?"

"Think that you are in the house of true friends, who

would neither see you harmed nor insulted," said Josephine.

"Oh, I am sure of *that*," answered her companion.

"Then listen to me," said Josephine,, "and whatever surprise you may feel, pray do not *say* it until you have heard
all. Mrs. Halstead is not sick, and the note sent to you was
written at my request, as the only means within my knowledge
of inducing you to visit this house *immediately*."

"Mrs. Halstead not sick ? a falsehood—a cruel falsehood !"
said the young girl, with some indignation, and rising from
her chair as if to leave the room.

"Miss Mary Crawford, I implore you to resume your seat,"
said Josephine, her voice now broken and husky with her
great agitation. "For the sake of your own happiness and
the happiness of those dearer to you than your own life, I
implore you to hear me out."

"This is all so strange !—what *can* you mean ?" she uttered, but she sunk back, nevertheless, into the chair again.

"It *is* strange—it is all strange—it is of crime and suffering that I am about to tell you," answered Josephine. "To
tell you for your own sake and no interest of my own."

"For *my* sake ?" asked Mary Crawford, now visibly trembling, and with a look of startled wonder upon her face that
was really pitiable to behold. "What can you know of me,
and what interest can you take in me ?"

"I know nearly everything of you, and I take the same
interest in you that I would do in a dear sister," replied the
city girl, striving to use the words that would most reassure
and invite confidence. "Will you understand me when I say
that two of the dearest friends I have in the world are your
cousins Isabel and *Richard Crawford ?*"

She purposely laid a peculiar stress on the latter name, and
fixed her eyes keenly on the other as she did so. She saw
the young girl flush to the very temples, then pale as suddenly, make another movement to rise from her chair, then
sink back again as if from sheer exhaustion. Oh, it was not
difficult to see how nearly that word touched with agony the
very fountains of her life ! She seemed trying to speak, but

the words, if any were intended, died upon her lips, and her helpless agitation was really fearful to witness. Josephine Harris retained sufficient coolness to mark every indication, and though her young heart bled for the misery before her, after a moment's silence she repeated the names :

"Did you hear me, Miss Mary? I said that two of my dearest friends were Isabel and Richard Crawford."

This time the young girl did manage to stagger to her feet, by a mighty effort, her face white and her expression piteous. Her voice had broken almost to hoarse sobs, as she said, leaning one hand on the arm of the chair :

"I do not know why you have sent for me, or why you should torture me so cruelly ! If you know anything of me and of the man you have named, you know that every word you speak is an unkindness, and that he is the last man in the world whose name should sound in my ears !"

"He is the *first* man in the world whose name should pass your lips, with a prayer for forgiveness of your own cruelty joined with it !" said his advocate, all her ardent spirit now thrown into her words.

"*My* cruelty ? *His* forgiveness ?" echoed Mary Crawford. as if really stunned.

"I said those words," repeated Josephine. "One of the best and noblest men that God ever made is lying on his sick-bed, nearly dying. He loved you—he loves you still. You pretended to love *him ;* and now you have allowed the words of falsehood to estrange your heart, if you *have* one ! It to save you from doing what you will repent to your dying day, that I have meddled in your affairs and placed myself in this false position."

"The words of falsehood ?" again echoed the young girl If she had heard the other words of the sentence, these were the ones which seemed to have fixed themselves most deeply on her attention. She had not again resumed her place in the chair, but stood with her hand on its arm, in the same attitude of trouble and indecision.

"Falsehood — the worst and blackest !" said Josephine Harris. "Come here a moment, will you ?" She took the hand of the young girl in hers, and led her close to the win-
23

dow, where the warm light of the summer day streamed in more brightly and countenances could be better discerned. " Look in my face. What do you see there ?—tell me frankly —truth or deception ?"

It is doubtful whether Mary Crawford had yet closely scanned the face before her. Now the troubled eyes looked closely into those that were sometimes so radiant with mischief, but now so solemnly earnest. The look was very long and silent—an evident acceptance of the strange invitation given. Before it was ended, that subtle magnetism which truth and goodness radiate to the true, had done its work. She cast down her eyes.

" I believe you to be true and good !" she said.

" Thank heaven that you do !" spoke Josephine. " Now sit down in that chair once more, and do not rise again until I have spoken what I must speak and you must hear. Do not shrink, faint or shudder, though I may say a few terrible words !" She led the young girl back to her chair, pressed her down into it, and drew her own still closer. She did not release her hand when she had placed her in that position, and she fixed her eyes full upon those of the other, which made an effort to escape, and then surrendered to the influence.

" Let me show you that I know *all*," she said. " Yet stop —let me first assure you that neither Richard Crawford nor his sister knows of my presence in this place—that neither of them has the least suspicion that I know one word of your family relations."

Mary Crawford's eyes looked into hers with one instant of close question ; then again they surrendered, and were gently reliant though still full of trouble.

" I said that I would prove to you that I knew *all*," Josephine went on. " I will do so. You loved Richard Crawford, I think, and he loved you with his whole heart. You were to be married, and the large property of your father would thus be kept in the family. A few months ago he ceased coming here any more, and you heard of him as plunged into riot and dissipation. Then you heard of him as sick, and that his sickness was the result of the foulest excesses, that had broken down his constitution and made him unfit for the society of any true woman. You began to answe: his letters briefly and coldly, and then you ceased answering them at all. You heard those reports—you scarcely knew yourself how you heard them, but I *do*,—through another cousin, Egbert Crawford, who has taken the place of Richard."

The young girl's eyes stared, now, and she moved as if to rise, but the hand of Josephine on her arm held her gently down, and her words went on, that steady gaze still fixed upon her as before :

"Every one of those words was a lie, and Egbert Crawford was trying to break your heart and the heart of the man who truly loved you, that he might win you and your wealth !"

"How do you know this ?—woman, how do you know this ?" broke out the poor girl, her agony of doubt and suffering terrible to behold.

"I know it as if God had revealed it to me from heaven !" said Josephine Harris, casting up her eyes and lifting her hand momentarily, as if invoking that heaven for the truth she was uttering. "Not one word of these stories of Richard Crawford was true. He was pure and good. He is so, in spite of wrong and neglect. He loves you still, though he is almost broken-hearted."

"Oh, you cannot prove these things to me !" again spoke Mary Crawford, the trouble in her eyes still deeper than before, and still that trouble now strangely compounded of joy and fear.

"I can and I will !" said the strange mentor. "Your own heart is proving them to you at this moment. You see how blind you have been, but you do not yet know all."

"All ? what more can there be, whether I am to believe you or not ?" asked the young girl.

"More—much more !" said Josephine Harris, speaking now almost in a whisper. "Do not shriek or run away from me ; but I tell you, before God, Mary Crawford, that for weeks past—perhaps for months, Egbert Crawford has been attempting to murder the relative he wished to rival, by *poison*."

"Poison ? oh no, oh my God !" cried the young girl, now no longer to be restrained, and starting from her chair in uucontrollable agitation. "You are mad—mad—and you are trying to make *me* so !"

"I have seen him apply the poison," said the strange compound of womanly weakness and more than manly strength —"seen him apply it, under the pretence of healing. I have seen the racking pains those fiendish practices have produced, and that no doctor's skill could combat. I have saved him—yes, I believe that I have saved him ! You do not yet quite believe all the wickedness of this man ! I see by your eyes that you do not ! But you shall ! See here !" and with the word she drew from the pocket of her dress the very bandage which she had exhibited in the office of Doctor La Turque, and unrolled its dark loathsomeness—"here is the very poison that I saw him apply to Richard Crawford's heart, warning him not to let the doctors suspect it, because they would laugh at him for *superstition*. I have stolen this—yes, *stolen it*, from the spot where Richard Crawford had hidden it when he first began to be aware of the terrible truth ; I have tested the powers of the unseen world to bear witness to his guilt ; I have had this bandage examined by one of the ablest physicians in America, and it is *poison—insidious, deadly poison*. Egbert Crawford is not only a liar, but a *murderer !*"

"Help me ! help me ! oh, my God, what shall I do ?" cried the poor girl, staggering as if about to fall, and only prevented by the quick arm of Josephine. "Do you know what you have been saying to me ? My father is sinking fast—his will is made—Egbert Crawford, whom you call a murderer, is at this moment at my home—I am to marry him this very day !"

"You *are* to marry him, after this warning ?" said Josephine Harris, looking at her with surprise not unmingled with horror. "Then you do not believe me, or you would marry a villain ! You are *not* glad to know that the man you once loved, and who yet loves you so dearly, is true and loyal ? I have indeed meddled where I was not wanted, and Richard Crawford—indeed—indeed she was not worthy of you !"

"Oh no, no ! do not say so !" cried the young girl, changing so suddenly from the icy misery in which she had before stood, that Josephine Harris was literally bewildered. "I do love Richard Crawford. I have never known one happy day since I believed him unworthy to be my husband. I do believe you, dear, good girl, and I do thank you from my soul for all you have done to serve me! But oh, I am so miserable and so helpless! What shall I do? what shall I do?" Before she had ceased speaking, she had literally flung herself on her knees, embracing the bottom of Josephine's garment, clinging to her as if there was no dependence in the world beyond, and sobbing as if her heart would break.

Josephine Harris was melted in a moment, and nearly heart-broken herself, at the sight of the young girl's misery; but oh, what a gleam of joy underlay the sorrow! She was *not* misunderstood!—she had *not* been laboring in vain! Happy Joe—even in the midst of her pain and anxiety!

. She raised the poor alarmed and sorrowing girl from her position of pleading and humiliation, took the chair that had just been vacated, and drew her down upon her own lap as if she had been a mother or an elder sister.

. "What shall I do?" still repeated the troubled lips, through choking sobs. "I cannot escape now. It is too late. Poor Richard!—poor wronged Richard! I have deserved my fate, for being so untrue to him. What shall I do? What shall I do?"

"Do?" said Josephine Harris, smoothing down her hair and striving to comfort her at the same time that she braced up her nerves for what must follow. "Do? Why send Colonel Egbert Crawford packing—that is the first step."

"Oh, I cannot!" moaned the young girl. "It would kill my poor old father, to have any trouble in the house, now; and I must marry that man, though I have never loved him—and he, oh heavens!—a murderer!"

"Well, if you *do* marry him," said Joe, with something of her old manner, justifying the resumption of her pet name, "all that I can say, is, that I hope you will have a happy time of it!"

"Why do you speak so?" asked the poor girl. "Why do you speak so lightly when I am so wretched?"

"Because I do not mean that you shall *remain* wretched,'

was the answer. "Hold up your head, now, Mary—may I
not call you Mary, *dear* Mary! Hold up your head, like a
brave girl, and listen to me."

Her frightened companion made an effort to do so, and
she went on:

"You believe that I have been right in what I have said;
do you not? And that I am a true friend?"

"Yes, indeed I do!"

"Then obey me now!" she continued, rapidly shaping
into words the thoughts that had been for a few moments
assuming consistency in her brain. "Do precisely as I tell
you, nothing less and nothing more, and this marriage will
break itself, without one word from you."

"Oh, how can that be possible?" asked the trembler.

"Sit down in that chair for a few minutes, and don't mind
me!" and in a moment she had transferred her burden to the
chair. In another she had flung open one of the end shutters
of the room, drawn a small table towards the window, opened
upon it her portable writing-desk (an article of use without
which she never travelled), and was hastily scribbling, though
with a hand that shook a little at its own boldness—the following note:—

WEST FALLS, Sunday, July 6th (noon).

Col. Egbert Crawford:—

You will probably recognize the name at the bottom of this, as
that of one you have often seen, but of whom you know very little.
No one but myself knows anything of the contents. You are discovered—detected. I have watched you and overheard your conversation, for days past, at the house of Richard Crawford. What is
more. I have the *poisoned bandage* in my pocket, after having had it
analyzed by a chemist. If you leave at once, without attempting
to consummate any more of your designs, you are safe from any
exposure—I promise you so much, on the honor of a true woman
If you are not gone before to-morrow morning, without any further
attempt at entangling Mary Crawford, I promise you, in the name
of God who sees us both at this moment, that I will not only expose
you before John Crawford and his family, but that I will do what
I can to bring you to justice. Mary Crawford knows all your falsehood and crime, but she, like myself, will keep silence when you
are gone.   JOSEPHINE HARRIS.

Mary Crawford had been sitting still in her chair, leaning her head upon her hand and not even looking up, while Josephine's pen was rapidly running over the paper. (The phrase is a proper one—Joseph's pen *ran*, always, when she attempted to write, and as a consequence her chirography was not the easiest in the world to be deciphered. No fear, however, but that what she wrote in this instance could be read!) When she had concluded and was rising from the desk, Mary first looked up, and there was such an expression of abject and almost hopeless helplessness upon her face, that had Josephine not pitied her before, she must now have done so. That look said so plainly: "*Can* you indeed help me? Is it possible that I can ever be lifted out of this pit of despair?"—that the city girl accepted it instead of words, and answered it.

"Yes, you need not look so doleful, my dear girl! I think you will find that this little epistle will do more than an ordinary volume could do. See—I have sealed it, as is best. I have said, within, that you knew nothing whatever of the contents, and at the same time I have said that you knew all his baseness and treachery."

"Oh, have you?" said the suffering girl. "How can I ever meet him, after that—when he knows that I have heard him spoken of in so terrible a manner?"

"You can even do that, a little better than you could lay your hand in his and promise to be his wife, I should think!" said the other, and there was even some sternness in her tone.

"Oh yes, yes, anything rather than become his beyond hope!" cried Mary, and there was such a shudder running over her frame for the instant, that her guide and mentor fully understood what must be the depth of the fear with which she had become inspired. "You have been so good to me—so kind and generous, that I can never thank you for what you have done. Command me, now—tell me what I must do, and I will obey you like a child—a poor, weak child as I am."

"I do believe that you thank and trust me," said Josephine, all her tender self again instantly, and grasping her warmly by the hand. "Many people think me a rattle-bra'n, I suppose, and my advice may sometimes seem very odd and rash; but I am sure that heaven has intended me for the instrument of foiling that man who would be your destroyer, and I know that I shall not fail. Please do precisely as I ask—give Egbert Crawford that letter without a word, and see if it does not produce the effect I have intended."

"I will do so, and trust that Heaven upon which you call, to save me from wrong and bring about the right!" answered Mary Crawford.

"The omens are all good," said Josephine, who really had in her nature a shade of *impressibility*, if not of superstition. "This is Sunday—a day for good deeds and not for evil ones. This night you were to have been married: I arrived just in time to put you on your guard. All will go well, and I shall see you free from a fetter so hateful and the wife of an honorable man whom I love as if he were my own brother."

"God bless you for all!" said Mary. "Kiss me before I go—my more than sister."

"Just what I was going to ask of *you*" said Joe Harris, who had great faith, and was not ashamed to own the fact, in the magnetism of the lips. The kiss was exchanged, with a warm embrace as an accompaniment, and then Mary Crawford said:

"I must go at once, before 1 am missed and too much wonder excited. I will try to obey all your directions. I shall see you again?—you will not leave West Falls until—until—"

"Until *you are safe*? No! Not if I stay a month!" was the reply. "If that letter fails, something else shall *not!* Good-bye, and let me hear from you to-morrow, or even to-day if anything occurs. But remember, no marriage to-night, if you have to run away here to escape it!"

"Oh, no! no! no! Good-bye!" and the young girl had passed out of the door and into the street, bearing the second letter which had that day left the little house for the great one on the hill, and bearing—oh, what a terrible change in knowledge and feeling since she had entered the door less than an hour before! Her brain throbbed almost to bursting, and every nerve in her body seemed to be strung to an unendurable tension, as she left the little gate and took her way homeward. She was wretched, in the knowledge of

guilt and wrong which had been imparted to her, and in the
fear of the future, which she could not shake away ; but she
confided, spite of herself, in the counsel which had been given
her, and there was a happiness out-weighing all the misery,
in the knowledge that the idol of her young heart was not a
base and miserable counterfeit. The gulf between Richard
Crawford and herself might have grown too wide to be over-
leaped—she might have become, to him, only a name to be
regretted and yet despised—but it was still something in life
to know that he was true and worthy, even if he was to be
nothing more to *her;* and the foot of the young girl trod
more firmly upon the green sward of the pathway than it
had done for many a long month, and half the languor was
gone from eye and nerve, as she walked slowly homeward
through the summer noon, to try that strange experiment
upon which she felt that the happiness or misery of her
whole future life might depend.

As for Josephine Harris, those who know the depressions
which sometimes fall upon high nervous organizations after
severe and continued effort, scarcely need be told that she was
almost prostrated the moment she felt that her work was for
the time concluded. She had been suffering with throbbing
temples and a too-rapid motion about the heart, during a
large part of her conversation with Mary Crawford ; and when
Aunt Betsey, seeing from the window the departure of Mary,
and little Susan, recalled by the voice of her cousin, re-entered
the sitting-room, they found Joe shedding tears like a great
baby and sobbing a little, with a fair prospect of an afternoon
and night in the company of that most unromantic of companions—*sick-headache.*

It is a matter of no consequence how much of the conversation which had just passed, Josephine narrated to her aunt
and cousin. Enough to satisfy their proper curiosity and give
them assurance that she had succeeded in her attempt at first
alarming and then winning the confidence of the young girl,
and nothing more. Neither asked more, for both felt, beyond
a doubt, that there might have been confidences in that conversation, too sacred to be revealed to other ears.

The sick-headache did come, as it had promised ; and Joe

Harris, her temples bathed with cologne by the willing hands of little Susy, went up to an enforced *siesta* in her little bed-room. But she had the satisfaction, as the drowsy hum of the summer afternoon gradually lulled her into slumber, of saying to herself—the best of all auditors for those who have sound hearts and clear consciences :

"I thought I would do it—I meant to do it—and may I never play detective again if I don't believe I that I have *done* it !"

CHAPTER XXIV.

JOHN CRAWFORD AND HIS NEPHEW—THE WRECK OF A WORK-ING MAN—THE EPISODE OF THE COCK—THE EFFECT OF JOSEPHINE HARRIS'S LETTER, AND AN EXODUS.

IN order to demonstrate more clearly the state of affairs be-fore existing at the house of John Crawford, and the effect really produced by the missive (it might almost as well have been called a *missile*) of Josephine Harris,—it will be neces-sary to change the point of view to the big house on the hill, at a little before noon on that pleasant Sunday of summer.

The back piazza of the house looked north and eastward over a slight depression which might almost be called a valley. and then at the range of hills rising behind and stretching downward on the other side almost to the Mohawk. Nearer, it looked out upon an extensive garden, carefully laid out and thriftily in growth with all the ground-fruits and vegetables natural to the climate, at that time in full luxuriance. Around the high board fences of the garden stood an almost endless variety of fruit-trees, the cherry-trees at that moment literally red, or black, or amber, as the case might be, with those delicious little globules of pulpy fruit-flesh which seem like drops of fragrant sweetness squeezed from the very heart of Nature. Among them stood apple and pear-trees, each loaded with the growing fruit of that wonderful fruit-season, in which the smile of God seemed resting broadly on the whole American continent in the wealth and variety of its productions, however his hand may have been smiting it with the desolations of personal strife and bloodshed. .

Digressions have become so common during the course of this narration, that if the later ones are not excusable on the score of propriety, they at least have that excuse which is held to be so important by the lawyers and the statesmen—*precedent*. And having already sinned in that regard, beyond any hope of forgiveness and almost beyond any feeling of accountability for the erraticism of the pen—let us pause here, under the reminder of those hanging fruits in John Crawford's garden, to say that while perhaps no nation has ever before been so cursed with an extended civil war as this once free and happy republic during the past two years—yet no nation, plunged into any description of conflict, has ever been so favored of Heaven with the means for carrying it on and so delivered of Heaven from the dangers of famine and pestilence which so often accompany the other affliction.

At no period in the history of any nation in the world, could the statistics of that country exhibit the same amount of material wealth and power of production as those shown by the loyal States of the American Union at the moment of the breaking out of the Rebellion—the capabilities of the seceding States being left entirely out of the question. Private coffers and the vaults of our banks were alike full of gold, which had been for years flowing in and amassing from the mines of California and the favorable course of foreign exchanges. We had been feeding the world, and at the same time supplying ourselves and the world with more than half the precious metals yearly contributed to the hoards of the nations; and that the country should literally have become "full of money," was inevitable. But more especially did we hold power over the whole world in our capacities for fruit-growing and in our stores of bread-stuffs already amassed. With proper management of our resources, the latter fact alone might have made the whole world tributary to us, and we could have dictated terms in war as well as in peace.

When a certain young Lieutenant in the British naval service, from the China fleet, crossed from Hong Kong to San Francisco on his way home on leave, in 1861, and then came by the overland route from San Francisco to New York, he fell into conversation in this city with a friend whom he had known in England; and as there were then rumors of trouble with Great Britain growing out of her expected help to the rebels, that conversation very naturally turned towards the relative wealth and power of the two countries.

"Well, I do hope," said the young English officer, "that there will not be any trouble between the two countries, because we don't want to fight you, you know!"

"And so do I," said his friend. "The *people* of America do not bear any ill will to the people or the government of England."

"But we should beat you if we *did* fight, you know," pursued the Englishman, with John Bull's tenacity of national pride.

"Think so?" asked the other, with the slightest suspicion of a sneer upon his lip.

"Oh, no, I don't think anything about it—I *know* it," said the Englishman. "Why, you haven't got any navy."

"The deuce we haven't!" observed the other. "I guess you have not *seen* our navy!"

"No!—nor has any one else seen an armament worthy of the name," said the Englishman, of course supposing that he referred to the dozen of old and worm-eaten wooden ships that then made up our whole preparation for contesting the empire of the seas. "Why any one of our half dozen fleets would eat up your whole navy in half an hour. If you had seen our Baltic fleet reviewed at Spithead, as I did just at the close of the Crimean war, you would know something of what the word 'navy' meant, and you would also have some idea, you know, of what a chance you would have at fighting England!"

"Humph! well, yes, you *have* a pretty long string of vessels, such as they are," said his American friend. "But I told you that you did not know anything about *our* navy, and you do not. You speak of the 'Baltic fleet.' Now what

will you say when I tell you that at one point on the Missis-
sippi we have a line of gun-boats that would knock not only
your Baltic fleet but all the rest of your fleets into smithe-
reens, without even firing a gun ?"

"Why I should only say that you were crazy, as I think
you *are!*" said the Englishman, really expecting that his
friend would by-and-bye attempt to demonstrate that the
easiest way of travelling was by walking on the head instead
of the feet.

. "Yes, I dare-say you do," said the American. "And yet
I am *not* crazy. The only thing is that you do not yet understand me. The line of gun-boats of which I speak, is a
line of warehouses at Chicago, containing at this moment
from six to ten millions of bushels of grain, constantly emptying and constantly being replenished. *That* is the line of
gun-boats to fight the world, and we can conquer the world
if we only use them correctly. We can live within ourselves,
without buying one dollar's-worth of anything from any
nation abroad, except possibly *tea* (for we can make our own
coffee while we can grow *peas* and *beans*); and there is not
another nation on the globe that can do the same. Not a
nation of you all but must have our breadstuffs or go hungry.;
and the sailors of your 'Baltic fleet' would not fight well,
I fancy, on empty stomachs."

"Humph !" said the Englishman. "That is an odd view
to take of war." But he said no more, and was evidently
thinking. He had grounds for thought, and so had the
whole world. We had the element of success in our own
hands, in the capacity of living within ourselves. Had our
resources been properly managed, the importation of all
foreign goods prohibited during the period of the war, and
the exportation of gold and breadstuffs forbidden and guarded
against by the closest watch and the most stringent penalties,
with our people practicing the self-denial and economy of the
men and women of the Revolution, setting their spinning-
wheels and looms once more in motion and wearing home-
spuns instead of imported broadcloths and satins,—had these
steps been taken, as they should have been taken, starvation
would have fallen upon half Europe, and the rebellion would

long before this time* have perished from its own weakness
or been crushed out, from sheer necessity, by the European
powers whose very existence its continuance was perilling.

The smile of God has not been withdrawn from our fields
and orchards; we have been continued in national health
and still supplied with all the luxuries of production and
abundance; and yet what is the use which we have made of
these immense advantages, and what thanks have we rendered to the Supreme Being in those two most acceptable of
worships, *labor* and *success*, for the health and wealth thus
given and continued?

But these reflections over, which have sprung from the
fruit glistening on the trees in John Crawford's garden, the
course of this narration reverts to two who occupied the back
piazza of the mansion at that hour of Sunday noon. The
piazza was a broad one, old-fashioned like the house, with
pillars of locust, planed and cornered instead of being turned
or fluted in the more modern fashion. Both the ends and
the side for a considerable distance towards the centre, were
enclosed by a low railing *in pale;* and the western end had
lattice-work extending to the tops of the pillars, with the
leaves and tendrils of a large grape-vine that had been planted
many years before at the corner, running over, twisting and
interlacing in the lattice, and making a pleasant flickering
shade of the summer sunshine on the floor of the piazza.
A few birds, not yet thoroughly exhausted by the noon-day
heat, were chirping in the thick branches of the fruit-trees
near, and the drowsy hum and chirp of insect life made such
a sleepy undertone as could not fail to bring rest and quiet to
any mind not preternaturally active. A more charming place
could not have been devised, for a half-dreamy and lazy
student of either sex to sit down in an easy chair with a
pleasant book, read and muse until the flickering of the sunshine and the shadows on the floor began to be blended with
the type of the page, and then fall away to the lightest and
happiest of slumbers.

There were two figures on the western end of the piazza.

* March 7th, 1863.

under the shade of the grape-vine. The first was that of an old man, sitting in a high-backed easy-chair, his feet upon a carpet-covered ottoman, leaning back, and if not in physical slumber, at least in that inertiæ of the mind which denotes failing physical faculties and marks a slumber more complete than that of shut eyes and stertorous breathing. Apparently he was very old, for his hair was thin and nearly white, as it showed from beneath the colored silk handkerchief thrown loosely over the back of his head; his skin had that shrivelled and wrinkled appearance, denoting that the life-fluids had been exhausted beneath it; his eyes, when opened, had that white opacity more melancholy than apparent blindness, because it shows a sight which after all takes in and recognizes nothing; and his thin lips had that constant tremulous motion which indicates a continual desire to speak, with scarcely the power of doing so and with little more than the remnants of a mind left to dictate what shall be uttered. John Crawford was, in short, a miserable human wreck, all its pride, beauty and power shorn and swept away, and drifting helplessly on to that lee-shore which is called death.

There was one peculiar feature of his situation which has not yet been named, and yet it was the most noticeable of all connected with him. From head to foot, sleeping or waking, at all times and under all circumstances, his nervous system was shaking and shivering, keeping the head in that, continual quiver which is so melancholy to behold because it suggests involuntary labor that must exhaust and wear out the system, and making the weak hand so ungovernable that even the cup of tea put to his mouth required to be held and guided by others to prevent the contents being spilled and the vessel falling to the floor. Nothing could be more pitiable, when watched for a considerable time and when the impression forced itself upon the observer that at no single moment would that tremor ever grow still until the spoiler had completed his work, and the limbs should stiffen and straighten in the last chill of mortality.

And yet John Crawford was really by no means the very old man indicated by his white hairs, his dimmed eyes and his palsied shiverings. He was very little past sixty, and at an age when under ordinary circumstances several years of pleasant life might have been calculated upon. Nor was he the victim of constitutional disease, which had been fought and combatted until it had at last triumphed and brought down the torn banner of manhood trailing in the dust. And still less had a life of early indulgence and evil courses laid the mine for this after-destruction. He was not old to senility; he belonged to a family that had been noted for their long life, continued vigor and freedom from hereditary disease; and he had carefully avoided those errors in drink, food and personal indulgence which open the doors of life's citadel to the invader from beyond the dark valley. What, then, was the fatal secret? John Crawford was a suicide, and he had chosen a peculiarly American mode of self-immolation. Or perhaps it may with more propriety be said that he was a Faust in ordinary life, and that he had called upon a national demon to be his aid and his foe. He had *worked himself to death*— a phrase by many supposed to be hollow and unmeaning, but one too sadly illustrated every day in our modern life.

Born wealthy, he seemed to have imbibed with his earliest breath the impression that he was comparatively poor, and that only the most laborious drudgery of mind and body, to which the toil of the slave in the cotton-field is little more than play, could keep him from becoming still poorer. He had been a miser at once of his pennies and his hours, when a boy; and as he had grown older he had become a still worse miser in every opportunity for gain, and a reckless spendthrift of his own comfort and energy. No laborer on his farm had worked so many hours or so laboriously, the impression having seemed all the while to abide with him that if *he* did not labor he would have only eye-service, and nothing would be left him. When others had slept, and he had been debarred from laboring with his hands, he had still toiled with his brain, turning restlessly on his bed when he should have slept, and planning to make his fertile acres still more productive or to add to them others that lay in tempting proximity. When hours of relaxation had been demanded by the calls of friendship, and even by the inexorable demands of his own system, he had shut his ears and refused, as if putting behind his back some tempter of the soul. Friends had said to him : "John, you are killing yourself !" or " John, you are working too hard and too steadily ! Some day you will pay for all this." And one day a blunt-spoken rustic neighbor, observing him at his toil early and late, had said : " John Crawford, you are a fool ! You do too much work ! You have a fine constitution, and think that you can take liberties with it; but some day it will pay you, mark my words ! You will find yourself, one fine morning, doubled up like an old horse that has been over-driven ; and that will be the end of *you !* But go on, if you like it !"

John Crawford *had* "gone on." He had married very late in life, principally on account of his belief that no man should marry until he had done his life-work and placed himself beyond anxiety on the score of property. When the day of his marriage came, after an engagement of nearly ten years, people had long been saying that the woman of his choice, his "Mary," had already worried away the best part of her life in anxiety for him and in fears for the final prevention of their union. Then, when the marriage was finally consummated and those who loved him best hoped that he would relax in his life-wearing toil, he had merely commenced to work the harder, because a married man needed to be better circumstanced than a single one ! And when, five or six years after his marriage, and after giving birth to his one daughter and only child, Mary, his wife died, he had gone to work still harder, it seemed, as the only means of forgetting his bereavement ! Rain or shine—early and late—year after year, he had labored on, enriching his lands and increasing his out-buildings, adding new acres and putting a few more thousands to those already out at interest on good bond-and mortgage.

One day—some two years before the date of this story— the crash had come. The "old horse" had "doubled up." John Crawford had not come down to breakfast at his usual time, and those who went up to look after him had first dis- covered what ruin could do in a single night. The hale man of the night before had become a partial paralytic, helpless from that day forward—never again to lift hand in any em-

24

ployment, and scarcely permitted brain enough to realize all
that he had won and all that he had lost. Gradually, afterwards,
his mind had cleared and his speech returned, though feebly;
but during all the two years his nervous prostration had been
increasing and his bodily strength declining, until for weeks
before that Sunday of July the physicians had pronounced
him gradually dying and expected him to drop away at any
moment.

Such was half the picture presented at the end of the
piazza, the other half being made up of Colonel Egbert Crawford, his military coat changed to a blouse of brown linen and
his boots replaced by a pair of embroidered slippers, but in
all other regards quite as we have before seen him, and altogether the legitimate commander of the Two Hundredth
Volunteers. During all his late visits to the farm, and especially since the defection and ostracism of Richard, he had
made his "strong point" in paying great attention to the
infirm-old gentleman; and as personal attention is always
pleasant and flattering, and more particularly so to the old,
crippled, tedious and tiresome, he had succeeded in winning
a place in the old man's regard, by this course, which he
might have failed to secure by any other means.

On this particular morning he was rather well pleased than
otherwise to see Mary throw on her flat and run out to make
a call on some one of the neighbors, as this gave him an opportunity, on this his last day of probation, of making himself very devoted to his prospective father-in-law, without any
serious drain upon his own personal comfort and energy. To
wait upon the old man, after he had been got up and dressed
for the morning and assisted out to the cool piazza, as in this
instance—consisted of very little more than answering the
few words which the invalid might happen to address him
(and they were likely to be very few),—brushing away a
troublesome fly when the old man sunk into a doze and the
pest came too near his nose,—moving him a little if the sun
happened to become troublesome through the vines,—or picking up and restoring a dropped handkerchief. The Colonel
was rather well pleased to have something to employ him in
this manner on this particular morning, especially when he

could combine the employment with a book and a lounge with his feet upon the piazza-railing; for the house was a little ticklish for indiscriminate roaming about, owing to the arrangements which he knew to be in progress. The dare-devil Major Lally, of the French revolutionary time, is said to have laid his head upon the block with many doubts as to the grace of his position, and with an apology to the executioner if he should have happened to transgress any of the rules of mortuary good-breeding,—on the ground that "he never had had his head cut off before;" and Colonel Egbert Crawford, never having been married before, may be excused if he had some sort of indefinite impression that all the rooms in the house were full of awful preparations, liable to be run against at any moment, and altogether fatal to matrimonial prospects if accidentally disturbed. So the piazza and the old man furnished him with a means of killing time that was "devilish dull," and at the same time with a certainty of being kept in a place where he could not possibly "run foul of anything" or do any harm. \

The old man had scarcely spoken for half an hour. He had been lulled by the drowsy sounds of the summer noon, and by the growing listlessness of his own nature, into a few moments of doze, in which the Colonel, closing his eyes to the pages of his book, seemed on the point of joining him. Suddenly a rooster, that had strolled around from the barn-yard and flown up to a cool location on the top of the garden fence, and under the shade of one of the cherry-trees (at which elevation no doubt his numerous harem in the yard regarded him with the same reverent respect paid to the Prophet Brigham, when at a distance, by his fifty-six wives and a fraction)—suddenly this rooster, forgetting the proprieties of the place and the hour, lazily flapped his big wings and emitted a crow of such magnificent dimensions as might have startled the whole neighborhood. Colonel Egbert Crawford started and opened his eyes: the old man straightened up his shaking head and did likewise. The sound was like an icy sword-blade thrust into a slumbering and tepid fountain—startling all the water spirits from repose and propriety,—or like Christmas suddenly obtruded, keen and pure, into the

sluggish rest of midsummer. Of what the old man mused
as his waking thoughts recognized the sound, can never be
known—possibly of the wealth which he had garnered and
of the broad lands over which that sound went ringing—all
his own, but his own in what miserable mockery! Of what
Colonel Egbert Crawford thought when the sound smote his
ears, is much more certain. The cock-crow and *betrayal!*
He had been brought up in the country, and many a time, in
his younger and better days, when intercourse with the world
had not yet developed the evil germ in his character, he had
read and pondered over the mysterious connection between
the cock, Shakspeare's "bird of dawning," and the scenes
which preceded the Crucifixion. Remembering that the cock
had seemed to appear and speak as the accuser of Peter, he
had insensibly come to connect those events with the blacker
guilt of Iscariot, and to look upon the bird as the watcher
and detecter. In olden days this had not troubled him:
perhaps it would not have done so, only four or five months
before, when his hands were so much nearer stainless than
they could be called at that hour. Now, on the verge of his
marriage, and when the double tree of murder that he had
planted (murder of character and murder of person!) was
about bearing welcome and triumphant fruit, the rooster's cry,
so sharp, sudden and unexpected, came to him like the voice
of an accusing spirit. It may be taken as a proof of his
cowardice when we say that momentarily his cheek whitened
and his limbs trembled; and perhaps every criminal *is* a
coward, because he dares not do right and trust the event
with the overruling providences. But Egbert Crawford was
no *physical* coward, as we may have occasion to know before
we have closed this relation. Yet he did whiten, and he did
tremble. Was there something ominous in this sudden disturbance of the Sabbath quiet? Did it foreshadow another
and a more startling disturbance, through which the dark,
silent current of the river of guilt would be splashed into by
the falling stones of the temple of error overhanging it?
Was there in it an omen of the sudden flash of a bright and
unendurable light through those black caverns, hitherto sup-

posed to be impenetrable, where crawl the loathsome and
slimy reptiles of deceit and treachery?

Pshaw! why should there be anything of this involved?
Cocks had crowed before, even at noon-tide in summer, and
the world had outlived the omen! Nevertheless the sound,
especially so loud and grating a one, in which the bray of
the donkey was so evenly mixed with the hideous scream of
the peacock before rain, was an inopportune and impudent
one; and the Colonel would have been very likely to wring
chanticleer's neck if it had happened to come within the
clutch of his fingers. As it was, he determined to cause an
immediate abandonment of that stronghold, and sprung up to
look for a club or a stone with which the enemy could be dis-
lodged; when the rooster espying danger afar off, evacuated
his Manassas before the enemy could reach him, and went
back to his cackling harem. To them he no doubt related, in
the appropriate language of the bipeds *with* feathers, what a
couple of sleepy-heads he had seen upon the piazza, and how
he had startled them both with a voluntary upon his private
organ. Meanwhile the Colonel had dropped back into his
seat.

But old John Crawford, fully awakened by the sound, did
not seem likely to fall away into slumber again. As Egbert
resumed his place in the chair, the old man said, feebly:

"Egbert."

Instantly the Colonel, never forgetting his cue of attention
to the invalid, drew closer to his side.

"Yes, Uncle, what can I do for you?"

"Where is Mary?" asked the old man, who had probably
before asked the question half a dozen times since she had left
the house.

"Gone out for a walk, Uncle," said the expectant son-in-
law "I suppose she is calling upon some of the neighbors.
It is her last day, you know, Uncle."

"Her last day?—yes, you are going to be married to-night.
I know," whispered the old man, with the air of a child to
whom the intelligence has been communicated as a great
secret—not that of a father who had thus willed for the happiness of a dear child

"Domine Rodgers is to come at six," said the Colonel. "And then I hope I shall have the pleasure of calling you by a dearer name than that of Uncle."

"Yes, yes—Mary is a good girl," said the old man. "Take good care of her, Egbert. I am afraid I shan't live long, my-self—not many years—(Poor old man!—no efforts had been sufficient to awake him to the fact that his remaining time on the earth was probably to be measured by days or hours in-stead of years!) "I am going to have my will made, Egbert, the moment you are married, and I am going to leave all my property to her—her—her and you. You will have it all. Don't waste it, and don't let it go out of the family—not out of the family, Egbert! You are a Crawford, and I want to keep the property in the family. Eh, Egbert?"

"I will *try* to do everything that you wish, Uncle!" said the Colonel; and no doubt that he really meant to obey that portion of his Uncle's injunctions—to *keep the property in the family.*

"And look here, Egbert," said the old man, who seemed to speak with less difficulty than was usual to him, though there were hindrances in his delivery very painful to the hearer and which we cannot caricature age and decrepitude by attempt-ing to convey. "Look here—there is one thing more. Not a dollar to that scoundrel, Richard!—not a dollar, if he starves!"

"Not a dollar, Uncle; I promise you this, solemnly." And this promise, too, he meant to keep, beyond a question.

"And, Egbert, keep Mary away from him. Don't let him even see her if you can avoid it. They used to be together a great deal, and I don't know—I don't know!" What the old man did not know, must remain among the other mysteries not yet to be revealed. "Keep her away from him—don't let her go near him."

Though there were words in this last sentence of his Uncle's which did not entirely please the Colonel, yet there were others which did please him thoroughly. He made the third promise with the same alacrity. How easy the old man was making his path! To keep the property in the family (that meant, to keep it himself!) to give Richard no part of it under any circumstances (a tning not very likely)—and to keep his young wife from the presence of a man from whom he had only won her by the basest falsehood (a thing he was certain to do at all events)—these were the three injunctions: how easy to fulfil! The cup of the young man's content was at that moment brimming over, and the impudent chanticleer who only five minutes before had tortured him from the garden palings. was quite forgotten.

Just then there was a light foot-fall on the piazza behind the two speakers. The dulled senses of John Crawford were too dim to recognize it, but the keener faculties of the Colonel heard the beat of the little foot at once and knew it to be Mary's. He was just opening his mouth to say to his uncle, "Here is Mary, now!" when he caught a glimpse of her face; and then he remained gazing and said nothing. Mary had returned from her walk, had thrown off her bonnet, and stepped out to the piazza to look after the comfort of her father, and perhaps for some other purpose. She was at that moment just outside the door, and from the position of the Colonel, framed between the pillars at the other end of the piazza and against the dark green foliage of an arborvitæ standing beyond. What was it that the quick eye of the Colonel saw, as he turned; that stopped the words upon his lips and made him look in silence on the young girl's face and figure? She had been absent from the house less than an hour—what could have occurred to her, within that space of time, to change their relative positions? And yet their relative positions *were* changed—he felt the truth in an instant. He had parted with her less than two hours before—he the successful deceiver and she the blind victim. They met again, and she had gone beyond his power and his knowledge. We have often before had occasion, in the course of this narration, to speak of sudden changes in the human face and demeanor, so marked as to be absolutely startling. None of those changes could have been more marked than that shown by the face and figure of this young girl, as glanced at by the practiced eye of this man of the world. She looked taller, straighter in form, and no longer drooping and inelastic. Her glorious auburn hair was partially shaken loose

from its confinement, as it had become during the exciting
interview with Josephine Harris; and while the negligence
added to the charm of her appearance, the very fact that she
had not displayed a woman's coquetry in smoothing it rapidly into order before the glass when she threw off her bonnet, betrayed that she was much more awake and excited than
usual. Was this on account of the near approach of the hour
of her marriage? Egbert Crawford scarcely thought so, for
the eye was not that of an expectant bride. That soft, sweet
hazel eye still looked sad and troubled, but there seemed to
be a spark of something fiercer and sharper than love, amid
the trouble. Once more, what was it? Never before had
she seemed so handsome, but never so unapproachable; and
if the unscrupulous man had really held a true sentiment of
love for her, at the bottom of all his selfish and evil designs
(and who shall say that he had *not?*) there came the sharpest
and deepest pang of his life in the first awakening of the
thought that she was *slipping away from him* even at the
moment when he had apparently clutched her.

The Colonel, thoroughly mystified and a little alarmed,
rose from his seat and was advancing towards the young
girl, when she moved a pace towards him, her eyes first
downcast and then even sternly raised to his face. She did
not call him by name, nor wait until he had so addressed her,
but held close to him, as if to avoid any possible observation,
a small sealed note—and said, her voice trembling and husky:

"A private note for you. Please read it at once."

Passing by him without another word and without waiting
for any reply, she advanced towards the end of the piazza
where her father was sitting, and knelt down beside him.
Colonel Egbert Crawford noted every feature of the movement, and saw that his fancy of the change in her appearance was not fancy alone. There *was* something threatening.
Mechanically he had taken the note as she had handed it to
him and passed by. He glanced at the superscription, and
though his wonder was increased, his fears of a rupture with
Mary were partially dissipated, for the hand was totally unknown to him. Ha! he had it! The hand-writing on the
note was that of a woman—the note had come to the house

for him—she had seen it and conceived a sudden spasm of jealousy on account of it! How easily he could dissipate that idea by showing her the note, which he was certain could not be from any illicit female correspondent who had brought him within her power. The note was almost certain to be from some lady on professional business, or from the wife, sister or mother of some recruit who had enlisted in the famous Two Hundredth, asking for his influence towards a discharge or a furlough. He would show her the note at once, after he had read it, and with some kind of laughing excuse for showing it which would not betray the fact that he knew of her having any interest in it; and then this sudden but not dangerous hurricane would be over.

He glanced round at the pair on the end of the piazza, a smile of triumph on his face, as he came to this conclusion. Mary was kneeling beside her father, her back towards himself, fondling the old man's poor withered face, and paying so little attention to the man so soon to be her husband, that the jealousy hypothesis might have seemed well supported. What was it that the little girl had said to Josephine Harris, not half an hour before ?—that "she could never meet Egbert Crawford after such a revelation ?"- Something of the kind, certainly. And she had met him, and unconsciously and without calculation gone through the very brief interview in a manner worthy of the most finished actress—say of La Heron, La Hoey or La Bateman, to name three of the most dissimilar but ablest representatives of dramatic character on the American stage. Oh, these little women, who make a boast of their weakness—there is very little that they cannot do when brought to the test !

Colonel Egbert Crawford tore open the note, walking towards the upper or eastern end of the piazza as he did so. His back was towards the two on the other end, and perhaps it was well that he should have been so positioned at that moment. Naturally, he glanced first at the bottom, and saw a name which he immediately recognized as that of one who had been *in the way* sometimes at the Crawfords. He had never liked her, or held any more intercourse with her than was unavoidable with a very frequent guest at the same

house with himself.   He had considered her a little loud in
voice, rather rapid, and *a fool.*   He had been satisfied that
she told all that she knew, and he would not have been surprised to find that sometimes she told considerably more.
He had considered her utterly incapable of keen research,
and the very last person in the world to keep a secret, supposing that such a thing could come into her possession.
What did he find here, and from her?

He read that note three times over, standing on the extreme east end of the piazza, leaning against the corner-
board of the house, and with his face so averted from those
at the other end that even if Mary Crawford once or twice
threw a quick glance around, she could see nothing.   Then
he turned, shoving the letter into his vest-pocket as he did
so, and walked slowly down the piazza to the hall-door, his
face calm, to all distant appearance, and whistling "*Strida
la Vampa.*"

If Mary Crawford had not before been able to see his
movements, she arose from her knees as he came down the
piazza, and saw him *then.*   She saw him as he passed in at
the hall-door, heard him whistle without an apparent tremor
in a note, and heard his slippered steps as he slowly lounged
up the stair towards the room on the second floor which had
been for some months kept as *his.*   The young girl was disappointed—astonished—astounded !   She had seen no agitation—had heard and seen the indications of the opposite !
The blow had not been effectual—it had either been feebly
struck or delivered from a false aim !   He was not guilty, or
he was beyond fear and knew himself to be beyond the reach
of public exposure !   She had hoped too soon—the bond she
dreaded was not broken or even deferred ; and God help her,
after all !

Such were the impressions of the young girl, as the man
within a few hours to be her husband disappeared into the
hall.   Were they well founded ?   Ah, young eyes !—you
may be schooled to do your part, very early, but you cannot
at once be schooled to read the eyes of others aright.   Perhaps you *never* learn to read aright, until you lose the
brightness of your own truth and beauty.   Seventeen cannot

well realize, to-night at Mrs. Pearl Dowlas's hop, when Mr. Pearl Dowlas, the eminent merchant, supposed to be worth a million, caresses his handsome side-whiskers with his faultless hand and interchanges pleasant nothings with the fashionable women who all admire him and all hate his wife,—that Mr. Pearl Dowlas is suffering, all the while, the intense agonies of ruin; and that he has the revolver already loaded and capped with which he intends to blow out his brains after the last carriage has rolled away. And Seventeen will be quite as slow to discover, unless Seventeen has lived too fast for her own self-respect and eventual happiness, that Lady Flora, patting her white-gloved hands to-night at the Opera, with the blonde Emperor by her side, apparently the happiest and the most truly envied woman in all that brilliant house, has such pangs of rage and jealousy tugging at her heart-strings, when she looks over at a much plainer woman in the opposite row of boxes, that could the terror of the law be removed, she would sacrifice self-respect, dignity, hope, everything; and bury a knife in the heart of that plainer woman as they brush by each other in the lobby. Seventeen will be slow to discover these things. Twenty-five may have a nearer appreciation of them, though yet dim as compared with the reality: alas!—it needs Forty-five or Fifty, or a younger age made so old by sad experience—Forty-five or Fifty, with the bloom gone, the gray hair here and the wrinkles coming, to look beneath the surface and see the agony writhing at the bottom. Thank God that some agonies never can be discovered at all, until they break forth in uncontrollable madness: the world might be sadder if we *could* look in through transparent flesh into our neighbors' hearts, as we do through glass windows into their houses!

" *Strida la Vampa*" had been bravely whistled. Not braver the conduct of the poor cartman at the hospital a few months ago, when he looked calmly on without a groan or a wince; while the surgeon sawed off the ends of the bone of his fractured arm, drilled holes through them and screwed them together with a fastening of gold wire! That was physical bravery, or perhaps stolid exemption from pain: this was that moral bravery, in a bad cause, but none the less real,

which could see wholesale and undeniable ruin fall without
betraying one sign of agony to the observer most interested.
Though he had read that letter three times to fix the words in
his mind, he had understood it at the first reading.   It told
him all that needed to be known. Mary's changed look and her
averted face were now accounted for—accounted for at once
and forever.   No word of explanation was necessary and none
would be given or demanded.   Some men might have hesitated, and questioned whether the blow could not be softened
or averted.   This was not Egbert Crawford.   He had played,
boldly, wickedly and recklessly, though apparently with all
care.   At the very moment when he seemed to have won all,
he had lost all.   At the bar he had always been known as
contesting a case unscrupulously and to the bitter end, but as
giving up gracefully and bearing a defeat without complaint,
when defeated.   A suspicion once aroused, and backed as was
this suspicion, the wearer of the eyes he had just seen could
never again be deceived.   Had he been less of a resolute man
he might have dared the other threats of the young girl, perhaps impotent.   But the one great stake lost, in the hand and
fortune of Mary Crawford, there was nothing left to play for,
worth even hazarding exposure.

We will not say that in his own chamber, and while changing his slippers for boots and his linen-wrapper to a coat more
fit for the street, he did not more than once gnash his teeth,
utter an oath below his breath, and curse the whole race of
meddling women.   But if he did so, he said nothing aloud ;
and if his dark brows were darker than usual, no human eye
saw them.   He had writing materials upon the table in that
room—*that room*, the best in the house, and into which, on
the night to follow, he had expected to be accompanied by
his bride.   He sat down at the table but a moment, but in
that moment he dashed off, with a hand wonderfully steady
under the circumstances, the following note :

SUNDAY, 1 P.M.

Miss Harris :—
You have meddled successfully, and whether you are right or
wrong in what you allege, I shall not be here to contest the question. If your husband, if you ever get one, keeps half as close a

watch over you, he will probably see quite enough to satisfy him. Perhaps you will be kind enough to communicate *this* to Miss Mary Crawford, and thus finish the obligations under which I rest.

Yours, humbly,

EGBERT CRAWFORD.

In a moment more this note was sealed and directed to "Miss Josephine Harris—Care of Miss Crawford" and left lying on the table, with the superscription upward. Then Colonel Egbert Crawford put on his hat, walked deliberately down-stairs and out at the front of the house. No one seemed to observe him—not even a domestic, and probably nothing could have pleased him better at that moment. Walking down the lane to the road, he turned up the road to the left, went up to a little country tavern where he had sometimes hired a riding-horse on previous visits, and hired a horse and buggy, with a driver, to go at once to Utica. Ten minutes completed the negotiation, and ten more harnessed up the horse to the vehicle; so that before the call to dinner was made at the Crawford mansion, before old John Crawford was assisted in from the portico, or Mary thought of the arbiter of her destiny as elsewhere than in his own room,—he was bowling down the dusty road towards Utica. When the down-train from Suspension Bridge left Utica for Albany that afternoon, the detected and beaten gambler in reputations, lives and matrimonial ventures, was a passenger.

CHAPTER XXV.

AFFAIRS IN THE CRAWFORD FAMILY IN NEW YORK—THE TWO BROTHERS—MARION HOBART THE ENIGMA—NIAGARA BY WAY OF THE CENTRAL PARK.

IT has been already said that John Crawford, wounded, and with the poor little Virginian orphan-girl in his company, reached New York on the evening of the Fourth of July—

the same evening, it will be remembered, on whi.h Tom
Leslie and Josephine Harris left the city, the one for Niagara
and the other for her matrimonial operations at West Falls.
It is just possible that their not arriving earlier was a lucky
event, as Joe Harris, had she once set eyes on the delicate and singular-looking Virginian girl, would have been
almost certainly attracted towards her, and in that event her
pet hobby for the time might have been neglected—her
departure for the North might have been delayed for a day
or two—and Mary Crawford might have been left to meet
her fate in helplessness and ignorance.

And yet all this is an array of "mights" that have no real
propriety, for events occur but once in the world, and they
only occur in one mode. Human will is free, and human
responsibility is never to be ignored; and still no human
hand changes in any degree the inevitable. "Oh, if I had !"
and "Oh, if I had not !" are very common exclamations, and
those who have committed terrible errors or met with severe
misfortunes will continue to make them until the whole
course of human existence is run; and yet they are none the
less *follies*. The events of yesterday were part of that general
plan on which the world was first formed and on which it
may have been conducted through all the hundreds of centuries which puzzle Agassiz and frighten the theologists. The
downfall of an empire and the picking up of a basket of chips
by a ragged child in a ship-yard, may each have equally
formed part of it, and each been equally impossible to avert.
Human will seemed to move each event, and human responsibility certainly attached to each ; but the event itself, unknown until accomplished, moved in its appointed course and
could no more be jarred from it than one of the planets from
its orbit.

But all this by the way. Joe Harris had her own odd
work to do, hundreds of miles away, and there was no hin-
drance in the way of her accomplishing it, from any new ties
suddenly added to bind her to the city.

Of course that strange and unexpected arrival from the
seat of war (for John Crawford had not even taken the precaution to telegraph from Fortress Monroe or Washington)

created a sensation in the Crawford household. A mixed sensation—for while both the brothers were heartily glad to meet, each had a cause for sorrow on meeting the other. Richard was naturally sorry to see John, who had passed through so many fights without harm, wounded at last and disabled for an indefinite period; and John was correspondingly sorry to see Richard, whom he had left in such high health and spirits, a broken-down and house-ridden invalid. Not long before he had another cause for anxiety; for in the first half hour of private conference which ensued, on the very evening of their arrival, in response to a question from John, as to the health of the family at West Falls and the progress of his expected marriage with Mary, Richard revealed the unaccountable state of coldness which had sprung up, Mary's neglect to answer his late letters, and the fact that Egbert remained all the visiting-link between the city and country branches of the family.

"Egbert, eh ?" asked John, whose service at looking out for skulking enemies when on picket-duty, might have made him more watchful and suspicious than he would have been under other circumstances. "Egbert, eh ? Well, all I can say is that I don't like the link !"

Richard Crawford started, as he lay reclining upon the sofa. He was decidedly better than he had been a week before, and kept his little room less closely, though he was fearfully weak and the racking pain had not entirely left his system. "You never liked Egbert," he said.

"No," said John, "I never liked him, a bit more than Dean Swift liked Doctor Fell, though perhaps I could not tell *why*, any better than the Dean."

"No, I suppose not," said Richard, musingly. And here the conversation dropped, on that point. Whatever may have been Richard Crawford's suspicions of his cousin, forced on him by circumstances and by the young girl who had so strangely volunteered to disenchant him—he had no intention of communicating them even to his brother.

If there was a mixed feeling in the meeting of the brothers, there was one quite as complicated in that of Isabel Crawford and Marion Hobart—two total strangers so unexpectedly

flung together. Bell Crawford was better fitted to receive
and care for the orphan girl, than she would have been a
month before, when the mysterious turning-point of her existence had not been reached ; and there had been no time
since she had become the mistress of her brother's mansion,
when she would not have used every exertion to make one
comfortable and happy who had been so strangely recom-
mended to her sympathy. What she would before have
lacked, was discipline and thoughtfulness. These she had
attained to some degree, in a manner which she could not
much more comprehend than those who surrounded her. But
it was impossible that she could be able at once to supply the
double want of sister and mother to one who had been so
differently nurtured and educated as Marion Hobart ; and the
very desire to be even kinder than she would have cared to
be to one who had more claims upon her, necessarily placed
her in embarrassment which was very likely to produce the
opposite effect. The young Virginian girl could not do otherwise than receive those attentions with gratitude, and yet her
very desire not to be obtrusive and not to seem to demand
more attention than was necessary, placed her in an equally
anomalous position. The two girls consequently became
much less intimately acquainted within the first few days, than
they might have done if thrown together under different
auspices.

Marion Hobart was, as her conversation and conduct on
the night of her grandfather's death so plainly indicated, a
most singular person, and one who might have been studied
for years without being fully understood. She talked but
little, and yet her silence seemed to be more the result of
having nothing to say and no sympathy with the ordinary
topics of conversation, than from dislike or inability to converse. When she did speak, the same childlike curtness and
immobility were observable, that had been shown by the
couch of her dying relative. She seemed to be repeating set
words, that did not affect her heart or make any change in
the expression of her face ; even though she may have been
deeply moved in reality. She received kindnesses with thankfulness, and yet that thankfulness was generally too set and

formal in its phrase to create the impression of gushing warm from the heart, and to give that exquisite pleasure that a simple "Thank you!" will often convey when it seems to leap out unbidden.

Of course in the double disaster of the fire and the death, the poor girl found herself almost entirely unprovided with clothes. Isabel, with thoughtful care, the next day after her arrival, spoke of making arrangements for procuring the services of a dressmaker at once.

"Yes, thank you, I have no clothes. I shall want some," answered the young girl.

"Excuse my touching upon your grief," said Bell, "but I suppose that you will wish black? You will wear mourning?"

"No, if you please," was the reply. "My family never wear mourning. My grandmother never did. I have been told so. I do not remember my grandmother. I do not know why we never wear mourning. But if you please, I wish to do as grandmother did."

Here was the same peculiarity again, that had been shown at the bedside of the dying grandfather—the grandmother spoken of, but no mention of a *mother*. Bell Crawford noticed the fact, as her brother had not done; but she could no more have asked that strange girl for an explanation, and risked the possible opening of some family wound, than she could have gone to the stake.

Nothing more was said upon the subject of the mourning; and Bell Crawford made the necessary arrangements for procuring her clothing that suggested no remembrance of her recent loss.

John Crawford had not forgotten the words of the old man, as to money in his granddaughter's name, lying in one of the city banks. He suggested the matter to her, aware that she would be anxious to rid herself from any feeling of absolute dependence,—and she answered him at once. She knew the name of the bank, and nearly the amount that should be standing to her credit, which was, as her grandfather had said, quite enough to make her comfortable for an ordinary life, ranging closely upon fifty thousand dollars. He

25

procured her some checks, and she filled up one in a hand of
crow-quill lightness, which looked indescribably like herself,
but with a readiness which showed that she must have been
before familiar with banking business. He presented the
check, and it was honored without enquiry, this fact proving
that her signature was known; and thus all anxiety on the
pecuniary question was set at rest.

The young girl had said, in that dreadful hour by the death-
couch, when speaking of her grandfather's fervent Union
sentiments, "I do not know anything about politics, myself!"
The truth that she had no knowledge or no feeling on the
subject of the struggle between the two sections, was made
manifest before she had been twenty-four hours an inmate of
Richard Crawford's house. John continued to fight, mentally,
though wounded and absent from the army. Richard was
an ardent loyalist, as we have seen. The brothers naturally
ran into warm denunciations of rebellion, and confident prophecies of the success of the Union cause, in spite of all
past disasters. Bell and Marion were both present when they
launched into the first of these; but before the conversation
had lasted many minutes, the young Virginian girl rose and
left the room with a word of apology. Both the brothers
noticed the act and her manner. It did not indicate anger
or dissatisfaction—simply a total want of interest.

The next morning something still more conclusive on this
subject occurred. Richard Crawford had been much in the
habit, during his illness, of being read to by his sister, Joe
Harris, or any other friend who would take the trouble to
amuse him in that manner. As he began to recover, he did
not lose the relish for that description of lazy luxury. On the
morning in question, John had gone out, Bell was busy, and
Marion and her host happened to be alone in the room, when
the morning papers were brought in.

"Miss Hobart, will you be so kind as to read the news to
me?" suggested the invalid.

"If you wish, Mr. Crawford," she said at once. "I do not
read very well aloud. But I will do my best." She picked
up one of the papers and commenced reading. European
news—news from Central and South America—railroad ac-

cidents—dramatic notices—everything except the news from Washington and the war, which happened to be all that he cared to hear at all ! He looked at her in some surprise, but watched her closely and saw that she did not do this by chance, but that she carefully avoided the columns containing the news from the army. Directly Bell entered the room, and *she* began, at his request, to read the war news. Then Marion left the room, with an apology, as she had done the day before.

When John returned, his brother related the incident to him. In return John informed him of her words on the first night of their meeting, and the two agreed that she had an unaccountable antipathy to everything connected with the war, and that nothing more should be said to her on the subject.

"What if she should be a little secesh ?" asked Richard, very much at random.

"She ?" said John. "The granddaughter of that man ? Not a bit of it ! She is a little of an oddity, and a very *pretty* little oddity—don't you think so, Richard ?" and so the conversation dropped.

The young girl had evidently had a fine musical education. She played very sweetly, though only upon request. Once she sang an English ballad, upon still more urgent request, but she seemed to do so with such unwillingness that she was not pressed again. Her voice, as shown on that occasion, was mournfully sweet and pure, and highly cultivated. She spoke French with singular facility and unusual correctness for an American. Bell and the brothers hoped that when the novelty of her position had worn away, she would more fully enter into their tastes and habits, and become less impracticable, if not happier.

A very neat little chamber on the second floor, which adjoined Bell's and had been standing empty except when occupied by chance visitors, was arranged for the young girl as soon as she entered the household, and she took possession of it with apparent satisfaction. And what a little "box' she made of it at once. The very next day she went into the street, without any consultation with Bell, and made purchases

.of not less than a hundred dollars worth of pictures and
articles of *vertu*, to ornament it. It was not difficult to see,
at once, that though she might be indolently content without
the surroundings of luxury, yet it was only *with* them, and
with them in somewhat aristocratic profusion, that she could
be spiritedly happy. When she had added her purchases to
the comforts and even luxuries already in her chamber, she
ran into Bell's room with something approaching to excitement upon her face, and called her in to see the arrangement.
Bell literally clapped her hands in delight, the young Virginian girl had shown such exquisite taste and made the
little room look so much like a cross between the sleeping
chamber of a very young princess, a museum, and an art
gallery. She had imagination enough to fancy how the scene
would appear, with the room so ornamented, the light turned
low and filtering through the white porcelain shade of the
burner, and that singularly beautiful little head lying in sleep
on the white pillow, the calm, childlike features in repose, and
the blonde hair a little dishevelled and insensibly fading away
into the white upon which it rested.

There were some articles of *vertu*, a very small statue of
Washington among them, lying on the bureau and not yet
arranged. Bell Crawford went up to the bureau and examined
them, while Marion was arranging a different loop to the curtains of her bed, which would enable her to look out, before
she rose, on a handsome little steel engraving of the white-
plumed Henry the Fourth at the battle of Ivry, which she
had just placed in position on the wall. Among the articles
on the bureau lay a locket, in gold with a band of blue enamel
crossing it diagonally. It was unclasped, and almost without
a thought whether she was doing right or wrong, Bell (as
woman, and even *man*, will often do in such cases) took it
up in her hand, threw open the case and looked at the face
of the miniature within. This was simply the head from an
admirable *carte de visite*, artistic enough to have been made
by Gurney or Fredericks, and showing that it must have been
taken within a very few months,—cut out in a circle and
placed within the glass. The face was that of a man who
might have been thirty ; ears of age, dark complexioned but

strongly handsome, indicating size and sinew in figure, with the cheek-bones a little high, fiery dark eyes under heavy brows, heavy black hair worn long and curling, and a very heavy and yet graceful dark moustache. In the picture he had a broad white collar turned down under the velvet of his dark coat, giving him a peculiar look which may have been Southern or South-western and was certainly not of the North and the "great citie." Bell Crawford had only a moment to notice the picture, and though she supposed it to be the portrait of some near relative of the young girl, she could not help thinking how completely and exactly her opposite it was in every particular—black hair for blonde, strength for fragility, and the fire of those dark eyes for the calm, childlike innocence of Marion Hobart's.

Only a moment sufficed to make these observations: the next instant the young girl saw the picture in her hand and sprung down from the chair upon which she had been standing, with an agitation entirely different from anything which she had before exhibited. Her pale face was for the instant deeply flushed—Bell Crawford was sure of it—and there was something more passionate than usual in the sad eyes. Her lips 'trembled, and her hostess grew both pained and alarmed in the belief that she was about to utter harsh and angry words. But if the eyes of Bell had not been mistaken, and there had really been such an agitation raging in the breast of the young girl, certainly a most remarkable change had come over her before she had taken the two or three steps forward and reached the bureau where Miss Crawford was standing. She was herself again, completely; and her words, when they came, were such as might have been expected of her from previous observation.

"Please do not look at that!" she said, reaching out her hand to take it. Then she instantly added: "But you *have* seen it. It was my own fault. I should not have left it lying open in that manner. I did not wish you to see it, or any one."

"I am really sorry," said Bell. "I took it up without thinking, and I hope that you will not think that I wished to pry into any secret of yours." She was a little ashamed at

her slight breach of etiquette, and a good deal pained; and
her strange guest seemed to be at once aware of both feelings. Before Bell knew what she was about to do, Marion
had thrust the locket into her bosom, then laid (not *thrown*)
her arms around her neck, and kissed her on the cheek.

"Please do not be hurt or angry with me," she said, her
voice very low and her whole manner childlike. "It was
not wrong for you to look at the picture. It was wrong in
me to pain you. It is the picture of a very dear friend—of
my family." There was the least instant of hesitation before
adding the last three words. "If you do not wish very
much, I will not tell you his name, for—for reasons that you
would not understand." Another slight instant of hesitation
in the middle of the sentence.

"Oh, by no means—do not tell me the name. You would
pain me if you did so," answered Bell. "Now let us forget
all about it, and only think of the wilderness of pretty things
that you have been buying, to make this room the very neat-
est in the house."

"Do you think so?" said Marion. "I am very glad if
you like them. I am very glad when I please any one, and
very unhappy when I do not. I do not quite know how to
arrange them all. Will you help me?" and in a moment
more the episode of the picture seemed to be quite forgotten
in the bestowal of the remainder of Marion's "art-treasures."

Saturday afternoon saw a marked event in the history of
the Crawford family, in the crossing by Richard of the
threshold of the outer door, for the first time in so many
weeks. He was weak, faint and feeble, but the racking pains
of his disease seemed hourly to leave him more completely.
He had no more thought of leaving the house, however, than
of flying, until the tempter appeared in the shape of his
brother. John had been reading over the morning paper, a
little late; and after the news had been thoroughly exhausted,
he had happened upon the programme of the music at the
Central Park,

"Hallo!" he said. "Here, Dick! Dodworth's Band at
the Central Park this afternoon. I have heard plenty of
what they *called* music, all the while that I have been gone;

but not Dodworth. Let's go up and hear it! Besides, I want to see how much more they have wasted on the Park."

" I !" answered Richard Crawford, astounded. "You are not very kind, brother John, to speak of *my* going out, when you know that I have not left the house for months."

" No," said John, "indeed I did not think of that! But now that I do think of it, all the more reason why you should go."

"Why, I could not sit up to ride a block!" said Richard.

"Don't believe a word of it!" said John, gayly. "You never know what you can do, until you try. You are better —you *say* that you are better—and the more you stay within the house, the more you may. In my opinion, to get well rapidly, you should be out of the house more than half the time, regaining the strength you have lost."

Just then there was a ring at the bell, and Dr. Thompson, the old family physician who had attended both the brothers since boyhood, came in to look at Richard and after the dressing of John's wounded arm. John had made a personal call upon him that morning, and the genial, gray-haired, but young-hearted old doctor had been very glad to see him returned, with no worse wound than that in his arm.

"See here, Doctor," said John, the moment he entered, "I have been giving Richard good advice, and I wish you to bear me out in it."

"Advising me to kill myself, he means!" said Richard.

"Humph! let's hear what it is all about, and see how much you are both wrong!" answered the doctor, who had made that advance in philosophy which recognizes that neither side in an argument is at all likely to represent the whole truth.

" I have been telling him that he should go out, and bantering him to ride with me to the Central Park," said John.

"And I have been telling him that I had not strength enough to ride a single block, much less to the Central Park," said Richard.

"Let me see," said the doctor, taking the invalid's hand in his, examining his pulse, and subjecting him to a general scrutiny. "The proposal is a bold one, but I fancy that it is

sensible, after all. Yes, when you *can* go out, you can go
out to advantage, and I believe that time has come. You
had probably better accept your brother's proposal."

The result of all which was, that the carriage was ordered
between three and four o'clock, and that in spite of the
insufferable heat of the day the two invalids (so very differently disabled) were driven to the Central Park, were driven
around it, heard Dodworth's Band perform half a dozen
operatic selections as only that cornet-band can perform
them, saw the loungers on the grass, the promenaders on the
walks, the boats on the pond which is called a lake, and all
the picturesque features of that Saturday-afternoon gathering
which within the past two years has become a pleasant
feature of summer in the metropolis.

Richard Crawford did not experience the fatigue he had
expected. On the contrary he felt new life and vigor flowing
in with every breath of the yet early summer ; and when
they drove back to the house an hour before sunset, he had
the sensations of a school-boy whose play-hour is over and
who is just going back to school and his books. He was not
only better, but he was nearly well. He felt and realized the
fact for the first time. The wide, glorious, open world, with
its flowers, its waters, its sunshine, and its smiling human
faces worth them all, had once more called the man who had
so lately believed himself shut away from life and enjoyment
forever ; and he was answering the call.

Not that Richard Crawford was happy, even while the
music was sounding over the lake and nature was wooing
him with her midsummer smile. He had loved—he yet
loved—truly and devotedly ; and without his realizing what
evil influence could have fallen like a blight upon all his
hopes, those hopes were destroyed. He was not broken-
hearted, as he had believed himself to be while laboring under
more serious bodily illness : he was only *sad;* but that sadness, he believed, would remain during life. Ah, well !—if
life and health were still to be his, he must nerve himself to
meet whatever of sorrow or disappointment might come,
and bear what he could not conquer. So thought he as they
rode homeward, when John for a time ceased that constant

stream of chat for which a wounded arm did not in the least disable him. He little knew how a lumbering stage was at the same hour setting down a dusty little woman in a gray travelling-dress, at a country village hundreds of miles away, whose acts and words were to produce so marked an effect on his own destiny.

These details of very ordinary events in the Crawford family, which followed the re-union of the two brothers, may seem very uninteresting and common-place; and yet they are necessary for the possible understanding of what so soon followed. For the letting in of sunshine on a dark place may not only warm and illumine that place for a time but make the continuance of sunshine a necessity. And going out into the sunshine may have the same effect. The school-boy, once let out for his " play-spell," may have great objection to spending so many hours, thereafter, over his books in the dusky school-room ; and Nature, after a time, may develope the fact that he needed the reviving and strengthening education of the outer world, much more imperatively than the additional education of the brain which he would have ac-quired within the sound of the teacher's voice. Nature's hygiene is very little understood, but it is at the same time very simple and very powerful. The *sun* contains the great mystery of health and hardihood, and the man who carefully shuts himself away from its rays is arranging for the same kind of existence which the unfortunate plant is forced to experience, growing under the shelter of a rotten log, succulent, tender and perishable. The fire-worship of the Ghebers was founded upon common-sense; and no doubt the first kneeling adoration of the sun-worshippers both of Persia and Peru, was paid by some poor fellow who had been sick, attenuated and miserable, who had finally crawled out into the sunshine after long confinement, and who believed that there must be some supernatural influence in the life radiating from the great orb and bounding through every half-chilled vein. The inventor of parasols and sun-shades should have been executed immediately on the announcement of his in-vention, for he has been the means of shutting away the faces of more than half the world, and especially the fairer portion,

from their best inanimate friend, the sun, of making sallow
complexions and lack-lustre eyes, and of causing a demand for
cosmetics that would never have been known had the sun-god
been allowed to steal kisses from the cheek of beauty and
leave there the ruddy glow of health as a compensation for
the privilege.

To induce a belief on the part of Richard Crawford that
he was well enough and strong enough to leave the house to
which he had been so long confined, had been found a little
difficult. The ice once broken, the next adventure into the
summer sunshine would need far less inducement. So it
proved. And so it happened that within four days from the
time when he believed that he was committing suicide by
adventuring to the Central Park, he permitted himself to be
persuaded, under the sanction of the doctor, into taking a
step which was certain to test his powers of endurance pretty
thoroughly—nothing less than *going to Niagara Falls.*

Of course this movement originated with John Crawford
the Zouave, whose original restlessness had not been a whit
quieted by the ever-moving adventure of a year in the army.
The city was growing unendurably hot, he said, so that he
every day expected to find the paving-stones splitting to
pieces with the heat, and the fish boiling in the North River.
It was ten degrees worse, he averred, than he had experienced
in Virginia either season ; and such a thing as a hot day had
never been known at Niagara, even by the oldest inhabitant.
(Perhaps the young man altered his opinion on that point,
visiting it especially during the early days of July, 1862 !)
Dick would grow worse again—he knew he would—and lose
the little strength he had gained, sweltering in such an un-
ventilated pig-stye as the city. Come !—there were to be no
more words about it !—they should all go to Niagara !

Richard Crawford was at first alarmed—then puzzled—
then a little delighted. Bell, who did not often fall into the
peculiarly girlish weakness of clapping her hands, did so on
this occasion. She had missed Niagara for the previous two
years ; and this season, owing to the serious illness of her
brother, she had expected to be debarred the privilege of exhibiting her unimpeachable summer wardrobe (which she had

not *quite* forgotten) at any of the watering-places. Richard's rapid improvement and this restless suggestion of John, seemed like a god-send. *She* voted for Niagara, if Richard felt that he could endure the fatigue of the journey. His citadel surrounded on two sides in that manner, and the genial old doctor faithless, there was little else left than a surrender, and Richard Crawford surrendered.

Stop!—there was something of which neither had thought for a moment! They had a guest, whose wishes should be consulted the more religiously because she would make no parade of them. Would Marion Hobart, who mourned in heart if not in the sombre hue of her garments, for her last relative so lately dead—would *she* be pleased to go into the gay world of a fashionable watering-place? Not *content*, but *pleased?* If she would not, the project must be abandoned, whatever the temptations to go forward. Bell, who had the moment before been about commencing her action as a committee of one to overhaul Richard's laid-away warbrobe and discover what additions would be necessary, had the sphere of her operations suddenly changed by being sent up-stairs to sound the inclinations of the young Virginian girl on the subject.

She found Marion Hobart half *en deshabille*, lying upon the bed in her own little chamber, busily reading and comparing the letter-press with the coats-of-arms, in a copy of the English Peerage which she had found in Dick's little library, and to which she had exhibited a scandalously aristocratic taste by paying more attention than to all the other books in the house.

"Have you ever been at Niagara, Marion?" asked Bell Crawford, leaning over her with a sisterly caress

"No," answered the young girl, looking away from her book, but without any indication of rising or any sign of that anxious agitation which inevitably brightens the faces of most American girls who have not seen the world's-wonder, when that magic word is uttered in their presence. "Father and some friends were at Saratoga once, when I was a very little girl. But father was drowned at sea. Grandfather never came North.'

"Would you like to see Niagara?" was Bell's second ques
tion.

"I do not know," answered the young Virginian girl, with
strange coolness and candor. "I think I should like to see
it as well as anything else. I have not seen many waterfalls.
I once saw the Falls of the Black Fork of Cheat; and I saw
the Natural Bridge. They are both in Virginia. I do not
know whether I should like Niagara or not."

"Would you like to go there. Suppose brother and myself
were going to Niagara and should ask you to go with us—
would you be pleased to go?"

"I would as lief go as stay here or go anywhere else," said
the singular girl.

"I thought you might possibly have objections to going,
because there is so much company at Niagara, and because
you have so lately lost your grandfather—that is why I asked,"
explained Bell.

"I do not mind the company. They are nothing to me. I
do not mourn for my poor grandfather *aloud*. But you are
very kind to think of me," answered the little enigma. And
with that very unenthusiastic endorsement of the Niagara
project, Bell Crawford was compelled to descend the stairs
and make report of the event of her embassy. But the result
was held to be rather satisfactory than otherwise, and the
hastily-devised arrangements for Niagara went forward.

To pass rapidly over that movement, the manner of which
does not in any degree affect the progress of this narration,
let it be said that on Wednesday, the 9th of July, the two
brothers, the sister and their guest, with the proper array of
the "great North River travelling-trunks" and other baggage,
took the steamer Daniel Drew for a sail by daylight up the
Hudson, as the mode of making half the journey least fatiguing
to the recovering invalid. That the three New Yorkers, to
whom the scenery of that noble river was thoroughly familiar,
clapped hands and shouted their joy once more, nearly all
day, at the flashing blue of the river, the rafts of steamboats,
sloops and tows that continually came sweeping down it, the
rugged frowning of the Palisades, the narrow-passes and rugged peaks of the Highlands, and the long, blue, uneven line

of the Cattskills, with the white glimmering of the Mountain House,—while the young Virginian girl, introduced to that scenery for the first time in her life, seemed to maintain her calmness and comparative insensibility. That they rested for the night at Albany, out of respect to the comfort of the invalid—John Crawford submitting under protest, and declaring Albany, after Washington, the most unendurable "one-horse town" in the universe. That they took the cars of the Central Road in the morning, Richard being so pillowed among cloaks and blankets and shawls, that he had quite the comfort of lying in an ordinary bed ; and that on Thursday night, the Tenth of July, when the full moon had risen so high in heaven as to make the coming midnight a very mockery of day, they rolled into the village of Niagara Falls, and found a resting-place at the still wide-awake and ever-lively Cataract.

CHAPTER XXVI.

Tom Leslie at Niagara—A Dash at Scenery There— A Rencontre—Dexter Ralston Once More—Union Man or Rebel ?—Tom Leslie Discounted.

It will be remembered that Tom Leslie, leaving Josephine Harris with a sigh of regret at Utica (tnose jolly fellows do sigh sometimes, after all !) went on to Niagara on the afternoon of the Fifth of July. Walter Lane Harding had promised to join him at the Cataract, early in the following week, if he could so arrange his business as to leave the city on Sunday or Monday ; but just now Leslie was alone—worse alone than he ever remembered to have been at any former period of his life. Lost one night in a pass of the Apennines, with some doubts whether he should ever be able to find his way to supper and civilization, he had been lonely enough for comfort ; and pacing his solitary night round as a sentinel

under the frowning guns of Sebastopol, he had felt that another friendly human face would be pleasant to see and a
friendly human voice something not be despised ; but neither
of those situations could for a moment compare with the loneliness of that summer afternoon and evening, while he was
bowling along through the Genesee Valley.

The absence of the whole world is a grief, when we do not
wish to be alone, but that is a grief in the *general*. The
coming of any one person will break the spell and fill the
void. But the absence of the *one*, immediately after earth
and air have seemed to be full of the sacred presence, is grief
in the *particular*. Only one can fill that void, and the coming
of that one is for the time impossible. The company of
thousands of others is then an aggravation and an insult,
making the loneliness worse by contrast with the apparent
companionship of all others.

Tom Leslie (this fact may have been sufficiently indicated
before)—Tom Leslie was deeply, irrevocably, hopelessly in love,
and he had not even taken the ordinary pains to deceive himself on the subject. He had found his destiny and submitted
to it, after a long period of immunity. He had every reason
to know that his regard was returned ; and he had no reason
to doubt, though not an explicit word had been spoken to
warrant the belief—that when he asked the corresponding
question of Josephine Harris, as he certainly meant to do at
a very early day, her answer would be a frank and satisfactory
—yes ! So much for content and the future. But Tom, like
many another child, had no propensity for waiting, and liked
his sugar-plums *now* as well as to-morrow. He would have
liked to give up business, ignore propriety, and have the company of the odd combination of female graces and weaknesses
who had won him, all the while for the present, and afterwards by way of variety. So he felt at that moment, at
least ; and it was with more than one, or two, or a dozen
yawns and " Heighos !" and several short naps that happened
along on his travel like cities of refuge, that he managed to
wear through the last hours of his journey.

But Tom Leslie, the cosmopolitan and journalist, would
have been unworthy the experience through which he had

passed, had he lacked the power to endure what he disliked. He could never have digested horse-beef among the Kalmucks, or stomached the rancid sour-krout of Old Haarlem, without this indispensable qualification. So, though on the night of his arrival at the Cataract he allowed the thunder of the fall to call him in vain to a view by the broken moonlight, and though he tumbled into bed within ten minutes after his late and light supper and went sullenly to sleep as if there had not been a woman in the world worth thinking of,—yet he was in quite another mood the next morning.

Niagara was unusually full for so early a period in the season, the leading houses being already crowded, though principally by transient visitors. The Fourth of July, then just passed, had been kept with unusual vigor and display, in the way of powder, fireworks and general patriotism at the International, the Cataract and all the other more popular houses—partially, no doubt, because the evil eyes from across the river began to be noticeable, and because the red-cross flag had been more conspicuously displayed at the Clifton House and on the flag-staff at the Museum at Table Rock, than in ordinary seasons.

But whatever changes might have occurred in personal and national feeling, Tom Leslie felt, as he strolled across the bridge and over Goat Island, on the morning after his arrival, that there had been no change which the human eye could perceive, in the great cataract or its surroundings, since he had looked upon it for the last time before his departure for Europe, when that narrow river supplied the northern boundary of what seemed to be a united and happy nation. Humanity is changing, inconsistent and unreliable: Nature is calm, grand, and verges on the eternal. He saw that the great American Rapid still came thundering down, "like a herd of white buffaloes with wild eyes and sea-green manes," as a graphic writer has described it; that the grand old trees with their gloomy immensity of shade and the-thousands of unknown and long-forgotten names carved upon their bark, still stood as sentinels along the beaten pathways over the Island ; that the thunder of the Fall still kept the whole solid mass of the Island in one creeping and trembling shudder, as

if a slight earthquake was just passing, with a dull, heavy
boom like that of a continuous distant cannonade, coming up
in the pauses of the wind.

He saw, too, as he paid his inevitable quarter at the
toll-house on the causeway, that the course of "honest industry" (*i. e.*, that blatant humbug which eternally taxes the
pockets for superfluities) had not been checked ; for the usual
amount of birchen-canoes, bead-caps and feather-fans with
sprawled birds in the centre, were on sale under peculiarly
aboriginal auspices. And that the whole race of Jehus had
not relieved society by going to be killed-off in the war, he
became painfully aware by the number of villainous-looking
wretches armed with dilapidated whips, who beset him on
the bridge and offered to convey him anywhere for something
less than the mere pleasure of his company. Tom Leslie had
been somewhat too familiar in other lands as well as his own,
with such human vermin as those with the whips, and such
fungi temptations to extravagance as those that hung from
the tawny hands, and beckoned from shelves and glass cases,—
to pay them much attention or receive much annoyance from
them ; and so he passed on across the Island, to look once
more upon the great English Fall and the Canada shore
beyond.

Emerging from the woods upon the high bank overlooking
the English rapids, the whole unequalled scene burst once
more on his view, as he had patriotically tried to remember it
when looking at Terni and Schaffhausen. He had carried
the sight and almost the roar with him, in memory, ready to
dwarf with them all that the European world could present ;
and so sacred seemed the thought of that wonder of nature
which could form such a talisman, that the broad hat was insensibly lifted from his brow as he caught the first new
glimpse, and he stood before the Fall fairly uncovered as he
might have done on the crest of the Judean hills, overlooking
the first-seen Jerusalem.

The dark and rugged Canadian shore was full in view on
the other side of the river, with the Clifton House and the
Museum glimmering brightly in the morning sunlight, and
the red-cross flag waving sluggishly from both as if in defi-

ance of the great nation that lay so near and yet could not possess the little patch of land over which it floated. The Horse-Shoe Tower stood as of old, still unconquered by the fierce rapids striving to undermine it; and around base and balcony swarmed visitors who seemed like pigmies not so much on account of the distance as because they were dwarfed and belittled in the presence of the immense and the immeasurable. All these things lay broadly in sight of the journalist on that glorious Sunday morning, and perhaps at another time he might have seen and attempted to describe them; but not *then*. He for the moment failed to see what was before him, and he saw something else not revealed to every eye.

Tom Leslie was either the master or the slave of a powerful imagination. Some who knew him said the one, and some the other. But all agreed as to the possession of the faculty; and it was not always that his soberest and most conscientious relations (in type) were received without a shade of suspicion on that account. It may have been that the loneliness of the night before had not quite worn away, and that it left him sadder and more impressible than usual; and it may have been that the one element before wanting in his nature, that of earnest and undivided human love, had changed him when it was supplied. At all events, there was a something in that wondrous scene, that came to him that morning as he had never before known it—something that came to him from dream-land, and made the sight of his eyes only the exercise of a secondary faculty. He saw, with this peculiar sight, all the features of the scene that we have noted, and another and one strikingly unusual, in a shipwreck in the rapids.

Two days before, on the Fourth, and in honor of the day, a knot of gay fellows had procured an old schooner, hoisted white streamers at the tops of her stripped masts, and sent her down the river into the rapids from Chippewa Creek, expecting to enjoy the rare pleasure of seeing her leap over the Falls and emerge in little fragments and splinters of timber in the river below. Thousands had gathered on the Canadian shore, and on Goat Island, to witness a prank never matched in audacity since the British "guerrillas" from the other side,

26

in the time of the Canadian rebellion, seized the steamer
" Caroline " at Schlosser, set her on fire, and sent her down
the Falls—an act which almost lit the torch of war so effectually between the two countries, that all the waters which over-
whelmed the " Caroline " would not have been enough to
quench it.

But with reference to the old schooner, sent down from
Chippewa Creek on the Fourth of July. She had only shown
that human calculations are not infallible, even when they
presage disaster. The thousands assembled to witness the
destruction, had been doomed to disappointment. The current
had swept the boat well over on the Canadian side, and there
some unknown eddy had seized and driven her between two
sunken rocks, where she lay as safe from any danger of the
Falls as if she had been ten miles below them, instead of half
a mile above. She lay, bow up the river, inclined lengthwise,
as if she had been caught when shooting down the Lachine
Rapids, and the white streamers on her bare masts fluttering
out to the winds as signals of distress that would have been—
ah ! so hopeless and useless with human life on board and in
peril.

At the first moment of beholding the old wreck, Tom Leslie
found her a prominent feature in the spectacle, and his reflections took a shape which may have been taken by those of
many sojourners at the Falls, who saw her during the season :

"There she lies to-day, and there she may lie for many a
long month, gradually weakening and breaking apart from the
action of the rapids surging around her, until some night when
the wind comes fiercely down the river, and heavy storms
have increased the volume of water as well as loosened the
last bolt that yet holds her securely together,—then, when
there is none to witness the death-throe of wood and iron,
she will heave and labor and at last break apart. The two
fragments will go sweeping down, whirled over like playthings—touching the points of the rocks and giving out groans
and shrieks like those which precede dissolution ; then for
one moment there will be a dark mass poised on the edge of
the Fall, and the next there will be one more deafening crash
added even to the thunder of the waters. A few broken

splinters will go sweeping away down the dark river, and all will be over."

But what was it that Tom Leslie saw, more than is revealed to the natural eyes, looking on that scene when he had contemplated it for a few moments? This and only this—but quite enough to make the memory of that moment immortal. He saw it *applied to the human heart and human life.* The water pouring over the Horse-shoe Fall ceased for the moment to be the falling water of this real world, and became some weird stream falling thunderously and in white glory through the land of dreams. The dark misty gulf into which it poured below was not the physical abyss over which the natural man must stand with a shudder, but the unfathomed pit of woe and sorrow into which, in nightmare dreams, man has been ever falling yet never destroyed, since the first visions of early childhood. The tower ceased to be a palpable mass of wood and stone, and became human hope and energy, with the clear blue sky of God's providence above, beaten by storms and undermined by fierce currents every moment threatening it with destruction, but standing yet through all. And the old wrecked schooner above had ceased to be a mere material wreck of plank and timber and iron—it was one of those unreal but sadder wrecks of a human life and a human soul, stranded for the moment on the rock of some great calamity, and eventually to be swept away and engulphed by the inevitable.

There had been a slight veil of haze shrouding the sun for the previous half hour; but as Tom Leslie partially awakened from his dream and listlessly descended the stairs cut in the bank, towards the bridge leading to the Tower, the mist rolled away, the sun broke forth in the glory of high-noon, and out of the darkness below sprang an arch of light that almost made the journalist, who was too old and too world-hardened for such exhibitions, clap his hands and cry: "The rainbow! the rainbow!" Of old he had seen the rainbow spanning the eastern heaven when looking out at early evening from the home of his childhood, and when the thunder-storms of summer were dying away over the Atlantic; but here it was, a thing of arms' reach, and at his feet!

At one moment it merely glimmered up through the mist from the bed of the river, a little broken space of the arch, and the colors dim and indistinct; anon the sky grew brighter and the column of mist rose higher; and now it formed more than the half circle, the top a little above the level of the Fall,—and the blue, and gold, and green, and orange, and purple, painted so brightly on the retina of the eye that they seemed to be a part of the very air the observer was inhaling. How near he stood, impressible Tom, at that moment, to the eternal mystery!—how near to the workshop in which seem to be flashed out from eternal forges the beauties of the sunshine and the storm! Climbing down from the bridge to the end of the rock, leaning tremblingly over and looking down into the misty gulf below with that Jacob's Ladder of faith set therein—it is not strange that the journalist for one moment wished for a line and plummet to drop into that reservoir of golden glory and bring up some memento of what seemed so near to the celestial;—just as one wishes, sometimes when the midnight heaven is darkest and the stars are burning most purely there, to be able to stretch forth a hand among the stellar lights and bring it back bathed with that radiance which is so fearfully beautiful.

Leslie had no intention of ascending the tower that day—other days would be his at Niagara, and something must be saved for each. Besides, he had breakfasted lightly and an unromantic call for lunch was being made on faculties quite as delicate as his mental perceptions. He had accordingly just turned again and ascended the stairs to the bank in front of the Pavilion, when the fates (ever kind to him in this regard, as to every other true lover of nature) vouchsafed him one moment's glimpse of a spectacle often wished for and seen but seldom. Turning for one last glimpse as he walked away, at that instant his eye was resting on the sharpest point of the curve of the Horse-shoe Fall, where the volume of water is evidently deepest, and where from that depth it makes one broad unbroken sweep of amber green as it plunges over, without one fleck of foam to mar it. He was just scanning for an instant that calm depth, and saying that *there* was after all the majesty of Niagara—there, where the great

green flood approaches the awful precipice, impelled by a re-
sistless force from above, but unruffled and untroubled by the
approaching fate—bends gracefully and proudly at the verge,
as some dusky Antoinette might do her proud neck when
the axe of the executioner was impending—then, still without a ripple or a tremor takes the last long plunge as Curtius
may have done when the gulf was open in the Forum and he
rode down the Aventine and spurred out into thin air to
fulfil the omens of the augurs and save the perilled life of
Rome,—he was just feeling and saying this, when a dark
speck appeared at the very edge of the green. It was a log,
perhaps fifteen or twenty feet in length, over the Fall!—a
mere log, nothing in another place, but everything in the place
it for that moment occupied. For one instant he saw it hang
trembling on the verge, then for another its dark outlines
were thrown into clear relief against the bright green water
with the sunshine glimmering through; and then down, down
it was hurled, rushing like an arrow's flight into the feathery
foam of the broken water below, and at last (so far as
human eye could ever know) into the blinding mist at the
bottom of the cataract. What a reed upon the brook had
been that log, that might have required the strength of a
dozen men to lift it from the ground!—what is the might
with which the elements make playthings of what seem to
mortal strength dense and immoveable—even as the great
Power that is equally above nature and above man, " holdeth
the mountains in the hollow of his hand, and taketh up the
isles as a very little thing !"

"By George !" said Leslie. "What a lucky dog I am !
I have known a thousand people who wished for just such a
view, and I have had it all alone, after all !" He was not in
the habit of holding conversations aloud with himself; but
he had been so impressed as to speak aloud involuntarily, in
this instance.

"No, not quite alone, if you please, Mr. Leslie !" said a
deep voice behind him, and at the same instant a hand was
laid upon his shoulder. He turned, and met the powerful
form and singular face of Dexter Ralston, the Virginian.

It was not unnatural that Leslie should be surprised ; and

it would be idle to say that he was not even startled at this most unexpected meeting, remembering what he did of the last three occasions on which he had met this man—in each instance, as he had reason to suppose, his observation being unknown to the other.   He might have been pardoned if he even shuddered, remembering the connection which he believed Ralston to bear towards the "red woman"; and he was too ardent a Union man, as we have seen, not instantly to remember the ambiguous circumstances under which he had twice seen him, and the chase after him and his companions which had cost him so long a ride only a few days before.   It may be said, in this place, that he had heard nothing from Superintendent Kennedy, before leaving the city, of the watch placed upon the house and its result,—and that after the second adventure of the house on Prince Street, and the opening of the new channel into which his thoughts and feelings had been led by the meeting with Joe Harris, he had not thought proper to follow up the mystery, and consequently had no knowledge that any of the parties had left New York.

All these thoughts, and the counter one that the man before him had really done him no harm but had once rendered him an important service—passed through the mind of Leslie so quickly that the other must have been a close observer to know that they were passing at all.   As a result, by the time that they became fairly confronted and Dexter Ralston held out his hand, that of Tom Leslie met him with all apparent frankness.

"Mr. Ralston," he said, owning a part of the truth, "really you surprised me."

"So I suppose," said the other; "and yet I have been standing here, leaning against one of the posts of the Pavilion, for several minutes; and I am certainly not so small of stature as to be easily overlooked."

"No," laughed Leslie.   And then he added.   "But yonder is something larger.   The Falls dwarf everything, and I suppose *hide* everything."

"Very probably," said Ralston.   "Were you walking back towards the bridge?   Shall I walk with you?   That is—I mean to ask—are you alone?"

"Oh yes, all alone!" said Leslie. "I am at the Cataract. And you—are you staying here?"

"I *have* been staying at the Clifton," answered the other, as they strolled back across the Island. "But just now I am at the Monteagle. It is long since we met," he added. "You have been in Europe, have you not? I think you told me you were going, when I saw you last."

"Yes," said Leslie, "I have been in Europe again, and only came back last spring." But he added a mental enquiry that was by no means shaped into words: "*Did* I say to him that I was going to Europe? or does he keep watch of me and know my every movment, through the mysterious agency of the woman of the Rue la Reynie Ogniard?"

"You are a newspaper man still?" asked Ralston, after a momentary silence, as they walked on.

"Yes," said Leslie, "I am still at that drudgery, in my own way, and shall probably never be freed from it. But you see that I do not stick so closely to the desk as to injure my health very much! And you—excuse my asking the question," and he tried, walking at his side though he was, to mark closely whether the question produced any effect on the face of the other—"but the truth is, Ralston, that I scarcely expected to meet you in the North at the present moment. I thought you so incarnate a Southerner, as well as a slave-holder, that you would have been likely to join in the rebellion!"

"No, did you?" asked Ralston; and if his face changed, certainly Leslie, close observer as he thought himself, could not detect the difference. "Well, I must say that you, put the matter plainly. You *should* have thought better of an old friend, and remembered that if I was a *Virginian* I was also and still more an *American*."

How openly and with what apparent honesty the man spoke! And how impossible it seemed that he *could* be uttering other words than those of entire truth? But Tom Leslie remembered the night under the arches of the Capitol, the stars-and-bars and the mystic circlet of the house on Prince Street, and the mysterious words that procured admission to the house up-town · and he had seen and heard

enough of double faces not to be *too* sure of his ground on
any man's word.

"Well, I am glad to know it," he said, in reply to Ralston's
disclaimer. "We have not too many true Union men, who
have *forgotten the particular part of the Union in which they
were born, for the sake of the country and the whole country.*
I am glad to know that you are one of them. He laid
peculiar stress on the more important words of the last sentence, and bent his eyes still more searchingly on the countenance of the singular man before him.

"How long do you remain?" asked Ralston, as they neared
the end of the bridge.

"A few days only," answered Leslie—"perhaps a week or
two. I came up to catch the moon on the Falls.

"You should have come in time, then, and seen the eclipse,"
said the Virginian.

"Aha!" said Tom Leslie to himself. "One point of information gained, if no more! He is a little in the *habit* of
being at Niagara, for he was here at the full moon in June
and he has since been absent! One touch inside your armor,
old fellow, if no more! You were here to see the eclipse,
then?" he asked aloud of Ralston. "I tried to come myself,
but could not manage it. What was it like, if you saw it over
the Falls?"

"I was staying at the Clifton House, then," said Ralston,
"and I came down to Table Rock, alone, just after midnight,
and sat there from the beginning to the end of the obscuration. You should have seen"—and here his undeniable
though repressed poetical temperament began to show itself
in his cheek and eye—"you should have seen the dull, dismal shadow gradually creeping over the rapids as the disk
grew smaller, every flashing wave seeming to be touched with
a ghastly reflection that said: 'Daylight and moonlight are
both gone forever—the last darkness is creeping on—the end
of all things is at hand.' The spray below the cataract seemed
dun and lead-colored, as if it might have been the sulphurous
smoke rolling up from a battle-field. All was splendidly dismal, let me tell you!—such a spectacle as few men see and
no man who sees ever forgets!"

"And what was the appearance of the moon when fully obscured?" asked Leslie, almost breathless with interest at the strangely graphic words of the Virginian, and no longer wondering, after those words, that there should have been a connection between the mysterious "red woman" and one who seemed so nearly of her mental kin.

"It was *no* moon," answered Ralston, and his dark eyes seemed to lose all their fierceness and grow inexpressibly sad and solemn as he spoke. "It was *no* moon! It was a mere unreal shadow and mockery—the dead ghost of a moon that had been, perished long ago, and embodying all the griefs and all the sorrows that had weighed down the heart of man since the Creation. The waters of Niagara lay beneath it, as if under a pall that had settled over a dead world!"

"I should have liked to see it—I would have travelled a thousand miles to see it, had I thought so far!" said Leslie, with the earnestness of a lover of Nature under all her aspects.

"Would you?" said Ralston. "Well, it was something to see *once*: I should scarcely like to trust the brain of the man who saw it much oftener. I must leave you, but I hope I shall meet you again. Here boy!" beckoning to one of the lounging hack-drivers at the hotel-end of the bridge, "Drive me to the Monteagle. Good-bye!" and away he whirled, leaving Leslie to look after him until out of sight, and to say to himself as he walked up the esplanade over the rapids:

"I thought that *I* was an oddity and a contradiction, but that fellow can *discount* me! I don't know half as much about him now, as I did the first moment I saw him!"

CHAPTER XXVII.

TOM LESLIE was not left to loneliness and his own resources
very long at the Cataract, for Walter Lane Harding reached
Niagara at noon on Monday, having left New York on Sunday evening. Though even had Leslie been left to his "own
resources," these resources were somewhat more numerous than
usual, and he was never much in the habit of being so bored
by Time as to be obliged to lay plots against its life. In the
first place—no, that should be the *second* place—he had his
duties as a newspaper-correspondent at a leading and fashionable resort, which entailed a letter every day, but which did
not entail, let, us say, the chronicling of the details of hops
and evening assemblies, after a manner somewhat scandalously
prevalent, with descriptions of the "charming dress worn by
Miss A——," the "elegance and grace of the accomplished
Miss B——," and all the other disgusting and indecent Jenk-
insism of the initials, together with fulsome laudations of the
table and even the laundry of the hotel, leading to the impression that the correspondent is upon free board and even free
washing! Our cosmopolitan had outlived that phase of cal-
low journalism, long before ; and the managing-editor would
have been a bold one who should now have proposed to him
to re-enter that most contemptible of all literary harness.
What he was to write and what he *did* write, catching up the
prevailing topics of conversation and tones of feeling, with
sensational descriptions of scenery and incident interspersed
like under-tones to joyous music,—men who have hearts,
brains and breeding will at once recognize, and others will
never know under any detail of information.
    What Tom Leslie found it necessary to do in the *first* place,
was to write a letter per day, and occasionally two, to a certain lady temporarily located at West Falls, Oneida County,

that lady having very kindly given him her address with permission to use it, and having promised to answer these epis-
tles with brief and maidenly little notes of her own. When
it is said that as early as Monday he received one of those
notes, and that for an hour thereafter he had very indefinite
ideas as to which end of the human figure was intended for
the purposes of locomotion, it will be understood that both
parties to the compact were carrying out their agreement
with praiseworthy faithfulness.

But even without the duties devolved upon him by love or
newspapers, Tom Leslie, a trained observer of society around
him, would have found plenty of occupation on the favorite
promenades and in the parlors and halls of the International
and Cataract. Such a complete and total revolution in society was beginning to show itself, in the gradual dropping
away of the old "good families" who years before had made
Niagara, Saratoga and Newport their Meccas at midsummer;
such bloated pretenders, with unlicked cubs of families, the
"shoddy aristocracy" who had first aided to make the war,
and then make dishonest fortunes from it, had come up to
take their places, with everything about them, sire and son,
mother and daughter, new, arrogant and unpleasant; and
there was such a marked absence of that Southern element
which in other days had supplied money to obsequious waiters
and green girls to needy fortune-hunters,—that there seemed
to have been a complete turn of the kaleidoscope, and it almost
puzzled an old habitue to know whether he had not exchanged
lands as well as years.

And something else, of no secondary importance, presented
its claims to notice. This was the "blue and buttons"—the
"absenteeism" to which notice has been before so often called
during the progress of this narration. The result of the
Seven Days' Battles was just coming to the sojourners at Niagara, through the Buffalo and New York papers; and while
the Fourth of July address of McClellan to his soldiers, which
came among the other items of news from the army, and which
was then and there being read and commented upon, showed
that the last chance of victory was not yet lost, it showed at the
same time how fearfully the ranks of our armies had been

thinned and what a necessity there was that every man who
had pretended to be a soldier, and who had from any cause
been so far absent from the field, should return at once and
aid to sustain the perilled cause. And yet through every
corridor of the leading houses at Niagara, in every parlor, on
every walk and on every piazza, sat, stood, walked, read,
smoked or flirted, the blue-clothed, buttoned, shoulder-strapped, jaunty-capped, natty-whiskered and killingly-moustached
officers of the Union army, who had sworn to serve the country and aid to defend the republic,—but who paid no more
attention to the pleading call of the generals in the field or
the authoritative voice of the President, than they would have
done to a blind piper playing in the street! It was easier to
dawdle than to fight or even do duty in camp : it was more
pleasant to bask in the admiring smiles of silly girls who
should have turned their eyes into basilisks to blast the indo-
lent and miserable cowards—than to dare the July sun on the
banks of the James, or run the risk of a flash from the enemy's
cannon. Men who had the welfare of the republic at heart,
turned sick when they looked at these hale, hearty and unwounded absentees from an honorable service, every man of
them daily breaking his oath to his country and his obligations to his own conscience. This was one more of the phases
of society at Niagara, which Tom Leslie was called upon to
note down and study during those opening days of July, and
one of the evils which—shame to the nation that it should be
so!—is only now * beginning to find a partial remedy.

But it has been said that Walter Harding reached Niagara
at noon on Monday, and thenceforth Leslie had a companion
in most of his strolls and observations. Harding's calm face
looked a little jaded with close attention to business in hot
weather and a time of financial trouble; he had not been
quite so frequent a rambler at the Falls as Leslie, and had
some points of interest yet to visit in the neighborhood especially on the Canada side ; he was fonder of the road and
less fond of observations among the crowd of sight-seers and
summer-loungers, than his friend ; and as a consequence, after

March 14th, 1863.

his coming, riding took the place of lounging to a great degree. Nothing with reference to these rides, most of which took place along the green lanes and among the fertile fields of Brantford County, deserves notice in this place, except one phase of the peculiar character of Leslie, half-earnest patriotism and half-tormenting mischief. He found plenty of ill-feeling towards the United States, among the Canadians, and as much effort as possible to depreciate the Federal currency. Thenceforth his special anxiety was to vex and annoy as many of the Canadians and native English as possible, and verbally, at least, to annex the two Canadas to the Union.

Going up to the top of the Observatory at Lundy's Lane, on their Tuesday-morning ride, among the other visitors who were listening to the ten-thousandth repetition of the story of the battle of Niagara (varied to suit customers), told by the old soldier who either was or was not a participant in the battle, they found one true John Bull from the mother country,—a stout, thick-set, florid-faced man of middle-age, not over-intelligent but very earnest and enthusiastic. Leslie marked him as a victim and began at him at once.

"I suppose you have not heard the telegraphic reports from Washington, this morning ?" he said to the Englishman, after some conversation with reference to the battle had brought them to terms of speaking acquaintance.

"No," answered the Englishman. "Anything of consequence ?"

"I should think so!" said Leslie, very gravely. "War between the United States and England, beyond a doubt."

"God bless my soul!" said John Bull. "No ?"

"Sure as you live!" said Leslie, while Harding shook his head and knitted his brows at him as a hint to be careful how far he went with his mischief—a signal which was misinterpreted by some of the bystanders to mean that he should not have betrayed the intelligence. "Lord Lyons made a demand on Secretary Seward, yesterday morning, to open the ports of Charleston and Savannah within twenty-four hours, for the free exportation of cotton. Secretary Seward at once refused to open them at all before the conclusion of the war or the First of January 1900 ; and Lord Lyons immediately exhibited his instructions to come home by the first steamer if the demand was not acceded to. He left Washington last evening, and will sail for England by the steamer of to-morrow."

Some of the auditors—intelligent visitors from the hotels, and other well-informed people, saw the joke and humored it. Others, prepared for almost any item of startling news, and not too well up in national affairs, took it all for sober earnest. John Bull was completely mystified.

"Good heavens !" he said. " Can this be possible ?"

" I must hurry back !" said Leslie, warming into broader mischief, and pulling out his watch. " Non-intercourse between the two countries may be proclaimed at any moment, and in that case I should be a prisoner !"

" God bless me " said the Englishman. " In that case I had better get over to the International and look after getting part of my baggage that is there, over on this side of the river !"

"I should advise you to do so at once," answered Leslie, quite as gravely as before. " I wonder whether we shall be stopped on our way back, or not ?   However, it is a matter of not much consequence. If any of us *should* be taken prisoners and kept over here, it would not be for long. Our people will of course overrun Canada within a week, and annex it to the Northern States."

" Oh, they couldn't do *that*, you know !" said John Bull, who might believe anything else, but who could not possibly be brought to believe anything against the power of the British Government or its colonies, when in arms.

" I believe that you are an Englishman by birth ? Am I mistaken ?" asked Leslie, in a tone of ministerial gravity and dignity.

" Not at all mistaken, sir," said the Englishman, proudly. " John Hazelton Butts, Leakington, Monmouthshire."

" John Thompson, Jr., late Secretary of Legation to the Duchy of Parma," said Leslie, picking up the first names that happened to come into mind, and bowing in return. " You seem, Mr. Butts, to be a highly intelligent gentleman—"

" Thank you, Mr. Secretary," said the Englishman, who had at least caught the fictitious title.

"But, sir," Leslie went on, "it is impossible that any foreign resident should know, concerning affairs on this continent, what necessarily comes under *our* knowledge. Perhaps you will be a little surprised when I tell you that there is a secret order existing all along the borders of the States adjoining these provinces, numbering more than three hundred thousand men, all drilled weekly, and all sworn, in the event of any opportunity occurring, to seize upon the Canadas and New Brunswick at once?"

"Indeed I *am* surprised," said the Englishman. "This is really the case?"

"Really and incontestably, sir," answered Leslie. "You will see at once, sir, what chance there could be of defending these provinces against such an inroad. But come, Smith!" addressing Harding, "we must really hurry back before the bridge closes. Good morning, Mr. Butts!—good morning, gentlemen!" and Leslie hurried down from the observatory and away, accompanied by Harding. Whether the Englishman at once went over after his baggage, or not, is uncertain.

"What *is* the use of all that, Tom?" asked Harding, when they were once more in the carriage and rolling along the privet-hedged lanes.

"Use? oh, plenty of use!—*fun!* I have been as grave as a judge for nearly a week; and besides, every Englishman whom I succeed in making thoroughly uncomfortable, is one scion of the stock of *perfidé Albion* paid off for all old scores!"

"Humph!" said Harding. "You are incorrigible, and that is all that can be said about it."

Close to the edge of one of the fields along which they were driving, some laborers were at work, hoeing potatoes. There were some splendid grain-fields adjoining, and at a little distance stood a handsome farm-house with thrifty-looking out-buildings. Leslie's spirit of mischief was now up, and nothing but exercise could calm it.

"Hallo, there!" he called to the laborers, stopping the carriage at the same time. One of the working-men stopped his work and came up to the fence

"Whose farm is this?"

"Mr. Bardeleau's, sir."

"Oh, Bardeleau! I know him. Crops look finely."

"Yes, very finely, sir," answered the workman.

"Going to the house soon?"

"Yes, sir, going in to dinner before long," answered the man.

"Well, my good man," said Leslie, "be good enough to give Mr. Bardeleau the regards of Mr. Thompson, International Hotel, an old friend of his, and to tell him that war has just broken out between England and the United States, and that the President has this morning issued a proclamation annexing Canada to the State of New York. Good morning."

Mischief of this character varied and enlivened the performances of that day and the next, Harding alternately enjoying and protesting against it. But on the third day there was a decided change in the programme. Running over the register at the desk, before breakfast on Friday morning, Leslie found the following four names, arrivals of the night before: "Richard Crawford—John Crawford—Miss Isabel Crawford—Miss Marion Hobart—New York City."

"Why, here are acquaintances—or at least one of them!" he called to Harding, who was at a little distance. He might have said more than one acquaintance, with propriety, for though he had met none of the Crawfords except Bell, he knew so much of them from Josephine Harris that he seemed to have known them for a twelvemonth.

"Who are they?" asked Harding, busy with a carriage-order.

"The Crawfords—and somebody else with them," answered Leslie. "You remember the young ladies on Broadway, the impudent scoundrel and the caning, a few days ago—one of them a Miss Crawford"—

"Yes, I remember," said Harding, with a little flush rising suddenly to his face. He also remembered, beyond a doubt, that he had been very much impressed by that young lady, and that had he dared, he would have called at her house before leaving the city. Here she was, brought accidentally into the same hotel with himself, and—. What else he thought may be left to the imagination. "Yes, I remember," he said. "And the other lady—Miss Harris, is she in the company?"

"No," said Leslie, "she does not appear to be." ("Appear to be!"—just as if that scamp did not know where she was, and as if he had not a letter in his pocket from her!) "No, see—Miss Crawford and her two brothers, with another lady whose name I have never heard before."

The result of this discovery was that the parties met at breakfast, a slight flush (corresponding to that of Harding a little while before) mounting to the face of Bell Crawford as she introduced the two friends to her brothers and Miss Hobart. Very naturally, thereafter, though there was an overplus of males and a deficiency of females to make the association perfect, the two parties blended, and in the future plans for sight-seeing and amusement each made arrangements for and calculated upon the other.

They were just passing from the breakfast-room—that cool breakfast and dining-room of the Cataract, overlooking the lower rapids with the clumped little islands near the bridge—when Leslie caught sight of a figure crossing the hall.

"Look—quick!" he said, touching the arm of Harding. "Look down the hall! There he is, now! Do you not recognize him?"

Harding, to whom Leslie had of course told the story of his late rencontre, looked in the direction indicated. Just for one instant the face of the person alluded to was turned towards them, and Harding plainly distinguished that it was that of the Virginian whom they had seen at the corner of Houston Street on the night of the opening of this story. He had but a moment to observe, for the tall man was almost at the office-door, and in an instant he had disappeared through it. At the same instant Marion Hobart uttered a quick, sharp cry, and staggered against John Crawford, as if about to fall. All the party gathered around her instantly, two or three of the waiters came up, and for the moment attention was distracted from everything beside.

"I had a sudden pain here. I do not feel very well. If you please I will go up to my room and lie down a little while. But I shall soon be better," said the young Virginian

27

girl, in response to the anxious inquiries of her friends as to
the cause of the sudden cry and the evident paleness of her
face.

In compliance with her wish Bell Crawford accompanied
her up-stairs; and the moment after, Tom Leslie stepped
into the office-door through which he had seen Dexter Ralston
disappear. He was not there. In reply to an inquiry, the
clerk said that a tall man, whom he had seen several times
before, had come into the room and stepped to the counter a
moment, perhaps to examine the register, but that he had
almost instantly gone out again. Leslie looked through the
halls and upon the piazza, a little perplexed by the sudden
appearances and disappearances of this man; but he was not
in sight anywhere—he had evidently left the house.

Before quitting the breakfast-table, it had been arranged
that the whole reinforced party should use the fine morning
for a ride over the bridge into Canada, a three-seated carriage being called into requisition. But after the gentlemen
had waited a few moments for tidings from the sudden invalid, Bell Crawford came down-stairs again and announced
that they would be obliged to take the ride without female
company, as Miss Hobart felt too much indisposed to ride
and would remain in her room, and she could not think of
leaving her entirely alone in a strange house on the first day
of their arrival. Marion, she said, had proclaimed her willing-
ness to remain alone, and had even urged her to go, but she
had refused and would remain.

This arrangement did not precisely please any of the gentlemen, and least of all it pleased Walter Lane Harding, who
had lately ridden over all that ground quite often enough
unless he was to go over it this time in peculiarly pleasant
company. He had an insane belief, by this time, that Miss
Bell Crawford was "very pleasant company." But there was
little else to do, than to obey the decrees of fate; one of the
ladies was temporarily an invalid, and the other, for humanity's sake, must play nurse; the gentlemen could have
little of their society, at least for the morning; and so half
an hour afterwards, while Bell Crawford returned up-stairs,
fortified with a novel and two Buffalo papers, to perform her

self-denying office of Good Samaritan, the four gentlemen took an open landau and were whirled down to the Suspension Bridge and over to the Canada side.

Their drive had lasted perhaps three hours and covered nearly twenty miles, when, hastening back to dinner, they drove in at the gate-house on the Canada side of the Suspension Bridge. A close-carriage was just leaving the bridge at the same moment. Between this and the carriage in which the four friends were seated, a clumsy furniture-wagon attempted to pass at the moment when they stopped to show tickets, and in doing so the driver locked his wheel with that of the close-carriage coming over. The friends noticed that there were trunks on the rack of this carriage, and that though the day was so hot and sultry, the windows were closed. As the wheels locked, one of the windows was dashed down with some petulance, and a head appeared through it, while a sharp, strong voice cried:

"Why the d—l don't you drive on?"

Both Tom Leslie and Walter Harding recognized the face and voice of Dexter Ralston. The latter, glancing at the figures in the landau, observed Leslie, and made a sign of recognition. By this time the wheel was cleared, Ralston again shut the window sharply, and the carriage dashed away at full speed towards the custom-house on which "V.R." is displayed for the benefit of those who never tread upon British soil to see it more liberally distributed.

"There he is again!" said Leslie to Harding.

"And apparently going away, by the trunks on the rack," replied Harding.

"Who is it?" asked John Crawford.

"An odd character, about whom we will tell you by-and-bye," said Tom Leslie. "He is a Southerner, but he must have been born in a *very* hot climate, to need the windows closed on such a day as this."

"And he must be in a hurry," said Harding, "by his impatience and the speed at which the carriage drove away."

They drove slowly over the bridge and then hurried back towards the Cataract. It was nearly two o'clock when they reached the house, and the riders and strollers had come back from their various wanderings and filled the halls and parlors, chatting, looking at the stereoscopic views arranged for the destruction 'of eyes, and waiting for dinner. As the four friends entered the hall after dismissing the carriage, they were met by Bell Crawford, who seemed to have been looking out for them from the head of the stairs—her face pale, her voice thick and troubled, and her general appearance frightened and "flustered."   ·

"What is the matter?" asked Richard Crawford, who had, even in that short space of exposure to the outer air, so much improved that fatigue rather made him fresher than otherwise, and who might even then have been called "almost a well man."

"She is gone!" cried Bell, drawing John and Richard, and the others insensibly following, into an unoccupied corner of the parlor, which was, however, vacated the moment after, in answer to the dinner-call.

"Who is gone?" asked John Crawford, alarmed.

"Marion Hobart—gone—gone away. Oh, what can it all mean?" said poor Bell, almost distracted with trouble and wonder.

"Marion Hobart gone? gone where—gone how?" asked John, grasping Bell by the arm with his one unwounded hand.

"I do not know—oh, I am half crazy!" said the poor girl. "All that I know is, that she has left this house in such a manner that she evidently never means to return to it."

"My God!" said John. "My oath!—I swore to take care of her! Tell me, quick, what is it that has happened?"

"I will tell you all that I know," said poor Bell, "only give me time and do not frighten me any worse if you can help it. You know Marion was unwell, and that she went up-stairs and lay down on her bed. Her room is up yonder on the next floor, number Fifteen, very near the head of the stairs. Mine is number Sixteen, adjoining. She lay on the bed, and I sat beside her, chatting with her, though she seemed to speak wildly and as if frightened. After a while she seemed drowsy and appeared to wish to go to sleep. I thought I would leave her alone, then, for a little while, to sleep; and

I took my book and went out on the little balcony at the end of that corridor. I was reading 'John Brent,' and I suppose I got crazy over the galloping horses going down to Luggernel Alley, for I read for perhaps an hour without hearing or seeing anything else than the things in my book. Then I went back to Marion's room—it was not an hour ago—and she was gone!"

"But she may have gone down on the Island—she is a strange little mortal—she may be out on the balcony over the rapids. What makes you think that she is *gone*, as you call it?" asked John, terribly excited, while all the others listened with strange interest.

"Oh," said Bell, "I know that she is gone for good" [*Americanice*, "finally"] "and I knew it the moment I entered her room. Her large trunk was gone—the one you bought her the other day, John; her clothing was gone—everything."

"Astonishing!" said Richard Crawford.

"This beats romance!" said Tom Leslie.

"It just beats the *d—ll*" said John Crawford, who must be excused for using such words in the presence of a lady,—because he was only a rough soldier. "And that is all you know, is it, sister?"

"No," answered Bell Crawford. "I know a good deal more, and it is all worse and worse. I got the chambermaid to enquire, and she found that a tall man came with a close carriage—"

"A tall man? a close carriage?" almost gasped Tom Leslie, though he only spoke to Walter Harding. "Do you hear what she says? This was a Virginian girl—he is a Virginian—his being here this morning—over the Suspension Bridge—those trunks on the rack—by George, Harding—don't you see?"

"But what could *he* have been to *her?*" asked Harding, who did not yet see it in the same clear light.

Bell Crawford had meanwhile gone on with her story.— "That the tall man went up-stairs, asking one of the waiters for number Fifteen, and that five minutes afterwards he came down with a very small lady, dressed for travelling, ordered

down the baggage from that room, put her into the carriage
and got in himself after throwing a dollar to the waiter who
brought down the trunks ; and that then the carriage drove
rapidly away towards the Bridge."

"By George, I knew it!" said Tom Leslie, this time so
loudly that all could hear him. All turned to him in surprise.

"What do you mean ?" asked Richard Crawford.

"That I believe I know the man who has taken away this
girl!" answered Tom Leslie.

"And I believe that *I* do, *now*," said Walter Harding, at last
fairly convinced.

"Stop," said Bell. "There was one thing I forgot to tell
you. She had evidently left in great haste, and two or three
little things were left scattered around the room. Here are
two of them, that I picked up and put in my pocket—one of
her tiny little shoes, and this locket. The locket I have before seen in her possession. She seemed to be sorry that I
had seen it, as I accidentally did, and said that it was the portrait of a dear friend of her family." She took out a little
slipper, scarcely too large for an ordinary child of ten years,
yet retaining the mould of the graceful atom of foot that had
rested warm within it ; and with it she took out the enamelled
locket we have before seen, and handed it to the gentlemen.
Tom Leslie grasped it with an almost frantic haste and threw
it open.

"Dexter Ralston!" he cried. "Look, Harding ! It is all
explained ! I know, now, why he haunted this house, and
what the sharp cry meant when he crossed the hall this
morning ! Don't you see !"

They did see, as little by little, while the dinner-dishes were
rattling in the dining-room adjoining, Tom Leslie explained
to his wondering auditors (Harding only excepted—who
yawned and was hungry) so much of the antecedents and
character of the strange Virginian as could bear any relation
to the abduction—though abduction it could not be properly
called. That that singular and commanding man and that
equally singular mere child had been friends, perhaps lovers,
was evident ; that they had fled away, with the girl's consent,
beyond the hope of successful pursuit, was equally evident:

and here the mystery for the time shut completely down, and they knew no more.

But what was it that Mazeppa said, through the lips of his self-appointed spokesman, Byron, of the impossibility of escaping the patient search and long vigil of the man seeking revenge for wrong? He might have cited another motive, less fierce but quite as powerful—*curiosity!* *Job Thornberry* may give up his search for the name of the destroyer of his daughter, and allow her to break her heart in quiet; but not so *Paul Pry*, who needs a full explanation of the scandal for retail purposes. John Crawford, in spite of the oath which he could now no longer keep, might possibly have allowed the mystery to rest here, had not Tom Leslie, who had sworn no oath whatever, been in his way. Balked in New York and mystified everywhere, the latter gentleman determined to know more—or less! John Crawford only needed this companionship; and an hour after the discovery of the abduction, the two once more whirled over into Canada, possibly on a longer ride than the one they had just concluded.

----◆----

CHAPTER XXVIII.

The Sequel at West Falls—Colonel Crawford's Flight, and How it was Accounted For—Josephine Harris's Return to New York, and Her Disappointment—Another Conspiracy.

THE length to which this narration, involving the fortunes of so many different persons, has already extended, renders it necessary that some of the succeeding incidents should be passed over with great rapidity and in some instances even grouped together without order or arrangement.

Were the opportunity otherwise, a forcible picture might be drawn of the events at West Falls, following the departure of Colonel Egbert Crawford and the discovery of his flight through the means of one of the farm-hands who had seen him driving rapidly away towards Utica. Nearly an hour after his departure had elapsed, before Mary Crawford was aware of it; and naturally her first step, on being informed that he had left the village, was to run up to his chamber. She knocked at the half-open door, her heart beating with as much anxiety for *fear* the knock should be answered, as many another heart has beaten in fear that such a signal would *not* meet a response. But there was no reply. She flung the door timidly open, and went in. Everything in the apartment remained as she had arranged it in the morning for (as she supposed) her own bridal chamber. The Colonel's valise and some portions of his clothing, had not been removed, and this seemed to render impossible the supposition that he had really left the village. But his sudden absence *at all*, after what had occurred, gave ground to believe that some extraordinary movement had really been made; and on the little table, after a moment, the young girl discovered the note to Josephine Harris, directed under her own care. It was sealed, and even had it not been, propriety would have prevented her ascertaining the contents; but the very fact of there being such a reply left, for *her* to deliver, told that the shot must have sped home, and that the expected bridegroom had indeed fled from his bridal.

How the young girl managed to walk to her own room and once more array herself for the street, with that dizzy sensation in her head, half of joy, half of fright—how she silently and swiftly quitted the house again, and made her way through the blazing afternoon sunshine, once more to the little house of Mrs. Halstead,—she will probably never know. People have walked in dreams, and others have done acts while under the influence of *waking* sleep, for which they were scarcely responsible. It is enough to say that at three o'clock that afternoon Josephine Harris was aroused from the sound slumber by which her sick-headache was being rapidly cured—once more to receive the young girl, whom she had little expected to see so soon.

When she descended the stairs, she found Mary Crawford standing alone within the door of the sitting-room, Susan,

who had admitted her, having shown the innate delicacy of
the good by retiring with only a kind word and a sisterly kiss.
The moment Josephine entered the room and saw Mary
standing there, her eyes full of unnatural brightness, her
cheeks all aglow with excitement like that of fever, and her
glorious auburn hair rudely dishevelled under her gipsy hat,—
she knew that her own effort had not failed—that surprise,
and not disappointment, was the feeling written upon that
speaking face.

Without a word Mary Crawford threw herself into Joe
Harris's arms, then slid slowly to her knees, holding her arms
still around the stranger of only a few hours before, now
dearer and more precious to her than any sister could ever
have been. At length she recovered herself sufficiently to
thrust one hand into the bosom of her dress, take out the
note, and hold it out to Joe, with the pleading words :

"Read! read! do read and tell me what he has done !"

"Why, you dear girl, how agitated you are !" said Josephine, stooping down and kissing her on the forehead.
"This letter for me, and from *him?* Stop—answer me one
question—has he gone ?"

"He has gone !" spoke the young girl, almost with a gasp.

A veritable cry of joy escaped Joe Harris. Often defeated and not seldom misunderstood, she knew then that she
had succeeded in the boldest and most erratic act of her life ;
and that moment of triumph was worth years of ordinary
existence.

"He has gone ! you are saved ! Don't cry or tremble, pet,
for it is all right—I know it ! See here !" and she tore open
the note with such an expression of gladness as some heroine
of old may have vented when she rushed in with her father's
or her husband's pardon, at the very moment when the axe
was depending above his head.

Josephine Harris's eyes had run rapidly over the brief note.
She extended it to Mary:

"See ! it is as I told you !"

Mary Crawford clutched the note in her hand, staggered to
her feet, and attempted to read. But she only saw a few
words—heart and brain had been overtasked—and with

a low moaning cry she sunk fainting into the arms of Josephine.

The hurrying feet of little Susy responsive to Joe's sudden call—the glass of cool water from the well that in a moment touched Mary Crawford's lips and sparkled on her forehead—these were the things of a moment. That which had a memory in it, worthy to endure for all time, was the return of recollection to the young girl, and the fervency with which she threw herself again into Josephine's arms, embracing her almost painfully, and saying, over and over again:

"Oh, you dear good friend! God bless you! God bless you!"

Mary Crawford was back at home again within the hour, happier than she had been for many a long day, and after a few moments more of earnest conversation with Josephine, too sacred for revelation. It may be believed that she who had gone so far for the young girl's happiness and that of her "brother" Richard, would not falter now in finishing her task; and the truth is that had she had no benevolence extending further, she had the fox-hunter's anxiety to be "in at the death," and the feminine fancy for her own peculiar "reward," which could only be obtained at the end of the course.

Instructed by the diplomatic Joe on one particular point, the moment she reached her own house again Mary Crawford despatched a messenger to inform Domine Rodgers that his services would not be needed that evening for the marriage, as Colonel Crawford had been called to Albany by telegraph, at a moment's notice, on government business. It seemed idle to attempt, in her father's senile and helpless condition, to make him acquainted with the real circumstances of the case; and so Joe's suggestion was carried much further than she had intended, and the old man and all the household were led to the same understanding, with the additional belief that the Colonel had left so suddenly as only to make Mary his confidant, after the arrival of a special (imaginary) messenger from the telegraph-office at Utica.

Old John Crawford seemed a little disappointed, and weary of waiting for the final arrangement of his family affairs;

but he had not life enough left in him to make his disappointment very painful, and Mary, inspired with a new hope which gave her energy to brave almost anything, trusted to something in a coming day which might enable her to remove that disappointment entirely. So that somewhat eventful day closed upon the Crawford mansion and upon the humbler one near it which had that day exercised so powerful an influence on the fortunes of its inmates.

Here again it is necessary to pass on with unamiable if not inexcusable rapidity, omitting any details of the time remaining of Josephine Harris's visit at West Falls. When the city girl went up to that place, she had considered her stay there likely to extend to at least a week and possibly to twice that period. But her errand had been done so much sooner than she could have expected, and she was so unwilling to communicate with Richard in any other way than personally, with reference to affairs at West Falls and her own action in the matter,—that within an hour after Mary Crawford had left the house the second time, her visit was really over. That is, the *heart* in her visit was gone. The shade and the quiet might be very pretty and pleasant, and precisely what she could have enjoyed for a month under other circumstances; but her restless brain was too busy to make rest possible until all was done. Aunt Betsey's cares and little Susan's attentions, joined with the society of the calf, the pigs and the chickens (with occasional excursions into the cherry trees) enabled her to wear through Monday. But every glance that she caught of the big house on the hill, reminded her that Richard Crawford was lying (as she supposed) a discouraged invalid, while she had a draught of hope at her command that might be put to his pale lips and furnish him with new life.

With the daybreak of Tuesday the robins woke her, and she slept no more. Anxiety and restlessness had conquered, and not even the expectation of receiving a letter from Tom Leslie that day (how enraged that gentleman might have been, had he only known it!) could detain her longer. Aunt Betsey plead and Susan pouted and scolded; but the laws of the Medes and Persians were not more irrevocable than some of

Miss Josey's notions; and promising to come again if possible before the summer was over, and exacting a promise
from Susy to forward to her address in New York any letters
that might come for her from her *cousin* at Niagara (sly-
boots !)—she flitted away. The morning stage from West
Falls took her down to Utica; and the train at the Thirty-
second Street Station at New York, that evening, landed her
at home again, dustier even than when she went North, and
this time alone, except as pleasant thoughts may have been
her companions. Long before midnight she burst in upon
good Mrs. Harris, with a fearful jangling of carriage-steps
and ringing of door-bells, leading that lady to believe, at first,
that she had been brought home in a sick or dying condition.
But the maternal embrace was warm, those red lips had never
forgotten the kiss of dear love and confidence upon those that
had first caressed her when she came into the world; and odd,
wild, erratic Joe had a habit which many people with more
opportunities have managed to escape—that of being *always
welcome.*

It was of course too late, that night, for any conference
with Richard Crawford. But the next morning, before nine
o'clock, his house was treated to a repetition of the same
ringing of bells that had sounded in her own the night before,
and Joe, all breathless eagerness (another one of the bad
habits of her childhood, that she had never been able to overcome) stood talking in the hall with the domestic who had
admitted her. Much good her hurry had done ! Much good
was it for her to fly hither and yon, transacting business for
invalids ! Some persons run away from happiness—do they
not ?—as others try to escape from known misery ! Richard
Crawford and his companions were then two hours up the
Hudson, on their way to Niagara ! Crawford was going
to pass West Falls, within a few hours, so near it and yet
ignorant of all that had occurred !

To say that Joe Harris raved at this announcement, might
be too strong a word. But it is not too much to say that her
springy foot (Joe had not the proverbially "little" one of the
novelists, but a very well-shaped pedal of the Arab pattern,
under the sole of which water could have run with as much

freedom as under the Starucca Viaduct or the High Bridge);
patted the ball floor with vexation, impatience and "botheration." There was not much use in blurting out her vexation
before a servant, but she did say:

." Confound your picture, Dick Crawford! Why did you
not let me know that you were going away?" Which was
not very elegant or very reasonable, especially as wild Josey
had for certain well-known reasons studiously kept away from
the house for some days before leaving for the North, and still
more especially because she had so concealed the direction of
her own journey that Dick Crawford could not have communicated with her if he had tried never so earnestly.

Then and thereupon Joe Harris turned about indignantly
and went to the door. Then she changed her mind, went into
the deserted parlor, opened the piano and banged away upon
it for a few minutes as if she was taking the physical revenge
of a drubbing. on the whole Crawford family. If Dick Crawford could have heard *that* performance, he would have gone
mad to a certainty! Then she flung to the piano with a slam
(forgive her, Steinway!—it was not your piano that she was
abusing, but an imaginary owner) and flung herself out of the
house so precipitately that Bridget only heard the violent shutting of two doors and knew nothing more.

By the time she had reached her own house again, the young
girl was somewhat calmer and a great deal more reasonable.
The fault was not that of Richard Crawford, after all; and
God bless him!—she was heartily glad that he had recovered
sufficiently to be able to leave the house for a ride of four
or five hundred miles. So she summoned back all the patient
and benevolent elements of her own nature (she had plenty
of them, but they were sometimes like badly-trained troops,
and needed a *recall*),—sat down and wrote a letter to Richard,
giving him a brief account of what had occurred, abusing him
playfully for going off without informing her of his intention,
and ordering him to West Falls immediately, in such terms
as a commander-in-chief might have employed towards a recruiting sergeant. That done, and the letter despatched, she
felt partially relieved.

But what a fool she had made of herself—she thought—by

leaving West Falls so soon! Neither her mother nor herself was yet ready to leave for Newport (she much less than her mother, until certain half-finished arrangements, in which Mr Tom Leslie bore a part, were more satisfactorily settled); the city was growing dull as well as hot, and most of the "people one cares for," flitting to one or another of the sea-shore or mountain resorts; and there were the pigs and chickens at Aunt Betsey's all lying neglected. Joe Harris was nearer to being *ennuyeé*—absolutely bored, for the next hour, than she had before been for a twelvemonth

There is an old adage that some of us may have read in the primer (or was it the hymn-book?) that "Satan finds some mischief still for idle hands to do." · Josephine's late life had been sufficiently exciting to make her undeniably restless; and it was while ruminating upon the misery of being too quietly happy, that she remembered her rencoutre with Emily Owen, at Wallack's, the magnificently bearish manner in which Judge Owen had lugged his daughter out from the theatre, and the promise she had made the mortified and abashed girl that she would run up and call upon her some day. Why not now? Not much sooner thought of than done; and in less than an hour thereafter she was ringing at the door of Judge Owen's house near the Harlem River, having endured the smashing of toes and disorder of dresses incident to a ride by car on a hot afternoon when half the city was rushing to the Central Park and the cool places over in Westchester.

She had better fortune, here, than she had experienced at the Crawfords'. Emily was at home, sewing by the open window in her little chamber, while by the other window of the same room showed the tall figure and placid face of Aunt Martha. The meeting between the two school-mates was very warm and cordial, and accompanied by those embraces which, when they occur between two young girls and an unfortunate masculine friend happens to be an observer, are so likely to destroy his equanimity for a long period. Emily's cheek reddened a little, to be sure, with shame at remembering where she had last met her visitor; but perhaps this evidence of sensibility broke down all barriers between the two, much easier than they could have been removed

under other circumstances. Josephine Harris had accidentally become aware of the one secret of Emily's life, and so
long as warm friendship existed this fact could not be otherwise than a tie, just as it could not fail to be a cause for
avoidance if the two hearts once became separated. Aunt
Martha, something of an oddity among women, and Joe
Harris, an oddity without any qualification, were pleased
with each other at once; and a pleasant chat sprung up in
the little room, which lasted until Aunt Martha thought it
proper to make an excuse for absence and leave the young
girls alone together.

It would have been something more or less than natural, if
within a minute afterwards the conversation of the two had
not been running upon the topic of which both had been thinking, but of which neither would speak before the third person.
Josephine broke into the theme at once:

"Who was he?"

"Who was *who?*" and the face of pretty Emily Owen was
red enough in a moment to show that she knew who was intended.

"Oh, you know that I saw part of it," said Joe. "I want
to know the rest. Who was the young man from whom your
father took you away? A lover, of course, or he would not
have taken the trouble."

"It was—it was—Frank—Mr. Frank Wallace," said the
young girl, the color on her face by no means diminishing.

"Oh, don't blush so," said Josey. "We all get into some
such scrape, at one time or another—that is, so many of us
as can find any one to form the other half of the pair of scissors. He was your lover, of course?"

"You are a strange girl, and you ask such odd questions!"
said Emily. Then, looking into the face of Josephine, and
seeing how true and earnest, in spite of their mischief, were
the eyes bent upon her, she added: "But I *do* remember how
good and kind you were to me at school, and I *will* tell you
all about it!"

"That's a dear!" said diplomatic Josey, and only casting
down her eyes a little and blushing occasionally, Emily Owen
told the story of her love and her persecutions—of her

father's pride and prejudice—of Aunt Martha's sympathy—of
the relations borne towards the family by the young printer
and Col. Bancker—and of the unpleasant affairs which had
already occurred, culminating in that outrage at the theatre,
since which time (not many days, however,) the lovers had
had no meeting.

"Why, it is as good as a play!" said Joe, when her friend
had finished her relation, and thinking, at the same time, how
there was an unaccountable something in her own fortune or
character, which drew her into acquaintance with so much
that was dramatic in the lives of others.

"I am afraid you think me very weak and silly," said
Emily. "You *must* do so, unless—unless—"

"Oh, I understand you!" said Joe. "You mean that I
must think your love silly, unless I happen to be in love
myself?"

"Yes, that was what I meant to say," answered the young
girl.

"Oh, make yourself easy on that point!" said the incarnate mischief. "It has not been very long under way, but
I have picked up a *fellow*."

"Oh, I am so glad! Then I know that you will understand me!" answered Emily.

"I understand you, and I do not think you silly at all,"
said her mentor. "I saw the young man's face that evening,
and I fancy that he is decidedly good-looking That is something. You say that he is honest, industrious and *brave:*
that is a good deal more. Then you love him, and that is of
much more consequence still. Never marry a man whom
you cannot love, my dear, if you remain an old maid so
long that they date from your birth instead of the Christian
era."

Emily Owen looked up for an instant, to see how old this
mentor could be, who talked with the confidence of experience and the gravity of fifty (so much like Aunt Martha) ;
but she met a face very little older than her own, and she
merely said :

.   "I am so glad you think that I am right!"

"You say that you have not seen him since that evening

at Wallack's," said Josephine. "Have you not *heard* from him since?"

"Yes," said Emily, "we—"

"Write?"

"Yes," again said the young girl. "I hope you do not think that is wrong. Frank does not wish to come here, and I do not wish him to come here, possibly to be abused by my father; and so—"

"I wish I knew him," said Josephine, who by this time had some odd idea running through her head. "What is he like? No, I do not mean how he looks, for you know that I saw him for a moment; but what is his disposition? Grave or gay?"

"Gay—very gay, I should think," replied Emily.

"You go to theatres: is he fond of theatrical performances?"

"Very," answered the young girl.

"So far, so good," said Josephine, in whose mind the thought, whatever it was, seemed to be shaping itself with great rapidity. "Now, is he a mimic? Could he play a part if he should attempt it?"

"I should think so," answered Emily. "He is very droll and a great mimic—too much so, I sometimes think. But what do you mean?"

"Why this," said Joe, whose plan had now grown to its full proportions—as odd and reckless a plan as the most *outré* could have wished, but quite consistent with her own sense of benevolent mischief. She had not quite recovered from the influence of her "amateur detective" exploit for the benefit of Richard Crawford, and masquerades seemed to her, for the time, the only realities. Conjoined with the memory of her late exploits as a volunteer detective, was a thought of the very effectual manner in which she had seen Tom Leslie disguise himself on the day of the visit to the fortune-teller; and she had hit upon a plan—nothing more nor less—to introduce the young girl's lover into that house, under her own protection, and in such a disguise that not even the suspicious eyes of Judge Owen could know that they had ever looked at him before! As for any ultimate good

28

to flow from the frolic—it must be confessed that she scarcely thought of it. She did think of throwing the two lovers together, for once or twice, at least, and of playing a prank which he well deserved, upon the imperious and not-over-reasonable Judge—that was all. She did not foresee the real results which were to follow the operation; as which of us ever did, when we began a frolic, imagine what earnest that frolic might become before it was concluded ?

"Why, this is what I mean—a plan that will at least give you an occasional sight of your ' Frank,' that no doubt you think more of than a Congressman of his, and wouldn't lend it to anybody. Scribble him a little note at once, tell him who I am and what I am going to do. Put in this card of mine, so that he can know where to find me. Then tell him to get a soldier's uniform—(say a Captain's) a crutch, a cane, and a green patch for one eye, and come to my house to-morrow afternoon. No—if he only gets the crutch and the cane, I will make the patch for his eye, to-night. You are not going out anywhere to-morrow evening ?"

"No," answered the young girl, a little bewildered by such an arrangement.

"Then I will bring him up to-morrow evening, equipped in that manner, and introduce him as my cousin, Captain—Captain—Captain—what shall I call him ?—Captain Robert Slivers—that will be a good name enough—of the Sickles Brigade, wounded in one of the late battles and home on furlough. Don't you think that will do, dear ?"

"I should like it, of all things in the world," said Emily Owen, "if I was only sure that they would not know him. But no—to-morrow evening will not do ! I remember hearing that hateful Colonel Bancker tell Pa that he was coming again to-morrow evening."

"Well, all that is none the worse," said the schemer. "If the gallant Colonel is as old as you think, his eyes cannot be any sharper than other people's ; and if your Frank Wallace is half smart enough to deserve such a pretty girl as you, he can manufacture some war stories that will do the Colonel good."

"But I am afraid—" again began Emily.

"Afraid of your shadow !" said the plotter. "There, run away and do as I tell you, and mind that your note goes this afternoon and that you do not forget to put in my card. Stop ! you are not afraid to trust me with him, are you ?"

"Oh, Josephine, you ought to be ashamed to ask such a question !" replied Emily ; and having given that assurance, and being really carried off her feet by the plausible mischief of her friend, she set about performing her part of the arrangement, though not without some question how it would all end, and whether the frolic might not eventually give excuse for additional severity on the part of Judge Owen.

It was agreed between the young girls, before they parted, that the arrival should not take place until evening, when there would be the advantage of gas-light in concealing the personality of the masquerader,—and that Aunt Martha, who had already proved herself too firm and consistent a friend to her niece, to be played falsely with in the matter, should be made acquainted with the whole arrangement, even at the risk of the disapprobation that she was almost certain to express against a proceeding that would certainly be better suited to the stage than the drawing-room.

Having set this mischief on foot and shaken off the ennui which had oppressed her in the morning, Josephine Harris left the house where she had paid so remarkable a first visit, and returned to her own, to astonish her mother with the knowledge of an intended prank somewhat more reckless and outrageous than any upon which she had before ventured.

CHAPTER XXIX.

FIVE MINUTES WITH THE MOONLIGHT—THE LAST SCENE AT
JUDGE OWEN'S—CAPT. SLIVERS, OF THE SICKLES BRIGADE—
TWO RIVALS DISGUISED, AND THE RESULT OF THEIR REN-
CONTRE.

THERE was no terrible portent in the air, hanging over the
city of New York on that Thursday evening the Tenth of July,
to which allusion has before been made as the same on which
Richard Crawford and his companions reached Niagara. On
the contrary, as some of the summer tourists may remember,
that evening was remarkably and even wondrously beautiful.
Not a clearer full moon ever rose than that which beamed
over nearly the whole of the Northern States that night;
and those, especially, who had the privilege of seeing that
moon rise over the brow of Eagle Cliff at the Franconia
Notch of the White Mountains, standing on the plateau in
front of the Profile House and seeing the disk of glittering
silver heaving slowly up beyond the crest, with the great
trees on the summits defined against it so sharply, with the
dark mountain brows frowning and the upturned human faces
radiant in the silver light, and with every aspect and.influence
of the scene something wildly and weirdly beautiful—those
who enjoyed that privilege will not be likely soon to lose the
memory of one of the loveliest nights that ever dropped
down out of heaven. How many souls, in one place and
another, and under influences akin to those we have named,
may have bowed down that night in worship before denied
to the Almighty Hand that, not content with making a world
instinct with life and usefulness, endowed it with such marvellous beauty ! And how many young hearts, before that
hour partial strangers to each other or divided by prudence or by ignorance, standing under that silver sheen may
have acknowledged the influence of the time, melted into
tenderness, and flowed together to be no more separated forever !
  Moonlight is an enchanter as well as a beautifier, and the

old fancy of partial madness when the moon was at the full
(from which the word "lunacy") was not altogether unwarranted by reality.   At sea, in the tropics, a night on deck
under the broad full moon stiffens and entirely maddens, if it
does not kill; here the madness is only partial and it has a
general reference to mischief and the opposite sex; but the
influence is the same, under different degrees of development.

On how many lands and waters is such a broad full moon
shining, and what varied scenes it throws into flickering light
and shadow—the very thought being a part of the permitted
madness of the time!   Think of that strange variety for a
moment.   Far out on the ocean tired sailors throw themselves
under the lee of the bulwarks and gaze up into its face, while
the light plays fantastic tricks among the masts and cordage.
Out of pleasant groves in the country light-robed figures are
flitting, and under that marvellous sheen words are spoken
that would long have been frightened back in the brighter
glare of day—words that may make the happiness or misery
of a lifetime.   Ringing laughter breaks from merry groups
that glance in and out under the shade-trees and the vine-
arbors that surround stately old mansions in the valleys of
wheat and corn.   Rough shouts and loud peals of laughter
break from the rough throats of the raccoon and opossum
hunters in the wild back-woods.   A broken-hearted woman
sits at her chamber-window and gazes out into the weird
atmosphere, thinking of falsehood and sorrow and the incon-
stancy of one year.   Half in the sheen and half in the shadow
lies a little grave, its light and shade fit type of the love and
grief of two who sit on a vine-covered porch and think of the
day when they buried the dear little sleeper.   In the dark
passes of the Apennines lurks a bandit, poniard in hand,
ready to spring on the unwary traveller as he emerges from
the shadow.   On the gardens and jalousies of fair Granada
falls the silver beam, and guitars tinkle and white arms wave
in recognition.   Under the gloom of the palazzo of St. Mark,
at Venice, a gondola is shooting, while the boatman hums a
drowsy air and the lover anxiously watches for the waving
of the white scarf of his mistress.   Cascades leap down the
mountain gorges, unheard of mortal car and unseen by mortal

eye, but scattering their diamond drops in air as a full libation
to the glory of night.   Far away at sea, on a drifting raft, a
sailor eats his last biscuit and smiles sorrowfully back to the
placid face that will look down next night upon his corpse !

All which may have very little to do with this story, and
vet it may be fully warranted by the occasion.   And at least
it is justifiable to say that the full of the moon may have made
Joe Harris madder than usual and readier than ever to indulge in frolics of the most reprehensible character.   What
we began to indicate, especially, was that no portent loomed
in the heavens above the doomed city or even above the
house of Judge Owen, and that still an earthquake was muttering and rumbling under it, destined to tumble it into the
most fatal confusion.

At about half-past eight that evening, a ring at the door
announced visitors.   Judge Owen had not yet returned, but
all the other members of the family, and one who expected to
become a member of the family—of course, Colonel John
Boadley Bancker,—were sitting at that moment in the front
parlor.   For some reason or other, not necessary to be here
explained, Emily went herself to the door and admitted the
visitors.   They proved to be Miss Josephine Harris, who had
just alighted from a carriage at the door, and a male companion in uniform.   Some time elapsed before the military
gentleman, who was introduced to the young hostess as
"Captain Robert Slivers," managed to get over the door-step,
so very lame was he.   But he managed to spare a hand for
one moment from one of his crutches, the instant after; for
Emily, who was half frightened out of her wits and half inclined to burst into uncontrollable laughter, felt a "pinch" on
her arm which nearly made her scream aloud.

The military gentleman hobbed along into the room after
them, and was introduced to the others there assembled.
One of the burners of the chandelier only had been lit, but it
quite sufficed to reveal an extraordinary figure.   Captain
Robert Slivers seemed to be about fifty to fifty-five, to judge
by his gray hair and moustache ; but any idea of the precise
looks of his face was rendered impossible, by an immense
green patch which concealed not only the right eye, but all

that side of the nose and the temple, while the string running around his forehead took away any expression from that important part of the human countenance, and an oblong strip of black court-plaster extended diagonally from the left eye nearly to the corner of the mouth, creating an impression of very severe tattooing. A pair of green spectacles were mounted on the bridge of the nose, and the left glass did duty over the corresponding eye, while the other was unseen as relieved against the shade. So much for the facial appearance and adornments of this hero, and his other claims to notice were not less extraordinary. Sartorially, he wore an undress military cap, with the "U. S." on the front, and a dingy blue uniform with the shoulder-straps of a Captain of infantry. Physically he seemed nearly as much out of order as facially. He carried a heavy cane in his right hand, and the right foot was enclosed in a sort of moccasin or spatterdash which might have belonged to one of the conductors on an avenue railroad, for use in very severe weather. In shoemakers' measurement this foot-gear would probably have been rated about number sixteen. Under the left arm, which was swathed below the elbow, he carried a crutch, and though the foot on that side seemed to be uninjured, the leg had not escaped so fortunately. It was stiffened and drawn up so that the toe merely touched the ground and the principal dependence was made upon the crutch. According to this arrangement, the left leg limped and the right foot shuffled, and the style of locomotion may be imagined.

But for the "pinch," which was a little characteristic, Emily Owen might have had grave doubts, even after the warning of the day before, whether this could be the sprightly young man whom she had known so well; and the very mother who bore him, if she could have seen him in that situation, would have been almost as excusable for not recognizing her offspring, as that traditional matron who defeated all the theories about "intuition" by not recognizing her son when "done up with pepper and onions, in a stew."

This interesting person was finally ushered into the parlor and introduced to the trio sitting there, as well as manœuvered into a chair. Aunt Martha, behind the curtain, was not pre-

vented by her fright at the possible consequences, from nearly
smothering with concealed laughter at the wonderful metamorphosis which had been accomplished. Mrs. Owen, a weak
woman with a soft heart, was dreadfully affected by the
"reality of war" thus brought home to her, and uttered
many ejaculations of pity, carefully under her breath for fear
the "poor fellow" should hear her and be pained.

Colonel Bancker—there is no use disguising the fact—
was literally horrified at the spectacle. A miserable old beau,
with unlimited vanity and a desire to appear everything that
other people admired, but without any other positive personal
vices—he was, as Frank Wallace had always believed, an incarnate, unmitigated poltroon—a coward of the first water.
He never had fought for anything, with hand or weapon—he
never intended to fight for anything—he never *could* fight for
anything. He could not bear to think of being hurt himself,
and he was pained beyond measure at the thought of seeing
any one else injured or in suffering. One hour of the battle-
field, with its sights and sounds of horror, would have killed
him without any aid from sword or bullet. He could have
been robbed in a dark street by a boy of ten years, who presented a knife or a pistol; and in any time of danger to himself or others (as may have been indicated by the adventure
of the carriage before recorded) he could be of no more use
than a baby in arms. Such men are not very common, but
they do exist; and under any ordinary circumstances, as they
cannot help the infirmities with which they are born, they
should be pitied and not ridiculed. It is only when they attempt to disguise themselves in the characters of bolder and
better men, that they deserve lashing without mercy.

Colonel Bancker had never had the least intention of going
to the war, nor had he ever connected himself, except in the
most vague description of talk, with any organization. He
had never come nearer to a commission than to think about
one—that is, think that he did not want one. He saw hundreds of others wearing uniforms and the insignia of rank
without any intention of fighting, and thought that he could
do as they did, sport borrowed plumes without too much enquiry being made into the source whence they were derived,

and throw them off when he pleased, under any excuse which he might choose to invent—sickness, business engagements, or *dissatisfaction with the mode in which the war was being conducted.*

With the before-named dislike to being pained, Colonel Bancker had so far avoided all the painful sights of the war. He had not visited the wounded at the Park Barracks or in any of the hospitals—he had managed to see none of the maimed living and none of the glorious dead—he had even escaped the hungry wives of the soldiers, clamoring for their husbands' pay and the means to buy bread, along the cross-walks of the Park and at the entrances of the City Hall. So far he had escaped easily from what he most dreaded.

But within the last day or two a terrible disquiet had sprung up. The army was to be reinforced and a stringent conscription was talked of. Among the unpleasant rumors in circulation, was one that the Provost-Marshals were to be directed to arrest every man in officer's uniform found in the streets, and if he could exhibit no commission, force him to immediate service in the ranks! Here was a dilemma—a dilemma none the less for having two well-defined horns. His uniform was becoming dangerous, but how give it up? He was determined to win Emily Owen, and he had discovered that one of his strongest claims to the favor of her pig-headed father lay in the wearing of that very uniform and pretending to be a soldier. To give it up was to acknowledge that he had no intention of joining the army, and perhaps to lose all. No—he *must* stick to those dangerous insignia of war, at least until he had accomplished his grand purpose, and then—. But they made him uncomfortable—very uncomfortable.

It was under such circumstances that Captain Robert Slivers, of the Sickles Brigade, came under his notice that evening, and he was horrified to see what wrecks war really made of men. One eye gone—a face cut to pieces—crippled in one leg, one arm and one foot—good heavens! For the moment the fright of such a spectacle almost overcame every other consideration, and Emily Owen and all her material charms became secondary to the thought of being placed beyond the danger of becoming a thing like *that!*

To add to the Colonel's horror, Captain Slivers seemed to take a decided fancy to him, and edged along his chair, the best he could do in his crippled condition, until he had brought it into very close juxtaposition to that of the Colonel ; while the four ladies, conversing together, formed a circle of their own a little in the background. It may be said, here, that Frank Wallace, even through his one green spectacle-glass, had seen and recognized the disgust and terror on the face of the Colonel, and that he had determined to dose him thoroughly with such flippant horrors as his fertile imagination could readily manufacture for the occasion, but such as no battle-field on earth has ever had much chance of witnessing.

Near as they had been brought together, and inviting as was the chance for conversation between two members of the same profession, the gallant Colonel did not seem disposed to enter upon it with so fearful an object as the Captain. The latter was obliged to commence the attack, after all.

"Very glad to meet a brother in arms," said the pseudo-Captain, in an assumed bass, taking up his cane and giving a slight punch to the Colonel, who seemed pre-occupied.

"Oh ! ah ! yes, very glad, to be sure," answered the Colonel, who scarcely knew whether he was talking English or Choctaw at that moment. Then partially recovering himself and remembering that something in the shape of conversation must be carried on, he said : "Very pretty girl that—cousin of yours, didn't they say, Captain ? What is her name ?"

"Eh ?" said the Captain. "Oh, my cousin yonder? yes, Miss Harris, Miss Joe Harris—daughter of Mrs. Harris." It is supposed that in the latter name he alluded to a somewhat doubtful character of Charles Dickens. "Devil of a girl, Colonel, I tell you !"

"Ah, what do you mean ?" asked the Colonel.

"Mean ? why I mean that when I came home two or three days ago, she seemed rather glad than otherwise to see that I had been cut up. Stuck her finger in my eye, or rather in the place where my eye had been, to see whether they had made a clean operation of it, and nearly broke that bone of my left arm again, trying to discover whether they had set it entirely straight. Said I must have been a splendid subject in the hospital. Devil of a girl—going into one of the hospitals to nurse, directly. Says that she is never happy except she has a few broken limbs, and smashed heads, and gunshot wounds through the body, and holes made by Minie bullets, under her especial care."

"Horrible!" gasped the Colonel, who could no longer sit silent under such a revelation of female character

"Yes, it *is* a little horrible, but a fact, though!" said the Captain. "Devil of a girl, I tell you! I believe that she would just as lieve see my head amputated as not, provided she could stand by and witness a 'beautiful operation.'"

"I say this is dreadful!" said the Colonel.

"Dreadful, of course," said the Captain. "Still, nothing when you once get used to it. Plenty of women just like her —all female devils, though they manage to conceal the fact, sometimes, until they get a man under their thumbs, especially for the purpose of practising on him. But we *want* women who have some nerve, for these bloody times. Don't you think so, Colonel?"

"Yes—I can't say—that is, really I don't know!" answered the Colonel, who did not at that particular moment, know much else than that he was a little sick at the stomach and that the whole world seemed to be a kind of hideous mockery.

"Oh yes, fact!" continued the Captain, who saw the white face and did not intend that it should regain any fresher color, in a hurry. "Bloody times, I tell you, Colonel! Make me think, sometimes, when the dead are lying in heaps around me and the blood running like small brooks, of that time prophesied for the Valley of Armageddon, when the blood is to run deep enough to reach to the horse-bridles."

"Captain," said the Colonel, "really I would rather—"

"Rather that I should talk about the present war, than anything in Scripture? of course—very natural and quite correct. Let me see—you were not at Fair Oaks, were you?"

"No," said the Colonel, emphatically.

"No, I suppose not," continued the pseudo-Captain. "Well, you ought to have been there—that is all! Highest old fight that any man ever heard of. When we went into battle

we had not had a wink of sleep for ten nights, but I tell you
that it kept us wide awake while it lasted! In the middle of
the day the air was so thick with bullets and shells that it
seemed to be as dark as twilight, and the blood at one time
made such a river down one of the gulleys that dozens of men
and horses were drowned in it!"

"Oh, this is too much!" gasped the Colonel, who thought
of getting up and running away, anywhere beyond the sound
of the voice of this sanguinary madman.

"Too much? of course it was too much!" echoed the veracious narrator. "But who could help it? Couldn't have so
many dead men, you know, without plenty of blood! At one
time there were so many of our fellows lying in a long win-
row near the top of the hill, that when the rebels made an
advance we punched holes through the wall of corpses and
used them for breast-works."

The Colonel made an effort to stagger to his feet, but his
nerves were too terribly unstrung to allow him that escape.
He sunk back upon his chair in a state of partial syncope,
aware that the terrible fellow was talking, and that he must
be *lying,* but that there might be truth enough at the base of
his stories to make them a fearful warning to all who had
ever thought of tempting the field.

"Talk about the *chances* of war!" the incorrigible romancer
went on—"there was no chance about it, in such a fight as
that at Fair Oaks or at Gaines' Mills! We went into Fair
Oaks nine hundred and eighty-four strong, and came out *four*
—three men and one officer! *I* was the officer. I only had
one Minie bullet through the left breast, too high to do much
harm, two bullets in the left leg and right foot, my left arm
broken by a fragment of shell and my right eye punched out
by another   That was all that ailed *me!*"

"Heavens! heavens!" was all that the stupified Colonel
could articulate.

"Yes," continued the Captain, "think of being obliged to
fight like that on two meals a week, the meals consisting of
boiled horse and mouldy crackers, drinking the same swamp
water you have been standing in all day! And I suppose
you think that our regiment lost heavily, Colonel? Eh?

Well, you are mistaken! We had the crack regiment and scarcely suffered at all, in comparison with some of the others. They took a tally the day before I left, and found eight sound eyes, twelve legs that were good for anything, and six usable arms, in the whole division."

"Oh good Lord! he will kill me!" cried the Colonel, starting at last to his feet and utterly unable to endure such torture one moment longer.

By this time Frank Wallace, carried away by the excitement of the lies he had already vented, and observing how horrified he had succeeded in making his auditor, began to get a little reckless, and concluded that it was time to play the indignant. The ladies had been in conversation on the opposite side of the room, the elder members delighted with the new acquaintance to whom Emily had introduced them in Josephine ; and though it may be supposed that at least two of them kept their regards pretty closely directed to the "military" corner of the room, much of the past conversation had been carried on in so subdued a tone as to be drowned by their own. What followed, however, they could not very well avoid hearing.

As the Colonel staggered to his feet and attempted to get away, the pseudo-Captain managed to crutch-and-cane himself to a standing position and confronted his superior.

"That last remark was offensive!" he said, speaking so that all in the room could hear him.

"What is offensive? What do you mean, sir?" asked the poor Colonel, now having thorough surprise added to his other emotions.

"Why this, sir?" cried the Captain, letting his big cane come down on the floor with such a thump as he had observed at the hands of enraged East Indian uncles and heavy fathers in old comedies. "You said in so many words, sir, that I was a bore and a humbug, and I do not take that from any man, sir!"

"I said nothing of the kind!" disclaimed the Colonel, who certainly had not used any such expression.

"What did you mean, then, sir, by the offensive expression : 'Good Lord! he will kill me!' I have not fought for nothing,

sir! J know what such words mean, and I would fight any
man who used them, if I had only one arm and no leg to
stand on!"

"Captain Slivers," said the Colonel, "you are unreasonable!"

"There he goes! another insult!" cried the disabled soldier, partially appealing to the ladies. Under any other circumstances than those just then existing, either or all the
four would have made some attempt to prevent what they
believed would eventuate in an outright quarrel; but Mrs.
Owen, as the hostess, did not like to interfere with the right
of a guest to quarrel or even to fight, if he thought proper to
do so, and neither of the others dared say a word for fear of
forcing a betrayal of the disguise.

"Well, then," said the Colonel, who had spirit enough,
sometimes, as we have before seen, to grow angry and be even
threatening when he saw no personal danger before him. "If
you do not like that, I will say something more. You are
either crazy or drunk, Captain Slivers, and I do not know or
care which!"

"I will fight you to-morrow, cripple as I am!" cried the
Captain, while the ladies had now all risen to their feet in
real alarm. Then, as if suddenly recollecting: "Stop! no, 1
will punish you in another way. You wear a Colonel's uniform—where is your regiment, sir? I will make you join it
to-morrow and march within the week. Every regiment in
the city is to be ordered off at once. See if I have not influence enough with my uncle, the Governor, to send *you*
packing!"

"*Find* my regiment first—*find* it, sir!" said the Colonel,
now fairly (and reasonably) exasperated beyond any recollection of what he was saying.

"Ah!—h!—h!" cried the Captain with one of those tones
of stage exultation which he had so often heard proclaiming
the final triumph of the villain or the discovery of that lost
will which was to restore the flagging fortunes of persecuted
virtue. "Ah!—h!—h! now I *have* got you! You have
no commission, you do not belong to any regiment, and you
are subject to the draft that is already ordered! Do you hear

me ?—the *draft!* the *draft!*" and he howled it out towards
the Colonel as if he suspected him of a very material failure
in his sense of hearing.

Achilles had his vulnerable heel, and there are times in the
lives of each of us when the arrow of accident, harmless at
all other periods, can enter and ruin. Colonel Bancker had
kept his secret, or believed that he had kept it, inviolate; but
his fatal moment had come. Whether really frightened out
of all recollection at the thought of that terrible "draft"
which has already twice re-peopled Canada* at the expense
of the population of the United States, or whether exultant
beyond bounds at the knowledge that he could escape it, by
his age, in spite of them all,—he uttered the fatal word, oblivious that Judge Owen stood angry and astonished at the
parlor door, and that others to whom he had so roundly sworn
that he was only thirty-two, were within hearing:

"You meddling fool!—what can that draft do to *me?* I
am exempt by age!"

"It is false! it is false!" cried the pseudo-Captain, driving
the victim to the wall more closely than even *he* knew. "You
are not an exempt, and the Governor shall take care of *you.*"

"It is a lie!" yelled the Colonel, now incensed beyond all
recollection of time, place or auditors. "I am fifty-four!"

"Fifty-four!" There seemed to be a chorus of that compound word coming from the group of ladies; and even
Judge Owen, who had been so solemnly assured that his intended son-in-law was more than twenty years younger, could
not avoid joining in the astonished exclamation: "Fifty-
four!"

But the climax had not yet been reached. There had long
been a suspicion which almost amounted to a certainty, in
the mind of Frank Wallace, with reference to one point of
the gallant Colonel's personal adornment; and he was now
quite enough carried away by the reckless mischief of his
nature, to determine that that suspicion should be verified or
disproved.

"Fifty-four?" echoed the scapegrace. "Impossible! No

* March 20th, 1863.

Commissioner will believe any such story! Look at your
hair—not a thread of gray in it! Bah!" and before the Colonel
could make any effectual attempt to prevent the movement,
the Captain had allowed his cane to fall to the floor and made
a sudden and determined grab at the head-covering of the
man of exempt years.   Any *effectual* attempt to prevent the
movement, it has been said: he did make an attempt to prevent it, however, as with a newly-awakened consciousness of
danger.   The only result of this sudden throwing out of his
hands and scrambling with them, was that they came in sudden and violent contact with the head-covering and facial
adornments of the pseudo-Captain, and that before any one
else in the room could become fully aware of what had happened, the green patch, the green spectacles and gray wig
which had metamorphosed the young man were all cleared
away, and the curly head and bright face of Frank Wallace,
printer and mischief-maker, stood fully revealed.

But it must be recorded that at that moment no one saw
him.   All eyes were turned in another direction, and yet one
not very far removed.   The sudden and vigorous jerk of the
young man, which had been so determinedly guarded against,
had yet produced its effect.   In his hand he held a dark mass
of hair, at the moment that his own pushed-off incumbrances
tumbled to the floor; and a state of affairs was revealed on
the cranium of the Colonel, for which not more than one of
the company, or possibly two, could have been in the least
degree prepared.   What Virginia would have been, if cleared
of all its woods and swamps and made into fair fighting-ground,
and what Virginia is, with all its woods and swamps, while
the Union soldiers fight over it at so terrible a disadvantage
—may fitly present the contrast between Colonel John Boadley Bancker's head as it was and as it had been supposed.
Not a spear of hair on it, from forehead to spine, so far as the
eye could see by gas-light; and the head one of those fearful
botches of nature when not over-well instructed in her work,
—with the forehead retreating like the roof of a house, and
the skull coming to a dull point at the top, like the end of a
gigantic cucumber, and glossy and yellow like that cucumber
ripening for seed!   The total baldness of the head was bad

enough, under the circumstances (especially for thirty-two!)
but the *shape* of that head!—oh father of that man, what right
had you to visit your own sins upon a succeeding generation
in such a manner?

The reception of this revelation was as varied, at first, as
the characters of those who received it. Frank Wallace was
so astounded at the extraordinary success of his manœuvre,
and at the same time at his own detection, that he dropped
crutch and cane, allowed his sham wounded leg to straighten,
and stood holding the wig in his hand as if he had no power
to lay it down. Mrs. Owen screamed, that seeming to be the
duty of hospitality when such a breach of good manners had
been committed in her parlor. Josephine Harris paled, flushed,
and finally fell back into a chair in such convulsions of laughter that she cried like a child. Emily Owen tried to look
grave, but looked at Joe and soon followed her lead. Aunt
Martha happened to have her handkerchief in her hand, and
stuffed it into her mouth so tightly that she came near suffocating. Judge Owen still stood in the door-way, his face ju-
dicially severe and portentous, as if he felt that some awful
desecration had been committed, for which the full severity of
the criminal law could scarcely be an adequate punishment.

Not an instant, however, before the two young girls found
recruits for their "forward movement." Aunt Martha's handkerchief flew from her mouth, and she laughed from cap to
slipper. Mrs. Owen, thus deserted by her reserve, caught the
infection and laughed still louder than Aunt Martha. Frank
Wallace directly came in with a baritone which chimed well
with the soprano of the young girls and the contralto of the
middle-aged ladies. And Judge Owen, at last, having satisfied his judicial dignity by keeping his gravity longer than
any one else, rung in with a gruff heavy bass that might have
been contracted for in the damp vault of his own court-room.

There are said to be some occasions in which the highest
order of eloquence is shown in total silence, and others in
which the most indomitable bravery is shown by immediately
running away. Certainly this was an opportunity for the
display of the latter quality. Just when the laugh had
fairly burst, Colonel John Boadley Bancker clapped his hand
29

to his head, satisfied himself that the catastrophe had really
occurred, then made a grab at the wig and caught it out of
the hands of his tormentor, took three steps out of the room
to the hat-rack in the hall, and a few more out into the bright
moonlight. Napoleon had left Waterloo !

CHAPTER XXX.

THE LAST TIT-BITS OF THE BANQUET—SUBSEQUENT EVENTS
IN THE HISTORIES OF DIFFERENT CHARACTERS—A CA-
VALRY CHARGE AT ANTIETAM—AND THE END.

WHEN the banquet is over, whether the guests have been
fully satisfied or the opposite, there may still remain a few
trifles which must be discussed, if the proper respect is to be
shown to each other and the entertainer. When a story is
almost ended, there may still remain a fragmentary portion,
perhaps not altogether worthy of attention from those who
have so far followed the fortunes of the different personages
involved, and yet impossible to ignore without manifesting a
disregard of the whole entertainment. To that stage this
narrative has reached, and all that remains is a hasty group-
ing together of those closing events for which all that have
preceded them would seem to have been intended by the
fates that overruled them.

It will be remembered that Josephine Harris, when first
recovered from the disappointment of Richard Crawford's
absence from the city, penned a letter and mailed it to
Niagara, giving him a rapid detail of all that she had been
doing in his behalf—of events at West Falls—and of the
absolute necessity that he should at once apply some of his
marvellously recovered strength to the purposes of a journey
thither. That letter, which should have reached Niagara as

soon as the travellers themselves, suffered the fate of many
letters that are sent upon matters of life and death with the
magic word "haste" in the lower left-hand corner; and was
not delivered at the Cataract House until Saturday morning.
Perhaps it was quite as well that the detention had occurred
on the road, for by that means the partially-recovered invalid was spared two excitements in one day, which might
have seriously prostrated him.

Even as it was, the shock was a sudden and hazardous
one, to a system no more thoroughly restored than Richard
Crawford's. He received that letter on Saturday morning,
with several others from the city, and went up to his own
room to read them. From prudential reasons, Bell, on the
disappearance of Marion Hobart, had taken the vacated
room, adjoining that of her brother; and when he had been
for a few moments alone after his return from the hotel
"post-office," she was startled by what seemed to be a groan
issuing from his room. Instantly running to the door and
tapping, when she entered she found him sitting on the side
of the bed, white as the counterpane that covered it, and
breathing heavily. She flew at once to his side, applied the
restoratives at hand, and had the joy of seeing him almost
instantly recover breath and voice. Then it was that she
observed that he held a letter in his hand, and that letter he
tendered her. She read, and her own excitement was
scarcely less than that of her brother. Now for the first
time she understood the strange words with reference to the
destinies of her family, which had been uttered by the sybil,
and which had done so much to change the very nature of
her womanhood. And what a revelation was here to her, of
the mental torture which Richard must have experienced
through all his long hopeless illness—of the uncomplaining
patience with which he had borne what must have seemed to
him the crushing out of all the best hopes of his life—of the
murderous depravity which could exist in the heart of one
connected with her by the dear ties of blood, and daily taken
by the hand and trusted—and of the singular character of
that young girl whom she had observed so much and known
so little, and to whose efforts seemed to be owing all this

happiness budding and blossoming out of the ashes of past
misery.

An hour restored the equanimity of Richard Crawford,
though several would be needed before he could recover all
the strength of which he had been temporarily deprived by
the shock. But joy does not kill, like grief; nor does it even
enervate for any long period. Only a little time elapsed-be-
fore the steadfast lover, to whom the promise of joy was again
open after so long an obscuration, decided that he must and
would be strong enough to ride to Utica that night and to
West Falls on Sunday morning. He could not be allowed
to go alone, and of course Bell, who would not dissuade him,
had no alternative but to accompany him   With a few words
of apology to Walter Harding, for thus making a last break
into what would otherwise have been a pleasant sojourn of
some days at the Falls, and leaving him entirely alone,—
but with the explanation that family affairs of the gravest importance demanded their presence in the neighborhood of
Utica,—they left Niagara on Saturday afternoon, slept a portion of the night at Utica, and reached West Falls on Sunday
morning, the Twelfth—a week from that eventful Sunday on
which the destinies of the whole Crawford family seemed to
have been played for, lost and won, in the little parlor of Aunt
Betsey Halstead.

It is an old story which can never be told over half so well
as it can be acted—that of the meeting of lovers who have
been once estranged by wrong or misunderstanding.   It
was a trying moment when Mary Crawford, altogether ignorant of the time of his coming, even if he would ever again
come at all,—was called to meet the man whom she had so
wronged and misunderstood.   But how to perform the rites
of reconciliation, is one of the sublime mysteries which Nature
teaches when she gives us the other holy lessons of love ; and
who doubts that the cousin-lovers clasped each other more
fondly, and with a better knowledge of what each was worth
to the other, in the meeting embrace of that Sunday morning,
than they might ever have done during their whole lives if the
tongue of slander and the hand of injustice had not come temporarily between them ?

Their connection with this narration closes here. Poor old
John Crawford is yet living, though dying daily with weakness and the gradual wearing away of the very power of life.
Mary Crawford is a wife, and has been since Wednesday, the
twenty-sixth of November, 1862, on which day—the day preceding the annual Thanksgiving—Richard Crawford religiously believes that he repaid himself for all by-gone wrongs
and misunderstandings. For some cause, with which his
past sufferings and his changed domestic relations may have
had more or less to do, he has never yet joined the army of
which he has always been thinking with a longing desire.
His pen has not been idle, even in his happiness—may not
that have done *his* appointed work? It need scarcely be said
that the friendship between the people of the big house on the
hill, and those of the little Halstead house in the village,
though for a time interrupted by pride and neglect, has since
been more warmly cemented than ever before,—and that
when little Susy marries the engineer, as she will probably
do before the summer closes, there will be no warmer prayers
put up for their happiness, than those uttered by two who
have trodden the same path but a little while before them.

We have not chosen to depict the storm which followed
the sudden departure of Colonel John Boadley Bancker from
the house of Judge Owen, near the Harlem River. That there
was a storm, is undeniable—such a storm as the burly Judge
had (and still retains) the faculty of getting up at the shortest
notice. One of those blind, indiscriminate storms, which
having no justice have no direction, and which consequently
hurt no one, though they offend all. Frank Wallace, for
daring to play such a masquerade in his house and offend a
guest—Josephine Harris, for being an accessory before or
after the fact, to the plot (the pompous man never knew
which)—Emily for having been always a disobedient daughter
and a disgrace to the family, this event being another of the
abundant proofs thereof—Mrs. Owen and Aunt Martha for
daring to live in the same house where such things were about

to occur, without preventing them, whether they knew of the
arrangement or not,—all received their share in this blast of
denunciation ; and yet, strangely enough, all survived it, and
not one even quitted the house in disgust.

Colonel John Boadley Bancker has never since entered the
house or held any intercourse with its inmates. He would
quite as soon, we suspect, change places with Driesbach and
tame a few tigers and hyenas for exhibition, as trust himself
once more to the tender mercies of people who *detected and
laughed at him.* If he prays (which is doubtful) he prays
first to be delivered from the wiles and machinations of a demon in petticoats named Joe Harris. He does not wear
shoulder-straps or a blue uniform. He has not been drafted,
and probably will not be, even in the new eight-hundred-thou-
sand levy. He is said to be still speculating, and making
money ; and there have been rumors that he is looking for a
"job" in the operations of the Harbor-Defence Commissioners
of the City of New York.* But as those Commissioners are
well known to be beyond the reach of those evil influences
which have made other operations of the war a little costly
beyond their return,—he cannot do otherwise than fail in this
instance.

Frank Wallace has not been banished the house of Judge
Owen, since that memorable night of July. He visits it, even
takes Emily to the theatres, and is neither insulted nor interrupted. It is supposed that the Judge did not rule him out
of the house, because he believed it to be of no use, holding
that a man who had begun to come in disguise might continue
the game if not allowed to come openly, and that to keep him
out he would be obliged to remain at home all the time himself, and keep a sharp eye on the supposed milkman, the
baker, the butcher, and even the man who carried in the coal.
It may be that after this lapse of time, the Judge even
tolerates the scapegrace. Emily does, it is very evident, and
as she has never since swerved in her warm friendship with the
wild girl who arranged the masquerade, she is not at all likely
to recede from her old position or to marry otherwise than as
she pleases. The Judge had better reconsider his old deci-

* March 21, 1863.

sion, gracefully, for he is certainly overruled by that "full bench" consisting of Emily herself (Mrs. Owen reserving her opinion), Josephine Harris and Aunt Martha; and Frank Wallace will "take judgment" some day before he is aware of it, in the shape of pretty Emily Owen!

This is not a clergyman's or a county clerk's record of marriages; and it is a matter of regret that we cannot carry out the system inaugurated by Southworth and followed by Wood, of marrying off all the couples at the close of the relation, even down to the footman and the kitchen-girl. If we put then en train for that pleasant consummation, shall it not be held sufficient?

It would have been one of the pleasantest tasks of this narration to marry Walter Lane Harding, merchant and good fellow, to Bell Crawford, much more worthy to be his wife than when she was leaving the couch of her sick brother, with the gallant-Colonel-of-the Two Hundredth as her attendant, in search of a peculiar shade of red ribbon. But Harding is a man of mercantile regularity of idea, and not even a novelist can move him more rapidly than he chooses. He left Niagara on the Monday following the departure of Bell Crawford and her brother on Saturday, but business may have had more to do with his return to this city than any outsider can know. He has since been very much in her society, and friends believe that they are sincerely attached to each other. It is highly probable that they will be at Kittatinny or the White Mountains together, during the summer; and a marriage between them, which is one of the eventual certainties, may take place at a moment when it is least expected by others, but when they (the parties most deeply interested, after all) happen to fancy that the time has come for such a culmination of the pleasant acquaintance. Walter Harding, meanwhile, has forsaken none of his old ways, and finds the same pleasure as of old, in the street, in the country or at places of intellectual amusement, in the company (when he can manage to light upon that ever-busy person) of his friend and companion Tom Leslie.

It has already been said, in a previous chapter, that Tom Leslie and John Crawford left the Cataract House within an hour after the discovery of the abduction of Marion Hobart, taking carriage into Canada. Perhaps neither of the two knew precisely what was his motive in the pursuit, except the one before named—curiosity. If Crawford felt that he had a duty to the young Virginia girl, and some claim upon her, under the bequest of her dying grandfather, he was yet fully satisfied that she had left with her own consent, and that she was now where he could take no legal steps to reclaim her from any false position in which she might have placed herself. Leslie had, and knew that he had, no right whatever to meddle with the movements of the suspicious parties, except that he might have obtained some description of Columbus' right by *discovery*. However, the reasons being what they might, the fact was patent—they were now in full chase of a will-of-the-wisp of most magnificent dimensions.

There was not much difficulty, on enquiry, to find that the carriage they were following (Leslie remembered that this was the *second* carriage *he* had followed, in that connection) had taken the road to St. Catharine's; and thither the pursuers posted. Parties who bore the description of those they named—one large, dark man and one very small lady—had taken refreshments at the principal hotel there, two hours before; and then they had apparently gone on to Toronto. They followed to Toronto. Some hours were spent at Toronto, in discovering that they had taken the rail to Montreal. The pursuers followed to Montreal, and late at night, on the day following the departure from Niagara, were at Donnegana's Hotel. No concealment had here been considered necessary by the fugitives, whatever they might have practised before; and on the register of Donnegana's, Leslie found an entry of the names of "Dexter Ralston *and wife !*"

"Phew !" he said, calling the attention of Crawford to the book, "they have been rapid. All my suspicious were correct, as usual. There never was such a match; but they have now acquired a legal right to remain together, even if there was power to separate them otherwise. They are married !"

"The d—l they are!" said John Crawford, leaning over to examine the register. "True enough! Then my guardianship is ended, with a witness. But is *she* his wife? Is it Marion Hobart, or may he not have been married before?"

"No, said Leslie," remembering the picture, "she and no other."

They had not been aware that they were speaking loudly enough to be easily overheard; but as the last words were spoken a well-known voice sounded behind them, and Tom Leslie, as he turned, saw Dexter Ralston, cigar in mouth, coming up from the door.

"You were speaking of my wife, gentlemen," he said, as he bowed to Leslie. "Well, what of her?"

"If your wife is Marion Hobart," said John Crawford, turning, "we were speaking of *my ward*, entrusted to my guardianship by her grandfather, her last surviving relative, on his death-bed, and stolen away by you from the Cataract House yesterday."

The words of Crawford were somewhat loud, and the face of the Virginian flushed, though the office of the hotel was almost deserted and probably no one but themselves understood what was being uttered. "*Stolen* is a hard word," he said, after a moment, "but if you are John Crawford, who brought Marion Hobart safely away from Glendale, in Virginia, you are licensed to say almost anything."

Tom Leslie spoke.

"Where shall I meet you next, Ralston?"

"That depends upon where you follow me," said the Virginian, in a tone of dignified pleasantry which came near bringing the blood to Leslie's cheek as it had lately been brought to that of the Virginian. The journalist shook off the feeling, however, and laughed.

"Well, we *have* followed you, of course," he said—"perhaps played *spy* upon you. But if I am not mistaken, I saw you playing very nearly the same game on Goat Island and at the Cataract."

The Virginian echoed the laugh.

"Fairly hit back," he said. "I *have* played the spy, more than once. Who has not, I wonder?"

"What are you to-night?" asked Leslie, with a marked banter in his tone. "It is none of my business, of course, here on Canadian ground, but the other day, on Goat Island, you were—"

"A loyal American," answered Ralston, interrupting him. "To-night, and on Canadian ground, I am a loyal *Virginian*, true to my own State, first, last and forever."

"By George! I thought so all the while!" said Leslie, though there was certainly no anger in his tone. (It is a matter of doubt whether within the preceding few days that young man had not found himself so pleasantly situated in some regards, as to be incapable of becoming very easily vexed, even for the sake of *patriotism*.

"We differ on the national question, and I suppose conscientiously," said Ralston. "I hold the extreme doctrine of State Rights, and you that of centralization. I am a rebel— you are a loyalist. All right—don't let us quarrel, especially as we have been friends and as you are certainly a jolly good fellow and I *ought* to be."

"I ought to hate you and wish for your extermination," said Leslie, in the same frank tone; "and if I heard you professing the same sentiments at the St. Nicholas I should certainly help send you to Fort Lafayette. And yet I rather like you, in spite of the fact that I believe you have been concerned in some of the nests of secession in New York, through which the enemy—that's your friends!—obtained knowledge of all that was going on at the North."

"Never nearer right in your life!" said the Virginian. "In fact you are more nearly correct than even you imagine. One of the reasons why the Union cause can never succeed, is that the 'rebellion,' as you call it, has emissaries among you in every class of society, from the club-house to the brothel. You will scarcely believe, even with your experience, how society is getting mixed up! I found Kate F——, the daughter of one of my rich old neighbors, seduced and lured away from home, the inmate of one of those houses I have just named; and as I could do nothing better to relieve her just then, I employed her for *the cause*. To-night she is asleep in this house, my wife's servant. You wouldn't trust her, would you?—I would. But you need not suppose that the machinery is all worked among the lower classes. Don't trust the brown-stone houses too far! We had a brown-stone house up-town, until not many days ago—".

"Yes, on East 5— Street, not far from the Eastern Dispensary," said Leslie, breaking in upon the Virginian in turn; "and another on Prince Street, and—".

"Oh, you seem to know a good deal about it," said Ralston, trying to keep up his tone of banter, but his voice showing that he was really a little surprised. "And yet I do not think that you can be altogether behind the curtain after all. The worst foes of what you call the 'Union cause' have not been those who declared themselves secessionists. Some of your leading officials, it may be pleasant to you to know, are as arrant 'rebels' as even Virginia can furnish; and with them and the correspondence carried on through their offices, we have worked more effectively than in almost any other way."

"Yes," said Leslie, looking steadily at Ralston, and with a wicked smile peeping out from under his moustache. "Yes —not only local officials, but Congressmen, judging by the conversation that you held with the Honorable ——— ———, under the arches of the Capitol, the night before Lincoln's inauguration."

"What!" cried the Virginian, for once surprised out of his equanimity. "The d—l! You know that?" Then he laughed and grew placid again. The instant after he held out his hand to Leslie. "Leslie, you are keener than I thought, and perhaps it is just as well that we are not to play against each other any more. I am going to Europe by the next steamer from Quebec. It is late—I must go to bed. Let me say good-bye."

"To Europe?" asked Leslie. "Eh? oh! more ships, cotton and tobacco loans, I suppose."

"No!" said Ralston, and his voice sunk into a low tone of concentrated bitterness, very different from the manner he had recently displayed. "No! I am going to Europe to reside. I am done with the Confederate cause, though I hate the Federal as much as ever. It was *Virginia* I was striving for, not to change the despotism of Lincoln to another and a worse under Jeff Davis. That is enough—once more good night and good-bye!"

"Stop!" said John Crawford, who had stood very near during all this conversation, but taken no part in it. "You have yet a word or two to answer to me. I charged you, a few moments ago, with the abduction of a lady left to my care and under my solemn oath to protect her, by her last living relative. I know there is no law here in my behalf; but as a *man* answering to a *man*, what have you to say to this?"

"Her last living relative?" said the Virginian, as if he had heard nothing else of the words addressed to him. "Humph! as I said before, if you are John Crawford, my wife and myself both owe you much, and perhaps you are entitled to be satisfied before you go. Come up-stairs with me a moment, and you shall see what foundation there is for your words."

He led the way from the office of the hotel, through the hall and up a broad flight of steps to the next floor, the two friends following. Turning to the left he tapped with his knuckles on the door of one of the private parlors. There was no answer from within. He tapped again, and still there was no answer. He turned the knob of the door and peeped within, then opened the door a little wider and beckoned to Leslie and Crawford.

"Look!"

The two companions looked within. Two of the burners of the chandelier dependent from the ceiling were lit, and a flood of softened light from the ground-shades filled the apartment. On a sofa at the left sat the red woman of the Rue la Reynie Ogniard, red no longer now, but with the matchless beauty of her face displayed as it had been for a moment when Tom Leslie saw her unmasked at the house on Prince Street. But her dark hair lay all dishevelled; and in the eyes, that seemed to be looking down with a fixed and almost *hungry* expression of love that could never gaze enough, there were traces of late weeping. At her feet, on a low ottoman, half sat and half knelt Marion Hobart—or she who had so lately borne that name—her blonde hair thrown back from her brow, and her eyes looking up with

an answering expression of yearning affection that would
need years to satisfy. She was in white, and around her
waist were thrown the arms of the other, holding her in a
clasp of agonized force and intensity. Neither seemed to be
aware that others were near—apparently neither had heard
the knock or the opening of the door—for the time they
seemed to be alone upon earth. A moment Leslie and Crawford gazed upon this picture : then Ralston closed the door
again.

Leslie, who had for an instant started and trembled when
the picture met his view, as he had never failed to do in the
presence of that marvellous woman, uttered no word as the
door closed.

"Well ?" asked John Crawford, to whom nothing had as
yet been revealed.

"You do not understand," said the Virginian. "I think
that your friend sees farther. I married Marion Hobart
yesterday, at Toronto. You said that you held a right over
her by the bequest of her last living relative—her grandfather : I tell you that I have to-night restored her to a
dearer relative, in whose arms she lies——".

"Her *mother*," said Leslie, the two words breaking from
his lips as if involuntarily.

"Her mother ? Oh Lord !" broke out John Crawford,
surprise completely overmastering him.

"Her mother—a French lady by birth, and something of
whose character you know, Leslie. Her mother, the re-
pudiated wife of Charles Hampden Hobart, from whom
Marion has been separated since childhood, and to whom
you unwittingly, and I of my own will, have just given her
back. Have I a right to her, now ? Are you satisfied ?"

"Yes," said John Crawford. "My duty is done, though
I should rather have seen it end differently. Good-night !"

"Good-night and good-bye !" said Tom Leslie, holding
out his hand. Dexter Ralston shook it, bowed to Crawford,
and entered the parlor, closing the door behind him. The
two companions descended the stairs ; and so closed Tom
Leslie's long adventure, which it must be confessed that he
had not brought to quite so practical an end as that reached

by his female counterpart in another direction. But then who ever heard of a man managing a mystery or an intrigue with the same effective dexterity as a woman, or making as much good or evil out of it in the end?

Tom Leslie left Montreal almost as suddenly as he had arrived there, in company with John Crawford. He reached New York still in company with the Zouave. His re-union with Joe Harris took place at that auspicious time when the comedy at Judge Owen's had just come to a conclusion; and one can very well imagine what a clatter of tongues and a ringing of merry laughter there must have been in the parlor of Mrs. Harris's cozy little house, as the two compared notes since their separation at Utica, and as each revealed what had yet been necessarily kept hidden from the other. Mrs. Harris, good soul, listened to the two rattle-pates on that first evening, and laughed as merrily as either; but after a time the good lady stole away, perhaps to her early bed; and then, strangely enough, the merriment soon ceased, and they were silent. Were their voices only for others, and did eye speak to eye, lip to lip, and heart to heart, when they were alone together? One who knew both passed them closely by without being observed, and arrived at that impression, when they had stolen away from Mrs. Harris and the Ocean House at Newport, a month later, on the night of the full moon of August, and were sitting silent together, on the almost deserted piazza of the Stone Bridge House, at the extreme north end of Rhode Island, and under the shadow of Mount Hope, looking at the moon shining in placid beauty on the still waters of the East River, and thinking of Indian canoes and the romance of old history, as the little boats of the pleasure-seekers glided in and out among the wooded islands, and the shouts of merriment rung out ever and anon on the night air from lips that were bubbling over with enjoyment.

And this brings us to a matter of no slight embarrassment. If this narration has a heroine (which may be held as a matter of doubt) that heroine is Josephine Harris, the wild, impulsive, loving girl, ever ready for help or mischief, whose madcap pranks have played so important a part in the fortunes of all. And if we have not been all the while entirely without a hero, Tom Leslie, the journalist, cosmopolitan; lover of nature, and strange mixture of boyish gayety and manly experience, must supply that important place. The meeting of these two oddities has been narrated, and their lives have seemed to blend together from that moment; and yet the strange spectacle has been presented, of two who are talking always and on all subjects, saying no word of love to each other that reaches the pen of the narrator. There is one long pressure of the hand on the first day of their meeting—one long, confiding pressure, in which the two palms might almost grow together; and that is all. Thenceforth they belong to each other, and yet without a single question openly asked or answered. If the narrator should be asked, Why this reticence?—he might not be able to explain the restraint which holds his hand. They love each other dearly —so dearly that the blotting out of one from existence would be leaving that existence a blank to the other, for so many weary months and years that the very heart would grow sick at contemplating the long expanse of bereavement yet to be travelled over.

But they are not married? No. Months have passed over them, since each knew each so thoroughly that often the one speaks the unbreathed thought of the other; and yet they are not married. When will that marriage vow be spoken? To-morrow? Next year? Never? Who knows, except God in heaven? Perhaps there is something in this strange, wild, wayward love, between two who may not dream of any reward beyond its existence, too sacred even for its words to be recorded if they should fall upon the ear or enter the mind of the romancer. Neither of them, perhaps, could attract a love beside: neither of them might value another love, if it should come at any call. Both of them will be Pariahs from the caste of hard propriety, while the world lives or they exist. Both will chatter, laugh, weep at times, fill unacknowledged places in the world, and weave unreal ro-

mances of loving mischief in real life: And yet, married or
unmarried, they rest in each other—*rest*, in the truest and
holiest sense of that sacred word which almost encompasses
heaven. Absent, they will wish for each other: together,
they will sometimes forget the blessing that has been confer-
red, to remember it again some time through sobs and kisses.
And here let the record close.

No—let the record bear one more important suggestion.
If they do marry, for the protection of society let conspicuous
labels be pinned on the backs of their children: "Don't let
these little people get into any chance for mischief."

John Crawford, the Zouave, returned to New York within
the succeeding three days. Among the first of his researches
in the city, was one as to the state of the bank-account of
Marion Hobart. The account was closed—every dollar had
been drawn, by check under her own hand, and the fact gave
only another proof that her abduction had been accomplished
without much violence, if not indeed with her own connivance.

John Crawford rejoined the Advance Guard in October,
and has since shared in all the perils and glories of that gallant corps. He is still a private—it may be because no commission has offered on such terms as a true man could accept;
and it may be because he believes the true romance and glory
of war to lie with the *soldier*, and not the *officer*—the danger
of the lonely picket-guard and the song and story of camp and
bivouac, supplying a fresh and glorious excitement to which
the superior must always remain a stranger.

From the moment when Colonel Egbert Crawford left West
Falls so suddenly, and took his way Southward by the cars of
the New York Central road on that Sunday evening of July,
he seems to have passed away entirely from the course of this
narration. Let it not be supposed that he has passed away
from memory or that these closing words can be complete without a knowledge of his subsequent movements

It has been seen how calmly, to all outward appearance, the baffled and detected man bore the knowledge of his ruin. *Ruin*, because nothing less was involved in the failure of his plans. He had long been embarrassed in money affairs, and for months before his business as a Tombs lawyer had been falling away under that worst of all cankers—neglect. The hand of Mary Crawford would have satisfied his heart, and her fortune would have repaired the weakness of his own. Failing both, he was hopelessly bankrupt. The Two Hundredth Regiment was a failure, and he had known the fact for weeks. Perhaps he had never believed that it would be otherwise. At all events, as may have been suspected from his forced submission to the unpardonable insolence of the Adjutant, he had been deceiving the authorities as to the number and condition of the regiment, and applying to his own use sums that might need to be some day strictly accounted for. The previous word will bear repetition—this event in his life was absolute ruin.

Some men commit suicide under such circumstances. Others make one more and a still greater departure from the path of honesty, and victimizing all whom they can influence by the holiest of pleas and the most sacred claims of friendship, flee away to bury their shame among strangers. A few find such positions the turning-points in their lives, and thenceforward develope some startling virtues which almost redeem the lamentable past.

Egbert Crawford had proved himself a villain, even as the world goes. He had trampled upon the dearest ties of blood, and been a constructive murderer, only withheld from the actual crime by circumstances over which he had no control. He had murdered character, and would have murdered the happiness of a poor, weak, unoffending woman, who had the double claim of youth and of kindred blood, demanding consideration at his hands. He had trifled with the public service and defrauded the government, as too many others were and have since been doing on every hand—draining his Mother Country of her life-blood in her very hour of need, and so aiding to commit that most deadly and horrible of

crimes—*matricide*. Could this man still have one virtue re
maining? Let this be seen.

He reached New York on Monday night, after a stay of a
few hours at Albany. What he did at the latter place has
never been known and perhaps will never be.   On Tuesday,
for an hour, he was at Camp Lyon, and some of the other
officers saw him walking backward and forward, on the piazza
of the hotel, in conversation with the Adjutant. Once, or
twice their voices were heard to rise louder than good-feeling
would have allowed, though the words they uttered were not
caught by any listener. Were they haggling, as robbers have
been known to do after successful operations in plundering,
over the division of the spoils?   At nightfall the Colonel returned to the city, and Camp Lyon and the Two Hundredth
Regiment saw him no more.

The morning papers of a day or two after announced that
the Two Hundredth Regiment, which seemed to have been
lagging in the way of recruits, for a few days before, had
been abandoned as a separate organization and would be con-
solidated with the One Hundred and Ninety-ninth, then in
the course of successful formation at a camp within half a
mile of its disbanded rival. With this addition, the One
Hundred and Ninety-ninth would be full and able to leave
within a week. The Colonel of the Two Hundredth, it was
added, had accepted a commission on staff-service, and had
already left for the seat of war.

All this was true, except so much of it as was mere speculation for the future. Whether the One Hundred and Ninety-
ninth did profit by the consolidation and move within the
week—whether any money, and if so how much, was received
by those who "sold out" the Two Hundredth—and whether
the One Hundred and Ninety-ninth (*not* including Lieut.
Woodruff, who threw up his commission in disgust) entered
and honored the service, or was yet frittered away by the
gross mismanagement of those in command,—all these are
matters that have no connection whatever with the present
relation. The gist of the newspaper paragraph was true—
the consolidation of the two regiments had been effected, and

Colonel Egbert Crawford had left New York for Washington, on staff-service.

When he left his legal office on the day of his departure for Washington, he carried with him a package the shape of which none could mistake. It contained a sword. So much any eye could see. But no eye could see what lay beneath. It has been more than once indicated that so far as an evil man could love purely, Egbert Crawford really loved the little cousin for whom he was playing so unfairly. Sword-factories had sprung up, since the breaking out of the war, along the little streams which emptied into the Mohawk, through the Oneida Valley; and some of them kept up the clink of the trip-hammers and the whirr of the emory-wheels that shaped and polished sword-blades, not far from West Falls. One day, in June, while his star seemed to be so certainly in the ascendant in the family of John Crawford, Mary and himself had visited one of those factories. Impressed by the intelligence of his remarks on the manufacture, and perhaps willing to curry favor with the commander of a regiment just going into the field, the superintendent of the sword-factory had presented the officer with a splendid plain light-cavalry sabre with its brazen hilt and heavy steel scabbard—a most deadly and effective weapon, upon which one could depend in battle almost as well as upon the best blade forged in Damascus. That sword Mary had carried home in her own hands, presenting it to him afterwards, in a moment of good feeling, with a playful word of confidence in his valor, which he had never forgotten. That blade, hallowed by the little hand of Mary Crawford which had once pressed its hilt, was the one which he carried with him that day as he left his office for no imaginary "field," but one of bloody reality.

Would he have been superstitious enough to connect the fact with his own past or future fate, had he known that Aunt Synchy, the old Obi woman of Thomas Street, was that very day lying dead on the floor of her miserable room, having had a dose of one of her own insidious poisons administered in her tea by Master Jeffy, who had become almost too much of an expert in the art,—because she would not allow him the extravagance of a whole penny to buy a top?

Josephine Harris, painfully correct in her general estimation of the character of Egbert Crawford, had pronounced
him, in addition to his other vices, " a coward," and " amounting to nothing, as a soldier, except his shoulder-straps and
sword-belts." She " did not believe that he would ever go
to the war." How very easily, seeing one half the truth, we
can overleap too much intervening space and falsify the
remaining half! Egbert Crawford *did* " go to the war," and
under such circumstances that his " shoulder-straps" and
" sword-belts" counted for very little in comparison with
himself. Three days after he left New York, he joined the
army at Harrison's Landing, as a volunteer aid-de-camp to
any officer who needed rough-riding and sharp fighting. He
was a dashing rider—thanks to the education received many
years before in the country, and the steadiness with which he
had since kept up the habit of riding, at an expenditure of
time and money which he could ill afford. He bore excellent
endorsements from Albany and New York, and he had lately
held a commission as Colonel. Besides these advantages,
Hooker saw something in the dark face of the lawyer—something in the set lips and clouded brow, which while it might
not have commanded confidence in the selection of an agent
to be specially trusted in matters of delicate issue, told that
there was desperation and *fight*. He joined the staff of that
General, with the honorary rank of Captain.

Then followed that terrible blunder which removed the
Army of the Potomac from the James River, unloosed the
grasp of the Federals from the very throat of the rebel power,
and re-opened the Pandora's Box of incursion which had been
almost closed by the investiture of Richmond. Then followed the still more terrible blunder of the appointment of
Pope to the leading command, and the commencement of that
chain of disasters which culminated in the disgraceful retreat
of the Union forces towards Washington, after the second
battle of Bull Run, on the twenty-ninth of August—a retreat
which was only checked by the momentary return of the
" young Napoleon" from his temporary Elba, and a demoralization which was only forgotten when the Potomac army
once more re-organized under the old commander, moved up

into Maryland to break the threatened invasion of the Middle States.

The young aid-de-camp proved himself a man and a soldier, however raw and unaccustomed, in the removal from Harrison's Landing and the disastrous fights of Pope's campaign; but there was little opportunity, indeed, for dash amid demoralization. And so matters passed rapidly on until the morning of Antietam. One of the captains of General Pleasanton's cavalry fell at Sharpsburg, leaving a vacancy which that gallant officer filled, by General Hooker's consent, with his volunteer aid-de-camp. Mary Crawford's cavalry sabre had at last found its true field, though he had worn it through all, instead of the more showy regulation blade, when on staff duty.

Antietam had begun to thunder, though the height of that terrible battle, which up to this time* divides with Malvern Hill and Shiloh the fearful honor of being the most destructive of any fought on the American continent, had not yet been reached. One hundred and twenty thousand of the Union troops held the eastern bank of Antietam Creek, ready to cross and complete the expulsion of the rebels from Maryland, while it was believed that not less than two hundred thousand of the rebels held the high lands opposite. The slaughter of the day was fairly commencing. Pleasanton held the upper of the three bridges over the Creek, that at the Hagerstown road, over which Hooker was sweeping forward to make his crossing. He had been ordered by Hooker to hold his position without fail and at all hazards. The rebels seemed to be in heavy force on the heights behind and farther up the creek, and evidently they were prepared to make a desperate resistance to the crossing of Hooker. The position of the cavalry was a painful one. Hooker seemed slow in coming, and shot and shell kept continually dropping among them, knocking from their saddles one and another of the brave fellows who were so chafing with impatience and inaction. At length, and just at the moment when the head of Hooker's column appeared from behind the woods on the other side, a squadron of rebel horse, two or three hundred strong, came into view, down the creek and a little behind, on a low plateau which stretched from it towards the hills. The advance guard came pricking in at the same moment. Pleasanton, who had been anxiously observing the advance of Hooker, caught a word behind him and turned. As he did so, and saw the rebel cavalry, he caught the word repeated.-

"Damnation!"

"Who spoke?" asked the General.

"I!" answered Captain Crawford, commanding the right company, and consequently very near the commander.

"And what did you mean?" asked Pleasanton.

"My word was not for your ear, General, of course," said the young officer. "What I meant was that it was a shame that Hooker was coming just at this moment, and that we could not have a brush with those rebels on horseback, yonder."

"Eh?" said the General. "What consequence?"

"This," answered Crawford. "They brag of the rebel cavalry—they say that we have *none*. I should like to try them, if not more than two to one."

"Good!" said Pleasanton. "The right feeling, though a little imprudent. You are a young officer, Captain Crawford, but they tell me you have dash, and that sounds like it. Dash is what we want, if we can only have steadiness with it. Your eyes are younger than mine—how many of those rebels are there?"

The rebel cavalry were now within four hundred yards, and still advancing, though at moderate speed. Crawford looked at them closely a moment.

"From two to three hundred, I should think," was the answer.

"By the Lord you shall have a chance!" said the veteran. "You think you can scatter them with less than two hundred. Try it, steel against steel. Take two squadrons, and away with you!"

"Squadrons on the right—attention!" rung out the sharp voice of the Captain, no despondency or vexation in it now! "Draw sabres! Squadrons forward! Column to the left—march!" and rapidly as the words were uttered the movement

was executed. Other words of command followed and were
executed with equal rapidity, as the squadrons moved down
to the left, then formed on the right into line facing the. foe ;
and it seemed but an instant after, when the concluding
words rung out: " Squadrons forward ! trot—march ! . Gallop
—march! Charge !" and the two squadrons of the. light
dragoons, headed by the new Captain, were sweeping across
the plateau to meet the advancing rebels. Their long line of
white steel glittered ominously, and the solid, earth of the
plateau shook under the hoofs of their galloping horses, few
in number as they were. As they swept on, coming nearer
they discovered that their scant one hundred and fifty were
even more fearfully outnumbered than they had at first believed; but no man drew rein and every one grasped the
hilt of his blade with a fiercer determination, as he drove
the cruel spurs still deeper into the flanks of his. flying
horse — lacerating the animal in haste perhaps to impale
himself !

In the more important details of the main battle of Antietam, this cavalry charge has been almost overlooked by the
newspaper chroniclers; and yet it is doubtful whether even
the Galloping Second when they dashed into Fairfax Court-
House, or Zagonyi's "Body-Guard" and Frank White's "Prai-
rie Scouts," at Springfield, displayed more of the true dash of
this undervalued arm of the American service, than those two
squadrons of Pleasanton on the little plateau over Antietam
Creek. The rebels met them with fierce determination and
the inspiring consciousness of superior numbers, but nothing
could break that headlong charge. Scarcely a pistol-shot was
fired, until the rebel ranks were completely broken. Like
tongues of white flame those fierce blades rose and fell,
lopping arms, crashing through brains and emptying saddles ;
and scarce once that they rose without some new stain caught
from the reeking life-blood. Poor little Mary Crawford's
sword, before so bright and spotless, caught terrible flames
of red in its course, as the Captain sped onward at the head
of his destroying angels ; and it was only when the rebels
were completely broken and in full flight, and the Union
cavalry wheeling to rejoin the main body with their sadly

diminished number, that the blade so bloodily baptized grew
still.

Crawford, at the very head of the charge, had passed beyond many of the rebel horsemen, now flying fugitives ; and
as he turned to ride back, drawing a long breath of exhaustion
and relief, two or three of the escaping rebels dashed towards
him.   He raised his sword and spurred forward, for the
moment unconscious of personal danger at the moment of
victory.   But at that instant the hand of one of the rebel
horsemen dropped to his holster—before the Union officer
could meet the motion there was a quick flash, a report, and
the bullet struck him full in the throat.   One gasp, one convulsive spouting of blood from the great arteries, in which
the whole flood of life seemed to be discharging itself—and
he reeled in his saddle and fell headlong from the stirrup, his
eyes already glazing in death, and the stained sword of the
Oneida Valley falling useless from his stiffening right hand.

Let the Koran be true, for him at least.   Let the death of
a patriot soldier on the battle-field, when striking for the
perilled land at its sorest need, be held to atone for much of
wrong and error, and even something of *crime*, in the past.
And let us say of him, as the master-dramatist says of the
perished Cawdor, and as some tired reader may be disposed
to say of this long and desultory narration—that "nothing in
his life became him like the leaving it."

THE END.

www.ingramcontent.com/pod-product-compliance
Lightning Source LLC
Chambersburg PA
CBHW052346110726
47901CB00005B/1375